KU-193-714

THE LOVING BROTHERS

"A blessed companion is a book"—JERROLD

Also by

LOUIS GOLDING

Fiction

FORWARD FROM BABYLON
SEACOAST OF BOHEMIA
DAY OF ATONEMENT
STORE OF LADIES
THE MIRACLE BOY
THE PRINCE OR SOMEBODY
GIVE UP YOUR LOVERS
MAGNOLIA STREET
FIVE SILVER DAUGHTERS
THE CAMBERWELL BEAUTY
THE PURSUER
THE DANCE GOES ON
MR. EMMANUEL
WHO'S THERE WITHIN?
NO NEWS FROM HELEN
THE GLORY OF ELSIE SILVER
THREE JOLLY GENTLEMEN
HONEY FOR THE GHOST
THE DANGEROUS PLACES
TO THE QUAYSIDE

Short Stories

THE DOOMINGTON WANDERER
PALE BLUE NIGHTGOWN
PARIS CALLING

Verse

SORROW OF WAR
SHEPHERD SINGING RAGTIME
PROPHET AND FOOL
THE SONG OF SONGS, RENDERED AS A MASQUE
POEMS DRUNK AND DROWSY

Travel

SUNWARD: ADVENTURES IN ITALY
SICILIAN NOON
THOSE ANCIENT LANDS: A JOURNEY TO PALESTINE
LOUIS GOLDING GOES TRAVELLING
IN THE STEPS OF MOSES THE LAW-GIVER
IN THE STEPS OF MOSES THE CONQUEROR

Belles-Lettres

ADVENTURES IN LIVING DANGEROUSLY
LETTER TO ADOLF HITLER
WE SHALL EAT AND DRINK AGAIN (WITH ANDRÉ SIMON)
JAMES JOYCE
THE JEWISH PROBLEM
HITLER THROUGH THE AGES
THE WORLD I KNEW

Sport

LOUIS GOLDING'S BOXING TALES
MY SPORTING DAYS AND NIGHTS
THE BARE-KNUCKLE BREED

THE LOVING BROTHERS

*

LOUIS GOLDING

THE COMPANION BOOK CLUB
LONDON

For
Cherry and Emanuel Litvinoff
this book
affectionately
to read on their boat

THIS edition, issued in 1953, is for members of The Companion Book Club, 29–30 Bedford Street, London, W.C.2, from which address particulars of membership may be obtained. The book is published by arrangement with the original publishers, Hutchinson & Co. (Publishers) Ltd.

CHAPTER I

I

THE telephone-bell rang, but no-one moved. The Secretary would be in from lunch, and she would take it, in the office beyond the landing. She came in a few moments later.

"It's for you, Warden," she said. "The Duke of Lechdale."

"Very well," said Dr. Browne. "I'll take it here." He tried to keep his satisfaction out of his voice and face; but he did not quite succeed. The twins winked at each other. There was no getting away from it. The old man liked to be telephoned by dukes.

He rose and went over to the telephone.

"The Warden here," he said. "Yes, Edward?" Then, not more than a few seconds later, the time it took him to recognize whose voice this really was, darkness came into his face. He made a gesture as if to replace the receiver, then restored it to his ear again. The invisible speaker went on for a little time, then stopped speaking.

"Well, Henry?" the others overheard. The instrument was half-an-inch from the Warden's ear. They had no doubt whose voice it was.

"I say *well*, Henry?" the voice repeated.

Then at last the Warden was able to set the vocal cords working.

"I'm sorry, it slipped my memory. We'll send them on by post at once, whatever we can find."

The voice expostulated. Apparently the post would not be quick enough. "One moment," the Warden said, and put his hand over the instrument. Then he turned to his wife.

"He's started," he said. "I knew it would happen. All right. Let him come. I'm not going to be blackmailed by him." A flush started in his cheeks and seeped slowly over the cheek-bones. He was going to explode with fury. Nobody would get anywhere that way. It was going to be very unpleasant for everyone.

Then Marian, the elder daughter, broke in.

"No, Father. There's no need to force anything. I'll go. Tell him that. I'll go today. I'd like to see Aunt Edith in any case. Ask him exactly where it is." The Warden hesitated. "Really, Father," she urged. "You've no need to worry. I'm not a baby." He still hesitated. The other might ring off any moment. "I'll tell him myself," she said, and rose from her chair. Her father removed his hand from the receiver. "Are you there?" he asked. "Marian says she'll come over some time today." His voice was cold and thin. The flush had receded from his face, leaving it pale as ivory. "When? I don't know. When can you be there, Marian? It's a hard place to find, he says."

Marian came up to the telephone with pad and pencil, and took the instrument from her father's hand.

"It's me, Uncle Matthew, Marian. I'm very well, thank you." She shut her eyes while the voice had its say. Then she resumed: "No, I haven't petrol enough. I'll take the bus. Have you a time-table there?" Apparently he had. She put down times and directions, said good-bye and replaced the receiver.

There was silence while Marian went back to her chair. She raised her cup of coffee to her lips, but it was cold, and she put it down again.

"Shall we get some more made?" asked her mother. But no. No-one wanted any more. The air had gone sour, despite the roses in the rose-bowls and the smell of lavender that came in through the open windows from the Fellows' Garden.

"I shouldn't have let you go," the Warden said. "I have no right to."

"Daddy," his daughter insisted. "I'm not a baby. I'm twenty-six, you know."

"Did he say he wanted to come here?" asked Robert, the boy twin. He was seventeen. "Why didn't you let him?" He clenched his fists. "I'd show him!"

"Don't be a fool!" said Marian roughly. "What use would that be to anybody! If we wanted to rough-house him, we could always collect a gang of huskies, here in College."

"What is he asking for?" asked their mother faintly.

"It's that old damask linen Aunt Emily left," the Warden said. "You remember. It was to be divided among her nephews. The table-cloths can wait. It's the napkins he wants. Aunt Emily never remembered to cut him out of the will. He must have got hold of a copy at Somerset House."

"Yes," said Marian. "He doesn't mind using the law when it suits his purpose. He just wants to throw his weight about, I suppose." Her father nodded. "Well, he shall have his table-napkins."

"I don't know where they all are," wailed Mrs. Browne. "Some have been lost in the wash. I'm sure of it."

"There'll be some to be going on with, won't there?" asked Marian. "Try and find them, Mother. I must go back to the shop and tell Cecily I'll be leaving early."

"Can I come with you?" the girl twin, Anna, asked suddenly. "I'd like to see what he looks like."

"Over my dead body," said Marian.

"Anna, how *could* you!" protested her mother. Her father looked up as if he might burst a blood-vessel.

"Oh, very well," Anna pouted. "I only wanted to be useful."

"Of course, darling, of course." Marian went up to Anna and passed her hand along her fine-spun hair. "But you know how it is, don't you?"

"Yes, Marian. I know. It's dreadful."

"Poor old Aunt Edith," said Robert. "She's a decent old stick, isn't she?"

"That's why I thought——" Anna started.

"Come along, Mother dear," said Marian briskly. "Let's see what we can do about those table-napkins."

Mrs. Browne rose and made for the door. Then she turned. Her husband was slumped deep into his chair. She hesitated a moment, as if she had it in her mind to go back to him, and breathe some word of comfort into his ear. But she knew well there was no word of comfort. The twins rose, too, and followed her. Only Marian was left with him.

"Daddy!" she whispered. He did not raise his head. "Daddy!" she said again. She would not leave him in that darkness. "It's not your fault! It's not anybody's fault!"

"You're a good girl, Marian," he whispered. "Where are my spectacles? Will you get them for me?"

She got them for him, then went out. There was a flurry

going on among chests of drawers and in the cistern-cupboard, but only ten of the table-napkins had turned up. They went neat and easy into Marian's brief-case. It was believed there should be another eight.

II

How did he get that way, Marian asked herself, as she walked across the quadrangle, and past the porter's lodge. How did he get that way? How? When?

"Good afternoon, Miss Marian," old Bennison called after her. He was senior Porter, and very conservative. She was still Miss Marian to him, though she was, in fact, married. And not merely married, but a widow. But, poor dear, you could hardly call that a marriage, could you? Married three days, then he's out in the North Sea, and he's boarding one of those little German E-boats, and there's half-a-dozen machine-gun bullets in his head. "Did you make a nice lunch, Miss Marian?"

She smiled, and raised two thumbs. Not a bit like a Warden's daughter, she wasn't. Probably her time in the Wrens had something to do with it. Having lowered the thumbs, she crossed the road and turned left along the High towards the Turl.

'Has old Bennison already heard Matthew has contacted us?' she asked herself. 'Is that why he was so extra nice just now?' But she knew that was nonsense. People didn't listen in to telephone conversations in Oxford colleges. And they couldn't listen in in the Porter's lodge. And Bennison hadn't been extra nice. He always had a smile for her.

She met two or three undergraduates she knew, and one or two dons, and some young women. How many of them knew Matthew Browne was her uncle? Probably none. People don't know that sort of thing. Or if they do, somehow they don't remember it. Any more than she remembered it herself, excepting just now and again, when the question would come pinging out at her, like a mosquito. How, how did he *get* that way? Did he start out like that from his mother's womb? Or was there a moment when something was born inside him, or, alternatively, something died?

She tried not to think about it, and practically never did.

After all, she had other griefs. But what about Daddy? There must be times when he thought everybody must be whispering about it behind their hands . . . the undergraduates in the Junior Common Room, the dons over their port, the tradesmen's boys on their bicycles.

But they weren't. She was certain of that. People are very decent on the whole. God knows, it can happen to anyone.

She had reached the little book-shop they ran in the Broad, Cecilia Bruton and herself—the Easy Chair, they called it. Marian had thought it a good idea to accept the offer of a partnership in the enterprise, a month or two after she was demobilized. It would be one way, perhaps, of taking one's thought off Bertie's death. Cecilia, also, wanted to forget a young man, though in her case he had not died, he had merely gone off with another girl. The Easy Chair wasn't going very well. There were too few books about it, and too much easy chair. And why buy books at all when you can sit flicking the pages and sipping sherry? That was Cecilia's attitude to business, and she was the senior partner.

"Do you mind, Cecilia?" Marian said. "I've got a job of work to do. Will you take over for me?"

Cecilia was polishing her finger-nails. She said nothing for a moment or two, then slowly raised her eyes. She kept them fixed on Marian's for some moments, then slowly lowered them.

"Certainly not, darling," she said languidly. "I've got some chocolates. And a poppet of a novel." She held it up to show the title. "Have you read it?"

"Tell me, Cecilia," asked Marian suddenly. "Have you heard of Matthew Browne?"

"Who?"

"Matthew Browne."

"With an 'e' or without an 'e'?"

"With an 'e.' "

"A relative?"

Marian's courage failed her.

"I must tidy up that desk," she said.

"O.K.," said Cecilia. She wasn't an Oxford girl, and they had hardly known each other a year. But she probably knew.

Or *did* she?

Oh hell, thought Marian. I mustn't let it get me down. Daddy hasn't.

III

The stopping place was opposite the Blue Lion, on the road to Witney. A deep wood marches for some distance along the south side of the main road. The lane leading down to 'Hatchetts' was some ten minutes walk away, where the small cross is.

Marian waited for half a minute by the cross, as arranged. No-one came. Another half-minute passed. Then at last someone appeared, a woman: it was Aunt Edith, in fact. It was almost as if at the last moment her nerve had failed. You could still see what a pretty woman she had been, though she looked so haggard now, and there were dark half-moons under her eyes.

"Hullo, Aunt Edith!" cried Marian, and ran forward and kissed her. Her cheek was cold, though it was a warm June evening. "You shouldn't have bothered. I'd have found my way. How are you?"

"I'm very well, thank you," said Aunt Edith. "You don't know how. . . . It's so *nice* of you!"

Marian slipped her free arm round her aunt's waist, and squeezed it.

"I've brought the napkins," she said. "But I really wanted to see you . . . now we're sort of neighbours. They all wanted me to come. You know how fond they are of you. You mustn't, my dear," she brought out urgently. She was aware of the quick catch in Aunt Edith's throat. She couldn't bear it if Aunt Edith broke down and started sobbing on her shoulder. Aunt Edith bit her lip. The danger was over. They turned into the lane. It had not rained for some time and the ridges were sharp and hard. The odour of small flowers, ground ivy and agrimony and pimpernel, came up from under the thick undergrowth.

"I've brought the table-napkins he asked for," Marian said. "They're here." She showed her brief-case. "It's not many. Mother couldn't find any more. They'll have to do for the time being." Aunt Edith did not say anything. There was not much one could say, was there?

"I understand it's quite a beautiful house," said Marian. "What do you call it? Hatchetts?"

"Yes. Your mother didn't mind my writing, did she? We were very lucky. It's modern, of course. But there are some rather lovely old things."

"And quite a decent piece of land?" Marian went on.

Aunt Edith's mind was not working very quickly. She was still thinking about the lovely things. "My grandfather died some months ago. He was a collector." Then her brain registered the other theme. "Oh, land? Yes, about fifteen acres, on the other side, beyond these woods." There was silence for some time. A dove cooed in a high elm near at hand. A dove answered from a tree further away.

"Enough to keep him busy," said Marian. "Yet not enough to bore him."

"No," Aunt Edith murmured, and the silence fell again.

Hatchetts was a good half-mile away. Yes, Aunt Edith had been quite right. You needed some-one to guide you there. It was not even a lane in places, just a track. You came upon the house quite suddenly. The woodland dipped down into a dingle, with a stream running under a rustic bridge, and a little pool in a basin, dappled with water-lily leaves. The house was on the further slope, rising out of flowering espaliers. There were a great many hydrangeas. The late owner of the house had clearly been a specialist in hydrangeas.

"You'll just have time to tidy yourself up before dinner," said Aunt Edith. "He doesn't like to be kept waiting. We have a married couple," she went on. She was making a brave effort at conversation. "He insists on having a man wait at table."

"I wouldn't dream of putting you out. No, Aunt, no. I'll catch my bus." How could she bear to have dinner with him?

"He specially said you were to stay for dinner," Edith pleaded. "He can order a hire-car."

She ignored the hire-car. But she could not ignore the pathos in Edith's voice and eyes. She had better make easy weather of it.

"Well, thank you, if it's not putting you out. How enchanting it all is! You should be very happy here."

Aunt Edith looked away. Marian could have kicked herself. It was not quite the right thing to say, in that easy tone.

Uncle Matthew came out to greet them when they were within some thirty feet of the red-tiled terrace that fronted the porch above them. You noticed the beard at once, a chestnut-brown silken thing, elegantly pointed in the Vandyck mode. He had not previously affected that type of decoration, so far as she knew, but she could not be certain. The clothes were Savile Row, too, the steely blue-black dinner-jacket, the impeccably creased trousers, the beetle-shining shoes. It was a stiff shirt and stiff collar. No informal half-measures for Uncle Matthew. He was pale, with the sort of pallor you could expect, but his toilet preparations did something to mitigate that. He held out his arms to her.

"Marian," he said. "How very kind you are. You are most welcome." The formality of speech and manner suited the clothes. He came down towards her, and laid his lips soft as a leaf falling on her left temple. It might have been taken as a gesture of forgiveness towards Edith his wife, Marian his niece, Henry his brother, everybody, everything.

"It's very beautiful, Uncle Matthew." She looked round on the ornamental trees, the flower-beds, the sun-dial, the water-lily pool. "How lucky you are!" Quickly, without a change of tone, she explained: "A place like this coming into the market, so complete." You had to have your wits about you.

"One even has a little bathing-pool," he added, smiling. "You'll forgive me, won't you? One feels one has to put on a black tie in the evening. One does quite a lot of work in the garden. And there are the animals." Yes, she thought, it was very proper of one, and how impersonal one was. "It won't take Edith any time to dress, will it, Edith?" The tone of voice suggested that, on the whole, it had better not. "And, Marian, that *can't* be a little frock you have in the brief-case there?"

"No, Uncle. It's those table-napkins you asked for. Mother hopes some more will turn up."

"Of course! How stupid of me! Dear Marian! And you undertook to bring them over! Really, how kind you are! How many are there, if I may ask?"

"We found ten."

"*Ten*?" he repeated. "There should be eighteen!" There was a green flicker in his eyes, like a darting lizard. Then the lizard was in a cranny, out of sight. The eyes were urbane again. He turned to his wife. "Perhaps you'll let Marian tidy up? Dinner in half-an-hour, please." How completely he had taken it for granted! He turned and went off into the house.

The house was very charming, and it had every modern convenience. A great deal of money must have been collected from one source or another. It hardly seemed likely that Edith had been able to lay hands on it all herself. Perhaps Matthew had been able to help a little from certain sources? The speculation was hardly her affair.

"This way," Aunt Edith said, and led her into her room. It was not the same as her husband's room. Marian tidied up and went down into the sitting-room.

"A gin and something?" asked Uncle Matthew. His sang-froid was beyond praise.

"Pink," said Marian, "thank you." Aunt Edith, not Uncle Matthew, made the drink.

"There's one thing you must let me say," Uncle Matthew brought out. Marian looked up.

"Yes?"

"I heard about your husband. I'm sorry. But you'd rather not talk about it?"

"I'd rather not."

He made no comment.

"An olive?"

"Thank you."

"She would like an olive, Edith."

How preposterous it all was! How could one human creature exert so hateful a fascination over another!

"Dinner is served," the man-servant announced. It might have been Londonderry House. Uncle Matthew *was* doing himself well. He held out his arm for her. There was possibly a hint of mockery in the gesture, because it was only a few feet from the sitting-room, across the hall, into the dining-room, and Marian's tweed skirt hardly lived up to such elaborateness. She placed her finger-tips against the side of his arm muscles, and went forward with him. The man threw the door open and stood by like an image. The dining-room unfolded. The Sheraton table glowed like copper bowls. The silver, the glass, the Dutch Still Life over the mantelpiece, the decanters and dishes on the sideboard, the rose-bowl on the table . . . it was conventional, but perfect. Really, it's such deadly *nonsense,* she said to herself.

Then she was aware of a slight stiffening of the muscle against her finger-tips. She turned her head. He was looking at the centre-piece of the table, a bowl of bright pink roses, in a Rose Japan Crown Derby bowl. The eyelids drooped over the eyes, the mouth stiffened. Everything was not perfect, not *quite* perfect. Perhaps the pink of the roses, cheerful, rather on the carmine side, *did* clash a trifle with the salmony pink of the bowl, beautiful though it was? It was the "Doctor," wasn't it, rather a blatant kind of rose, maybe? Uncle Matthew half-turned to his wife.

"Again?" he said. That was all. Edith's mouth puckered like a scolded child's. Again what? Marian asked herself. Was it the wrong vase? Were they the wrong roses? The salmony-pink and the carmine! Calamitous conjunctions!

"Will you sit here, Marian?" asked her uncle. The man pulled back her chair. Matthew sat down at the head of the table, Edith at the foot. Her chin was low on her breast.

"I'm sorry, dear——" she started.

He stroked his beard, and gazed at her unblinking for two or three seconds.

"We won't discuss it," he said. That presumably meant the flower-arrangement. Salmon-pink, carmine! There was some smoked trout, then a creamed fricassee of chicken. It tasted like real cream, too. Uncle Matthew was the sort of man who would get the best of what was going, wherever he might be. There was a pleasant bottle of Pouilly on ice. He lifted the glass to his lips. Yes, it was cold enough. Aunt Edith's sigh of relief was quite audible. He savoured the wine delicately.

"A Pouilly Fuissé, 1933, I think. Is it all right, Marian?" he asked. It was a rhetorical question.

"I suppose it is." She was not going to flatter him by assuming expertness. Besides, she was not happy about the treatment of Aunt Edith, though to be sure she had not expected a cooing among the wine-glasses. If he was aware of the chill in her reply, he gave no sign of it.

Conversation was not vigorous. He had something to say about the garden, the thinning and staking of the red roses. He seemed to know something about it. Edith started off about a washing-machine they had found in the kitchen in good order. But once again he stared at her, it did not seem to need more than three or four seconds, and the subject died on her lips. He did not like the washing-machine switched on over the Sheraton table. The meal came to an end with a green salad and a Camembert, at this time still a luxury. Aunt Edith rose. Marian rose, too.

"We'll have coffee in the sitting-room," said Edith.

Matthew moved his arm along the table and touched Marian's hand with his finger-tips.

"I hope you don't mind, my dear"—he was addressing his wife and his voice had the silky smoothness of his pointed beard—"I hope you don't mind. Could Marian stay on and crack a few walnuts for me? It would be quite like old times."

That was a fiction. There had never been an old time when Marian had cracked walnuts for him. Was this the moment to say something at last? Marian looked into her aunt's eyes. What could one say that would not make things even more sad than they were?

"Please do as he asks," Edith's eyes said. Without a word, Edith went out of the room. Without a word Marian sat down again. The man-servant brought a bowl of nuts over from the sideboard, and put down two fruit-plates. Then he brought the decanter.

"Here you are, my dear," said Matthew. That meant the nut-crackers. "Do you mind?"

"No," said Marian without warmth. But she did not mind. She was intensely interested.

He circled the decanter clock-wise and set it before her.

"A glass of port, surely? The daughter of an Oxford Common Room!"

"I think not," she said. "Thank you, I'll wait for coffee."

He shrugged his shoulders, then filled his glass.

"It's Dow '05, you know," he said, as if that might make a difference. He held the glass reverently to the light, then moved it to and fro under his nostrils. "Delicious," he murmured, and sipped it once, and again, and again. He had the faculty, it seemed, of completely absorbing himself in the moment's thought or act. She took a walnut from the bowl, and cracked it.

"Oh, yes, my dear," he said, as if the walnuts had quite gone out of his mind, in the intensity of his meditation on the Dow '05. He poured a little salt on his plate, she placed a cracked nut beside it, then a second, then a third. "Thank you," he murmured. "I don't really deserve it." No. Perhaps he did not.

The man came in with a taper, and hesitated a moment.

"Yes," said Uncle Matthew. The man lit the candles like a Venetian mute. A last few birds bickered in the evening sky. Then these, too, ceased, and there was no sound at all save the cracking of the walnuts and the clink of the decanter against the glass. And another sound. The tapping of the beak of the woodpecker against the side of her skull.

How had it come about? He was his father's son, and his father had been an eminent surgeon, and from all one knew of him as amiable a parent as the next one. He was his brother's brother, and his brother was Warden of St. Stephen's, Doctor of Divinity, Doctor of Letters. Did the Thing emerge with him from his mother's womb? Had it grown from tiny beginnings, subtly, like a canker, when he was a child? But who, what, had implanted the seed? Was there a moment when the growth could have been killed like a nerve in a tooth? Or was the first theft a sudden explosion, filling the deep secret crevices with a gas impossible from that moment to expel?

"Won't you have just a half-glass, Marian?"

"No, thank you."

"What are you thinking of?"

"Just thinking."

How long ago had Edith married him? Before the War, of course. Yes, well before the War. Edith had not known then he was a criminal, but she knew soon enough. In a few months there was an eighteen months sentence at Pentonville for safebreaking. He came out, and she had him to live with her again. Then the War happened. He managed, somehow, to get a commission. He stole jewels and cheque-books in country houses. He was cashiered. There was a long sentence to serve in Parkhurst. Here he was again, in a new house she had bought for him, terrifyingly near Oxford. Was he irretrievable, quite irretrievable? Were all Edith's labours a handful of grain thrown on to a field of gravel?

If there had been an Edith earlier, when he was a boy, might it have been different? Was he even now utterly irretrievable? Only one thing was sure. If every moral scruple, if every flicker of shame, were as dead inside him as dust, certainly the taste for luxury was not dead, the silk on the skin, the bouquet on the palate. How could he bear the gritty indigence, the scaly squalor?

"Wasn't it horrible," a voice asked, "over there?" She realized with embarrassment it was her own voice. There was no pity in it, merely a baffled curiosity.

He smiled. She saw the flash of his teeth in the candlelight. Then he raised his hand to his beard and stroked it affectionately.

"It was this," he said, meaning the beard. "The three years . . . in Siberia . . . weren't so bad at all. It was the six weeks it took me to get this right . . . they were the very devil. Shall we go in for our coffee now?"

IV

The man-servant was off-stage somewhere in the shadows. Within a minute of their entry into the sitting-room, the coffee was brought in, chuckling in the glass percolator.

"A little brandy, Marian?" asked Uncle Matthew.

"I think not," said Marian.

"You, my dear?" he asked his wife. Out of sight of the ill-suited roses, he was more affable. She shook her head.

"Not even a little crême de menthe?" Women might be deemed partial to that. They refused. They were not feeling very festive. Uncle Matthew permitted himself a cigar.

"Do you like the water-colours?" he was asking. "This is one of Edward Lear's. I think he's been rather underrated, don't you?"

"They're very pleasant," she said. "Did you find them here? And the books?" (She was standing by a bookcase without in the least remembering when she had risen from her chair to go across to it. The books were in good taste, too: the metaphysical poets, the travel books by the approved novelists.)

"Yes," he said. "We found them here. Oh, talking about

books. I seem to remember. You were to take over a book-shop in Oxford. Did you? In the Broad, I think. I can't remember how I found out. One does, you know." He smiled. "I went off, you see . . . to Siberia." He meant penal servitude in Parkhurst. It was the second time he had made the joke. That was so odd. Not that he had no sense of guilt, but that there was no shame, not even embarrassment.

"I did, Uncle Matthew," she told him. "I thought it would be a good thing to do."

"Going nicely?"

"Quite nicely."

"I've learned a lot about books—since I've left school, that is to say. I've been made librarian more than once. You may want to take me on, one of these days." His eyes twinkled.

"You're going to have your hands full here," Marian observed. "And you have chickens, did you say?" She looked at her watch. "Oh, dear, I'll miss my bus. They're so few and far between."

"My dear," he assured her. "I'll order a car for you."

"No, thank you." The firmness of her voice quite astonished her. She had plunged a can too deep down already into a bucket whose water quickly became dubious and murky. "I'll find my way. May I get my things, Aunt Edith?"

"Well, one of us will take you to the high road. I insist." One of them meant his wife, of course. She did not want the company of either of them. "You can't go through the woods alone, at this hour," he observed.

"I shall enjoy it. I can look after myself. Besides. Look. A moon's coming up." She went up with her aunt and got her things. They said good-bye to her on the terrace.

"Remember me to my brother, Henry," he told her. "And to your mother."

"Yes," she said. "Thank you." She made her way down the slope towards the lily-pool.

"And to the twins," he called after her.

"Yes. Good-bye."

"Good-bye."

He stood on the terrace waving to her, like any girl's favourite uncle. She turned once again as she reached the bottom of the slope where the artful little bridge crossed the artful little stream. He, too, turned at that moment into the house. The light over the front door flickered on his silken beard. His wife went before him, into the private hell she could not and would not break.

It was only a two minutes walk down to the stream, up the clearing, and into the wood. And within those two minutes the mist had fallen. Beech and lime and hawthorn might have been ilexes or lamp-standards for all she saw of them. All she saw, shining through the mist, was the light in the dead eyes and on the dead lips of her young sailor husband, who had been killed on the North Sea three days after the second day of their honeymoon. There was nothing to do about it, whether you were in a book-shop in the Broad or in a square in Bloomsbury, or in an Oxfordshire wood, nothing to do but to wait till the mist lifted: or till it thinned, at least, for it never quite lifted. And there you were at the centre of it, your brain empty, your heart empty. You went on living because the blood went on pumping, and the clock kept ticking over. There had been something so adorably, wistfully *comic* about him. Even his name. Cuthbert. Is it possible to address anyone as "Cuthbert"? "Cuth" is even more deadly. "Bert"? Hardly. Nothing left but "Bertie." His nose was comic, tip-tilted, the wide pale nostrils. There were freckles. The hair, too, was comedian-coloured, a washed-out ginger. The most comic element in him was the discrepancy between the stuttering timidity of his manner and the legendary derring-do of his career at sea, a sword-flash, a trumpet. There was something comic about his peace-time job, too. He was at the Reading branch of the Empire Home Stores; in sole charge of all matters relating to underwear, male and female. He had joined the Navy as a lower-deck rating; but he was one of those young men in whom active service releases all sorts of talents no-one had suspected, least of all himself. By the time Marian met him, he was Lieutenant-Commander Cuthbert Framley, in command of an M.T.B. She was an officer in the Wrens, and had met him at a dance in Harwich, early in 1943. They fell for each other in five seconds, or less. This was the first time that a girl had done this to him, and he stormed up to her, all guns blazing, as if she were a German E-boat. They did not discuss their respective jobs in the Navy. They had come to a dance to forget all about that. But they talked about everything else under the sun. They kidded each other. They laughed at each other's jokes. They danced as if they were put together out of moonbeams. They were transfigured.

It was only at the very end that there was a contretemps. She was saying good-bye to him on the moonlit gravel of the hotel yard when she suddenly remembered that she knew the people who owned the Empire Home Stores; the young men of the family usually went to Rugby and St. Stephen's. She had intended to mention this before, but only now, in this last moment, did the topic jump to her tongue.

"I wanted to tell you," she said. "I know the people who own the Empire Home Stores. I'll see them on leave. I'll tell them I met the Manager of their Reading branch."

His face blanched in the moonlight; his hair, somehow, turned pale as string. Then a fierce blush flapped across his cheeks.

"Not Manager," he whispered, "not Manager," for that was what he had told her. He was almost dead with embarrassment at the indecency of his overstatement. "Only Assistant-Manager. *Please don't tell them,*" he implored.

There seemed to be nothing to do but to throw her arms round him and kiss him. This she did. In some seconds he had recovered, for his reflexes were swift. He kissed her back, with a fervour which repaid the investment at a high rate of interest.

She did not for some time have the faintest idea of his quite legendary reputation among small ships. She was moved to Portsmouth only the next day, to a job where she did not meet the people who might have heard of it. Certainly, it did not occur to her to question them. It was when she was on leave some months later at home that she was put into the picture. The B.B.C. was broadcasting at that time a series of exploits performed by valiant service-men, dead or living. It had been a strenuous day for Marian. She was alone. It was dark. She switched the wireless on, and found herself plunged into an account of the exploits of a fabulous M.T.B. and its fabulous commanding officer. She listened, if only because she had a special interest in that branch of the service. The breathless story unrolled. It was a welter of boarding-parties, and shootings, and smashing up of engines, and blood and fire and glory. The story was brought to a close. The announcer read his codicil: "You have been listening to an episode in the career of Lieutenant-Commander Cuthbert Framley. . . ." She did not hear the rest of the announcement. A voice was speaking much closer to her ear.

"Not Manager. Not Manager. Only Assistant-Manager. *Please don't tell them. . . .*"

They were married the next time they had a leave together. He was called back on the second day after the honeymoon, and was killed on the third day. It was a brave death to die, and picturesque. But it would have been better if he had not died.

She rubbed her eyes. 'Where am I?' she asked herself. Yes, of course. She was on the Witney high road, headed towards Oxford. She must have been walking along the high road for several minutes already. The moon was up on her right hand, and the branches lay across it in a beaten wrought-iron pattern. Ahead of her on the left were the lights of the Blue Lion, where the bus-stop was. She looked at her watch. She could take it easy. There would be a few minutes to spare.

Then suddenly a young man appeared, hatless, a smile on the mouth, full chin, a broad brow, the moonlight pale on his face. You first saw the smile on the mouth. It was an attractive face, not at all a face to worry you, coming up against it suddenly by moonlight on a lonely road. The young man must have been approaching her for some time, for there was no side-road right or left; or maybe he had been sitting quietly on the grass verge till a moment or two ago. But she had not seen him till now.

"Beg your pardon," the young man said. "I'm looking for a . . . house, name of Hatchetts. You wouldn't . . . have an idea where it is, Miss, would you?" It was a working-class accent, Home Counties or Cockney. The young man had to pause before bringing out an "h" successfully.

"As a matter of fact . . ." she started. She was going on to say that she had just come from a house named Hatchetts, then it occurred to her one should not readily give information about a house tucked away in a wood; not to a young stranger at night on a high road, even if he seemed quite amiable.

He saw her hesitation.

"It's all right," he assured her. "I know Mr. Browne. He's an old friend of mine."

He was quick-witted. He had perceived the significance of the few words he had got out of her. Well, she would not give more information until she felt she ought to.

"Oh, you know the people who live there?" she asked.

"Yes." This time the sound was much nearer the Cockney *yus*. "It's the gentleman I know. As a matter of fact, I've met him more than once . . ." he hesitated for the fraction of a second, then an eye screwed up in a wink . . . "in Siberia."

"Well, if you know——" she started. Then the sentence broke on her lips. Her heart stopped beating. She was talking to a released convict, an associate of her uncle, Matthew Browne, in Parkhurst Prison, or wherever it was. She was not afraid, though he was a powerful, broad-shouldered young man, and they were quite alone on a long stretch of road. But she was astonished, and she was angry. The young man had had no reason to believe that his witticism would mean anything to her, a total stranger coming from anywhere at all. It was only by a thousand to one chance that it *did* mean something. Despite all that, with what easy insolence he had established a sense of intimacy, even of collusion!

But the brain worked quickly, despite the suspended heartbeating, and the suffocation in her throat, and the banging at her temples. It had clearly been arranged between the older and the younger man, somewhere, some time, that they should meet. The arrangement, as likely as not, would have been made in prison. It was not up to her to further whatever schemes their renewed association might portend.

She clenched her fists, and opened her mouth to speak. She was surprised to find that, in fact, words came.

"As a matter of fact," she said, "I'm a stranger in these parts." Then she moved on, her knees as soft as cushions.

The young man turned and looked after her.

"Sorry you've been trroubled, miss," the young man said

facetiously. He was being a telephone-operator for a moment. He raised his voice. "I'll be seein' yer," he declared. There was a pause. Then he raised his voice louder. "The name's Tommy."

The statement that he would be seeing her was not intended as prophecy, she knew that. Further, he had given his name exactly as he might have given his name to a little machine-hand in a Palais-de-Danse. It was just a counter in the game of boy-meets-girl, any boy meets any girl, and you might as well pass the counter as not.

Yes, she was depressed, and she was just a little frightened, too, as she stood waiting for the bus to come lurching down from Chipping Campden. For there was already a link between this young man and herself, and the link was the man who was her father's brother and this young man's friend. For this young man that would somehow be enough.

The name's Tommy. The name's Tommy. She tried all she knew to dispel the name and the face. She summoned her dead sweetheart to her aid. But he came only when he chose to, not when he was summoned.

The name was Tommy, all the way home to the Cornmarket, and half the night in her small bedroom over the book-shop. The moonlight glimmered on the white sprigged wallpaper as it had glimmered on the young man's smiling mouth.

Matthew, Tommy. . . . She got up next morning and had a cold, sharp shower. She tried to believe she was sluicing herself free of both of them, the two precious creatures that had come up out of the pit. But before an hour or two had passed she knew she had not achieved this. The question that had haunted all day yesterday haunted her today. But the object of reference was changed.

How had it come about? What had made a crook of this young man? Was he born in a thieves' den? Or were his miserable parents as decent and respectable in their world as the parents of Matthew Browne had been in theirs? Had he been thrown as a small boy among scallywags? Had they egged him on to some first fateful little snatch of an apple from a barrow? Then had they stationed him at a street-corner while they themselves nipped smartly down a back-alley to do some squalid little job?

Or had the thing come from nowhere, from anywhere, like the flying spore of dry rot in wood?

Then suddenly the memory came back to her. The blood pulsed across her cheek like flame. She, too, had been a thief in her time.

She was at that moment standing in the tiny kitchenette of the Broad Street flat, behind the bookshop. It was her morning to make the breakfast and do the washing-up. The memory came up out of its kennel like a shaggy little mongrel crawling with fleas. The milk-jug slipped from her hands and smashed in the sink. It was a dragon-blue milk-jug from the nice set, and the set belonged to Cecilia.

"I'm terribly sorry, Cecilia!" she called out. "It's the milk-jug! From the nice set!"

"Don't worry, Marian dear!" Cecilia replied. She was good at this sort of thing. "Plenty more where that came from!" It was Chinese china, and there weren't. "Shall I help you dry?"

"No, Cecilia! Smoke your cigarette! So sorry!"

Of course she had never really quite forgotten, though she tried hard to convince herself she had. Sometimes she would hear the horrid little mongrel stir and whimper. 'Down!' she would say inside herself. 'Down! Get back!'

And, of course, that was one reason, probably the chief reason, why she had plagued herself so about Uncle Matthew and this miserable Tommy, how they had started off. She had started off, too. But she had stopped.

It was the year they had been to Loch Tay during the long vac. Then she was eight, and it was the Michaelmas term. Her governess, Miss Fothergill, had asked her would she please go upstairs and get her reading-glasses for her. In wet weather Miss Fothergill's knee swelled up, and that made climbing stairs difficult for her. So Marian went upstairs and got the reading-glasses; but on the same table as the glasses there was a heap of copper coins and some bits of silver.

So she had stolen sixpence, thinking it would not be noticed. There had been no pangs of conscience. She bought sweets. In those days there were endless sweets to buy, and you could buy endless sweets for sixpence. That was the beginning. The stealing went on for two or three months; not only from Miss Fothergill, but from Smithson, the parlour-maid, as well; and her mother, too, towards the end. She never tried it on with Mrs. Rennitt, the cook, who was altogether too formidable a woman, without a scrap of sentiment inside her.

Miss Fothergill had a great deal of sentiment, far too much, and a lucky thing for Marian, too. Marian was soon aware of a certain constraint in Miss Fothergill's manner, and of a hurt expression in her eyes, like a dog who cannot believe that its master can really be meaning what he is saying. There was a period of insecurity, when Marian wondered whether Miss Fothergill was going to report the stealing to Daddy. But obviously Miss Fothergill did not report it to anybody, for nobody said anything.

Then she started stealing money from Smithson. Smithson had a tin chest under her bed, with a padlock. But the foolish creature kept the key on a nail just beside the tin chest. So Marian crept under the bed, unlocked the chest, and helped herself to those hardly-earned shillings and sixpences. Before long she was aware that a whispering was going on between Miss Fothergill and Smithson, which stopped as soon as she appeared on the scene. They were obviously discussing the stealing, but still they said nothing. Once or twice she surprised Smithson sniffling in a corner. Smithson could not afford, even less than Miss Fothergill, to lose those shillings and sixpences, for she was saving up to get married. And still neither Smithson nor Miss Fothergill said anything. And still she herself, Marian, had no pangs of conscience; no more than a cat stealing a lump of fish from the kitchen-table.

She bought sweets, she bought fairy-tale books, and what she did not spend she put on a cross-slat in the recesses of a sideboard. Somehow she did not arouse the suspicions of her parents. They were both stone-blind, of course. But then, one does not begin to think this sort of thing about the well-brought-up daughter of an Oxford don in holy orders, a little girl who goes to church eagerly every Sunday morning, with a face shining like a bar of soap.

Perhaps Daddy (she said to herself now, many years later)

might have been a little more on the *qui vive*. She stood there by the sink, the clock in one hand, working out a sum on her fingers. She was eight. Therefore these goings on were in nineteen-twenty-eight. When had the first open scandal with Uncle Matthew taken place . . . her mother had once given her some of the details of the grim Matthew story . . . when was it? The scandal of the stolen cigarette-cases at the week-end cricket party? It was nineteen-twenty-five, wasn't it? About then. He had not gone to prison that time. They had managed to hush up the scandal.

Oh yes. Being a thief could happen to Daddy's brother. Why should it not happen to Daddy's daughter? The old boy should have been more on the *qui vive*.

So the stealing went on for some more weeks. Then suddenly she realized how filthy she had been. A picture stood up before her of Miss Fothergill and Smithson in the kitchen removing their handkerchiefs from their eyes and pretending they had not been crying.

And Marian had gone out into the paddock at the back of the house, and been sick . . . never in the years to come had she been so sick in a heaving Channel sea. She spewed her insides up. She had never been a thief since then.

"Hello, Marian darling! Aspirin?" This was Cecilia calling out from the sitting-room. It was her way of saying: "Keep your chin up!" For during the times when the grief came down like a fog, and to all intents and purposes Marian wasn't there any more, it was the convention between them that Marian was to be presumed suffering from headache. It was necessary, sooner or later, to bring Marian back to the common clay. Sometimes she would say yes to aspirins, sometimes not.

"No, my dear! I'm all right! I'm coming in! I've finished!" She looked at the draining-board and, in fact, she had. She had put the cups away and the plates and saucers were draining in the rack.

She went across into the sitting-room. Beyond the sitting-room was the shop, with the easy chairs and the sherry. There should have been less easy chair and sherry, and more books. But that was Cecilia's theory on the business, and she had put the greater part of the money into it. The light was streaming in through the open door. The shop was empty.

"Anyone been in?" asked Marian doubtfully. She was doubtful because usually, if anyone came in, they stayed in, and sat down and smoked, and read. It was not often they merely came in, bought a book, paid for it, and went out.

"Oh, yes," Cecilia said enthusiastically. "That poppet from Trinity was in. What's his name?"

"Osterley?" Marian's heart sank. He owed a bill of thirty pounds already.

"Yes, that's his name. He said he wanted Green, and I said I'd order it."

"Which Green? Fiction? History?"

"Oh, I don't know. He was in an awful hurry. But it wouldn't be *history*! Fiction, I suppose. Isn't there a Julius?"

It was not a very dreadful mistake. There might well be a Julius, but Marian was certain that it was Julian who was wanted. None the less, at that moment the partnership snapped. As a business the 'Easy Chair' was too footling. As a book-woman, Cecilia was too giddy.

'Somewhere,' Marian said to herself, 'I'll start up a bookshop of my own, away from poppets, something I can get my teeth into. London, maybe. London's my place.'

CHAPTER II

THE next episode took place in October of that year. Marian was in London, doing a week of theatres. It was her turn for a week off. But on the Thursday night she was not doing a theatre; it was dinner at the flat of the Ernest Latimers in Mecklenburgh Square, in Bloomsbury. Ernest, and one or two of the others, had known Bertie, her dead husband, but they weren't talking about him. Nobody talked about Bertie when Marian was around, but it was always a comfort to her to be with people who had known and liked him.

Dinner was over. They were sitting round over coffee and brandy, when the telephone-bell rang, and Latimer rose to answer it. He had a housekeeper who usually took the calls, for his wife, Doris Latimer, had a 'thing' about the telephone; but the housekeeper lived out, and she was gone now.

"Yes, prees?" asked Latimer, in a high-pitched voice. "Who is that, prees?" It was clearly intended for a Japanese voice. The others took next to no notice. They had all known him long enough to know that when Ernest himself lifted the receiver, he pretended he was a Japanese man-servant, to give himself the opportunity to decide whether he was in or out.

Presumably the caller gave a name, and inquired whether Mr. Latimer was in. Or Latimer recognized the voice.

"One moment, prees," he said, and laid the receiver down. Then he turned. The call was obviously unwelcome. "Hell!" he muttered, and made a gesture of annoyance with his clenched fist. He looked very put out. Nobody said a word. Then his wife spoke.

"Who is it, Ernest?"

"You don't know," he said, shortly. "You don't know." He walked up and down the room several times, then shrugged his shoulders. The gesture implied: After all, the telephone has its embarrassments for us all. Then, aloud, he said: "I suppose I'll have to." He showed at once what he meant by that. He would have to stop being a Japanese man-servant to the caller, and admit to being himself. He lifted the receiver.

"Oh, yes," he said. "This is Mr. Latimer. Who's that?" There was no cordiality in the voice. On the contrary, there was constraint and embarrassment. It was really rather odd. If he had not wanted to speak to the caller, why hadn't he gone on being the Japanese man-servant? All he needed to say was: "Sorry, prees, Mr. Latimer is out." That would have been good enough.

By this time the caller had given his name. Latimer repeated it.

"Oh, it's you, Tommy, is it? I'm very well, thank you. Are you all right?" Presumably the caller admitted he was all right. Then for some moments a deadness seemed to have fallen on the interchange. Either there was a mechanical fault in the line, or for some reason at the other end as well as this end there was a pause. It was Latimer who resumed the conversation. "Have you got a job?" he asked. "Oh, I see." He pursed his lips. "You're doing all right. That's good. Well?" Latimer waited. Whether the other spoke or did not speak, nothing very satisfactory transpired. The situation was becoming embarrassing to everybody. "Is there anything special you wanted to say to me? No? Oh, very well. It was kind of you to ring. Good night, Tommy, good night."

Latimer replaced the receiver and sat down. He was pale. His forehead was moist with sweat, but in the silence his wife uttered three words, not more.

"Nothing wrong, Ernest?"

He shook his head. The gesture was not conclusive. But she said no more. It must be left to him to talk, if he wanted to. A certain Bill Hylan, one of the guests, reached forward and raised Latimer's glass from the table. With the other hand he brought the whisky decanter nearer.

"Shall I just top it up for you?" he asked, trying to make his voice sound as casual as possible. It was Ernest's business, really, not his, to suggest filling up the glasses. But Ernest looked as if he could do with a shot

"Yes, please," said Latimer. "Thank you. More than that. No soda."

"Me, too, please," came a faint voice from the depths of an easy-chair. It was the voice of Marian Browne. She had her whisky-glass stretched out before her, but her hand was trembling so, it looked as if the glass must slip through her fingers.

"Why, what's wrong?" asked Bill Hylan.

"Are you all right, Marian?" asked the girl, Angela.

"Oh, my dear!" said the third man in the company, young Stratton.

It was puzzling to them all. Why was Marian Browne looking so white about the gills? It was not to *her* that a disturbing call had come along the telephone-wire. Bill Hylan filled up her glass.

"Oh, it's nothing," murmured Marian. "Just a bit of a turn!" The others turned their eyes away. One does not let oneself probe into the reasons why a young woman goes into a dither all of a sudden, particularly when she is a war-widow, who had been terribly in love with her husband, and her husband had been swallowed up in the North Sea a day or two after the wedding. Probably it was of *him* that somehow or other she had been reminded. Had *his* name been Tommy, too? But it hadn't been, as one or two of them remembered. It had been Cuthbert, Bertie.

Attention switched back to Latimer.

"All right, Ernest?" asked Bill Hylan.

Latimer did not reply for several seconds, then the question registered.

"What? Me?" he said. "Of course I'm all right."

"O.K.," murmured Bill Hylan. Nobody was going to poke his nose where his nose wasn't wanted. The silence was resumed, and endured long enough to become uncomfortable. One was at the stage when somebody ought to appoint himself life-and-soul-of-the-party, and get things back on an even keel again.

"It's a bloody nuisance!" Latimer shouted, banging his fist down on the table beside him. "I wish to hell I knew what to do."

Nobody, of course, could begin to tell him, for nobody had the faintest idea what was biting him, not even his wife, apparently. It was something to do with Tommy, of course. Was this Tommy a cadger, a sponger? Who *was* this Tommy? Had Ernest incurred some obligation to him during the war, which had now become a pain in the neck to him?

"Listen!" said Latimer. "I'd like to tell you about him. I wonder what *you'd* have done. It's got me worried sick!"

"Just one thing——" Bill Hylan started out diffidently.

"Yes?"

"Who's 'him,' anyhow? Who *is* this fellow?"

"Oh, Tommy. Yes, of course. I was going to tell you about him. Tommy Smith. He's a young criminal; anyhow, an ex-criminal. He was in Parkhurst Gaol till a few months ago." He turned to his wife. "I've not spoken about him to you."

"No," she said. She was scrupulous to keep out of her voice any suggestion of reproach, or even of curiosity.

"Oh, *dear*," said the young man, Stratton, blinking. The very thought that he had been in the same room as someone who had received a telephone message from a gaolbird was like a smut in his eye. He would have liked to slide off then and there. But the someone who had received the message was Ernest Latimer, his pal. And he had just had a damn good meal with some damn nice people at Ernest Latimer's table. One would stay put, of course.

"Really?" said the girl, Angela. There was excitement in her eye. 'How fascinating!' her face said. But her mouth managed not to say it.

'Smith!' said Marian Browne to herself. 'So *that's* what the name is! Tommy Smith! Something told me I wasn't finished with him, he was going to crop up again somewhere. I mustn't scream! I mustn't!' She took a cigarette from the box in front of her.

"A match, please, Mr. Hylan!" He flicked his lighter for her. "Oh, thank you!"

"And yet I don't know," Latimer was saying. "I don't know whether I *ought* to tell you. I mean——" his ideas were not coming at all clearly to him—"you can only fight it out for yourself, inside yourself. It's not that it's a breach of confidence. Oh, no. It's nothing like that at all."

The ideas were not clear inside Marian's skull, either. They had been anything but clear from the moment she had turned away from the young man, there in the moonlight, at the bus-stop, in the lonely Oxfordshire road. She couldn't say it had been clear to her that some day, somewhere, she would meet him again. It wasn't so simple as that. Somehow she had become tied up with him. That was all. In fact, she *hadn't* met him again, not *yet*. The worst that had happened now was that she had been in the room of one of her friends when he had telephoned. And even then, was she certain, was she absolutely certain, it was the same Tommy? Yes. That she could answer straight away. She *was* absolutely certain. The two Tommies were the same Tommy. This was their second encounter, if you could call it an encounter. Somehow, somewhere, there would be another.

To what end? To what good to anybody? It was as if she were on the fringe of a swampy country at evening, and a mist was coming up, and at any moment the quagmire would be around her knees.

Bill Hylan was talking now. At least he was trying to. He was tugging at his collar as if it were chafing his neck.

"It isn't that . . . I mean . . . how can I put it? . . . You're not worried about something, Ernest—— Is that it?"

"But I've told you!" Latimer said rather shortly. "I'm damned worried! I'm miserable!"

"You don't see what I mean," Bill Hylan floundered. "What I'm trying to say is . . . it's absolutely idiotic, of course."

Then his meaning flashed into Latimer's mind, like a smell suddenly released from a bottle.

"You mean has this fellow got anything on me? Come on now! Is it?" He paused a moment, then he smiled. "No, Bill. The young man's got absolutely nothing on me. I haven't cracked a crib with him, or set up a plant to make five-pound notes. I've only met him once, in a public place, with anything up to sixty or seventy people there. It's not that at all, Bill old boy."

"I'm sorry," said Bill, pink with embarrassment. "I'm sorry," he muttered again. Then he was quiet.

"I'd like to tell you," said Latimer diffidently. "I wonder if you'll be bored." He turned to his wife. "I ought to have told you earlier, darling."

"It's up to you always, darling," she assured him. "Whenever you like."

"We *won't* be bored!" vowed Bill Hylan.

"Certainly we won't!" said Angela, almost clapping her hands.

Marian lit up her cigarette again, and settled back into her chair. That showed *she* wouldn't be bored, either. She scrutinized the others through narrowed lids. No, she was positive. Not one of them remembered, if they had ever known, that she, too, had a criminal in her life, her father's brother, in fact. Not even Doris Latimer, though they had been at college together. How lucky it was that the family name was Browne, even if there was an "e" to it! No, these people could not be such good actors. They just did not know about Matthew Browne.

"You know how keen I am on boxing, don't you?" began Latimer. "It's one of my side-lines." Yes, everybody knew that. "I know most of the promoters and managers, and the boxers, too, for that matter. Have you heard of Andy Patten who was Middleweight Champion till last year? Well, I suppose not. It was at his wedding I met Tommy Smith. When was that now . . . ? Yes, July, 1943, just over four years ago. Andy was on leave from the army at the time, and I was doing that job at the War Office.

"It was nice of Andy to ask me along. I was quite flattered. The wedding was going to take place at a pub in Hornsey, the Cross Keys. I liked the sound of it. You know, the boys on leave, and the girls on leave, and a few boxers with their little blondes, and a few slick-haired managers and trainers, and the old men with their clay pipes, and the old women getting merrier and merrier, lifting their skirts up, and singing: 'Knees up, Muvver Brahn.' You know, quite my cup of tea.

"I didn't flatter myself I was asked down entirely for my good looks. Andy was always a bit of a tuft-hunter, and he thought I'd add 'class' to the occasion. I did, in fact, bring down my latest masterpiece, duly autographed, as part of my wedding present, and they propped it up in front of the wedding-cake as if it was a First Folio. I also brought three bottles of gin, which were at least as popular. I felt I'd more or less paid my way. I ought to say I didn't come alone. I was looking round for a taxi in Tottenham Court Road, when I heard a voice hail me from the driving-seat of a little Ford van. It was a sergeant who'd been in my company in France and was discharged now. Bill, his name was. Frost-bite.

" 'Going anywhere, Captain?' he called out. 'Want a lift?'

"I got in. We both thought it would be a good idea to have one on the way, just to drink to old times. We had one or two, and by the time we got to the Nag's Head, Bill had picked up a mate of his, a sailor named Ted, I think. Yes, Ted. Well, you know how things were in war-time. All three of us turned up for the wedding. If I had any misgivings about bringing two uninvited guests, Andy and his bride put them to rest very speedily. Besides, I *did* bring three bottles of gin, as a sort of over-all entrance-fee. The young couple were charming to us. Bill and Ted just slipped into the party like a couple of minnows released into a pond from a schoolboy's jam-jar. As for myself, I was thoroughly happy, too, though I felt a bit self-conscious at first. I must have looked it, too, for Andy felt he ought to do something about it. There happened to be a young fellow near me, a pleasant-looking fellow, about twenty-two, in a dark civvy suit.

" 'Tommy,' said Andy. 'Will you look after my friend, Mr. Latimer? 'E's a book-writer.'

"Then Andy moved off. He was, after all, the bridegroom. There were a great many calls on his attention.

"How do you do, Tommy?' I said, and put my hand out.

" 'Pleased to meet you . . . er . . . er,' he said.

" 'Ernie,' supplied Andy; then he was engulfed.

" 'Pleased to meet you, Ernie,' Tommy resumed. 'What yer drinkin'?'

" 'Oh, just beer,' I said. 'Known Andy a long time?'

" 'Last Sunday in the gym,' replied Tommy. 'Old Wolff's gym. In Charlotte Street. But I've always *followed* 'im. Bung-ho!' He lifted his glass of beer.

" 'Bung-ho!' I replied.

"He seemed a nice lad, this Tommy. He had a rather broad, open face, slightly snub-nosed. He might have been a bit of a bruiser, too. He fulfilled his assignment very nicely, saw that I had enough to eat and drink, and worked me pleasantly into conversation with my neighbours. He made it all a lot easier for me than it might have been. The party duly advanced to the knees-up Muvver Brahn stage, and then I had to be off. It had been a jolly couple of hours. 'Good-bye,' I called out to everybody. The bride threw her arms round me and kissed me. So did her mother and sister and most of the girls there. 'Don't forget, Andy!' I called out to the bridegroom. 'The next party will be at *my* place! You, and Dolly, and your mum and dad, and Tommy, and all the boys and girls. Cheerio.' 'Cheeribye!' everybody called back.

"So off we went; for Bill, the sergeant, had to be away, too, and Ted, the sailor, wouldn't stay without him. Then, when we were in the doorway, my cicerone, Tommy, tapped me on the shoulder. Which way were we going, he wanted to know. Bloomsbury, I told him. Going through Camden Town? I I looked at the sergeant. Yes, that would be all right, nodded Bill. Did Tommy want a lift? Yes, please, Tommy did.

"So we set off. I got in front beside Bill, the sergeant, and Tommy went behind and stretched out alongside Ted, the sailor. We hadn't been moving more than a minute or two when Tommy touched me on the shoulder.

" 'Do you know, Ernie? I'm a sailor, too.'

" 'Oh, really?' I replied, not particularly interested. I was thinking of other things.

" 'Yes,' said Tommy. 'I am.'

"He obviously wanted to make conversation, so I pursued the theme.

" 'On leave?'

" 'No.'

" 'Then you're demobbed?' I was still only making conversation.

" 'No,' replied Tommy.

" 'Oh?' I couldn't get the hang of it. Not on leave, not demobbed, and yet he was a sailor. 'How's that?' It was a little dense of me, of course.

" 'I'm on the run,' said Tommy, without the faintest embarrassment. Some of you may not know the phrase. He meant he was a deserter.

"I don't know what any of you would have done. I suppose I wouldn't have hesitated, either, if he'd been Army instead of Navy. In that case it would have been my clear duty to stop the van and hand him over to the nearest policeman. But it wasn't so easy, somehow. He *might* have been pulling my leg, though I was quite certain he wasn't. Moreover, you've got to remember the circumstances I'd met him in. There was really nothing to do one way or the other but to let it slide. Nobody said anything for two or three minutes, then Tommy spoke again.

" 'Listen, Ernie,' he said. 'You know that book of yours that you gave Andy?'

"I wasn't quite so pleased this time with the jovial manner of address.

" 'Yes?' I asked.

" 'I'd like you to give me one of your books some time. I like your books.'

"Other writers might be impervious to that sort of thing. I'm not, I'm ashamed to say. I really was a bit flattered.

"Perhaps I will some time. Which one?' Then I realized it was perhaps putting a strain on him to remember a book-title. 'What about the one that's just been filmed?' I asked. '*Ashes of Terror*?'

" 'I've read that one,' he told me. 'I liked it.'

" 'Oh?' At all events I couldn't pretend I disapproved of his taste in modern fiction. 'Did they have it in the Ship's Library?'

" 'No.'

" 'The Public Library?'

" 'No!'

"I couldn't dare to believe that he'd actually bought a copy.

" 'The Twopenny Library?'

" 'No.'

"I was really quite puzzled by this time.

" 'Where did you get it from, Tommy?'

"He answered without the slightest hesitation:

" 'I read it when I was inside!' Inside prison, he meant.

" 'Oh!' I felt my heart drop a beat or two. He'd asked to be dropped at Camden Town, and I saw with pleasure that Camden Town wasn't far off now. I should have left it at that, but you know what an inquisitive idiot I am. I can't leave things alone.

" 'What were you inside for, Tommy?'

" 'Housebreakin',' he said simply.

"We were no distance at all from Camden Town, but I couldn't resist the temptation of letting him know that there are people who don't take housebreaking quite so lightly.

" 'I hope you've given it up, have you?' There was no friendliness in my voice now, but I thought it prudent not to sound too censorious. One had no idea what lurked behind that smooth façade.

" 'Yes,' said Tommy. 'I have—more or. . . .' Then he paused. Then an eye screwed up in a wink. Then he added one word . . . 'less.' He had given up housebreaking, more or . . . less. You can imagine with what relief I saw that the van had braked in front of Camden Town Station.

" 'Well, here I am,' said Tommy. He extricated himself from the rear of the van. 'Thanks, Bill. So long, Ted. So long, Ernie. Cheerio. I'll be seein' yer.' There was a pleasant grin on his broad, open face. He waved a hand, and was off."

Latimer was silent for a minute or two. No-one else spoke, though the girl, Angela, gave the impression she would explode if she didn't. Marian stubbed out her cigarette, and lit another. She was thinking of the wink, the hideously knowing wink. A wink is, after all, not an uncommon gesture. Yet she felt that the wink on the Oxfordshire road and the wink outside the Camden Town Station would have been enough by themselves to have established the identity of the Oxfordshire Tommy and the London Tommy.

The concluding words were the same, too.

I'll be seein' yer.

Yes, he would be seeing her. It was inevitable as the fogs that would be engulfing the city within a few weeks. And the thought was just as lugubrious.

"So what happened?" asked Bill Hylan. "How soon did he come to see you?" There was an edge of bitterness in his voice. Doris Latimer noticed it if Ernest didn't. She put her hand on his arm.

"Bill!" she murmured.

"He *is* an old mutt, isn't he?" Bill observed. "He *asks* for this sort of thing!"

"What were you saying?" Latimer broke in. "How soon did he come to see me? I've never seen him from that day to this!"

"Oh!" There was a general sigh of relief.

"So he just makes a nuisance of himself on the telephone?" Bill Hylan went on. "Is that it? You shouldn't have your name in the book. I've told you."

"That wouldn't stop a young man like this," murmured Marian. It was the first time she had spoken for some time.

"No, I suppose not," agreed Bill Hylan.

"Well, Ernest, he *did* telephone you pretty soon?" he ventured. "Or didn't he?"

"Yes, the next night," admitted Latimer. Doris looked at him inquiringly. "No, Doris!" her husband said. "You'd gone to bed. I told you nothing about it."

"What did he want?" asked Marian.

"Was he just being friendly?"

"*Friendly!*" said Ernest. "*Friendly!* I'd like to tell you exactly what happened. Shall I?"

"Do!" insisted everybody.

"Well. The telephone-bell rang. I answered it. I mean Sessue Hayakawa answered it. Just like just now.

"'Who is that, pree?' I asked.

"'Is Ernie there?' a voice said. 'I want to speak to Ernie.'

"I didn't recognize the voice straight away. I hadn't heard it before on the telephone.

"'Who I say it is, prees?'

"'Tell 'im it's Tommy, who he met at Andy's weddin'.'

"'One moment, prees.' I put the receiver down, and thought. Somehow the call was not entirely unexpected. I had a sort of premonition he'd ring up. But not quite so soon as that."

"Quick off the mark," murmured Bill Hylan.

"You had a sort of premonition?" asked Marian.

"Yes, I did," confirmed Latimer. "So I stood there thinking what I ought to do . . . like just now, exactly the same thing. If I said I was out, he'd ring again, maybe, and then again. He probably had a lot of time on his hands. Or perhaps he'd just call round, casting a trained eye over the windows and drain pipes. I decided there was only one thing to do . . . get the thing over. I'd have to freeze him off somehow.

"I picked up the receiver.

"'Yes?' My voice was pretty icy. 'This is Mr. Latimer. Tommy Smith, is it? What can I do for you?'

"'Is that you, Ernie?' He was exceedingly affable. He seemed about as insensitive to my tone of voice as a dray-horse. 'I've got them four bodgers,' he announced gleefully.

"'*Bodgers?*' I repeated, quite taken off my guard. Obviously I should have told him I was busy and rang off.

"'Yes, bodgers!' he repeated. 'You know, dames!'

"He clearly had four women for my delectation, and, presumably, his own. I made another false move.

"'Four?' I said. It was most inept. 'I don't understand.'

"'Yes, Ernie,' he said. 'You said we should have a party. So I've got four dames. One for you, one for me, one for the sergeant, and one for the matelot.'

"'I'm afraid you've got it entirely wrong,' I said. I don't know. I just couldn't put that wretched instrument down. And I suppose . . . I was a bit afraid, too? Anyhow, I was damned curious. I wanted to know how that preposterous mind of his worked.

"'Listen, Smith,' I said. 'If I should ever want to meet a woman other than my wife, I wouldn't ask someone else to arrange it for me. As for those two young men, what have they to do with the business? I was given a lift just the same as you were, and you know it.'

"'What?' he exclaimed. 'Aren't they diggin' with yer? I thought you was runnin' some racket together!'

"I resisted the temptation to roar 'go to hell!' down the 'phone. There *was* something funny about it. Was there, or wasn't there?"

Of course there was, but it was only a rhetorical question. They all just mumbled something, but he wasn't listening. He wiped his forehead and went on.

"I said to him, with all the patience I could muster: 'Look here, Smith! You saw me give a copy of one of my books to Andy, as part of his wedding-present. What's more—you've read some of my books yourself, you tell me. You know as well as I do I'm an author.'

"'Oh, yes,' he observed. 'I know you're an *author*! But what do you do for a *livin'*?'"

That was rather funny, too. There was no getting away from that. Latimer does quite well out of his books. Everyone smiled.

"And then?" asked Marian.

"I suddenly got bored and angry. Perhaps he touched my *amour-propre*. Maybe. Anyhow I said I was being called, and would have to go. 'Good night, Smith,' I said to him. 'Good night, Mr. Latimer,' he replied. He seemed quite subdued. 'Sorry if I've been a bit of a nuisance,' he said, and rang off."

"And that wasn't the end of it?" asked Marian.

"No," said Latimer. "You've seen for yourselves."

"I suppose the Japanese butler worked overtime after that?" ventured Bill Hylan. "On the telephone, I mean?"

"No. It wasn't a telephone-call, it was a letter next time. It went on for pages and pages."

"He had time to kill," murmured Marian.

"Yes, that was part of it. He was 'on the run,' as he put it."

"What was he after? Money?" asked Bill Hylan. "He wanted to go straight, and if you'd only give him a helping hand——"

"Easy, Bill. I'm trying to explain. He didn't ask for money. Even if I was an absolute idiot there was only one thing I could do—ask him to give himself up to the naval police."

"And you did, of course?"

"Bill!" he snapped. "Don't rush me! You miss the whole point. Was I going to answer his letter, or wasn't I? If I answered, I admitted that I was interested in him, I admitted he had some sort of claim on my time and attention."

"I quite see," said Marian. "It had nothing to do with the contents of the letter."

"Yes, Marian, you're quite right."

"You haven't got the letter?" she asked.

"It was an extraordinary letter," Latimer murmured. Then he answered the question. "No! I haven't got the letter! I destroyed it. As I destroyed all the others."

"There've been others?" his wife asked.

"Yes. About half-a-dozen. I destroyed them all. As if *that* would get rid of them for me. But it didn't. I've got whole passages here"—he pointed to his forehead. "Like a strip of film."

"What did that first letter say?" asked Marian, quietly. The initiative had passed from Bill Hylan to her. Bill was out in the cold for the time being.

"First, the style in which it was written. It was a bit like the Cockney in which he spoke, except that the spelling was bad. I suppose the spelling was the exact equivalent of the occasional dropped aitches and thickened dentals. He used much longer words than *I* care to use, although the meaning of the words was often just off-key. The sentences were elaborate, and often just petered out, after four or five lines. His thoughts were too involved for the medium he had to hand."

"But what did he *say*, dear?" his wife asked with mild reproof.

"Yes, I know, darling. I'm sorry. You think I'm boring you with an author's interest in a purely professional matter—style, words, sentences. But it's something deeper than that.

The man at the wedding and the man who wrote the letter seemed to be two different people."

There was a suppressed grunt from Bill Hylan's direction. Latimer smiled.

"All right, Bill, all right. I know what you wanted to say. Perhaps they *were* two different people!"

"How do you know they weren't?" asked Bill Hylan diffidently.

"It's true I've never seen Tommy Smith again, so I've never put him down to a sheet of paper with a pen to test his handwriting. But one *knows*. There's no argument about these things. Shall I tell you about that letter?"

"You've got to, now," his wife murmured.

"Yes," muttered Latimer. He was unhappy about her. He had touched with a whiff of sulphur the telephone she used, the letter-box in her door. "I'll give you the gist of it, because the actual sentences, as I've told you, are as twisted as the man himself. The first letter arrived about a fortnight after the wedding. There were some fifteen pages of it. It began 'Dear Sir.' That in itself was an extraordinary change from the familiarity of the personal attitude."

"Ernest!" said Bill Hylan.

"Yes?"

"May I say things when I feel like them? You did ask us for our views, I think?"

"Certainly."

"That 'Dear Sir.' It sticks in my throat. It's so mealy-mouthed, somehow."

"Yes, I see what you mean. My view is that people like this are infinitely less confident in themselves than they seem to be. It's a show they put on. They live in a pretty cut-throat world. Hence the swing between the cocky and the grovelling." Bill Hylan did not seem very convinced. "Not that this letter was grovelling. He didn't ask for money for himself or his sick mother or anybody. He asked could he come and see me, could he talk about books, could he borrow more of my own books. Try and call it a bit of clumsy flattery. You may be right."

"He'd changed his mind about your working a racket with your two young accomplices?"

"He went into that a great deal—it was the most tortuous part of the letter. He apologized for his mistake. As far as I could see he tried to explain that he lived in a world where it did not occur to you that anybody was honest, not *anybody*; he meant the world of the Approved School Home and Borstal and prison. It's a world, he made out, in which it's no use trying to go straight. If you get a job without letting your employer know you've got a record, you usually have to do it with false papers. Usually you're found out quite soon. Then you're out on your neck. If you *do* let the boss know, you're at his mercy. Even if he takes no advantage of his knowledge, somehow it leaks out. Your own crook pals manage to get it put across. They don't want to see you escape from the country of the damned. They want you back again."

"But all that was irrelevant, wasn't it?" asked Marian. "It was war-time." Her husband, too, had been a naval man, and he had had a different sort of record.

"Exactly, Marian," said Latimer eagerly. "No power on earth could do anything for him till he'd given himself up as a deserter. That's why I evaded the issue. That's why I didn't write."

"You *evaded* the issue?" repeated Bill Hylan. "But it wasn't *your* issue."

"It was my issue, and yours. It was everybody's issue."

"I don't see that," said the young man, Stratton.

"No," observed Latimer patiently. "I'll put it this way. I don't think anything would have been finally decided if he'd given himself up, and taken his disciplinary punishment. He'd have done his spell in cells, and emerged in course of time; that is, if there were no civil offences to take into reckoning. And then? Was he any further on than before?"

"But, darling," his wife said. "Would he have been any further on if he'd come to see you, and you'd have talked to him, and lent him books, and so?"

"Why particularly *you*?" asked Bill Hylan.

"I don't know. I just don't know. Perhaps to each one of us is given the chance to save *one* brand from the burning, if we'll only stretch out a hand. But we have to have courage, and we haven't. At least, *I* haven't. I was afraid I'd burn my hand."

"But, Ernest," Bill Hylan objected. "I say again. Why *you*? What claim had the fellow on you? He'd brought you over a couple of drinks at a pub wedding. You'd given him a lift to Camden Town. Why pick on *you*?"

"It might have been *you*. It might have been anyone here. I was perhaps the first fairly honest and stable person he'd ever met, outside his official contacts. Perhaps the fact, too, that I write has something to do with it. Words, sentences, ideas, fascinate him."

"Perhaps he does Crossword Puzzles, too," suggested Bill Hylan, "wherever he is."

"Quite so," Latimer agreed wearily. "Perhaps he was trying something on. Perhaps he wasn't. Don't you see that that's what's always got me down? If you see a man being swept away by a fierce current, and you're safe on the river-bank—have you any right to ask what sort of a man he is before reaching your hand out to him?"

"So you *didn't* write to him?" said Marian.

"No. I had the same misgivings as Bill. And the rest of you, for that matter. I felt the chances were he was" . . . he paused a moment . . . "as they say, 'playing me for a sucker.' Probably he was."

"And perhaps not?" asked Marian.

"Perhaps not. I got another letter, about ten days later. In its own way, it was a curiously dignified letter. He said he knew he couldn't expect me to see him in my house. Perhaps we could meet in the Park, or in a pub somewhere."

"Always forgetting he 'was on the run'?" ventured Bill Hylan.

"Yes. He seemed to forget that. If only we could talk things over, he said. . . ."

"And get you in a place where he could knock you on the head with a length of lead piping?"

"Yes, maybe, Bill." Latimer turned towards him. "I don't think you realize, old boy, I'm quite as sceptical about it as you—most of the time. That's why you're not really being very helpful."

Bill Hylan looked shamefaced.

"I'm sorry, Ernest. I'm sorry."

"So you didn't meet him, in the Park, or anywhere else?" asked Marian.

"I sat here in this chair, twiddling my thumbs, thinking it out, arguing one way or another, as I've been doing ever since. I never got round to it."

"The next thing you knew he was in prison again?" asked Marian.

"Yes," said Latimer, startled. "What made you say so?"

Marian was aware that a flush had spread across her cheeks. But she was in shadow. She did not think it could be seen.

"It's obvious, isn't it?" she asked, and realized in the same breath how very obvious it was. There was no reason why Ernest should have this wretched sense of guilt about the young man, unless he *had* gone back to prison.

"Yes," Latimer agreed. "It's quite obvious. It sticks out a mile. I met the boxer, Andy, at one of those Service tournaments, and he told me."

"Did Andy know what sort of customer he was," asked Bill Hylan, "when he had him at his wedding?"

"I don't know. I shouldn't think so," Latimer said rather sharply. "They'd just met the previous Sunday at Andy's gym. I told you, didn't I? A month or so afterwards I heard again from Tommy Smith. He was in Parkhurst."

"And what did he say? I told you so?" ventured Bill Hylan. "If only you'd given me a helping hand, I wouldn't be where I am now?"

"No, not a word of that sort. I appreciated it."

"Robbery with violence? Did *you* knock the night-watchman on the head?" Bill sounded very waspish.

"Perhaps I did, if you weigh the matter up properly."

"Darling!" objected his wife.

"It's wicked!" cried Stratton shrilly. "You've got no right to talk like that! You might as well say *I* knocked the night-watchman on the head!"

"I see what Ernest means," said Marian. "We *all* knocked him on the head!"

"I *couldn't*!" said the girl, Angela. "Honestly, I couldn't!"

"He gave no excuses," resumed Latimer. "He asked for

books again, and mentioned three or four of mine he'd like to read."

"He was still on that tack," growled Bill Hylan.

"He hoped to become a library 'redband,' he wrote. I suppose that means a sort of attendant. 'I might have wrote books myself,' he informed me, 'but *dis aliter visum*'."

"I don't understand," said Marian. "He used the Latin phrase?"

"Yes. He used others, too, in later letters. Tags from Horace and Virgil. Quotations from Shakespeare. I suppose there was a Dictionary of Quotations in the library."

"And he thought it would impress you?" suggested Bill Hylan.

"I suppose so. He went on writing."

"Then at last you answered?" asked Marian.

"I did. A short note. The most difficult piece of writing I ever did in my life. I think it was a great mistake."

"Why?"

"Either I steeled myself against his solicitations for a scrap of attention, and, sooner or later, they might have petered out. Perhaps. Perhaps not. I must have become something symbolical by this time—a symbol of the life he might have lived."

"*Might?* Why didn't he?" asked Stratton.

"It's a big question, isn't it?" Latimer looked round, and caught Marian's eye. "Isn't it, Marian?"

"It's a lot of questions, I think," she ventured.

"You said either you steeled yourself against him, or else . . . or else what?" Bill Hylan reminded him.

"Or I took the plunge. I allowed myself to believe that he genuinely wanted someone to help him, and I threw myself into the job for all I was worth."

"Don't they *have* people to help them?" asked his wife, Doris. "People whose job it is."

"I think that's the point, darling. People whose *job* it is."

"What did you write him?" asked Marian.

"Just a few lines. I hoped he was getting on all right; and when he'd finished his time, I hoped he'd be able to settle down in a decent job. If there was anything I could do when he came out, I'd look round and let him know. Yes, it was a tough letter to write. I didn't want it to be too . . . after all, I wasn't his mate. And I didn't want to preach at him. There are people who get paid to do that."

"How did he take it?" asked Marian.

"It was pathetic; or it was clever, as you choose. He jumped at it like a mother seizing a loaf to feed her starving children. He went on and on; his gratitude was only part of it; he discussed the dark tragedies and bleak little comedies of his background; he philosophized; he threw his little Latin tags all round the place. It was too much. It stifled me. I let the letter go. There were more letters. Again and again he came back to the theme: if only one person could be found to believe in him, he thought he could go straight."

"Did you believe him?" asked Marian.

"If I could answer that, it would all be so simple," said Latimer wearily. "Sometimes I believed him, most of the time I didn't. I asked advice of several people of great distinction and experience in these affairs. They practically agreed that I should leave well alone. It's a matter for the specialists, they said. The man's an invalid. Would you go to a T.B. sanatorium and think you could be of use to an advanced T.B. case? That was their line."

"Did you say they all agreed?" asked Marian.

"No, not all. The professionals all agreed. There was another expert, an amateur, who said: 'Take a risk, Latimer, take a risk!' But he was not only an amateur, he was a saint. I'm no saint." He paused. His hands were trembling. He looked hag-ridden.

"He came out of prison in due course," Latimer continued, "and rang me up. It was May of this year. He asked me would I meet him somewhere, and talk things over with him. The tone was dead and flat . . . not at all like it was just now, when he rang up." There was another pause.

"Did you go?" asked Marian.

"I did not go."

"A damn good thing, too!" said the young man, Stratton. "He'd have borrowed a fiver off you, if you'd been mug enough to lend it." He looked round, as if surprised to find it was he himself talking. But no-one stopped him, so he went on. "Next time it would have been ten. You'd have had him in your hair. You'd have never got him out again . . . not till next time they carted him off to gaol."

Latimer shrugged his shoulders.

"Maybe," he said. For the first time Marian noticed it was not merely a mobile and sensitive chin, it was a weak one. She found it odd she had not noticed it before.

"He wasn't after money when he rang up just now?" she asked.

"No. He just wanted to let me know he was there."

"He said he had a job, did he?"

"No. He said he was doing all right. I suppose he's met up with some of his old pals again."

"There weren't any new pals for him to meet up with?" Marian said softly. "Were there?"

"Hadn't we better have some drinks?" Latimer said. "What a hell of a host I've been! Hello!" There was a muffled sob from somewhere. "Oh, Angela! What's wrong?"

"The poor boy!" wept Angela, her handkerchief at her nose. "Nobody gave him a chance! The poor poor boy!"

"Stow it, Angela," said Bill Hylan. "Or I'll give you a kick in the pants!"

The dinner-party was over really. There was nothing to be done with it now.

CHAPTER III

It was in February of the following year that Marian saw Tommy Smith again. She had the conviction that sooner or later she would see him, but hoped that it would be later rather than sooner. Trying hard not to think about it, she had no mental picture of the circumstances in which the second meeting could take place; so that when in fact it took place in the Ritz, it surprised her no more than if it had been Paddington Station, or the Corner House.

It was in the Ritz, and he was not alone. He was, in fact, with her own dear uncle, Matthew. They were both in uniform to which, of course, they were not entitled, the uniform of the Royal Air Force. Matthew was a very natty Wing Commander, Tommy was a Sergeant. They both wore ribbons for valour, as well as service ribbons. You might presume that Matthew was one of those jolly officers who remember with pride and affection the tough time they went through with their men, presumably in bombers, rocking like mad over Berlin or Munich, and popping off the old Jerry night-fighters like coconuts.

There was also a lady with them, probably as old as the two *soi-disant* airmen put together. She was wearing too much make-up and too many jewels, and she would very probably pay the bill. She was whinnying like a foal, and having a very good time. So were her two friends. There would doubtless have been still better times to come for both of them, if Marian Framley had not turned up that evening for a glass of sherry with a friend.

Marian was a few minutes early, and was about to sit down, when she caught sight of the jolly trio half-a-dozen tables away. She was quite certain that her uncle had caught sight of her, too, and had promptly turned his eyes away, in the certainty that whoever else in the county of London might feel compelled to proclaim his identity it would not be his niece. One does not tell the world, in the Ritz perhaps less than elsewhere, that one's uncle is an ex-convict up to his tricks again. If one does not feel warmly about the tie of relationship, one is, at all events, a lady; one just does not make a fuss.

But he did not know Marian, as, probably, Marian did not, either. She was aware of a wave of anger more furious than anything she had known before. The anger, though at that moment she did not recognize it, was not primarily centred upon Matthew Browne. He was a crook, and would remain one till the end of his days. It had no connection with the whinnying female, who had been a dupe before, and would be again. The young man, Tommy Smith, was at the heart of it.

Marian strode straight over to her uncle's table, and laid both hands on it. Then, staring him straight in the eyes, she said: "I give you exactly ten seconds to clear out!" She made no effort to keep her voice down.

Matthew looked coolly into her eyes, then addressed himself to the lady beside him.

"Who is this person, Molly?" he asked. "A friend of yours?"

By this time the attention of a waiter some little distance away had been attracted to the little group. Somehow, the voices, the tension of the figures, presented themselves as not quite Ritz, not *comme il faut*. Without actually moving, the waiter produced the impression of having advanced a few steps. Several people had turned their heads, and, in the most well-bred manner, turned them away again.

"The waiter will bring the manager, and the manager will bring the police," said Marian.

"Excuse me a moment, Molly, will you?" said Matthew, and rose from his chair, as if he had remembered his cigarette-case in the cloak-room. In a few seconds, with the speed and silence of a cat on a back-yard wall, he had disappeared from the hotel.

Tommy Smith had risen, too. Within a couple of seconds he, too, would have disappeared.

"Stay here!" bade Marian. "I want to talk to you!"

"This is an outrage!" exclaimed the lady. "Who are you? What do you mean by this?" Her lips were trembling. She might burst into tears in a moment or two.

"I'll give you a full explanation if you really wish it," Marian said coldly.

"Waiter," cried the lady. The waiter came up. "My bill, please!" The lady was not so silly as she looked. She may have had similar experiences before, and she was able to profit by them.

"Hello, Marian!" a voice said. It was, in fact, the voice of Ernest Latimer, the novelist. "You've found some friends?" Then he caught sight of Tommy Smith. It was clear the face was familiar to him, but for several seconds he could not put a name to it. Tommy Smith had been some years younger on the one occasion they had met, and he had not been wearing an airman's rig. Then awareness flooded him.

"It's you! It's Tommy Smith!" he cried. His face was pale as paper. Tommy Smith said not a word. There was no bounce in him at all.

"Will you forgive me, Ernest?" requested Marian. "I'm not going to take that drink with you."

"Y-y-yes," he stammered. "Of course."

"Thank you," the jewelled lady said, and put a note down on the table, then flounced off, her nose high in the air.

"Is there . . . is there anything I can do?" mumbled Latimer.

"No," Marian said. He had already amply shown there was nothing he could do. She turned to Tommy Smith. He stood there, as if his feet were riveted to the ground. "Take your cap!" she said. It was on a chair close by. He looked round, but the thing seemed to make no impact on his eye. "There!" she pointed out. He lifted it. "Come! Let's get out of here!" She turned to Latimer again. "I'll ring you up!" She and the young man moved off.

Latimer suddenly was articulate again, in limb and voice. He hurried after her, and seized her arm.

"Marian!" he said. "Do you know who this is?"

"I know perfectly well!"

"You've gone mad! You can't! I won't let you!" He thrust his face into Tommy Smith's. "What game are you up to?" Then back to Marian. "How did it happen? How did he get hold of you?"

"I never met her before," mumbled Tommy Smith. "Not as I can remember."

"Is that true, Marian?"

"Practically true. I'll talk to you again, Ernest. Please sit down. Have your drink. I know what I'm doing."

She and the young man were at the doors now. The doorman got into action.

"Marian!" Latimer called out once more after her. But they were gone. He stared after her open-mouthed, then walked unevenly to a table, as if he had had too many of the cocktails he had not touched.

They stood for one moment on the pavement, Tommy Smith staring forward to the north side of Piccadilly, Marian Framley staring at his averted face.

"You can go off," she said. "I can't stop you."

"What do you want?" he asked without turning his face.

"I don't know what I want. I only know it's miserable and

stupid." He said nothing. "I'd like to talk to you," she said. "There's a café down there."

He turned to her.

"What's miserable and stupid?"

"You're intelligent. You know quite well what I mean."

"I'm a crook," he said. They were walking eastwards now along Piccadilly. "You don't want to be seen with the likes of me."

"We've met before. Don't you remember?"

"Yes, I know. On the road near the bus-stop."

"I see." She slackened her pace and thought it over. "You never let on, do you?"

"Not if I can 'elp it." Then he corrected himself. ". . . Help it." It was evident he had a talent for raising the status of his speech according to the company he was in. It was probably automatic. "Excuse me, miss . . ." he began.

"My name's Framley. Mrs. Framley. Yes?"

"No funny business?"

"Don't be foolish, Smith. What funny business could there be? I could have done something 'funny' in the Ritz, if I'd wanted to."

"You know my name, eh, Mrs. Framley? How do you know that?"

"You're forgetting we met Ernest Latimer."

"Yes." His face darkened. "He's been talking about me, has he?" They were at the door of the café by now. It looked as if the odds were that he would shove off and disappear into the night.

"Have more sense!" she rebuked him. "How should he know I'd ever come up against you? In the Ritz, too! Shall we have a cup of tea, or shan't we? I told you. You can clear off now, or any moment you like. Nobody's going to stop you."

He went up to the café door and moved his hand towards the handle. Then he stood there, his hand raised and motionless, as if obscurely aware that that would not be an ordinary opening of a door. Beyond, in the warm room, the sound muted by the misted glass panels, the wings of Fate flapped slow and heavy. He turned to her. "All right!" The door let them both in.

They sat down, any girl with any young man in the services. Here, in the run-of-the-mill café, he was much less at his ease than in the de luxe hotel, with the soft carpets and the flunkeys.

"A pot of tea, I think," she suggested. "Or would you like coffee?"

"Yes, please." He felt for his cigarette-case, and brought it out. It was an engine-turned Cartier. He saw her eyes alight upon it, then turn quickly away. He thrust the cigarette-case back hastily into his pocket, as if it had been a dirty handkerchief. She brought out a packet from her handbag.

"Have one?"

They puffed away in silence for some moments. The waitress came and took the order.

"You know the Professor, eh?" he asked.

"Yes, I know him quite well. I've known him a long time. So he told you he's a Professor, did he?"

"We all called him the Professor over at Maidstone, too."

"You say you've known him for some time?"

"You're always meeting old pals. I remember he told me. I always thought he was shooting a line. But you never know who you meet, actors, business-men, clergymen, all sorts of people." So long as he did not look her in the face, he had no difficulty in opening up.

"He told you he was a Professor, eh?"

"Yes. At St. Stephen's College, he said. That's in Oxford."

"Yes," she observed. "I know. So you've entered into partnership with him?"

"More or—" he paused, "less." She could decide whether the ghost of a wink followed the pause. But the inflection was exactly as Ernest Latimer had recorded it, the time he told the tale of the return from a Cockney wedding.

"Wasn't there anything else you could do except go in with that man? You're not going to get anywhere with him. You know that. Except to one place."

"He's all right. He's a mate of mine." He turned to her suddenly. "Look here. What have you brought me here for? It's about time you told me. Are you an author? I've had enough of authors. I'm blowing."

"Let me put you right about Mr. Latimer. I happened to

be at dinner with him the night you telephoned him. When was it? Last year, October, I think it was."

"*'Who is that, prees?'*" Tommy Smith mocked, in the falsetto voice of a Japanese butler.

"He worried about you a great deal. He was quite miserable."

"Fat lot of good it did anybody. There's no need for you to worry, missis."

Her cheeks flared.

"No, of course there isn't. It's no business of mine."

"Who are you? What's your job?" the voice was hard and not agreeable.

"I'm in business. I sell books."

"You're not a probation officer, or anything like that on the side?"

He was becoming impertinent. She suppressed her rising annoyance.

"Did *I* arrange that little business in the Ritz just now? Did *I* make it happen?"

She could almost hear the deflation, like the air escaping from a tyre.

"I'm sorry . . ." he fumbled for the name. ". . . Sorry, Mrs. Framley."

"Mr. Latimer told us about your letters to him. I thought you meant what you said."

"Didn't he?" he thrust out at her. "Didn't *he* mean what *he* said?"

"He couldn't make up his mind. He waited too long, I suppose. Today, seeing you in this uniform, I suppose his mind was made up for him."

"If he'd have done something about it when he said he would. . . ."

"Yes?"

"I mightn't have hitched up with the Professor, like we arranged."

"It doesn't occur to you there are some things you've got to do for yourself?"

"Sometimes you can't. You get it knocked out of you. You can't do things by yourself any more."

She thought for some time.

"In the last resort it's got to be yourself," she affirmed.

He turned on her suddenly.

"Listen, Mrs. Framley! Suppose I asked could I see you some time, to talk things over? I'd have to have your address. Maybe your telephone number."

"Yes," she said. "Of course you would." She hesitated. There were things to take into consideration. The address was Oxford, an address she shared with Cecilia Bruton. Would it be quite fair to Cecilia to give her address and telephone number to a young man of this sort? The Broad Street bookshop was only a few hundred yards away from St. Stephen's. What avenues of trouble did not that open up? Did not the Warden of St. Stephen's have his plate loaded enough already? Was it quite fair to introduce to Oxford his brother's trusted partner, from Maidstone and Parkhurst?

"Well?" a voice asked sharply in her ear.

She turned to him, quite nettled.

"You mustn't rush me! After all, it's not only me——"

She was aware of a series of movements by her side so swift and sure that they seemed only one movement. He had reached for his cap, he had risen from beside her; in almost the same instant he was at the door and through the door. She started after him, but, of course, it would be quite useless. She sank back on to the seat again, and drew the teapot towards her. She filled up her cup, but the tea was cold and tinny. It was not the taste of tea, she realized. Her mouth was bitter with folly and frustration. She got up a minute or so later, paid the bill, and went out. She turned left and was at the entrance to the Ritz again when she realized where she was.

"No!" she said to herself firmly. "No!" and turned sharp round again. It was possible Ernest Latimer would still be there, and if he was it would be impossible not to talk about Tommy Smith. There was no-one in the world she wanted less to talk about.

CHAPTER IV

I

IT WAS the first week of June this same year. Marian was still in partnership with Cecilia at The Easy Chair in Oxford, though she had been thinking for some time of starting a more propitious enterprise in London, where many of her friends were. However, she was still in Oxford, this pleasant June day. She was, in fact, in St. Stephen's, her father's college.

She had been lunching with the Warden, and he had been in good shape. There had been two marquises at the table, and it is to be supposed that two marquises are as good as one duke. She was on her way out of the College, when suddenly she remembered that a certain Jerry Holt, who lived in the Middle quad., was expecting her to tea that afternoon. There were no luncheon-parties in College these austere days, or you could hardly call them luncheon-parties. You could not ask your guests to bring their own rations, and your own did not go very far, particularly if, like Jerry Holt, you stroked the College boat. So you gave people afternoon-tea, or a glass of sherry.

But Jerry Holt gave tea-parties that *were* tea-parties. With money you could still find cakes and pastries and éclairs and meringues that were dream-like, and Jerry had plenty. He was good-looking, too, tall, with broad shoulders, and fair, close-curling hair. She was sorry she could not make the tea-party. She had to look in at the private showing of a library that was to go on the market.

So she retraced her steps, back along the central walk of the Front quad., under the archway to the Middle quad. She would tell him personally, she decided, how sorry she was, and he must ask her again, please, soon.

He shared rooms, she remembered, on staircase seven, second floor, with little Lord Hilbury. The Middle quad., like the Front, was deserted. Of course, everyone was out on the river, or was playing cricket or tennis. Neither Jerry nor young Hilbury would be in. Well, she had got so far as this. She would go into his room and leave a note for him. His room was left of the landing, on the first floor.

She did not knock and, of course, the door was open. It

is bad form in Oxford to lock one's door, to sport one's oak, as they say. She turned the handle and entered.

The room was not empty. A young man was present, his hand in the inside pocket of a hanging jacket. He was dressed in the standard undergraduate style, with a loose-fitting tweed coat, a pair of creased flannels, and a long woollen scarf in College colours flung round his neck. Balliol it was. Yes, Balliol. The young man turned at the click of the door-handle. It was neither Jerry Holt, nor Eddie Hilbury. It was not an undergraduate at all. It was Tommy Smith.

"Oh, hello!" he started, a grin on his face; it was obvious that he had got some lie pat on his tongue in case he was disturbed. Then, as the memory of who Marian was slowly came back to him, the grin dispersed into air, like steam on a mirror.

"Christ!" he said. "It's you again!" His free hand made a dive to his coat, as if he had a weapon there.

It was not at all unlikely, but she gave no thought to it. Her first reaction was neither fear nor anger. It was shame. She blushed to the roots of her hair.

"How filthy!" she cried, and pulled the stout oak door to, as if to isolate the infection, to prevent it seeping out up and down the staircases, along the cloisters, into the halls and libraries.

He turned to the windows and saw they were wide open. Then he thrust over to the width of wall that separated the windows, and stood with his back to it.

"What are you going to do?" he demanded. "Yell for the police? Eh, Mrs. Framley? That's your name, isn't it?"

She looked him straight in the eyes.

"Aren't you ashamed?" she asked.

"Don't you come that stuff on me!" he brought out. "What are you going to do? How did you get here? Are you having me tailed?"

She eyed him curiously. It was a different face from the one she had seen twice before. Even the bone-formation seemed different. She had not remembered the eyes were green, and bright green at that. They blazed like a cat's, out of the shadow between the windows.

"I don't want to hand you over to the police," she said.

"Try!" he challenged her.

"You'll just go to prison again, and in course of time you'll come out. Then you'll go back again. And then again. It won't get you anywhere."

"That's my business," he said.

"No. It's my business, too. It's everybody's business."

"What are you up to? Just keeping me talking till somebody comes?"

"Sit down," she said.

He stared at her for some moments, weighing her up.

"No!" he said, violently.

"What's in your pockets?"

He hesitated and thought the matter over. He seemed to make up his mind he had no alternative. Either he knocked her down, which at this stage would be noisy, or, without knocking her down, he could try for a get-away, which would be difficult. He emptied his pockets. There was a gold cigarette-case, a wallet, a gold pencil. She realized that there would not be many undergraduates in College other than Jerry Holt who would have litter of that sort lying around in their pockets.

"Who told you about these rooms?" she asked. But she knew the answer.

"Find out!"

"You know I'm going to let you go?"

"That's up to you!"

"Are you stone all through, Smith?"

He did not answer.

"So you were just shooting him a line, were you?"

His eyes swivelled round towards her, then back again.

"You know who I mean, of course, don't you? Mr. Latimer, the writer. *You* know."

"If you're going to let me go, let me go! The people will be coming back!"

"You know the trouble I can get into with the police?"

He shrugged his shoulders.

"*I'm* not asking you."

"You know why I'm doing it?"

He was silent.

"Because I think there's a chance it may do something to you. I don't suppose there's anyone in the world who wouldn't tell me I'm a thundering idiot. Put those things back where they came from." He obeyed her. "There's only one thing I'm going to ask you in return . . . though I hope that won't be the end of it."

"What is it?" he asked sullenly.

"How can I *believe* you?" she exclaimed in sudden despair. There was a break in her voice. "With anyone else I'd ask them to swear on something or somebody they hold dear. But what can I do with *you*?"

"What are you getting at?"

"I want you to swear to keep away from here. From this College, from Oxford. For God's sake keep away! We don't want you! I don't want ever to see you again!"

"All right! Let's get weaving out of here! I swear!"

She bit her lip. Her eyes were full of tears.

"Is your mother alive?"

He muttered something under his breath.

"What did you say?"

"I said—that old tart," he brought out venomously.

She uttered a deep sigh.

"If you were a Catholic . . . I'd have asked you to swear by the Holy Cross. Are you a Catholic?"

"Don't give me that stuff!" he growled.

"Is there *anything* you hold dear? Anything, anything?"

"What?"

"Is there anything you love in all the world?"

"What?" he said again. "What's tha' to do. . . ." Something had gone wrong with his speech. The green glitter had dulled in his eyes. "I'm no' . . . no' answering. . . ." The phrase remained suspended. The mouth remained open. A small clot of spittle was bubbling at one corner.

She felt her heart quicken and race and roar. Somehow she had thrust the point of a knife-blade through the thick dead casing. She must press it home deeper, deeper.

"There *is* somebody you love? Who *is* it? Tell me! Who *is* it, Tommy? Who *is* it?"

His lower lip was trembling like some broken plant hanging on a fibre or two. The skin was grey and blotched with goose-flesh.

"*Tell* me, Tommy!" she begged softly. "*Tell* me!"

"Cliff!" he murmured. "Cliff!"

"Who's Cliff, Tommy?"

"My . . . my brother."

"Yes, Tommy. Cliff. . . . For Cliff's sake will you try and go straight?"

"I'll try."

"You'll keep away from us, here?"

"Yes."

There was someone coming up the stairway. It might well be Jerry Holt, or Eddie Hilbury. Somebody called out: "Peter!" on the quad. below. From an upper window someone replied: "Yes, Robin?"

She went up to Tommy Smith and shook him by the shoulders. His eyelids were fluttering like someone going out under a narcotic.

"We'd better get out! Do you hear?"

He blinked and shook his head.

"Wha'?"

"They might come back any minute. Come!" She pulled him by the sleeve towards the door. He followed, his feet shuffling along the carpet. She went ahead of him down the stairway and into the quad.

"Keep with me!" she said. "It will be all right!"

"Yes." He still looked half-asleep. They turned left, and passed under the archway. A College scout passed.

"Good afternoon, Mrs. Framley."

"Good afternoon, Sutherland."

Sutherland took not the least notice of Tommy Smith. He was an undergraduate, like any other. They passed along down the central walk, between the long, narrow beds of forget-me-not and pansy and geranium that flanked the lawns. A young man cutting with his tennis-racket at an imaginary tennis-ball came up, smiled and went on. She smiled back. A knot of undergraduates was clustered round the Porter's lodge. Others were coming up the college steps, in twos and threes.

"Marian!" a voice called from across the lawn. She turned.

A young man was standing in the doorway of a staircase. "Have you found it?" It was doubtless some book he had asked her to get for him.

"No, Harry!" she called, and moved on. Then she became aware that Tommy Smith was no longer walking beside her. She looked round. She saw that he had stopped dead in his traces. He was staring straight before him, his eyes almost dropping from his head. At that moment once again her name was called, not by one voice, but by two. They were voices she recognized, the voices of the twins—her brother, Robert, her sister, Anna. She turned. It could not be possible that it was at them Tommy Smith was staring so.

It was not. He was staring at an undergraduate, Clifford Eckersley by name, now approaching the end of his second year. Eckersley was advancing with Robert on his right hand, Anna on his left. If Tommy Smith had recognized Clifford Eckersley, it soon became clear that Clifford Eckersley had recognized Tommy Smith. Eckersley went white as chalk. Then, for three, four seconds, he shut his eyes, then opened them again, as if hoping that he might convince himself he had seen a ghost, a figment of his own imagination, anything, anything but a living creature.

"Cliff!" Marian heard Tommy Smith stammer beside her ear. "Cliff!"

In that same instant, without a word to his two friends, Eckersley turned sharply round. At a pace quickening to a run, he moved towards the Porter's lodge, down the steps, and into the High. Then he disappeared.

"Wait for me, Cliff! Wait!" called Tommy Smith into the vacancy of green lawns and grey stone. He, too, ran a few yards towards the Porter's lodge. Then he stopped, then moved forward again, this time at a snail's pace. Marian Browne was close behind him.

"Marian! Marian! What's all this about?" she heard the twins shout after her. But this was not the time to tell them, if there would ever be a time. There was a tumult in her head like the sound of waters between two steel cliffs. Clifford Eckersley, undergraduate, was the brother of Tommy Smith, gaolbird. That was as manifest as a fire or a precipice. He was an undergraduate of a College where the Warden was the brother of a gaolbird. How could so deadly a pattern be pure coincidence? If it was not coincidence, how had it been arranged, this grotesque and dreadful conjunction?

She was still walking by Tommy Smith's side. They had descended the College steps, they had crossed the road and turned left, and were moving westwards along the High. She dared not leave him. What might he not do if he were left alone now? He was shambling alongside the gutter like an old man.

She pulled at his sleeve.

"Tommy!"

He did not answer.

"Tommy!"

He turned grey-glass eyes upon her.

"What do you want?"

"You had no idea he was . . . at that place?"

"No."

She felt it impossible he could be lying. An idea struck out at her.

"Did he send you here? . . . You know who I mean? . . . the 'Professor'?"

He stopped.

"What?" The intelligence was coming back into his eyes. He had heard and understood, but he wanted time to consider her question.

"You heard me, Tommy, didn't you? I asked was it the 'Professor'? Did he arrange this?"

The chin, that had been hanging loose, tightened upon the tendons.

"Leave me alone!" he barked at her. The change in his manner was like a sudden slap on the jaw. "I don't know nothing."

What had happened? Had she stumbled against taboo, the rumoured taboo of criminals? You do not in any circumstances give information about your accomplices.

She only knew her face was red with shame and fury. They were at the corner of the Turl now. It was all she could do to prevent herself turning sharp round, moving off up the Turl, and round to her little home there, where she could make tea, and there would be toast and honey. What compulsion was there to soil herself with all this dishonour and insolence? It was a compulsion that could not be denied. She was still beside him. They had crossed the street, and she was with him still. They were walking along the pavement towards Carfax, and she was looking sideways into his face as if she were a hospital nurse, and he a sick man . . . as assuredly he was.

What, then, was she going to do with him? Was it to be still another tea-party outing, to follow the tea-party in Piccadilly? Not in a public café, of course. She had her own flat in Oxford. Well, not quite. It was Cecilia's flat, too. Where, then, could she take him? She had got him safely away from her father's College, with the stolen things put back where they belonged. She had extracted a promise from him that he would at least give Oxford a miss from now on. He had sworn it on the one thing he loved. Then suddenly, as if a wand had been waved, the one loved thing had appeared, like a spirit rising between the thick stalks of geraniums.

Would he betray the promise he had made, as he had doubtless betrayed hundreds of promises before? Would he come back, not to steal, but because it would be totally impossible to keep away from the one loved thing?

She must find out, for everybody's sake, above all for Eckersley's. Eckersley, at least, unlike the 'Professor,' was no accomplice of his in crime. He must be outside the taboo she had infringed upon.

"Listen! Are you listening?" she demanded.

"Yes." The tone was very sullen. "Well?"

"You remember what you said?"

"What?"

"We wouldn't see you here again in Oxford. You remember—you promised. Will we?"

At that moment a bus drew up at a stop on the opposite side of the road.

"I'm getting out of it!" he cried, and dived suddenly across the road through a maze of bicycles that set up a shrill, indignant clamour. Then he jumped on the bus as it moved off, and was invisible.

She stood and looked after the retreating bus till it was

engulfed in the traffic that wallowed across Carfax. Then she turned up into Cornmarket. Her heart and limbs were heavy. She had met Tommy Smith three times now. On the first two occasions she had admitted to herself a premonition that she would meet him again; but she would have forgotten him sooner or later if she had *not* met him again. Now she knew he was bound up inextricably in the pattern of her life. It was true that he had promised her he would never show up in Oxford again. Whether he did or he did not England was a bigger place than Oxford. She would have to meet him again, it was inevitable, whether he sought her out, or she sought him. The chain that bound them together was a plaiting of diverse tough wires. She had caught him red-handed in the act of stealing, and had let him go. Therefore she had a responsibility both to him and to society. She must at some time and in some place take up her responsibility again.

But there were other strands more palpable than this. First, he was working hand in hand with her uncle. She was as certain of this as if she had listened to them plotting together, through the chink of a door. Further, he was the brother of Clifford Eckersley, one of the most prominent of her father's undergraduates.

Poor young Eckersley! She grieved for him.

She did not know much about Eckersley; not so much as her father, of course; or her brother, who seemed to be very friendly with him; or her sister, who, in the way of twins, was as often as might be with her brother, and therefore quite often with Eckersley. But she knew enough. She had quite a number of ties with St. Stephen's, and not only with the Senior Common Room. Also, she was part-owner of the Easy Chair, where more talking was done than book-selling. And she got around here and there. She was quite well-informed as dons' daughters go.

Poor young Eckersley! He seemed to have no outer skin at all, he was so sensitive. He was sensitive because he came from Baxendale, and had a Lancashire accent as thick as a railway-sleeper, for which reason he went out of his way to make it sound even thicker than it was. He was sensitive because he was always making mistakes in clothing and deportment, even now in his second year. He was sensitive because he was a poet, and they were less tolerant of poets at St. Stephen's than elsewhere. He did not make things easier for himself. He was arrogant, because he thought himself superior to most members of the College in most things, and was. He could be as silent in company as a log or as garrulous as a cricket. He could be a skinflint, and, within his limited means, prodigal to a lunatic degree. People disliked him or liked him a great deal, and most people disliked him.

Poor young Eckersley! To have Tommy Smith to put up with in addition to all this!

"Hello, Mrs. Framley! What can I sell you?" She looked up in surprise. She was mooning outside her own shop window. It was Cecilia Bruton, her partner, grinning in the doorway.

"Awfully sorry, Cecilia," she explained. "White wine for lunch! You know what it does for me!"

"I thought you were going to look at that library up the Iffley Road, darling? I'll go if you like!"

Marian jumped.

"Oh, of course, darling! Those books! That's what I've come for! My bicycle, I mean!"

"Take a taxi, darling!"

"Cecilia!" One shouldn't eat up in advance the profits that might not be there. In Oxford one still rode bicycles. She wheeled the object out from the alleyway beside the shop, and slid into the saddle. "So long, Cecilia!" and 'Damn!' she said to herself. She suddenly remembered Jerry Holt and his tea-party. She hadn't left that note for Jerry Holt, after all. She felt at that moment she would never be able to enter Jerry Holt's rooms in her life again.

II

At least twenty minutes had gone by, and Robert and Anna Browne had still not quite recovered from the shock of Clifford Eckersley's extraordinary behaviour. They were still walking the length of the Front Quad., then the Middle Quad., then the Front Quad. again.

"For crying out loud!" exclaimed Robert for the third time. He was addicted to American modes of speech.

"Not like him at all!" said Anna, throwing back her pretty head, though it was very like him indeed. It distressed them both to see Clifford behaving in this *gauche* way, though they had seen it before.

"I'm sure I've seen him at the Wilker's lectures," repeated Robert. This time he meant the young man who had caused the odd *contretemps*. "Haven't you?"

"I may have," mused Anna. "I'm not sure at all. He's probably from Pembroke." She had had a quarrel with a young man from Pembroke and since then the place had become a synonym for Brixton or Wormwood Scrubs.

"No, Balliol," said Robert. "That was a Balliol scarf."

"Pembroke," insisted Anna.

"Oh, very well, Pembroke," he agreed. He was interested in something else. "They hated each other's guts, those two. I wonder why. I suppose Marian will know something about it."

"You've already said they hate each other's guts," Anna pointed out. "Three times, I think. That doesn't excuse him behaving like an ape."

"Hello, Robert!" someone called out. It was Jerry Holt in flannels, coming in from tennis. "What about some tea?"

"Tied up," said Robert. "Thanks."

"You, Miss Browne?" The invitation did not sound very cordial. It was Marian rather than Anna that Jerry Holt had an eye on. He was the sort of young man who falls for young women rather older than himself.

"No, thanks, Mr. Holt! I'm tied up!"

"Awfully sorry," said Jerry, and went on.

Robert was fuming.

"You have no right to call Clifford an ape!" It had been on the tip of his tongue to call him something similar.

"Haven't I? Why haven't I?"

"Because you haven't!"

"Yes, I have!"

"No, you haven't!"

That was a type of controversy the twins had engaged in since the days when their tongues first formed more or less coherent sentences. Even nowadays it sometimes ended up in a bout of hair-tearing. But obviously not in the Front Quad. of St. Stephen's, their father's College.

"Oh, I hate you!" said Anna.

"I hate *you*!" said Robert.

Then one went right towards the Middle Quad., the other left towards the Porter's Lodge.

III

"What's the matter with him, now?" asked old Bennison, the porter, as Clifford Eckersley tore past the Lodge and down the steps into the High. He was a queer one, that one, as touchy as a cat on hot bricks, and old Bennison had met a few queer ones in his day. He remembered the time last year when this young Mr. Eckersley had taken a cup-ful of aspirins, after the College hearties had debagged him during the course of a Bump Supper. It was *said* it was an accident, but everyone knew different.

"It's caught up on me at last!" the young man muttered to himself, as he strode like a madman down the High towards Magdalen. At last! It had taken five years.

He was thirteen, no, thirteen and a half, some three years after he had been taken up north to Baxendale by Mum and Dad Eckersley. He was on his way home from school one day, when suddenly he heard someone whistle and call his name. He turned round, though he knew who it was before he turned round. He always knew. Yes, it was Tommy. So he had come out of prison. Yes, it was prison now. Maidstone. Borstal was too good for the likes of him, as Grannie had written, in an unwelcome letter full of Mercer Street news. Somehow, Tommy had found out where he, Clifford, had been taken to. Perhaps Grannie was responsible for that, too. There were not many bolts and bars on Grannie's mouth when she was in gin.

"Hello, Cliff," said Tommy. "It's me. It hasn't half been a job getting here."

Clifford walked on quickly, as if nobody had said a word to him. But Tommy could walk quickly, too.

"Don't be mean, Cliff. I just thought I'd like to see you, that's all."

Clifford turned round. Tears were in his eyes.

"I don't want to see you! Leave me alone! Go away!"

"Well, I'm here, see? I just want to give you something. You might as well have it."

"I don't want anything. You know I don't. I'll break it! I'll burn it! Go away!" For this was by no means the first time Tommy had offered presents to his younger brother, left them under his bed, sent them by other boys . . . stolen knives, watches, cameras. Once it had been a stolen bicycle. More than once it had been a screw of pound notes.

"Go away!" Clifford repeated, shrilly. "You know what the Magistrate said? He said——"

"Cut that out, Cliff boy, quick. What are they like, these people you're with, eh? What you going in for?"

"What's that got to do with you? I don't want to be seen with you! Go away!"

Tommy looked round carefully, then took an envelope out of his pocket.

"Here! Take this! You could do with a new whistle and flute. You could tell the people you're with——"

Once again Cliff had tried to run off, but it was no good. Tommy had his fingers round his arm. They were like steel.

"You've got no right to be treating me like this. I've not done *you* no harm. All right. If you don't want it, you don't need to have it. But I'm here, aren't I? So just let's go into a caff and have a cup of tea and a bit of a yarn. Then I'll blow. Matter of fact, I'm meeting a pal in Blackpool today. How about this place here? Come on, Cliff!"

Anything was better than drawing attention to themselves by making a scene. There was nothing for it. He followed Tommy into the café. There Tommy talked; not about anything in particular. He just talked. It was as if it was doing something to him just being with his brother. There were certain subjects he tried not to talk about, and for the most part he kept them out of the conversation. Grannie was safe, for instance, and air-raids, and the time they had been to the Zoo. But it was impossible for the other side of Tommy's life to be kept out completely. He had a high opinion of the padre at the place he had just come from, which was, in fact, Maidstone Gaol, and there was a bloke who had made an old-time cottage out of chips of wood that fitted into a tobacco-tin. There was also a pal of his, a Professor he was, from St. Stephen's College, in Oxford. The Professor could talk ten languages and when he read a book he could say whole pages at a time. Tommy told him his kid brother could talk off the whole of that poem about the Spanish Armada, at Flores in the Azores, Sir Richard Grenville lay, when he was seven.

Cliff sat and drank tea and tried to think of the Peasants' Revolt, and the Lollards, and the Wars of the Roses. And Tommy went on talking and then at last stopped talking. He was now paying for the tea and the cakes and the sandwiches.

"You're sure you won't, Cliff?" he asked. There was a sudden diffidence in his demeanour.

"Won't what?"

"You know." He patted his pocket. He meant the envelope, and the envelope, of course, contained stolen money.

"I've got an extra lot of homework. I want to go now, please. Let me go."

"O.K., damn you!" Tommy shouted with a sudden spurt of temper, and went off. Clifford waited for some minutes, afraid to go out. Then he emerged. Tommy was not to be seen.

That wasn't the end of the money-business, not by any means. Clifford tried to forget it, as he tried to forget everything connected with his brother, but it wasn't easy. Several years went by. Clifford was now a star pupil in the History Sixth at Baxendale Grammar School, and was to sit for a scholarship at Oxford. One morning the history candidates were assembled under Bailey, their master, to discuss the scholarship question.

"You know, boys," said Bailey, "the colleges that are offering scholarships are combined into groups. I'll read out the groups to you, and I'll ask you to give them to me in your order of preference, if you have any."

Bailey came to Clifford.

"And you, Eckersley?" he read out a list . . . Trinity St. Stephen's, Oriel, Queen's, whatever they were. They did not in any case have a sharp sense of the differences in colleges, up there in Baxendale. To Clifford the list was a collection of syllables. The name of only one College struck a bell—St. Stephen's. Somebody had once mentioned the place to him.

"St. Stephen's, sir," he said.

"Very well, St. Stephen's," said Bailey, making a note. "Pretty hard going, the standard's high, but you may make it."

It was only on his way home from school that day that Clifford remembered with a sudden gust of horror why the name of St. Stephen's had jumped to his tongue. It was because his brother, Tommy, had made a reference to it. He had a pal, he said, a Professor, from St. Stephen's College. He could talk ten languages and recite whole pages from a book. He had told his friend he himself had a brother who could recite all Tennyson's 'Revenge' when he was seven.

Clifford had striven hard to forget everything Tommy had said to him on that occasion in the "caff," but forgetting is merely to shove out of sight, it is not to destroy. He could bite his tongue off, he told himself angrily, for having specified St. Stephen's, when there were half a dozen other colleges he could have put his name down for. He didn't expect to get a scholarship at all, but if he did, he wanted it to be anywhere rather than St. Stephen's. He wanted nothing, least of all his Oxford College, to remind him of his brother; and though he had the gravest doubts about the so-called "Professor" having actually been a don at St. Stephen's, there was probably some sort of connection somewhere. As he was in course of time to find out.

So he turned and went straight back in the hope of finding Mr. Bailey still at school; but he was gone. Next morning he went up to Mr. Bailey and said he would like to alter his order of colleges, if it was not too much trouble. "Why?" Mr. Bailey snapped, his eyes glinting through his pince-nez. It was one of his days for a liver.

"Because," Clifford stammered, "because I don't think I'd make the grade for St. Stephen's. The standard's too high."

"Perhaps it is, perhaps it isn't!" shouted Mr. Bailey. "But I've already sent the lists off, and I can't muck about with them now. They won't stand for it. It's not done. Besides, who said you wouldn't make the grade for St. Stephen's?" He banged his fist on the desk. "It's your damned inferiority-complex! You make me sick, Eckersley!"

So the lists were not altered; the scholarship examinations were duly held; and Clifford Eckersley, having done extremely well, was snapped up by the first college he had put his name down for.

And he was at St. Stephen's, the college whose name his brother, the gaolbird, had first put into his head five years ago. He kicked violently, that June day in Oxford, against the trunk of a weeping willow that roofed over the nile-green shallows of the Cherwell. "It's caught up on me at last!" he muttered. "Sooner or later it was coming to me!"

"It's all tied up with the 'Professor,'" Clifford Eckersley told himself. "It stands out a mile." He knew all about the 'Professor.' Or at least he knew enough to be going on with. He had found out in his first term.

He remembered the night he had learned that the scholarship at St. Stephen's had been awarded him. The viva voce had been in the morning. They had announced that the results would be pinned up on the window at the Porter's Lodge that night. He was convinced that he could not possibly win. He was always like that about himself. Mr. Bailey up at Baxendale was quite right about the inferiority-complex. At first he could not make out the writing on the pinned-up list, it was so full of archaic flourishes. Then he started reading the list upward from the bottom, because he felt his name would only be at the bottom if it was anywhere. Then he got to the top of the list and read the name: Eckersley, Clifford. For several moments his mind resisted the patent affirmation. Then at last it broke through. He, himself, was, must be, the Clifford Eckersley who had been awarded a History Scholarship at St. Stephen's. He bounded into the air like a kangaroo, uttering a loud yell of triumph. Then he ran whooping along the cloisters for twenty yards, then back again, like an animal touched off with the tip of a red-hot poker. Then he drew up short again where the list was pinned on the lodge window. Eckersley, Clifford, he read again. He was aware of a pair of spectacles inside there, and the eyes beaming kindly through them. The beard was like the beard of an old Hebrew prophet.

"That's me," he said to the beard, trying to keep the jubilation out of his voice. "Here." He pointed to the name at the top of the list. "Clifford Eckersley."

"Very well done, sir," the old man said. "I'm sure you'll be very happy——" Then the words stopped dead on his lips. For something had happened to the youth. The colour had drained out of his face. He suddenly looked like a woebegone child, or like an old man, the way his head fell forward and the whole body sagged. "What is it, sir?" asked old Bennison. "Come inside here, sir, won't you? I'll get you some water." The boy was obviously one of those highly-strung ones the way he was carrying on. But he had seen them even worse than that, sometimes when they saw they had taken a scholarship, sometimes, too, when they saw they hadn't. Once or twice he had even seen them fall flat on their faces.

"What, sir? What's that you're saying?" asked old Bennison. The boy was trying to say something, but it wasn't coming at all easy.

"There isn't a Professor here who's been . . . who's been. . . ." It was no good. He could not say it, whatever it was.

"Bless your heart, sir. We have the Tenterden Professor of Greek studies, Front Quad., two, and we have the University Professor of Physics and . . . I beg your pardon, sir? Yes?"

"I think . . . I'll just go out and get some fresh air. . . . Thank you very much. Good night."

"Good night, sir. And good luck." Old Bennison pushed his spectacles up on to his forehead, and got down to his evening paper again. "They're a bit raw sometimes," he said to himself, "those boys from Lancashire and those places. But they turn out all right, bless 'em."

"Why are you taking on like that?" (Clifford Eckersley asked himself). "You could quite easily have put your name down for St. Stephen's, if Tommy had never mentioned the place. And supposing there *was* a Professor at St. Stephen's who was a bad lot and he went to prison and got to know Tommy there? Well, what then? What's all the fuss about? When the fellow came out, he certainly wouldn't come back to St. Stephen's. That's the last place he'd come back to. He probably went to South America somewhere. The same goes for Tommy. Perhaps Tommy's now in Australia. Or maybe he's in prison again. Or maybe he's joined the Merchant Navy. Anyway, there's nothing to bring him chasing after me to St. Stephen's, when I come up next year."

A motorist hooted sharply. Clifford pulled up short in the middle of the roadway. He looked round. Where was he? It was more like Baxendale than Oxford. It must be Cowley, he thought, where the motor-works are, a long way from Beaumont Street. He managed to get a late bus, but it was so late he had to knock up the landlady. A very forbidding lady she was. She did not like Grammar School boys. They let down the tone of her bed-and-breakfasts.

It was during his first term that Clifford found out more details about the Professor. He was having tea with Haygarth, now in his second year, and in the first rugger team. It was a duty tea, for Haygarth had been at Baxendale, too. One was supposed to give a hand to the freshmen of one's old school, even if they were poets, and had ambitions at the Union.

Tea was over, really. The last slice of seed-cake had been eaten, there was no more tea in the pot. Haygarth got up from his easy-chair, took up his scholar's gown, put it down again, shuffled among his papers. And still young Eckersley would not go. Very awkward, these freshmen from Baxendale. At last it occurred to Haygarth, who was excellent at scrum-half, but not quick-witted, that there was something on Eckersley's mind.

"Is there anything on your mind, Eckersley?" he called. "Shoot!"

"Oh, no, nothing!" said Clifford. "Not at all!"

"Very well, then," said Haygarth, and got up from his chair. Then he went to his desk. He looked at the door. His meaning should have been unmistakable.

Then Eckersley brought himself to the point.

"Please, Haygarth, there's something I'd like to ask you."

"I thought so. Well?" The blue eyes looked straight from under the thick black eyebrows.

"Was there once a don here, a Professor or something, who . . . . who. . . ."

"Who what?"

"Who had to go to prison for something?"

Haygarth did not answer. He got up from the desk and returned to the easy-chair where he had been sitting, and stared into Eckersley's eyes for some time. Then he spoke.

"It's not your idea of a joke, is it Eckersley?"

"No, no," Clifford assured him anxiously. "I just wanted to know. Somebody once said something." It was transparently no joke to Eckersley.

"I'm going to tell you something, Eckersley. It's not pleasant to talk about. Somebody'll tell you sooner or later. It might as well be me."

"Yes?" His heart quickened. There was a drumming in his temples.

"It wasn't a don at the College. It wasn't a don at all. Old Browne, the Warden. . . ."

"Yes?" asked Tommy's brother.

"He has a brother. I think the name's Matthew." He told him what he knew of the career of the Warden's brother.

"I see," whispered Clifford. "I see." He was in a position to see a good deal more than his ex-school mate.

"You won't talk about it, Eckersley," said Haygarth. "Not more than you can help."

"Of course not, Haygarth."

"Try not to talk about it at all."

"Certainly. Oh, Haygarth, why should I?"

Why should he? There was every reason why he should not. He sat hunched up in his chair that night, a green eye-shade over his eyes, trying to concentrate on Thucydides. But other themes ran hugger-mugger through his brain.

What a strange, sad business it was! The Warden and his brother, the freshman and his brother! Where was the Warden's brother now, and the freshman's brother, where was he? Had they gone their separate ways? Were they together again somewhere behind bars? To what end had this dreadful coupling been ordained. Surely, grotesque and wretched though it was, it was all nothing but blind coincidence? Surely it was. His mouth was twisted with pain.

"Oh, God, keep him away!" he muttered. "It wasn't my fault! Why should I have to suffer? Get him to forget me, God! That's all I ask!"

All that first year passed by, and a good deal of the second year, and no-one in any direction brought up the matter of the Warden and his brother. It was possible to believe that practically everyone knew about it, or that practically no-one knew about it. It was just not the sort of thing that anyone could possibly want to talk about.

The Warden was superb, Clifford told himself. As the old man sat at the centre of the High Table in Hall, flanked by his dons, it was totally impossible to believe that behind that high dome and those calm grey, slightly short-sighted eyes a horrid secret squatted like a toad. Excepting, of course, it was not a secret. *Some* people knew; Haygarth, for instance. He himself knew now. Suppose someone should some day find out about *his* toad? The idea made him shudder to his marrow like that night when, as a small boy, he had reached his hand under the table for a fallen pencil, and had laid his hand upon a dead cat. Suppose his toad found out that he was now a scholar at St. Stephen's and came to inflict upon him his odious kindnesses?

"I'd chuck myself into one of those jungles of weeds in the Cherwell backwaters," whispered Clifford Eckersley.

IV

It was five years since Tommy Smith had spoken of a 'Professor' at St. Stephen's College. It was two years since Clifford Eckersley had come into residence there. And now, on this lovely June day, there Tommy was, in the Front quad., with a Balliol scarf around his neck, and the Warden's daughter by his side, the Warden's daughter who was the 'Professor's' niece. Clifford Eckersley felt the scarf tightening around his throat, damp and slimy like water-weeds.

He must talk to Marian Framley at once. That before anything. She was not at her little bookshop in the Broad. There was no message, he told the other girl. He crossed the road, and took up his vigil, pacing the pavements, this way and that and back again, between Trinity and Balliol.

It was about half past five when Marian came back into the Broad from the house on the Iffley Road where, with other buyers, she had been inspecting a library that was up for sale. So far as she was concerned the inspection had not been very successful. She had had other things to think about.

"There he is!" she told herself. "I thought so!" There was Clifford Eckersley, lounging outside the gates of Trinity. If she had been with anyone he did not wish to see, his brother, for instance, he could have made himself invisible beyond Trinity gates, in a matter of seconds. No, it was no surprise to her. She had been certain he would be around.

She got off outside 'The Easy Chair' and, leaving the bicycle against the shop-window, she felt about in her bag for the key. It was not yet closing-time, but Cecilia had closed up. A few minutes later he was by her side.

"Excuse me, Mrs. Framley!" he said. She turned.

"Oh, it's you, Mr. Eckersley.

"I'd like to talk to you. Have you a moment?"

"Certainly. Won't you come in and have a drink? You've had tea, I suppose?"

"Will anyone be there?"

"No. My partner's out. Do come in."

"Are you expecting anyone?"

"No. I don't think so."

"Sure?"

"Quite sure."

"Thank you very much."

They entered and passed through the shop to the sitting-room beyond.

"Won't you sit down? A glass of sherry?"

He looked as if he could do with it. He did not answer. He came out straight away with the question she had already, twenty times that afternoon, with her mind's ear heard him framing.

"That fellow you were with this afternoon in College . . . do you know him, Mrs. Framley?"

She looked him straight in the eyes, and lied, as she had decided to. She did not know how well she would succeed, for she had not had much practice in lying. She was surprised how well she did it.

"Oh, *that* fellow. He'd come up for the day from somewhere. He was asking when the College was built, and all that."

"Mrs. Framley, he was up to something. He was dressed like an undergraduate . . . that scarf, it looked like Balliol. It *was*, I think. But he can't have taken you in. Not the way he speaks."

"There's some odd accents in Oxford nowadays," she pointed out. She changed the subject hurriedly. He might easily take this as a dig at his own flat speech. "It seemed to upset you seeing him there. I'm sorry."

"Please tell me." He was out of his chair swinging his arms around. "Was he asking after me?"

"He wouldn't ask *me,* would he. He'd ask old Bennison, I suppose."

"Yes," he muttered. "I suppose he would." He sat down again and passed his fingers through his hair. He said nothing for some moments, then suddenly he was at her again.

"Was there no-one else he asked for?"

"I assure you," she said slowly, "he asked after no-one. No-one at all."

"No," he muttered. "I suppose not." He realized how stupid it was for him to have imagined for even one moment that Tommy would be asking about his old friend, the so-called 'Professor,' here in an Oxford College, even though the old friend had so close a connection with it. "But still the fact remains——" he went on, and stopped. She waited for him to specify what fact remained. He told her a moment or two later. "The fact remains he now knows I'm up at St. Stephen's!"

"Why?" she asked. "There were quite a few people in the quad. who didn't belong to St. Stephen's."

"Anyhow, he knows I'm up at Oxford. He'll find out."

"I'm sorry," she murmured. "I'm terribly sorry." She did not dare to say more than that. "If there's anything I can *do* . . ." she started.

"There's nothing anyone can do," he told her. "Nothing." Then it occurred to him he owed her at least a syllable or two of explanation. "You know," he said. "One of those family things."

One of those family things. *She* knew.

She did not trust herself to speak. Within, the questions were fists beating on her brain, as they had been all afternoon. Does he know who my father's brother is? Does he know they are colleagues, his brother and my father's brother? Ought I to tell him what I know?

He got up from his chair.

"I'm sorry," he said. "Taking up your time like this." He looked so woebegone she could have taken and held him in her arms.

"You haven't touched your sherry," she pointed out. He raised his glass and drained it at a gulp. "I wish you'd believe me," she told him, looking him straight in the eyes. "I'd be happy to be of use, if you'd like me to." She dared go no closer than that.

"Thanks awfully, Mrs. Framley. Everybody's awfully decent, your father, and the dons, and everyone. Your brother and I are great friends."

She observed that for the first time his eyes were taking in some details of the room he was sitting in—the Severini drawing, the little Skeaping bronze.

"Yes," she said. "The twins talk about you all the time. I feel quite out of it. And what's this I hear about a walking-tour in Brittany?"

He did not seem to get the question.

He was now looking at the silver-framed photograph of her husband, Lieutenant-Commander Framley, who had been killed in the North Sea. The Lieutenant-Commander was in his uniform, with his decorations. Had young Eckersley the image of another sailor behind his eyes, an ignoble sailor, his brother? She saw the shadow pass across Eckersley's eyes, and the eyes turn back to the small bronze again. She hastened to pursue the conversation in the tenor it had attained. "I'm glad you're happy at St. Stephen's," she went on. "We've had a good year, haven't we? You've done very nicely for us yourself, of course. I ought to have congratulated you before. Give my regards to Robert, won't you?" she went on. "Tell him I'd like to see him some time. Well, goodbye, Mr. Eckersley."

She held out her hand. He was any undergraduate

taking his leave from any don's female connections in any red brick villa in North Oxford.

"Goodbye, Mrs. Framley, and thank you."

They had got nowhere at all with each other. Nowhere.

She was not through with visitors for the evening. The twins appeared, while she was clearing away her two eggshells. She had felt very hungry all of a sudden, and had decided to make a pig of herself on eggs, one egg being Cecilia's and hang the consequences. The twins looked thoroughly well-disposed towards each other. You could not have suspected that they had had a row not long ago, and had turned their backs on each other.

"Hello, Marian!" they said.

"Hello, twins! Sit down! Which of you wants to borrow how much?"

"That's unworthy of you," Robert reproached her, "though an odd ten bob *would* come in handy."

"When you give me back the last lot," Marian said.

"All right, no need to be shirty," said Anna, quick on the defensive.

"As a matter of fact we've come to ask you about that chap," explained Robert.

"What chap?"

"The chap you were with in the Front Quad. this afternoon. I could swear he was wearing a Balliol scarf. Anna thinks he's from Pembroke."

"Well, what about him?"

"We were with Clifford Eckersley. I wonder if you saw what happened?" asked Anna.

"Why, what?"

"Clifford looked as if he'd seen a ghost. So did the other fellow." It was Robert this time. "Do those two know each other?"

"How should I know?"

"Didn't you see the way Clifford bolted off?"

"I may have done. I didn't think twice about it." (Oh, dear, when one once starts lying, the way one has to keep on!)

"The chap with you looked pretty ghastly, too."

"But, my dear twin. what *is* all this about? What's it got to do with *me*?"

"Nothing much, really," conceded Robert.

"A glass of beer?" asked Marian.

"*I* will," said Anna. She considered herself the tough twin of the two, for though Robert played rugger very well, he still preferred lemon squash to beer.

"I'll tell you what," declared Robert. "Make it five bob, instead of ten."

"Very well," granted Marian. She opened her handbag and took out the purse inside it.

"Why not get it out of the till?" Robert asked. "Cecilia always does."

CHAPTER V

I

AUNT EMILY's table-napkins, which brought Matthew Browne to the telephone in the first page of this narrative, reappear at this point. It was because of these same table-napkins that Tommy Smith paid the fateful visit to St. Stephen's College which has just been described.

Matthew Browne wanted his table-napkins. He wanted the whole dozen-and-a-half which had been left him by Aunt Emily, not merely the ten which had been delivered to him by Marian. There had been table-cloths, too, and some bed-sheets and pillow-cases, and most of the things had been forwarded, after a lapse of time. It had not been possible to forward the linen earlier, because, at the time when they had been entrusted to the elder brother, Matthew's only address was Parkhurst Prison, an address where one does not forward fine linen. (There was no wife's address for the time being. Poor Edith had disappeared somewhere into a fog of misery and a seaside boarding-house.)

Matthew wanted the whole eighteen table-napkins, and he had only had ten. It meant nothing that he had received all the rest of the linen due to him. It meant nothing that he had robbed many people, including some who had been hosts and friends, of valuables totalling many thousands of pounds. He had been robbed of eight of the table-napkins that dear Aunt Emily had left him, and he was furious. They were a link with a Golden Age, the age when he still belonged to the world of good families, good schools, good weekend-parties, good church services, the good world he both loathed and grieved for.

Eight table-napkins were missing, for one reason or another; because it was war-time, and because laundries are what they are, and because the Warden's wife was what she was. Matthew wrote and demanded his table-napkins. The letter was answered by the Warden's Secretary, who explained the situation, and enclosed a cheque to cover the regretted losses. But Matthew did not want a cheque (though he duly retained and cashed it). He wanted his grievance. He wrote again, marking his letter Personal. The cheque having been cashed, the Warden thought the matter was settled and he might as well tear up the letter. But his brother did not think the matter settled at all.

It was on a night in June, nineteen hundred and forty-seven, that Tommy Smith fulfilled a long-standing invitation to seek out his old friend, the 'Professor,' to talk over old times, and prepare new ones. The arrival of the young man at that hour of the night filled Mrs. Matthew Browne with dire misgivings, in which, of course, she was justified. But Matthew rarely found it necessary, or desirable, to study her feelings in any matter. She went off to bed, and left the two associates, with a bottle of black-market whisky, to enjoy themselves.

"Sit down," said the 'Professor' heartily. He liked young Tommy Smith. They both liked each other. It made prison feel more like home for both of them, when each found the other one was already there. Only one of the two was a "gentleman," but they both had nicer feelings than many of their brother lodgers. They were not partial, for instance, to going about hitting people on the head with coshes. They liked books. They liked a bit of nice music now and again. Tchaikowsky and all that. When they came out, they both dressed reasonably, each in his own station. And they could usually see eye to eye with each other, you do this job, I'll do that.

Tommy Smith sat down in the easy-chair the 'Professor' pointed to, the same chair as the one Marian Framley had been sitting in, an hour or so earlier. Tommy Smith was not aware of this, nor was he aware that there was any connection between his talented friend and the young woman he had brushed up against in passing, outside on the Witney Road. It had been on the tip of his tongue to make a casual remark about the 'judy' he had brushed up against near the 'Green Lion,' but the moment passed, for there were many other things to talk about. It was, primarily, a social meeting, for both had reserves of ready money to draw on which would see them both comfortably through the next few months, each in the sphere the Lord had called him to. Later on there were certain jobs, as already agreed between them, upon which they could pleasantly co-operate. Others would develop from time to time. In the meantime one would take things easy; one might even provide oneself with the façade of a job from which the police could deduce one was going straight. The police always tended to be a little solicitous in the first months after discharge. Matthew had his little house farm to look after. That meant one had a car and a certain amount of legal petrol. The rest of the petrol was an easy matter, when real travelling became necessary. Tommy could run a little tobacconist's store, or even do an occasional turn with a fruit-barrow, they were there for the hiring on an agreed scale of charges. It was all a recognized routine among the "wide boys."

Later on, there were two or three first-rate jobs in the bag, real smashers. One had been in the bag for years, as is the way with the best jobs, which involve long-term strategy as well as short-term tactics. The months passed, six, seven, eight. The firm of Browne and Smith were having a good time even though fences were demanding outrageous rake-offs these days. They were paying good dividends to the fellow-directors that were occasionally co-opted. They were putting money away now and again into the kitty and spending it modestly when the spirit moved them. One learns how to spend money in such a way that the curiosity of the police is not aroused. It is a more difficult art than even higher-grade house-breaking, and many a fine artist has been brought low in the one, who has achieved three-star awards in the other.

The firm were doing well. But Matthew Browne was less happy than he should have been, because he was so intolerably riled about the table-napkins. He telephoned to St. Stephen's once or twice, but nothing happened. He wrote once or twice, too, and with extreme discretion, for he was aware that, with his past, the least hint of blackmail was inadvisable. Still nothing happened. Brother Henry apparently held the view that brother Matthew was bluffing, and he had called the bluff. Taking into consideration all these circumstances, it occurred to Matthew it would be only right and proper if brother Henry's house in College were broken into, and the stolen napkins returned to their rightful owner. Considered merely as a break-in job, it was peanuts, but there were several people at St. Stephen's, or connected with it, who knew what he looked like, and Matthew was not the one to court trouble for its own sake. So it was arranged that Tommy should undertake the assignment.

There was practically nothing in it but fun, but Tommy liked fun. You got into the College togged up like a real undergraduate, then you slipped over through an archway beyond the Front Quad. into the Fellows' Garden, as they call it. "You can get into most Colleges day or night," Matthew Browne pointed out, "because there's always scaffolding around, where they're facing up the old stone. But by day it's better just to walk in, Tommy. Three windows along to your right in the Fellows' Garden is a window with a stone canopy, which will be open as likely as not. A grand old wistaria runs like a carriage-drive straight up to the window, and there you are, in the Warden's dining-room. There'll be no one there after lunch. Have a look round for the napkins in the drawers of the sideboard. They're big ones, see, like this one, with this monogram in the corner. All right, serviettes. If anyone's around, there's an old junk cupboard, just outside, on the left. Do you get it, Tommy? All O.K.?"

"O.K. Prof." But Tommy hung about. There was something on his mind.

"What is it, Tommy? Out with it! It's not worth the risk? Is that it?"

Tommy spat.

"Risk! It's too easy! I like a job I can get my teeth into! You know that!"

"Sorry, Tommy boy. It's a *man's* college. No pearl necklaces, no mink coats. Though I don't think you'd find any of *those* things in a woman's college, either. It's just a lark, Tommy. If you don't really like it, I'll do it myself. It's just as easy to get in at night by that scaffolding as it is to get out. It's only this damn shoulder." He searched for his left shoulder blade with his finger-tips. "It's never got quite right after that Wendover job."

"You stick to your game, Prof.," said Tommy severely, "and I'll stick to mine. Climbing's mine. I was only thinking."

"What were you thinking of?"

"There's bound to be a few bits and pieces round, isn't there, Prof.? The odd gold cigarette-case and wristlet-watch. You know, things like that, for my collection. Just for a souvenir, like. It's not for the *value*. It's nice to flash around a little thing like that now and again, isn't it, Prof.?"

Matthew's eyes beamed.

"Of course, Tommy. How right you are. Why shouldn't you do yourself a bit of good while you're on the job? Help yourself, Tommy boy."

II

So Tommy had duly gone to St. Stephen's College, with the idea of helping both himself and the Professor. But, as we have seen, it had been one of his less successful forays.

It was now eight o'clock of that same day. The place was The Three Duchesses, a roadhouse outside Oxford, on the Eynsham Road. Matthew Browne looked at his watch. Yes. Eight o'clock. Tommy was an hour overdue. Matthew went up to the bar.

"A pink gin, Hermione!" he ordered. "And one for yourself!"

"Another? Oh, really sir, you *shouldn't*!" She handed Matthew's glass over to him, and put her own under the counter with the others. "He won't be coming now, sir. If it really *is* a he." She winked.

"I'll give him ten more minutes," he thought, and took his

gin back to the resin-smelling alcove. "I don't think anything can have happened to him, not possibly. A blindfold baby with a limp could crack an Oxford College wide open as easy as raspberries and cream." He took out a handkerchief from his breast pocket and waved the odour of lavender into the pitch-pine air. But he had given him fifteen minutes more, twenty minutes, and still Tommy had not come. "I wonder if it's got anything to do with Maid Marian?" he asked himself uneasily, not for the first time. "She *does* know his face. But I don't see why she should be hanging round. She's got a shop to look after. I'll find out soon enough. It's probably some little slut at a tea-shop. He felt like flashing his jewellery in her face, and she got her teeth in. I'd better beat it. It doesn't do to hang around too long." He waved a hand to the barmaid. "So long, Hermione," he called out. "What have you got that other girls haven't got?" He knew the barmaid language.

"You'd be surprised," she assured him, swivelling round on him the massive assault guns of her bust. "Goodbye, you beautiful blonde thing."

Matthew Browne was back at Hatchetts, his house in the wood, less than an hour later. He had a small parcel in his hand.

The door was open. He entered and went straight into the sitting-room.

"Edith!" he called, but she was not there. He went back into the hall. "Edith!" he shouted up the staircase.

"Yes, dear!" a faint voice replied to him. She obviously had one of her sick headaches and had gone to bed early. He went upstairs. She was lying on her bed, still dressed, a black eye-shade over her eyes. "I left some sandwiches under a damp napkin," she said. "I hope you don't mind. I've got one of my heads."

The reference to napkins was not fortunate, but he controlled himself.

He unwrapped the parcel he held. There was a handsome box inside, and inside the box was a bottle of Schiaparelli's most recent scent. He bent back the hinged lid.

"Look, dear!" he said.

She turned her head and lifted the eye-shade. The face was seared by tears, like a South Italian hillside by its *torrenti*.

"Oh, no!" she gasped incredulously. "Oh, no! Oh, no!" It was the sound a shut-in dog makes, yelping at the sudden blinding glory of the door opened and the loved one standing there in all the accoutrement of going-out. But perhaps it could not *really* be true? Perhaps the scent was for himself, for someone else?

"For *me*?" she asked. "For *me*?"

She reached out and took the bottle from him, then she turned away, the tears gushing down her face, like the sudden collapse of water from a blocked gutter.

"Matthew, Matthew," she moaned. "You shouldn't! Really, you shouldn't!"

He turned on his heel and left her.

"One has to do something about it now and again," he said to himself. "That'll keep her sweet for months."

III

"I've got to get out of it!" shouted Tommy Smith, as he dived across the road at Carfax. The cyclists swerved and swore. He got on to the bus as it gathered speed, and thrust a woman out of the way as he hurled himself up the stairs.

"Here! Here!" shouted the woman, and seized his coat-tails. He turned upon her a face so white and vicious she hastily released them. "These bloody undergraduates!" she muttered. "Think they own the world! Dead-drunk at this time!"

He sat down, and felt in his pockets for a cigarette, then immediately forgot about it.

"He thinks I've come after him! He thinks I've found out where he is, and I've come after him!" He was talking to himself quite loudly, as habitual prisoners, who spend a lot of time on their own in cells, get into the habit of doing. A man in a bowler hat was about to sit down beside him, then thought better of it, and moved along to the next seat. "Well, I haven't! I must tell him I haven't. I'm his own brother, ain't I? Just because he's a student at one of these la-di-da Oxford colleges! Oxford College, eh? Mercer Street ain't good enough——"

The conductor had come upstairs.

"Fares, please!" The little bell clanged. The pennies dropped into the satchel. He was standing beside Tommy. "Fares, please!"

"I didn't tail him!" he was saying quite loud. "He thinks I did. But I didn't!"

The conductor touched him on the shoulder.

"Fares, *please*!"

Tommy turned, his mouth twisted into a snarl. Then he saw who it was.

"Sorry, mate!" He felt in the hip-pocket where he kept his loose change. His fingers came upon a large ring inside there, where there was usually nothing but money. He realized at once it was part one of the objects he had stolen, back in the College there, and failed to put back. He sprang from his seat.

"I've got to put the damn thing back!" he said to himself. "I don't want to have anything to do with it. I ain't going to have Cliff saying I've been pinching things from the dump where he hangs out——"

"'Ere, 'ere!" shouted the conductor uglily. "What abart it?"

He took a half-crown out of his pocket and thrust it into the conductor's hands.

"Shut your trap!" he ground out, and flung off down the stairs. He jumped off before the bus stopped, and turned back towards Carfax.

"I've got to find him!" he told himself. "I'll give him what for! What does he think he is, running away from me as if I was a bad smell!" Then the thought turned on its tracks. "I hadn't the least idea, Cliff, honest I hadn't! I only want you to be happy, that's all I want! Don't be scared, Cliff. I don't intend to make you miserable among all your posh pals. Why should I? I'm going to get out of here, like I promised her, that dame that bust in on me. Almighty jeebers, that dame! What the hell's it all about? Why' she always getting in your hair, the way you can't get her out with a tooth-comb? What's the Prof. and her got to do with each other? Hello!"

He started. That was Cliff, wasn't it, just coming out of that tea-shop on the opposite side of the road? No, of course it wasn't! It wouldn't be no *tea-shop* Cliff would run off to, the day he met his long-lost brother again! Where *would* Cliff be? He'd got to see him! For Christ's sake, where *was* he? He might be in any of these Colleges, just look at them, crawling like rabbit-warrens. There were shops all round, libraries, post-offices, railway stations. He might be anywhere. He might be running like a madman out towards the country. He might have jumped on a bus, like he'd done himself, or gone to the station, and jumped on the first train. Hello! Was that him, the one near the church door with the twisted pillars? No, of course it wasn't! Why do all these damn students all tog up the same way, like a lot of prisoners? He looked down at the end of his own scarf, hanging down his front, and snorted. Posh, eh?

Hello. This place was familiar. The College with the round steps, and a bloke on top in the tower, holding a big stone! Yes. St. Stephen's College! The place where he'd seen Cliff! How long ago was it? Jeez, it seemed like hours! It couldn't be many minutes. Maybe half-an-hour, at most. Was it possible Cliff had cut back and was in his own rooms, behind a locked door? Wait a minute! How did he know Cliff belonged to this joint? Perhaps he belonged to one of the other joints? It would be easy enough to find out. It was clear each gate had a porter, just like at Brixton or the Scrubs.

He climbed the St. Stephen's steps and addressed himself to old Bennison.

"Clifford Eckersley, he *does* live here, don't he?" he asked.

"*Mr.* Eckersley does not live in College this term," stated old Bennison, a hint of reproof in his voice. The inquirer was obviously no gentleman, Balliol or no Balliol. But it was always like that after wars. The least said the sooner mended.

"Doesn't live here?" said the inquirer. Suddenly his bones felt as brittle as driftwood. "Doesn't live here, did you say?"

"That's right," the old man said. "Did you want to see Mr. Eckersley? I could give you his digs," he added, a little doubtfully. "But he's often in and out."

"No, no, that's all right," stammered Tommy Smith. "I'll be round again, tell him." He turned to leave, when a sense of the full meaning of his words shot through him like an electric needle. "No. Maybe I'll write," he brought out. He was aware he was blushing like a ten-year-old schoolgirl.

"Here, take this!" he muttered, and removed a pound-note from a screw of notes in his pocket.

"Well, sir, really——" started old Bennison. The fellow was already lungeing off towards the stairs. "What name shall I tell him?" But the fellow made no reply. He was gone. The old man scratched his head. "Really, the way undergraduates behave these days," he muttered. "Like regular spivs." He put the pound note away, but was not at all happy about it.

There was only one thought in Tommy Smith's head now. He must get out of Oxford and as quickly as possible. He knew that if his brother were suddenly to emerge from any of these doorways, he would run away from him as fast as he could make it, and hide till there was no chance they should come up against each other. He was not unaware that he had a date with the 'Professor' in an hour or two, in a road-house near Botley. But the 'Professor,' he muttered, could go and stuff himself.

He would go to the station, that was the best thing to do, and get back to London by the first train. In London you can get right with yourself. That was the place, London; the place for the whiskey and the women, and the good jobs, with a kick in them.

He was lucky. A train for London left ten minutes after he got to the station. He settled down to a book he had picked up on the bookstall. He was always partial to a good book.

A little time later the ticket-collector came round. "Tickets, please!" he demanded. Tommy put his fingers into the ticket-pocket, and once again came up against the stolen signet-ring he had failed to replace, back there at the College.

"Hell!" he muttered, and flung the ring through the open window as far as he could fling it. The ticket-collector blinked. So did one or two other passengers, who thought they had seen the young fellow throw through the window something that looked like a nice gold signet-ring. But probably it was some old piece of junk. Surely it was. Nobody could be such an idiot as all that.

"Here you are, mate," said Tommy Smith, handing over the ticket to the collector.

"Thank you, mate!" said the collector. The young fellow *looked* all right.

Tommy Smith took out a cigarette, and settled down to his book. He felt better already. Then another thought presented itself to him, which added to his satisfaction.

"You see, ma'am, I'm doing just like I said I would." The image in his mind was the image of Marian Framley. "I'm getting out of Oxford, see? Who says Tommy Smith doesn't keep his promises? Has anyone seen my halo hanging around anywhere?"

CHAPTER VI

I

THE first thing to do was to find Rosie. That was not difficult, for Rosie could generally be found in the fun-fair at the Angel, or in the Saloon Bar of the Pied Bull round the corner. She was at the Pied Bull, with a group of friends.

"Hello, there's Tommy!" she said, with a sinking of the heart which had both ecstasy and anguish in it. When Tommy came in with a face like that, so set and white and unsmiling, she knew exactly what she was in for. Her friends turned, then turned away again. They did not particularly wish to catch his eye. He did not come over to her. He merely summoned her with a toss of the head. She rose. "Be good, everybody!" she requested. "Be good, Rosie!" they replied. They preferred to seem as casual as might be.

She joined him at the door.

"Hello, Tommy," she said. "I hope you're all right."

"I'm all right," he told her. "We've stacked up."

He meant that he had provided all the bottles of whiskey they were likely to need.

"Shall I tell Maudie?" she asked.

"They'll tell her," he said briefly.

Yes, of course they would. The boys would tell her.

"I'd like to have a few sandwiches in," she murmured. "Last time I was that hungry in the middle of the night, my inside nearly dropped out."

"You won't need no sandwiches," he assured her. "Don't play up. All right," he conceded. "Get some."

"Thank you, Tommy," she said, humbly. There were sandwiches under glass lids. She had a packet made up. Then they went off to the room he had for these occasions. The main idea was to get drunk. But he found it good to have a dame around. Otherwise you might think you were in cells. They don't keep dames in cells. The session lasted a couple of days and nights—you didn't keep count of time. Then there was another couple of days during which slowly you pulled yourself together. You told Rosie to get the hell out of it, and Mrs. Blenkinsop, the landlady, made you tea. You didn't feel like eating, but you had gallons of strong black tea, no milk, but a lot of sugar. Then at last you staggered out again. You felt a bit weak in the knees at first, but soon you were all right. You could start looking round for some fun.

The debauch was over; the time of strong tea was over, too. Tommy was out in the light of day again, and thoughts of fun were top of the bill. But there was a job to be got through first.

The job was his brother, Cliff. Cliff was not dead, after all. He was alive. He had never particularly wanted Cliff to be dead, though he was pretty sure Cliff would have laughed his head off if he, Tommy, had kicked the bucket. But there was no getting away from it, it would have made things easier for either of them if the other had taken a powder.

There was no particular reason to think Cliff had died. He didn't think there'd been much bombing so far north as Baxendale, and in a place so small as that. But you never could tell. Perhaps a bomb had laid him out; or pneumonia; or something.

Well, no bomb and no pneumonia had done no such thing, not to either of them. So there the kid was, in a posh place like Oxford, and he'd have to send some money to him. After all, he *was* his big brother, wasn't he? Those people up in Baxendale might be his guardians . . . what was their name? Yes, Eckersley. But he *was* his born brother. Blood's thicker than water.

It wouldn't be the first time he'd sent money to Cliff. He'd sent along some wads of real dough several times, in between sentences, and had been more than once strongly tempted to arrange with a pal who was being discharged earlier than he was, to drop him a few nicker to be going on with. But he'd thought better of that. He knew well enough how much Cliff didn't want anyone to know he'd got a brother who was a regular gaolbird. So he'd sent on some dough himself, when it was convenient. Of course, he couldn't enclose an address for Cliff to write and say the dough had arrived safely. Knowing Cliff the way he knew him, ten to one Cliff would send the money back, or those Eckersley people would send it back for him. So the least said the soonest mended. The money went in chocolate-boxes neatly tied up. It looked like cigarette-cards, or packets of postage-stamps.

If Clifford had needed money in Baxendale, he'd need it fifty times more over in them Oxford colleges. Fancy Cliff Smith from Camden Town being with all the dukes and earls. Old man Smith, their father, if he *was* their father, and the old tart, their so-called mother, would burst a blood-vessel if they knew! The kid was clever, not half he wasn't, and no doubt he'd got a load of scholarships and things; but still, all those scholarships would do for him wouldn't ever be enough for him to hold his own among all them toffs. What he'd really like to do, of course, was to send Cliff a decent car, a sports model, all lovely paint and chromium, like a Wurlitzer. That's the sort of car you'd want at a place like Oxford. It needn't be a knocked-off job, either, although these days people were so clever at assembling parts, there was absolutely no risk at all. The papers, too, would be in apple-pie order. For money you can always get anything, and since when was there a money shortage? Still, you couldn't tell with Cliff. Unless the papers were triple-locked and then signed, sealed and spat on, he might put on a sour face. So you'd have to get him a real straight-up car. Latest model. Why not? For an extra two or three hundred you could always jump the queue.

Tommy sighed. He knew he'd never be able to drive the car up to Oxford himself, much as he would like to, and leave it there outside the steps of St. Stephen's College, low and sleek and shining. Cliff would throw a fit, the young bastard, same as he did that time in Baxendale. What was more, he, Tommy, had promised that Framley tart he would keep away from Oxford. And somehow, he couldn't say why, you can't ever understand these things, he felt he would like to keep his promise . . . for the time being anyhow. You could always think better of it, if you had to.

So he would have to send the car up with one of the boys. Freddie the Quiff, for instance. Freddie would certainly like the job. He was quite miserable at the thought that it would be Freddie, not himself, who would hand over that nice Lagonda—yes, it ought to be a Lagonda—to Cliff, outside the steps of St. Stephen's.

Then it suddenly occurred to Tommy that perhaps Cliff couldn't drive. He was never much use at anything with his hands. That *would* be a nice how d'you, all that trouble and the car would have to be towed off to a garage. No car, he told himself. Not till we find out whether Cliff can drive. If he can't he'll have to have driving-lessons first. He'll need money for that. And for a lot more, too . . . clothes, drinks, pictures, ornaments, all that sort of thing. Maybe, a nice gold cigarette-case or two. That would be easy. He had several gold cigarette-cases in cold storage. He'd always been partial to them. Pity about that one he'd nicked at St. Stephen's and Mother Framley had made him put it back. Better luck next time.

So we'll have to collect a bit of dough. Fifty pounds to be going on with? Yes. That'll do fine. We can manage that quite easy. And one or two "rabbits" on the side. ("Rabbits" is lower deck language for presents. The lower deck had left a permanent impression on his vocabulary, even more than the other disciplinary institutions which had claimed his time and a good deal more of it.)

He had dumps of money and things up and down the place. There had been times when it had been positively hard work to know what to do with the money he had made in his profession. He was cleverer than some blokes, who start chucking it around at such a rate, the very day after they've cashed in, they're simply bound to attract the attention of the cops. And he wasn't such a mug with the dolls as some of the boys, either. An expensive jane can get through anything for you; if you got your hands on the Crown Jewels, she'd be through them like a dose of salts. Dames were all right for an occasional bang. But he didn't reckon on them. He didn't reckon on anybody or anything. He was a bit of a lone wolf. He just liked thieving . . . when there was a kick in it.

He was quite certain that there were at least two or three dumping places he had completely forgotten about, and his career hadn't extended over so many years, either, particularly if you took away the time he had spent in "stir." Wasn't there a big biscuit-tin, crammed full of rings and brooches, that he had packed somewhere in a wood in High Wycombe? Or was it Great Missenden, perhaps? He didn't remember. He didn't care all that much about the profits after a job was over and done with. An artist, that's what he was, a bit of an artist. He was pretty sure there were one or two other dumps like that one in Berkshire somewhere. Well, he might remember where they were some day. Cliff might need a real load of dough. He might even want to buy a house or something, when he had a wife and wanted to settle down.

In the meantime, all that was needed was a wad of ready. The place to go for that, of course, was old Papa Gruncible, who had an antique shop in Notting Hill. A few decanters with or without stoppers, a few pictures of little girls dancing round lily-ponds, some clothes-hangers, soup-tureens, dancing-shoes, gramophone-records . . . *very* antique. But old Gruncible really made his money by a safe-deposit system. In the inner room were a wardrobe heeling over, an old-fashioned gas-stove, a couple of decrepit chests of drawers. You came in to sell a bit of junk, and you left a little fortune behind, tied up in string in a biscuit-tin, and stowed away in one of these receptacles. It was perfectly safe. Old Papa Gruncible was scrupulously honest. All Papa Gruncible wanted was his commission. The cops didn't suspect a thing. The place was never used by the Notting Dale boys, any more than the Hackney boys thought of using Mrs. Freese's tobacconist's shop in Mare Street. Any more than anyone thought twice of knocking old Papa Gruncible or Mrs. Freese on the head. There are certain things which are simply not done. The whole outfit was as safe as houses. You couldn't come unstuck.

Tommy had a Dundee-cake tin at Papa Gruncible's containing a packet of pound-notes in a sponge-bag. The cover of the tin was stuck down with insulating tape, but that was only a formality. He didn't have a very clear idea how much he had there; between eighty and a hundred quid, he thought. No, it turned out it wasn't so much. It was only sixty. He would have to get to work pretty soon, if only to keep himself in smokes. He took the sixty, kept twenty for himself, and sent the rest in a registered packet, addressed to Mr. Clifford Eckersley, St. Stephen's College, Oxford. The address was typed out in a little bureau in Holborn. The package was posted in Lambeth. The small boy who handed it over the counter was a complete stranger, and thought himself well-paid with half-a-crown.

"Not that you deserve it, Cliff," said Tommy a little severely, as he watched the small boy leave the post-office. "Well. There's plenty more where that came from." He spat in the palms of his hands in a business-like manner.

II

He met Freddie the Quiff that same evening, in the Kismet Salon de Danse. Freddie was an old friend. You would never have imagined he was an accomplished house-breaker, he was so blond and well-made and good-looking, and he had so carefree a curl in his hair. A Salon de Danse, over a glass of orangeade, is a much better place to talk jobs over than a dark back-street pub full of holes and corners, and you never know whether the man in overalls who's just ordered a pint is really a man in overalls, or a dick who's been switched to a new area, because the boys don't know his face yet.

"How's tricks, Freddie?" asked Tommy.

Freddie squeezed his arm tighter round the waist of the girl he had just brought in from the dance-floor.

"Peachy," said Freddie, and lifted both thumbs. He might be taken as meaning that the young lady was peachy, but he meant that the housebreaking business was doing fine. "Sit down, Tommy. Have an orangeade. Meet the girl friend. This is Doris. This is Tommy."

"Pleased to meet you," said Doris.

"Pleased to meet you," said Tommy. "I'll have a cuppa." They sat down. Freddie went off to the counter for the refreshments.

"A slice-a?" he called out.

No, Tommy did not feel like a slice of cake.

"Where did you get them eyes from, Doris?" he called.

"Now, naughty!" Doris reproved him, and touched the back of his hand with her finger-tips. "I'm with Freddie." Freddie was back again with the orangeade.

"Look out, wolf!" he cautioned Tommy. "What have I got here?" He patted his inside vest-pocket.

"A razor," said Tommy, as if he were being funny. All three roared with laughter.

"He's a fair caution, really," said Doris. And he was. They knew that at Borstal, the 'Ville,' the 'Scrubbs,' and several similar institutions. They sat down. Conversation had to be respectable, and that was not easy, for it was not the football season. They talked about snooker, and about the new drummer, who was an importation from another dance-band; then Doris said might she powder her nose. Doris went. Conversation got down to brass tacks. It was interrupted by the return of Doris, and an occasional excursion to the dance-floor on the part of Freddie and Doris. Tommy did not want to dance, though Freddie courteously assigned Doris to him for a samba. He wanted to dance least of all with Doris. He felt, if he did, it would be difficult not to break her spinal column in two. He was content to puff his cigarette, and sip his orangeade, and look on.

None the less, things got themselves said, in between dances. Business had been going nicely in the smoke, while Tommy and the 'Professor' were up-country. The smash-and-grab that Mike's boys had in mind for months had come off a fair treat. Bridlington's, the jewellers, that was, on the Kilburn High Road. The furrier job, Levene's, in Brondesbury, had been brought off, too, though there was a bit of a scare at the last minute, and one of the best bundles had been left behind. "How about you and the 'Prof.'?" Freddie wanted to know. The comb was out of his breast pocket again. The palm of the left hand was patting the wave over the left temple. But Tommy was not informative about the 'Professor.' On the contrary he seemed to have the needle on him. "Sugar the 'Professor'!" he said. Freddie's eyes opened wide. But he said nothing. Even brothers have a little disagreement with each other now and again. There was Alby and Micky O'Neill, for instance. He began to tell Tommy the tale of the O'Neill brothers, how Micky had run off in the middle of a job, leaving Alby to take the can. But Tommy wasn't interested in that, either. He seemed to be a bit on the short-tempered side. Well, what can you expect after two days and nights on whiskey and Rosie?

"What's new?" Tommy wanted to know. "What's cooking? Anything in my line?"

"Sure," said Freddie heartily, relieved to find himself on firm ground again. "I've been wondering when you'd turn up. It's an antique shop off Baker Street. It's run by an old man and woman, live on the premises. The old dame's been having chest trouble, so she's gone off to Hove for a week. Mike told me."

"Mike?"

"The paper-boy."

"Oh, *Mike*!" It was apparently not the first time Mike had been helpful. "Yes?"

"The old boy's deaf as a post. The job's as safe as houses. Can't go wrong."

Tommy stared Freddie in eyes, straight and contemptuous, for quite a time, then, still saying not a word, he stubbed his cigarette out in the ashtray, and got up.

"What's the matter, Tommy?" asked Freddie, a little uneasily.

Tommy bent over.

"Did you hear what I said, Freddie?"

"Why? What?"

"I said something in *my* line, Freddie. *Safe as houses!"* he mocked. "Safe as your Grannie's knickers! So long, Freddie. I'll be seeing you." He strode off towards the exit.

"Hello, Freddie! Is your friend gone?" This was Doris, who had just been escorted from the dance-floor.

"Yes, he's just gone."

"Can't say I like him, Freddie. He makes me feel a bit funny inside here." She got hold of Freddie's finger-tips and placed them under her left breast.

"Oh, he's all right," said Freddie. "He's fine." He had a genuine admiration for Tommy.

III

Two or three other jobs presented themselves for Tommy's approval during the next few days, but for one reason or another they did not make the grade. They were too easy, or they were too hare-brained, or they required hitting someone on the head, and he was not keen on that lark, it didn't read good in your record.

Then a pal told him one evening that Frankie the Toff was in town again. Tommy beamed.

"Good!" he said. "Have another split, mate?" For Frankie got to know things quicker than anyone. If anyone was likely to know about just the right sort of job, it was Frankie.

Frankie was an old gentleman now, well over seventy. He always wore a red carnation in his buttonhole, even if he hadn't enough money in his pocket for a cup of tea and a wad. Perhaps on these occasions he stole his red carnation; if he did, it was the only thing he stole, for he had finally made his peace with God and had gone irremediably honest. Now and again an old friend would point out that the red carnation was nothing more nor less than an advertisement; but he would just smile. He was not afraid these days of being advertised. The police knew all about his past, and his present did not interest them. They were aware that criminals of all ages sought him out, and if he liked them he did not at all mind having a good old jaw with them. He was very vain of his former prowess. He would talk for hours of his revolutionary application of the stethoscope to the art of safe-breaking, where he would claim firmly that he was the pioneer, the trail-blazer. With a light in his eyes, he would tell of the time he had forged tens of thousands of Bradbury pound-notes; or the more stirring episode in the desert south of Las Vegas, where he had held up the Western Mail. The police knew all that, and it did not worry them. To whom else, excepting perhaps a sympathetic reporter or two, could the old warrior show his scars?

The fact was (it was considered) the old boy was harmless now. He had made his peace with God, to whom he had always been partial, particularly during his spells in prison, where he had spent a good many years of his life. There was one occasion, in fact—it was in Wandsworth—when (as he phrased it): "God passed so close to me I touched the hem of His garment." Since then he had sung hymns, and not only sung them, but written new words for them, which were sung to this day in some of the best prisons in the country. Even at the height of his career, in between one sentence for forgery and another for robbery with violence, he had more than once got himself installed as a Sunday school teacher, with no other object in view than the salvation of the young souls consigned to his care. He spent a good deal of his time in London, which had been the scene of some of his most dazzling achievements, but now and again the Call came to him from one of the greater provincial cities, and he arose and went, the red carnation beaming in his buttonhole. He went. He came back again. He was a reformed character. The police were not worried.

Perhaps they should have been a little more worried than they were. Frankie had come to terms with God, and was ready to do anything for Him, within reason. But he hated Society. Society had consigned him to long terms of penal servitude, and had dressed him up in that horrible broad-arrowed suit and the knicker-bockers and the stockings ringed with red. For months at a time he had had to endure solitary confinement and on a derisory diet he had been condemned, with those sensitive fingers, to pick two and half pounds of oakum a day. It might be considered by some that Frankie had given Society a certain amount of provocation, but not by Frankie. He had never forgiven Society for those outrages, he told his intimates, and never would, not till his dying day. "From the moment the beak said to me: 'You are sentenced to six years penal servitude,' my heart and hand have been against Society." (His language always had a tendency towards the sententious, which might have been one reason for his success in his famous masquerade as the Bishop of the Falkland Islands.) "Society has struck back fiercely and spitefully, but she has had some nasty knocks from me. She showed me no mercy in my youth and I've got my own back again and again. No, no beer thank you, son. It seems to upset me these days. A cup of coffee, nearly all milk. Thank you."

He was an old man now. His nerves were not so steady as

they had been, nor his vision so sharp, his fingers so skilful. Besides, he had made his peace with God. But the fact remained that he enjoyed nothing more than the spectacle of Society getting a kick in the groin from his juniors. His eyes shone when he read the news of a spectacular smash-and-grab raid or a first-class bank robbery. There were times when he knew about these events before they actually happened, for craftmen would come to him for advice, if they were not sure of themselves. If an almost impossible job became practical politics, Frankie knew about it quicker than most. He had an ear on the ground and an eye on the drain-pipe.

If to be an artist means to do a thing entirely for its own sake, it could be said of Frankie that he was an artist. He expected no payment for services rendered, which were sometimes quite valuable. If payment was offered him, he would only turn it down. He had outgrown alike the need for danger and the itch for luxury. Only the consuming hatred survived. He had no use for money any longer. If he spent more than the few shillings a week he could knock up in easily verifiable ways, he would at once arouse suspicions in various quarters. He did not drink any more, and his stomach could not abide rich food. A single dark suit was good enough for him and it had almost fallen away from his shoulders by the time he felt it necessary to try and get another one somewhere. He had long ago outgrown women, and more recently outgrown dogs and horses.

There was really nothing you could do in return for Frankie when he handed you a good tip-off, excepting, perhaps slip him a packet of Weights or pay for a plate of sausage and chips. But it wasn't that he was after. You made the old boy happy when you did a good job. You and God between you were the only things that could bring a bit of a smile to that dour long-jowled face.

"Good old Frankie," Tommy Smith said to himself. "That's the boy for Tommy Smith."

So off he went to find Frankie.

First he made his way to Mother Harrington's, the Temperance Hotel in St. Pancras, where you could get a meal for next to nothing if you were ready to listen to the old dame preach for a couple of hours, and join in the hymns; and if you had actually been saved, there was a bed for you, too, if there was one to spare. Frankie had not been seen at Mother Harrington's. Tommy went on to Jack's Place, a milk-bar in St. Pancras, where the red carnation might sometimes be seen glowing among the cheese sandwiches. He was not there, either. "Tomorrow's also a day," Tommy murmured. "A glass of Horlick's, please." You would have thought him the honorary secretary of the local Y.M.C.A.

It was actually in Hyde Park, at Speaker's Corner, that Tommy finally ran Frankie down. In Hyde Park Frankie was not called Frankie. He was Uncle Dawkins. Uncle liked to sing hymns in public, particularly those he had written himself. Nobody asked him embarrassing questions in Hyde Park, as they had done more than once in the West End Church Choir where he had sung for a time. It had been one of his really down-and-out periods, when he looked more like a Bowery bum than an ex top-drawer crook; yet he sang the bass solos in Mozart's Requiem from memory so admirably that quite a few people had asked him where he had learned it. It was a question he preferred not to answer, for he had learned it in the Strangeways Prison Chapel Choir. These contretemps did not occur in Hyde Park. And there on a fine evening he would open out his chest with a will, feeling that he held tightly clenched a whole fistful of the hem of God's garment. And there he duly was, that July evening, with his meiny of devoted elderly females clapping their hands in time with his rhythm, and the usual handful of guardsmen, and the pale clerks from Tooting, and the gaggle of loose little girls, and the cyclists in reversed caps and white alpaca coats. Only the brash young hobbledehoy hecklers were not there. There was something in the cold grey eyes of Uncle Dawkins that disorganized them. They opened their mouths, but nothing came. They shifted from one foot to the other. Then they slunk off to more rewarding pastures.

Tommy waited on the outskirts of the crowd. He was in no hurry. Frankie was embarked on a hymn, one of his own. Tommy was quite familiar with it, for they still sang it in Parkhurst. The tune was the tune of "Sweet Genevieve."

"Come on," requested Uncle Dawkins. "Here's the refrain. Join in, everybody.

"I do not know where I would be
If 'twere not for God's kind mercy.
His goodness often makes me ask
How best to do my time and task."

Do his time and task. Tommy smiled obscurely in the shadows. A girl brushed by. She was cloudy with snaggles of hair and sweater.

"Hello, beautiful! Doing anything?" the girl asked.

"Go to hell!" said Tommy.

The dim large moth heeled over towards a Coldstream drummer.

"Hello, beautiful! Doing anything?"

" 'Ow mooch?" asked the young man. He seemed to be from Yorkshire.

"The time is long" (sang Frankie) *"but God is good*
Behind the bars where I now dwell.
But goodness in the end will tell—
It gives me joy, 'tis understood."

The crowd liked Uncle Dawkins. His religious services were much more singing than theology. There followed a traditional hymn. A woman cried out sharply, finding the mouth of her handbag yawning wide open. Tommy smiled. He, and he alone, had seen the job done, and it couldn't have been improved on. It was Smiler Harris, a real artist, of whom they said he was the second-best handbag tea-leaf in town. Frankie the Toff turned round, stared severely at the woman, then concluded his hymn. "Good night, Uncle Dawkins," the regular members of the congregation said. "Good night, dear. Good night. Good night." The crowd dispersed. On long legs Uncle Dawkins strode off towards the park gates. Only the woman with the rifled handbag, still unfastened, remained behind, the tears streaming down from her bewildered eyes.

"Hello, Frankie!"

Frankie whipped round, like a savage in a jungle hearing a strange sound. The eyes registered with lightning speed the identity of the object they lit upon; with the same speed the mind swivelled to a new area of association.

"Tommy! You want anything? Got a cigarette?"

Tommy held out a packet.

"Let's have a cup o' tea at Paddy's," suggested Tommy. Paddy's was a coffee-stall off the Edgware Road on the edge of a bombed site used as a car-park. You could talk nice and comfortable leaning against the car-bonnets. They got to Paddy's.

"Anything doing?" asked Tommy.

"Funny thing. I was only thinking of you yesterday."

"What's in it?"

"Necklaces, rings and brooches. The stuff's a bit on the fancy side."

"Actress?"

"Sort of. Singer. A couple of mink coats, too. Nobody's been able to get a smell in. Bayswater. Sixteen Corfe Terrace."

"Where does she sleep?"

"Second-floor front. A good deal of her jewellery's in the bank, but there's still enough left at home to make the job worth while."

"Don't she have a safe?"

"Yes. She has a safe. But she's been getting a bit careless lately, with all those alarms on every door and window. So she often keeps it in a jewel-box in her dressing-table."

"No husband?"

"No husband. A boy friend comes now and again. There's a housekeeper in the front room next to the chauffeur's." Frankie's eyes were alive with pleasure. He was feeling himself a boy of twenty again.

"How long's the job being going?"

"For years. Five years. Joe Donatti did her five years ago. Since then it's been tough, with bars on the windows and those burglar-alarms. Though I'm not so sure." He smiled secretly. The phrase probably meant there was a time when Frankie wouldn't have let a whole battery of burglar-alarms get in his way.

"How's the pipes?" asked Tommy.

"No good. That's what's always kept the boys off. There's a drainpipe goes within a couple of feet of the back windows. But it's loose at the clamps. A kitten'd bring it down. They don't repair it. They leave it that way."

"Have they fixed it all of a sudden?"

"No. The Council's got around to doing up the wall at the back. Bomb-damage. Let's walk. I think. . ."

He thought that the seedy-looking tramp scrabbling around for cigarette-ends was hovering around pretty close. Tommy thought so, too. They moved on to another car.

"There's scaffolding up at the back, then?" asked Tommy.

"That's right."

"But the windows are still wired?"

"Yes, they're all wired, but one gets switched off, the room at the top-back. The chauffeur sleeps there, a young chap. He's got a new bit, he's crazy on her. He gets out of his window every night, about one o'clock, and climbs down the scaffolding. The windows have separate alarms. He switches that one off, then switches it on again when he comes back, up the scaffolding again, a couple of hours later."

"He's away a couple of hours, eh?"

"About."

Tommy ruminated.

"Not so bad," he decided. "What about the get-away?"

"If you want the mink coats, you'll have to have one of the boys with you. It would be a suit-case job. There's a garage in the mews at the back, number eleven. The other bloke could be waiting in a car."

"To hell with the other bloke!" Tommy was silent for some moments. "Seems a bit on the easy side," he murmured, "isn't it?"

Frankie hesitated. He was aware of Tommy's penchant for jobs with a kick in them, a spice of real danger.

"There might be dogs," he said helpfully. "Anyhow, a dog."

"*Are* there any dogs? Do you know, or don't you?"

"They've not said anything. Maybe not."

"O.K." Dogs were a hazard he was quite ready to do without. "Let's move on, Frankie. You're a pal. How about a nice steak?"

"Hungry work, hymns," said Frankie. "It's very kind of you. Are you sure it's all right? Steaks aren't cheap."

"I can make it."

They moved along to one of the eating-places on the

Edgware Road, where you could sit down and work things out properly. It was beginning again, the odd, delightful, distressing tingle just below the knee-cap. Tommy stopped and whacked the place hard with the side of his hand.

"What's the matter, Tommy? Was it one of the damp ones?" He meant Tommy's last cell at Parkhurst.

"Dry as a bone. No, it just plays me up now and again. I think I'm going to like the job, Frankie."

"Look after yourself," enjoined Frankie. "Wish I was doing it with you."

"Why don't you?"

"The Lord wouldn't like it," said Frankie severely. "You know He wouldn't." They had reached the doors of the El Dorado Eatery. It didn't look much of a place, but they always had a good assortment under the counter. "They have eggs," Frankie said wistfully. "Could I have a couple of fried eggs on my steak?"

"You can have a dozen," said Tommy.

IV

It was no more than three days later, at about one-minute-past-one in the morning, that Tommy Smith might have been seen striding purposefully, with all the authority of a resident, down the mews which runs along the rear of the Corfe Terrace houses. So far as he knew, the occasional boy friend of the lady singer who lived at number sixteen had not put in an appearance that night. That left the singer herself, the housekeeper and the chauffeur. As he passed the garage of number twenty, the door opened, and a young man emerged. That was clearly the love-lorn chauffeur. That left only the singer and the housekeeper. Tommy slipped his gloves on, always the first thing to do. Then he paused for one quick moment. It would have been simple enough to pick the lock of the garage door. It was just a Yale lock, and a piece of the "loid"—that is to say, celluloid—would have been good enough. But it was just as simple to shin up the short drainpipe, and on to a flat roof. A moment later that was done. A moment later he was down into a sort of rockery there was at the back there. Beyond the rockery was a rose-wreathed trellis, and beyond the trellis extended a long strip of lawn, like a length of dark green carpet specially unrolled in Tommy's honour.

"Cushy!" Tommy murmured. He looked up into the sky. No moon, nothing. No need to hug the wall's shadow. He strode nonchalantly to the end of the lawn, where half-a-dozen brick steps led down into a cement-paved area. The scaffolding climbed broad and easy up to the top-back room. Two feet away the rigid snake of the drain-pipe ran up to the roof-guttering. The chauffeur was mad, or love had made him that way. The lower window of his room had not even been pulled down properly. He had left a gap nearly as deep as the window-sill. A whole ship's company could sidle up into the house without making more noise than a mouse.

"Cushy!" Tommy said to himself again. "Too cushy!" He started. Was that the sound of a dog somewhere close by dragging on a chain? It might be in that little out-house on the left there. He listened intently. Silence. He stooped and felt around for a nugget of fallen rubble, found one, and threw it softly against the outhouse door. Still silence. No moon. No dog, at least not on the outside here. No nothing. He felt a lump of something behind his ribs, and knew that it was a sense of sharp dissatisfaction that was gnawing at him. All the flesh of his body felt flabby, unexcited. He bent down and whacked himself behind the knee-cap with the side of his hand, in the way a doctor does to test the reflexes. It felt like the leg of a chair. There was none of the lovely tingling that sometimes, during the great jobs, ran in waves all up to the back of the neck and down again, a thrill more breathless than whiskey or women or anything at all in the world.

"Well," he told himself. "It's about time I was getting on with it. It's not in the bag *yet*. Besides, the boy friend might be on duty after all. Who knows?" The boy friend might just add that element of tension the adventure lacked. He advanced a few steps and got hold of one of the steel poles of the scaffolding. It was as firm as an oak-tree. Then suddenly a flash went off inside his skull, like a photographer's magnesium-flare. It seemed actually to illuminate the immediate neighbourhood, and in the light of it he saw the drain-pipe, two feet away from the scaffolding, mottled with tiny blisters of green-grey paint. Immediately his whole body thrilled, as if he had touched an exposed wire. He knew exactly what he was going to do, and in the same instant was doing it. He had seized the drain-pipe, he was hauling himself up, he was distributing his weight between hands, feet, chin, belly, with a skill as uncanny as a cat's. There was a moment, perhaps, even there were two moments or more, when the whole thing seemed certain to come away from its moorings and hurl him down to his death, or at least to a smashed spine. In the fraction of an instant he had shifted his point of gravity, found lodgement for the toe of his shoe or his finger-tips, or was pressed up against the wall immobile as a lizard, maintained, it seemed, only by the force of suction, or his demon will-power. At length he reached a steel pole just below the chauffeur's open window, and with a final convulsive thrust of every tendon and muscle he swung himself clear of the drain-pipe, and on to the scaffolding. There he stood for some seconds, the sweat pouring from his forehead in icy streams, and his finger-tips standing out like individual rods of fire.

"Christ!" he said to himself. His heart rose and fell like a drop-forge. "That was good-o!" He breathed deeply, not so much to fill his lungs, as to get the heart to stop making that clamour. He didn't want to wake the dame. Why wake her? He might as well help himself to the shiners while he was round the place.

The rest was dead easy. First he took his shoes off. They were, in fact, so torn they almost came away of themselves. Then he crept to the dame's door, one floor down and facing front. The same sort of muscular control as he had used in climbing the drain-pipe he used in descending the staircase which, under feet less deft, would have creaked like a wind-cracked tree. Here, then, was the dame's door. It would be dodgy if it was protected by a burglar-alarm, but he thought it probably was not. No. It was not. The door was not even locked. The door moved inward as silently as a handkerchief stroking a cheek. Practically no light came into the room from between the curtains; so he stood there, waiting, till his eyes could fill out the nothingness with the shapes that occupied it.

First, the bed. You could hear the dame breathing peacefully. Then the wardrobe, a chair, a cabinet, and, nearest the window, a dressing-table. Then he put a foot forward, lowered the heel, advanced the other foot. The blood sang sweetly in his veins. It was not the delicious delight of the drain-pipe climb, but it was fun, life was worth living. Now he was at the dressing-table. In two seconds his hands outlined the jewel-box, a shape not unfamiliar to him. The small key was in the lock. He turned it. It made a click so loud and clear it was hard to believe it would not waken the woman. She slept on. He lifted the outer lid and felt there a pleasing assortment of jewellery, rings and brooches. Below the inner lid were the larger pieces, necklaces and jewels. He dug in both hands, smiling. The jewels, slipping back between the fingers, brought back an episode of the long ago with such clarity it almost seemed to be raisins now, as it was then, and not jewels, that were slipping between his fingers. It was one of his earliest stealings, at a grocer's shop. What was the name? Clarkson. He used to play with little Dicky Clarkson in the living-room at the back of the Clarksons' shop. They kept surplus sacks of stores there. Sugar. Raisins. How old was he? Six, seven? Nobody was around. The neck of the raisin-sack gaped open. In went the two grubby little hands, up they came, the raisins slipping through the fingers. Next time it was Woolworth's. Remember? That pocket battery?

The jewel-box was now empty. The dame still slept sweetly. It was time to go now. He slipped out through the bedroom door, up the stairs, and into the chauffeur's room, where he put his shoes on again. He listened with pride to his own silence. Then he stepped out upon the builder's scaffolding, let himself down as if it were a flight of stairs. There was no point is going down the other way, by the drain-pipe. He'd had his fun.

In his more sententious moods Frankie the Toff had a lot to say about a crook's 'signature,' as he learnedly called it. "Thousands of crooks have fallen," he used to say, "because the police have known and studied their methods, and have been able to identify a certain crime with a certain crook. Some burglars assert their individuality so clearly, in the way they force open a window, or whether they make a clean job or a botched job, whether they leave the place tidy, or in a ransacked condition, whether they grab anything they can lay their hands on, or pick and choose the choicest titbits—it all speaks volumes to the trained eye of the police." So spake Frankie the Toff.

The job in Corfe Terrace eloquently proclaimed the 'signature' of Tommy Smith. Who else would have gratuitously climbed that deathly drain-pipe. Tommy Smith was duly questioned by the police, but his alibis were as cast-iron as they were expensive. Tommy Smith got away with it.

V

A week or two later Tommy was ensconced in a nice flat a pal had lent him, in Ship Street, Brighton, while the pal went off to Cannes to see what the pickings might be in the 'Zanzibar.' It was a comfortable flat, with an easy-to-run kitchenette, a radio, a gramophone, and a whole load of books, chiefly by Hadley Chase and Cheyney. There was a novel by Ernest Latimer, too, but he flung that out of the window. He felt he wanted no truck with Ernest Latimer. Now and again he had one of the girls in for a night or two. They were easy to pick up in Brighton, at Karno's dance-place, or across the road at the skating-rink. But on the whole he preferred to be on his own at a time like this, when he was relaxing. He brought in a load of novels of a somewhat more cerebral order, and made quite a pig of himself, with proper highbrows, like Cronin and Philip Gibbs. The gramophone was quite a new model, but the records were all just the old favourites, Bing and the Andrews Sisters and all those. So he would come in now and again with an armful of real classics; not only the "Warsaw Concerto," but even Handel's 'Water Music,' and Tchaikowsky's "Fifth." He thought Cliff might not turn his nose up quite so high if he could see him now, spread out on the couch, listening to Tchaikowsky, and having a bash at Aldous Huxley. He was a smart one, this Huxley, but Tommy didn't mind admitting he was a bit above him. He poured himself out another slug of Drambuie, a liquor he was very partial to, and read the passage again. It was from the book called *Point Counter Point*.

"The essential character of the self consisted precisely in that liquid and undeformable ubiquity; in that capacity to espouse all contours and yet remain unfixed in any form, to take, and with an equality facility efface, impressions. To such moulds as his spirit might from time to time occupy, to such hard and burning spectacles, as it might flow round, submerge, and, itself cold, penetrate to the fiery heart of. . . ."

No. It was no go. Tommy grinned, shoved the book aside, and reached for a still unread Cheyney. If you're going to relax, you might as well *relax*. He lit up another cigarette. Everything was fine. He was on top of the world.

Then one afternoon he met Shorty on the promenade, and everything started off again. Shorty had started life as a farm-hand in Essex, but he found he preferred the smell of petrol to the smell of pigsties and soon graduated from Finchingfield to Braintree, and from Braintree to Bermondsey; but it was actually in Borstal that Tommy and Shorty first met. After Borstal, Shorty managed to get into the Air Force, where he served as a fitter, and had the happiest time of his life, playing among engines like a pussy among daisies. As a side-line he stole clocks and radios, and often got away with it. He was less successful when he took to stealing ten-ton lorries, and was finishing a long term of detention when the war ended.

On his release, Shorty slipped into the second-hand car racket, as an eel from the mud-flats slips into the great sea. Being a country boy, he knew his way round among farms and farmers. He would locate in a barn some old car which looked like a derelict heap of junk, and buy it for a few pounds. Then he would get to work on it, supply it with some new parts, splash a pot of paint over it, and sell it for a hundred or two. The huge dumps of service left-overs at Great Missenden and elsewhere were more profitable. You would buy an old bone-shaker for the sake of the numbers on its log-book, and they would almost pay you to take it away. You would then steal a brand-new car, eliminate its old engine and chassis numbers and substitute new ones—the numbers on the log-book you had acquired at Great Missenden. You would change a few parts, too, and you were laughin', as Shorty put it. People began to look to you to supply them with cars for black-market night-work, even for smash-and-grab jobs. Shorty was thoroughly happy for some time, with his pliers and hammers and blow-lamps. Then it occurred to him that he might comfortably increase his dividends, if he eliminated the middle-man, and do a job or two himself, in one of his own jerked-up cars.

So he started looking round, and when you start looking round for that sort of job, it starts looking round for you. So he heard about Wheeler's, the tin box people, just off the Kilburn High Road. Wheeler's employed about a hundred people, whom they paid off Friday mornings. Friday mornings, a few minutes past eleven, they would send off their van to pick up the wages, at a bank less than a quarter of a mile away. They had sent the van off without any trouble for so long now, and the distance between works and bank was so short, that they often, quite often, sent the driver off on his own, though officially a bloke was supposed to sit in the rear of the van.

So Shorty thought it out. It was dead easy. You have to have a mate, of course, on this sort of job. You'd have this mate, and an old drag; it would have to be a lively one, something not very big and flash. You'd tiddle round on the Friday morning and find out if the driver was alone; probably he would be. When he moved off, you'd move up close. The mate would have to do a bit of a jump into Wheeler's van, but it shouldn't be too hard. Then he'd get hold of the bags and fling them in through the rear window. He'd have to be smart about it, sure, and when the job was done, he'd jump back into the drag. By that time someone might have noticed something. So you'd have to move plenty quick. It would all boil down to how quick you could do it. It would take a good car and hot driving. But no-one wasn't worried about *that*. You'd double this way and the other way, and in no time there was old Pete waiting for you with a wide-open smile at the wide-open doors of his garridge. Hail, smiling morn!

"Well?" asked Shorty, when his tale was ended, his tale being the push-over at Wheeler's.

"Well what?" asked Tommy.

"You know what," said Shorty.

"No good, Shorty. I'm taking things easy for a bit, see? Who sent you down to Brighton?"

"Nobody sent me down to Brighton. I was just browned off."

"What was you browned off for?"

"I fixed up an old tin can. I bought her for fifteen quid in a builder's yard in Poplar. You never saw such a miserable old 'as-been in your life. No inside, no outside, nothing. I've fixed 'er up so you could race 'er at Silverstone. Not *all* the way, mind. Just fifteen or twenty miles. After twenty miles she'll bust. She'll blow up like an old kettle. But for those twenty miles, oh, boy!"

"I've told you, Shorty, I'm all right!"

"Yus," said Shorty; by which he meant that he, and the other boys, had a good idea who'd done that job in Corfe Terrace, just as good an idea as the police had. But whose business was that? Certainly not Shorty's. His mind was on a different tack. "I've got to!" he proclaimed suddenly. "I've got to!" Was that a tear in his eye?

"Got to what?"

"I can't let her go to waste! It would be God's own bleedin' cryin' shame."

"Why don't you get Pop-eye in with you? He'll do it! He's out of nick."

"He's in again!" moaned Shorty. "Last Wednesday! I didn't know you was in Brighton, Tommy, honest I didn't. I just 'opped on the first train to anywhere, I was that miserable. Will *you* come in on the job? *Will* you, Tommy?"

The twitching under the knee-cap was going on and off like neon lighting. It was funny. He wanted to laugh. It was like tickling with a feather. Suddenly the laughter ripped the air as if it was a length of calico.

"Ha! Ha! Ha!" Tommy roared. "Ha! Ha! Ha!" He wiped his eyes with the ball of his thumb. "Of course I'll come in with you, Shorty! You think I'm chicken?" He clapped Shorty on the back so heartily the spine nearly came through on the other side.

This conversation took place on a Tuesday. The robbery took place on the following Friday. It was one of those squally days such as you get at the end of June. That would do no harm. The showers were sending people indoors. For just under a quarter of a mile everything went exactly as planned. Shorty's "drag" nuzzled under the van like a calf nuzzling under the udder of a cow. The transfer of the money-bags was witnessed by a number of people, but it was all going on in so matter-of-fact a way, it was thought to be some time-saving routine. Things went wrong when the car was held up at the entrance into Fowler Road. A water-main had burst, the workmen had just arrived to take the road up, and there had been no time to put up the detour notice. Wheeler's driver, turning to reverse, saw a young man leap from his own van into a vehicle behind. The second vehicle went into reverse with a bad crash of gears. A third vehicle was coming up behind. There was a squealing of brakes, a yelling of drivers and pedestrians, so frantic it was as if hell had emptied itself. But the little "drag," like a scalded cat, had already shot off into nowhere. And the hunt was in full cry.

The next few minutes were chiefly Shorty's. His eyes were wide with bliss. He was like a superb yachtsman riding a storm, or a horseman to whom the whole country gives itself, every fence and ditch and stream. To his right now, to his left now, back on his tracks again, overshooting the lights not more than once or twice, he was almost there, almost at the garage doors of old Pete, when the "drag" suddenly fell in on itself, with an almost human cry of grief, for there is no jacking-up of a car, however masterly, that can halt the demise of a big end, when its day is done.

"Oh, no!" wailed Shorty. "Oh, no!" with a pathos which could have torn from its roots the heart of Bloody Judge Jeffries himself.

"Scram!" cried Tommy, through his teeth; for already close at hand was a babble of voices, a loud gonging as of police-cars hot for the kill.

"Sorry!" said Shorty, and was gone in the very moment that the first police-car thrust round the corner. In that same moment Tommy was gone, too.

It was impossible to say if the cops had recognized him. If he managed to go to earth, which didn't seem easy, he'd find out soon enough, as soon as he came up again, whether they'd recognized him or not. He turned and twisted, there in the Kilburn back streets, then doubled, and turned and twisted again. The district was not very familiar to him, but the crisis was not new. He had a mate somewhere round here, in Canterbury Road, but there was no time to try and nose out which direction that was; all he could hope for was some sort of a bolt-hole, and he had an intuition of a sort that had rarely failed him before, that one would present itself. There was fear both in his eyes and heart, but not enough to dilate the one or constrict the other; and that was not only because of his anticipation of deliverance, but because he was exquisitely happy, as happy as he had been on the loose drain-pipe on the rear wall of Corfe Terrace, the happiness that only came to him when danger, like a radium needle on another plane, burned through all the layers, till even the deepest were for the time being anaesthetized. But while the acute bliss so twisted the upper lip that more than half the upper teeth were showing, the eyes took in every detail, large or minute, of the landscape. And in one moment of brilliant conjunction they registered exactly that, a detail large and small—on his right hand a static tank, of the sort which is still a familiar feature of the London scene, in the angle of tank and pavement a wind-blown straw. As the eye registered these things, the mind instantaneously recalled an episode in a pursuit-film. The Texas Rangers, or the Canadian Mounties, were thrusting down the tree-thick valley with all their cavalry. Totally invisible below a pool's surface, breathing placidly through a broken-off reed, the hero lay, the quarry—Tommy Smith, in fact. In action quick as the flickering image itself, Tommy had caught up the straw, he had vaulted over the low brick wall, he had lain himself down under the grey wind-smeared water, between a door and perambulator, on a bed of meat-tins, dead buckets, and objects softer and more grisly. Between his mouth and the vault of Kilburn sky stretched one thin straw. The nostrils were clamped between two fingers. Faintly, as from a world beyond woods and rivers, he heard the rumour of the hunt, thickening, bickering, and dispersed at last. The surface of the water was dark; from minute to minute it became darker. A school of water-beetles scurried hither and thither in terror. The rain-drops first, then the drops of hail thudded like knuckles on stretched skin. The sky was all gone. The water in the tank, the space between tank and sky, the sky itself, were almost all as wet as each other. It was the devil's own storm that was now raging. Tommy's heart bounded like a lamb. He need not wait more than five minutes or ten before he emerged. His wetness would hardly be more remarkable than that of any other honest citizen caught without his raincoat in this weather—and it was unlikely there would be many citizens around, honest or dishonest. He raised one ear above the water's level, a pale pulpy lotus among a thin grove of rushes that had taken root in the tank. There was no sound to hear but the drumming of rain on surfaces of slate and pavement and static tank water. Then he lifted the whole of himself, looked round, was further reassured, and jumped back to the pavement again. He paused a moment or two while he squeezed a few quarts of the more easily eliminated water from the ends of his jacket and trousers. Then he swung off through a solitude almost as complete as Stonehenge. That old mate of his on Canterbury Road was probably not far from there. He soon got his bearings, and in ten minutes was sitting by a cosy kitchen-grate, steaming like a boiled suet pudding.

CHAPTER VII

I

CLIFFORD ECKERSLEY had rooms, and rather squalid ones, in the Bullingdon Road, and most of his mail was delivered there. But things turned up in College, too—circulars, personal notes, invitations to meetings, and so on. He was on his way this morning to a lecture at Christ Church, but first he put his head in at the porter's window at St. Stephen's.

"Anything for me, Bennison?"

"Yes, sir," said Bennison. "Registered packet. I signed for it, sir."

One gets registered packets from time to time, even in College, though one would expect them to be delivered at one's digs. Why did the knees sag all of a sudden? Why did the tongue feel like a glove in the mouth? He took the packet and the two or three other things that were there, and went down the steps into the High.

There had been registered packets before, *this* sort of registered packet. He knew exactly whom it came from and what it contained. He could not bring himself to look at the wrapper till he had almost gone the length of the High. How pleasant it would have been to fling the thing under the wheels of a bus! But it is not safe to play tricks of that sort with that sort of parcel.

It was a lecture by Voysey, the philosopher at Christ Church, and he had very much indeed wanted to go to it. But it wouldn't be at all easy now for his mind to entertain divine philosophy. What was he to do then?

The police-station was not far off. Wouldn't it be best to go straight there, and get rid of the packet? Get rid of it? At a police-station? There's only one thing that happens at police-stations. You get things padlocked on to you. For keeps.

It occurred to him that perhaps the packet wasn't what he thought, after all. He looked at the address—typed, like the other times. The postmark was Lambeth. It could just as well have been Ayr or Uttoxeter.

It's no good being *afraid* of the damn thing. It couldn't bite you. And perhaps it *was* something else, after all. Some flowers, or something, in a nest of moss. Or someone felt he ought to send him a cigarette-lighter, God knows why. And why Lambeth? He turned into Cornmarket and went over to Pickering's, the café, where one often went for "elevenses." It was a bit early, of course; the women were still swabbing floors. He sat down at a corner table covered with an egg-stained tablecloth, and ordered some toast and coffee. The waitress brought it, put it down, disappeared. He was alone in the café now, apart from the swabbing women. Then at last he cut the string and unwrapped the packet. It was a box which had once held chocolates. It contained pound-notes now, a good fat wad.

He put back the lid again sharply, as if the box had held spiders which might get away. He tried to finish his coffee and toast, but they tasted like soot. He got up. Then he sat down again. What was he to do when he went out into the street? It needed thinking out, though it was hard work thinking with a noise going on in your brain like a car without a silencer.

It wasn't the first packet of that sort. No, alas. And before the packets of pound-notes, there had been the stolen watches, fountain-pens, cameras, in the time that preceded the first prison sentence, the time of the Approved School and Borstal. There had even been a shiny new bicycle left at the pavement's edge. He had been taken away to Granton Row, in Baxendale, and legally adopted by the Eckersleys by the time the first registered packet appeared on the scene. It happened to be a day when he was away from school, ill. When was it? Yes. Nineteen-forty. Soon after New Year. He was about twelve at the time. Dad Eckersley was at work, Mum was out shopping. So he himself signed for the parcel. Then, as now, the address was typed. Then, as now, he had a horrid premonition of what he would find inside the package. He went into the kitchen, cut the string, removed the paper. It had been a chocolate-box then, as now, and again there was a wad of notes inside it. He put the lid back on again, the way you put your foot on something burning.

What was he going to do? Tell his Mum and Dad? He knew he should, but he wasn't going to. What good would it do them to know that the Borstal crook had found out the whereabouts of the kid brother he had plagued for so long with these horrible horrible presents that no-one wanted? It might make Mum nervous, though it certainly wouldn't do that to Dad. Dad would insist on lugging him, together with the pound-notes, over to the police. And he didn't want any more police. There had been police enough, during all those wretched years in London, before the authorities had fixed up a new life for him. No more police, for God's sake!

What was the best thing to do? (he had asked himself, up there, in Granton Row). Give the money to a charity? That would be a fine thing, a small boy giving thirty pounds, or whatever it was, to a charity! Besides, young though he was, he knew one doesn't give stolen money to charity. What then? Tear it up? Burn it? Yes, burn it. You'd have to be very careful the way you did it. . . . At that moment the key grated in the front door key-hole. Mum was coming in from her shopping. In a flash he had thrown the box under the sofa. All morning he suffered agonies lest Mum should suddenly take it into her head to give the kitchen a clean-out, though, as usual, it was spick and span as a bar of soap. Fortunately, she had other things on hand. An hour later he retrieved the box and took it to his room, where he hid it in his cupboard. There it stayed that day and all the next day till he had got rid of the touch of temperature which had kept him home.

On the third day he went back to school. But he did not go straight there. He went first to Haxton Moor up above the town, and sought out a place he knew among the rocks, where he burned to ashes each pound note, and broke up the ashes in his fist.

That was the first packet. The second came just one month later, a registered cardboard box wrapped in paper as before.

But this time Dad was there. He was on night-shift, and had not long been in. It was Dad who signed for the thing.

"A registered parcel for thee, son. Why, what's come over thee? Aren'ta well, Clifford?"

"I'm all right, Dad."

"Th'art anything but. Tak t' parcel."

"Thank you, Dad." He took the parcel and made a move to go off upstairs.

"What's wrong, lad? Th'art as white as a sheet."

"Nothing, Dad, nothing." He moved from the kitchen into the lobby.

"Clifford!" Dad Eckersley called out. "Coom back 'ere! What's in parcel? Coom back, I say."

Clifford came back. Mum Eckersley looked on watchfully from beside the kitchen-grate. The boy's lips trembled.

"Well, Clifford? No-one's goin' to eat thee."

The boy could as easily have told the truth as the could have knocked out his front teeth. He told a lie, instead, which was foolish, for the lie would be found out at once. It wasn't entirely a lie, either. The boy, Mossop, had told him yesterday he could get Clifford, too, a set of dirty French postcards, like the set Mossop was showing round the class at a penny a time.

The postcards would come in a plain envelope, by registered post, said Mossop.

"It's some French cards," stammered Clifford. "A boy at school said he'd send them. They're horrid, Dad," he went on, seeing a chink of light in his darkness. "I don't want anyone to see them. I'll just give them back."

Dad's lower jaw was as stiff as a nut-cracker.

"Gi' me that parcel, Clifford!"

The boy hesitated.

"Gi' me that parcel." There was nothing to do but hand it over. Mr. Eckersley turned to his wife. "Mother!" he commanded. "Get into t'scullery." The Eckersleys were as strait-laced as only Primitive Methodists know how to be in a small Lancashire town. Mrs. Eckersley went off. Her husband, his face as black as shoe-polish, opened the parcel. It was not dirty postcards. It was a wad of pound-notes. For two or three minutes he sat looking at them, thinking hard, piecing things together. Then he lifted the wad out of the box between finger and thumb like something unclean, looked into the box to see if there was any letter. There was no letter. He replaced the notes in the box.

"Mother!" he called out to his wife. "Tha can coom in!" She came in from the scullery. "It's a wad o' pound-notes," he said. "We can guess wheer they coom from." No name was mentioned. "Is it first time, lad?" His voice was very gentle.

"No, Dad."

"How many times before?"

"Just one."

"Where did he send it?"

"Here. The day I was ill. Mum was out."

"What didsta do wi' it?"

"I took it up to Haxton Moor, and burned it."

Again Mr. Eckersley sat thinking for some time. Then he spoke again.

"I see, lad. I see. Tha didna want to upset us, like? eh?"

Clifford's chin was low on his chest.

"Yes, Dad."

"Clifford!"

"Yes?"

"Tha' shouldn't ha' told a lie, lad. Just now, I mean. It never helps. And besides that, it's wrong."

"Yes."

"So we'll do what tha should have done first time. We'll go to t'police. They may be able to trace numbers. They may be able to give 'em back where they coom from. It's oop to them. Coom on, lad. I'll tak thee over."

"Yes, Dad."

"Put your coats on, both of ye!" demanded Mrs. Eckersley.

They went to the police. It was horrible, like the bad times again. But there was nothing for it. From now on there was home, and there was school, and, always in the background, the police-station.

The next visitation was Tommy himself, in February, nineteen hundred and forty-one. That was when he had done his first prison sentence, in Maidstone. This time he brought the money personally, so it was possible to push it back into his teeth. A week or two later a letter came saying Tommy had joined the Navy, a letter which Clifford duly handed over to Dad Eckersley.

"Navy, eh?" Dad said shortly. "Maybe yes, maybe no. I suppose 'e's stole somebody's identity card. They wouldn't be signing 'im on in 'is own name, I fancy." No more was said on the subject, not even when a cardboard box containing thirty pounds was delivered at the Eckersley house in Granton Row, some three or four weeks after that, not even though the packet this time contained an honest-to-goodness note from the sender.

From my navy Pay with love to Cliff from Tommy.

As before, the notes were taken over to the police-station, within ten minutes of their arrival. There was a witticism from the sergeant: "Navy pay, eh? So they've made him a bloddy Admiral." That was all. Nothing more was heard after that all through nineteen hundred and forty-two. It was inferred in Granton Row that Tommy Smith was again behind bars, in either a naval detention barracks or a civil prison. Another parcel of pound-notes was delivered in August, nineteen hundred and forty-three. It was inferred that, for the time being, Tommy Smith was free again to carry on as before. Perhaps he had deserted from the Navy. Perhaps he had done another stretch in a civil prison, and been ignominiously dismissed from the Navy. Or, perhaps, he had never been in the Navy at all. Once more Clifford and his adopted father took the *via dolorosa* to the Baxendale Police Station. Clifford's sense of shame and guilt were so dreadful it might have been thought that it was he and not his brother who had sent still another present of dirty pound-notes. Two more packets came in the late autumn of nineteen hundred and forty-four. There was inaction for some months after that along the front up in Lancashire. And then, one Sunday at the end of that year or the beginning of the next, a report appeared, complete with the photograph of "Tommy" Smith. (A number of aliases were also given.) The report appeared in *Sunday News and Views,* a journal which was not delivered to the Eckersley household, for Mum and Dad deplored its addiction to sensational crime reports. Sometimes, on a Sunday evening, Clifford would find a copy at the house of one of his school-friends, whose parents were not so fastidious in their Sunday journalism.

It was a particularly foolhardy and vicious act of highway robbery *Sunday News and Views* recorded that weekend. The sentence was for three years, the longest sentence that had been passed upon Tommy Smith, so far as his brother knew. Three years is a long time. Tommy might die by then. He himself might die by then. Anybody might die by then. The boy went upstairs as if to wash his hands, but, instead, he filled the basin with cold water, so that he could sluice his eyes in it. There was a prickling like electric needles behind his eyelids. He was afraid, if he did not get them under cold water, he would start crying. And he would never forgive himself, never, never, if he started crying because his brother, a hardened and vicious criminal, had been sent to prison for three years.

He came downstairs, and though his heart was heavy, he was convinced this was the end of an epoch. There was no reason for thinking so. He had no idea of a criminal's scale of values, why three years should mean one thing and twelve months another. But he felt, he could not say why, excepting that the same womb had conceived and housed them, that his brother, wherever he was at that same moment, would be feeling as he did. An epoch was ended. His brother would never seek him out again. He would never more outrage him with his abominable gifts. They were out of each other's lives. That year he was less hag-ridden than he had ever been in all his life before. He applied himself to "swotting" for his scholarship with something of the devotion of a monk in the desert to his holy books.

And then the ill-omened day came on which Mr. Bailey, the history master, had put before him a choice of Oxford Colleges where he might sit for a scholarship, and Clifford had put St. Stephen's at the head of the list. He had tried to redeem the gaffe, but the mechanism had been ineluctably, as it now seemed, set in motion. He had won the St. Stephen's scholarship. He had duly gone up there. But a shadow was over the place, and the shadow had hung over it all through his first year, all through his second year. Now, not many days ago, in the Front Quad of St. Stephen's, the shadow had become substance. And now the ghastly wheel that had dropped the ghastly money was in motion again, here on the table with the egg-stained tablecloth, in the café in Cornmarket.

He brought his fist down on the table, and the coffee cup rattled in its saucer.

"All *right,* sir. All right!" observed the waitress sharply. She came up and made out his bill. He *might* be the famous Eckersley of St. Stephen's, but there was no point in him *creating.*

He hadn't the shadow of a doubt. He must go straight to the police-station, hand over the packet, and tell them the whole story. He had nothing to be ashamed of, or afraid of. He was sure they would be very understanding. The resolution went with him till he was within twenty yards of the station, then suddenly it stopped like a donkey digging in on its four hooves without any warning, and would not go an inch further.

"I can't face it!" he told himself. "I don't see why I should foul my nest in Oxford, too. Isn't it bad enough to have this mess up in Baxendale?" He remembered how beastly it had been on any number of occasions. Whenever there had been a robbery within fifty miles of Baxendale, a policeman would pay a visit to Granton Row to ask if Clifford Eckersley had been sent some jewellery or a wad of notes. It wasn't very intelligent of them, of course. It wasn't even likely that Tommy Smith, a thoroughly metropolitan character, would operate in the environs of Baxendale, nor that he would advertise his performance by sending his ever-loving brother an immediate *cadeau.* But that's how it is in police-stations. A routine once established is very hard to upset. And an inquiry might lead *somewhere.* You never know. No harm's done.

No harm's done. Clifford Eckersley would very nearly choke with anger. No harm done, with policemen calling at the front door, day in, day out, notebook in hand. No harm done, with himself dodging the policeman on his beat whenever he wore a new suit or a new pair of shoes, for fear the policeman might conclude there had been another registered packet that morning.

It was odious up in Baxendale. Why plant the nightmare here in Oxford? No. He would go straight back to his digs in Bullingdon Road, lock the packet up in his suitcase, and hand it over to the police in Baxendale within five minutes of his getting home the day term ended.

He went back to his digs, and at once locked the money up in his suitcase. Then he pushed the case under the bed as far as it could go. Then he came down the High again to carry on with his normal business.

But it didn't work out as simply as that. He had never been to a hot country, and for that reason had never had prickly heat. But that was exactly how he felt. He ached and itched all over.

It was no good waiting till he could go to the police in Baxendale. The point about going to the police in a case like this is much more to help them than to help yourself. What use was there in going to the police in Baxendale with the booty of a theft in the London area? Then another horrid thought presented itself. Supposing a hue-and-cry were suddenly raised? Supposing, somehow, the hue-and-cry led to St. Stephen's, and from St. Stephen's to his digs in Bullingdon Road? There it was, the tainted money, in the suitcase under the bed. The hue-and-cry wasn't likely. Of course it wasn't likely. But supposing it *did* happen? How could he explain the money away?

He dared not wait till he got to the police in Baxendale. On the other hand, he loathed the thought of going to the police in Oxford. Was there anything else he could do? Up and down the Iffley Road he walked, to Magdalen Bridge and back again, then back again to Magdalen Bridge. If only old Dad Eckersley weren't all those many miles away! If there were only someone here in Oxford!

Then suddenly he stopped and slapped his forehead hard. There *was* someone in Oxford. There was one other person in Oxford beside himself who knew of the existence of Tommy Smith. And this person, he was now absolutely convinced, knew that this same Tommy Smith, however at this moment he described himself, was the brother of Clifford Eckersley.

That person was, of course, Marian Framley, the Warden's daughter. He had been thinking over that fantastic encounter of a few days ago (it seemed like months now) in the Front Quad. at St. Stephen's. The misery had not left him, nor the apprehension which had succeeded it; but the panic of those first few hours was gone. He could think clearly about the situation now. These were the facts. He had seen Tommy coming towards him along the Front Quad., dressed up to look like an Oxford undergraduate. He had been walking alongside Marian Framley. Later, he, Clifford, had gone to Mrs. Framley to find out if there was anything she knew, and, if so, what. He had asked her point-blank if she knew who Tommy was, and she had said no, she didn't. Tommy was just a stranger, she said, who had come up from somewhere, and he was asking about the College. Later, in the course of the conversation, Clifford had himself told her that Tommy was a family connection of his, he had not dared to go any further than that. Finally, just when he was going, she had gone all out to give him the green light. *"I wish you'd believe me."* (He remembered each word, and the way she uttered it.) *"I'd be happy to be of use, if you'd like me to."*

That was the gist of what had happened, or, at least, of

that part of it which was visible, so to speak, to the naked eye.

That Balliol scarf Tommy had worn had been visible to the naked eye, too. So were those undergraduate flannels. The face that went with them might easily have belonged to them, but the voice certainly could not. If Tommy had tried to put on the sort of "posh" accent he might have fancied right for that costume, Marian Framley, of all people, would not have been taken in by it. She hadn't been taken in, then, yet she had told Clifford that Tommy was just a visitor up from the country. Why had she not told the truth?

Go back to Tommy a moment. What was Tommy up to in that fancy dress? He was clearly up to no good at all, there in St. Stephen's. But why St. Stephen's, and not one of the really rich colleges? That was an easy one. Because the Warden of St. Stephen's had a criminal brother, Matthew Browne, who used to make out that he had been a Professor at St. Stephen's. This Matthew Browne had met Tommy Smith in prison. They might have been partners in crime. They might have arranged to become partners again. This Matthew Browne, the uncle of Marian Framley, was therefore the link between St. Stephen's and Tommy.

What had Tommy been up to in those undergraduate flannels and that Balliol scarf? And had Mrs. Framley caught him at it? And if she had, why had she not handed him over to the police? Was it because that was bound to bring up the name of Matthew Browne again, and that name had caused heartbreak enough in her family? Had she any inkling that Tommy Smith had a brother who was an undergraduate at St. Stephen's, before he had himself told her that they were related? Had she refrained from admitting her knowledge because she knew how frightfully it might affect him?

One came back again to those words of hers, spoken so earnestly, the eyes looking with such candour into your eyes: "I wish you'd believe me. I'd be happy to be of use, if you'd like me to."

And now the horrible money was lying in its box in his suitcase, exactly like a box full of malignant insects that might eat their way out at any moment.

"Oh, yes, Mrs. Framley," he said to himself wretchedly. "I believe you. Please help me. You are kind and wise. I've no-one else to turn to." He made his way to the nearest public telephone.

"Is that you, Mrs. Framley! This is Clifford Eckersley."

"Of St. Stephen's? Oh, yes. How are you?"

"I'm fine, Mrs. Framley. Do you remember what you said?"

"I remember very well. Would you like to come and see me?"

"I would, please. Can it be today?"

"One moment." She turned to her partner. Was Cecilia likely to be in at six? She was not. "Would you like to come in at six, Mr. Eckersley?"

"Thank you. It's awfully good of you."

He was there exactly at six o'clock that evening.

"I can't tell you how grateful I am you let me come, Mrs. Framley." His eyes were quite bloodshot, she noticed.

"I've been very worried about you. Do sit down. Has anything fresh happened?"

"Mrs. Framley!"

"Yes?"

"I want to talk to you about that fellow who was with you last Monday."

"So I thought. Yes?"

"Did you know he was my brother?"

"Not till that moment, the moment you set eyes on each other."

"What did he come for?"

"You know, don't you, Clifford? I'm going to call you Clifford."

"Yes, Mrs. Framley."

"Marian. The whole College calls me Marian. You know what he'd come for. He was dressed up to look like an undergraduate. We mustn't spare each other any more, Clifford. I found him in Jerry Holt's rooms."

The youth bit his lip so hard he almost drew blood.

"What did he have to come *here* for?" His voice was hardly above a whisper. "What have I done to him?"

"I told you, Clifford, he hadn't the faintest idea you were here. You must take my word for it."

"Then, somehow, it's all tied up with. . . ."

She helped him out.

"He's a friend of my uncle, Matthew Browne. You knew all about Matthew Browne when you were talking to me the other day?"

"I knew the Warden had a brother . . . with a police record."

"They told you about him when you came up to St. Stephen's?"

"I heard about him a long time ago. From my brother, when he found out where I'd been taken to, up in Lancashire, and came to see me."

"You wanted to spare my feelings, so you didn't say anything about it? Is that right?"

"Yes, that's right."

"Some people know. Some people don't. I suppose most know. One gets used to it."

"I couldn't get used to it, Marian. I *couldn't*." His forehead shone with sweat. "I'd have to run away from Oxford if it got round."

"There's no particular reason for it to get round," she comforted him. "Your brother wouldn't say a word. He's far too fond of you."

"I know. That's been the trouble all along. If only he'd forget me. I thought he had."

"He'll never worry you in Oxford again. He promised me that."

He looked up and stared incredulously into her eyes.

"And you believe him?"

She shrugged her shoulders.

"I believe him," she said quietly.

He sighed. "I don't know how you possibly can," he murmured. "But what about the other one?"

"Matthew Browne? I don't suppose he's aware of the existence of Clifford Eckersley. I take it that's an adopted name? It was Tommy, Tommy Eckersley?"

"No, Smith. I was born Smith, too."

"There's no reason to imagine Matthew Browne will ever be aware there's any connection between Tommy Smith and Clifford Eckersley. Is that what's been worrying you?"

"No. Not that exactly, something else. But the 'Professor'——"

She raised her eyes.

"That's what Tommy called him, that time he came to see me, up in Baxendale. The 'Professor' knows that Tommy had a younger brother. He boasted about how clever I was."

"How long ago was that?"

"Let me see . . . six or seven years, I think."

"I shouldn't think of it again. How could the connection between you possibly be established? What's the other thing? Let's be frank now. I wanted to spare you last time, and you wanted to spare me. It got us nowhere."

"Can I ask you . . . how much you know about Tommy? And how did you *get* to know? I'm bewildered. I feel as if I was on a raft, and the currents were taking me this way and that."

"I'll tell you all I know. It'll make it easier for you. . . . And, it'll make it easier for me, too. Then we can talk about this new trouble. Let's have a drink. I think we'll both need it. Now settle down in that chair, will you? Put your feet up on the tuffet. I'll talk first. Then you'll talk."

As she promised, she told him all she knew. When she finished talking, it seemed as if he was asleep or in a faint, for his eyes were closed and he was still as the chair he sat in. But he was not asleep. He kept his eyes closed for several minutes. Then he spoke.

"What am I going to do with that money?" he asked. It was all she could do to catch the words.

A sudden flurry of temper whipped her face.

"Have you been listening?" she asked. "Did you hear what I was saying to you?"

He opened his eyes and shook his head, as if he were trying to expel the fume of some sleeping draught.

"I'm terribly sorry," he said. "You must try and forgive me. It often happens." She said nothing. He would probably explain what he meant. "I'm one of those people who can follow several conversations at the same time. Please don't be cross, Mrs. Framley."

"I'm not cross," she insisted. "I'm not cross."

No, she wasn't cross, she suddenly realized. She was disappointed. That was it. She hoped devoutly she had seen the last of Tommy Smith, but she had a numb and weary certainty that somewhere, somehow, he would present himself again. If and when he did, she would struggle and she would fall. She would be caught up in the skein, as her friend, Ernest Latimer, the novelist, had managed not to be. And if and when she was thus caught up again, it would have been helpful to have Clifford Eckersley as an ally. For Clifford was, after all, Tommy Smith's brother, however much he loathed him. She realized now it would be as hard to enlist Clifford's help as to cross the Pyrenees bare-foot.

"I'm not cross," she said once more, as if to underline to herself her own discovery. "And I won't let you call me Mrs. Framley again."

"I'm sorry, Marian," he begged. "You know, I sometimes play a game of chess inside my head, while I'm listening to a lecture, and I'm still following every word."

He was a queer youth. One must let him be himself.

"You were asking what to do with some money. What money? Has Tommy been sending you some?"

"That's what I've come about. It's your turn to listen. Will you?"

"I promise you. No games of chess." She pointed to her head. "Go on, then, Clifford."

He told her about the gifts straight from the beginning, all the way back to the apples stolen from barrows, to the fountain-pens, the bicycle, the cameras, the wads of notes. He told her about the latest wad, lurking in the suitcase under his bed like a phial with a mite of radium in it. He told her how the police had bedevilled his life in Baxendale, ever since he had handed over the first wad of notes to them, and how terrified he was they would poison Oxford for him, if he handed over the parcel that had reached him yesterday. "Though I know I *ought* to," he said miserably. "Of course I ought to."

She listened, her head bent slightly forward, her clasped fingers on her lap. She let him finish, but her chin thrust forward sharply on his last words.

"What's that?" she asked. "What did you say just then?"

"When?"

"Your last words?"

"As I ought to, I said."

"Well, then?"

"But, Marian, were you listening? Did you hear me tell you about the policeman in Baxendale, who slipped the camera off my shoulders, and hunted for the number? There were two prefects with me."

"I heard all right, Clifford. But there's only one thing we can do. You may think I'm a prig, and I'll have to lump it. But I don't think you will."

"You mean——"

"One can only do as one ought to."

"You're right," he said heavily. "I suppose I knew you'd say that."

"Don't look so down in the dumps," she requested him. "This old brain's simmering already. You mustn't forget you're not the only person in Oxford with doubtful connections."

"No, Marian. I think you're wonderful about it, all of you. If as many people knew about my brother——" He stopped awkwardly.

"We do our best. And that's all you're asked to do. Oh, dear!" A blush ran down her cheeks and reddened her neck all the way down to her collar-bones.

"What?" he asked.

"The way I'm talking. Like a Methodist local preacher."

"That's all right," he assured her. "That's exactly what my father is . . . the Eckersley one, I mean."

She threw her hands up in comic despair.

"I give up. Now listen. I'll tell you what I'm going to do." She reflected a few moments. "I suppose it's a bit of a wangle. That's my training in the Wrens. *Is* it? I don't know. You're going to go straight to your digs and bring back that little chocolate-box. While you're gone, I'm going to telephone the police. The Chief Constable is quite a friend of the family. I'll ask him to send somebody here. Or he might come himself. On the other hand, if they want you to go to the station, you'll go."

"Yes."

"But they'll be decent, I think. If ever the issue crops up again—while you're up at Oxford, I mean—we'll tackle it the same way. Is that all right, Clifford?"

He turned his head away, so that she should not see the tears that had started in his eyes.

"Oh, dear!" she said, turning to a small bureau littered with papers. "I've got some accounts to make out. They should have gone off yesterday. Off with you!"

He plunged off without a word.

II

In July, some weeks after the end of term, Marian received a letter from which she could conclude that the issue was not going to crop up again, not for some time at least. There would be no more wads of notes, for Tommy Smith was in prison again, this time in Brighton, awaiting trial.

This is what happened, according to the account contained in the letter to Marian. Tommy had been to the pictures one night, and when the show was over, feeling rather restless, he had gone mooching about, as he put it, not anywhere in particular, just up and around. He had fetched up somewhere in Hove, and a car had been parked in a side street there, just a few yards off the main road. A chute of light fell on it from an open window with no curtains. It was a smashing job, in fact a Lagonda, the sort of job he had always had in mind to get for his brother, young Cliff, if ever things got all right between them. So he stood there, looking at the gadgets on the dash-board, and weighing it all up, the upholstery, the line of the bonnet, when a cop came up and knocked him off. The charge was loitering with intent to steal. The sentence was six months.

Why I write this (the letter read) *is because I feel that I have known you for years and that you have a shrewd and understandable mind. I feel that in making an appeal to you I shan't go unrewarded and if possible you will help me. What I am arsking for is a solicitor to defend me at my trial. I swear on anything I hold dear there was no attempt on my part of nicking that car and I can prove it if I had a capable counsel. I have a perfect case providing—as is necessary in these things—a compitent counsel. Well that's my appeal and I pray to God you will grant it, though what right I have when you have allready been so good to me, but like you said where does it lead, nowhere? If you do not heed my appeal I shall understand it is a case of* dis aliter visum *but I pray and trust not.*

Humbly yours,
Tommy Smith.

The letter had been addressed to her at "St. Steven's Collage," and was brought over by one of the College servants, whose way home to Walton Street took him past the Easy Chair. She wondered if he had asked himself why the Warden's daughter should be receiving an envelope of that quality, addressed in so illiterate a hand, and in such uncouth spelling. Then she remembered that once or twice a year she did, in fact, receive envelopes not unlike this one in style. They came from former members of one or other of her husband's M.T.B. crews, who, like herself, had loved him this side of idolatry, though it did not prevent them, in their easy manner, from speaking of him as a "pig," in his capacity as officer. She conquered the impulse to tear to shreds this letter from this other ex-sailor, and thrust it into the centre of a thick folder marked: *Personal* (*Secondary*). The *Primary Personal* folder contained letters one had to deal with, if not today, tomorrow, or the day after. The *Secondary Personal* folder contained letters such as we all get, which are a bore, yet we cannot destroy them out of hand. Sooner or later we my get round to them, or the mere lapse of time will provide them with all the answer they need.

But within half an hour Tommy Smith's letter was already kicking in the folder, like a fish in the net, or the child in the womb. It refused to be treated like a personal letter, secondary. There was a party at a don's house that night in Charlbury Road. He was an alert don and the wife was delightful. Marian usually enjoyed the Charlbury Road parties, but that night she hardly spoke. It was assumed that this was one of the nights when Marian Framley was out in the North Sea, among the screaming gulls and the blown spray, so no-one worried her. At ten o'clock she excused herself and went home. At eleven, twelve, one, two, she heard all the bells striking.

It was the impertinence, she kept on saying to herself, which was so shocking to her. What sort of a claim did it institute on her time and money that she had twice caught the young man in *flagrante delicto,* once in the Ritz masquerading as an Air Force Sergeant, the other time in St. Stephen's masquerading as an undergraduate? That was not the only impertinence. Why should he expect her to accept his version of the episode, and not the police's version? What had he been doing that time in Jerry Holt's room, with his hand in Jerry Holt's pocket? Had he been distributing circulars?

She did not hear the bells toll three o'clock, nor four o'clock. But she heard five. . . . She knew that her mood had changed. She was racked with doubt, so acute it was like a toothache. Had Tommy intended to steal that car? Perhaps he had. It was hard to doubt it when you remembered Jerry Holt's rooms, Jerry Holt's pockets. On the other hand . . . on the other hand, perhaps he had *not* intended to steal that car? Perhaps it was *true* that he saw himself giving that car as a present to his brother, as he had given him apples, cameras, wads of notes. Did it make him less of a thief that he wanted to steal the car for his brother, not himself? But did he *want* to steal it? Was it anything more than a vision of his brother, the slum boy gone grand and Oxford, sitting at the wheel of a grand car?

She heard six toll in all the Oxford steeples. She heard seven toll. She did not hear eight, nine, ten. And, of course, Cecilia never heard them, either. You always had to get Cecilia up with a coal hammer. So the Easy Chair did not open up at all that morning. (Not opening up did not make much difference to the amount of business done there, even in term time.) One of the girls usually put up some sort of sandwich meal for lunch, or, in case of necessity, went round and bought some glazed buns from a café round in Cornmarket. Marian did not want to stay in for lunch that day, so she pretended she had a date and went to a bus-stop with the idea of thinking things out on the top of a bus.

But she did not get on to any bus. There was no thinking

out to do. She was aware that she had, in fact, made up her mind what she was going to do the moment she had finished reading Tommy's letter. It was not indecision that had kept her awake, but pure irritation. She had condemned herself —that was the word—to a certain course of action, if not that evening in the Ritz then that afternoon in College; for she had entered into a sort of complicity with him. He had asked for a lawyer, and it was up to her to try and get him one—at all events, if it should be considered advisable and useful.

She would have liked to talk the matter over with someone before she telephoned old Dunstable, the family lawyer, and the only possible someone was her friend, Ernest Latimer, the novelist, with whom she had long since discussed the fantastic episode in the Ritz in all its bearings. The thought suddenly pricked her that Tommy might have written a frantic letter to Ernest, too. She shrugged her shoulders. She did not think it likely, though the workings of a mind like Tommy's were totally inscrutable to a run-of-the-mill mind like hers. Anyhow, Ernest was a long way off and, in any case, he had been very sour indeed about the way she had taken on the Tommy Smith assignment. He thought she was a lunatic, and said so. Well, she was not going to make a special journey to town to see Ernest and be insulted. She had an appointment pending *re* the new book-shop, but that was not till next month some time. She might see him then. She went back home and telephoned old Dunstable.

The matter she wanted to see him about, she told him, was complicated and might take up a lot of his time. Come in at four o'clock, he told her, you can have the rest of the day. She went in at four, and he let her talk for well over an hour, listening patiently. At length she stopped. "Is that all you want to say?" he asked, quizzing her through his pince-nez. She said she could go on talking about the case for hours, but she knew he wanted to get home, and she thought she had given the essence of the matter. He got up from his chair, and behaved in a manner rare in lawyers, and almost shocking in the solemn and proper Mr. Dunstable. He moved her back hair aside with his finger-tips and with those same finger-tips started feeling around the base of her skull.

"What are you doing, Mr. Dunstable?" she asked faintly.

"I'm feeling your bumps, young lady," he said. "Good afternoon, Marian."

"Thank you. Good afternoon," she said. She had expected that answer in general terms, but not the phrenological investigation. He got down to his papers, attacking them under the cut-away section of his spectacle lenses. Her hand was on the door-handle, when he lifted his head and spoke again.

"One should remember whose niece one is, too," he said, severely.

"Yes," she breathed and went out.

That evening she wrote to Tommy Smith. The mode of address needed some working out. "Dear Mr. Smith"? It was the formality of people who have some sort of business relationship with each other. "Dear Tommy Smith"? It was only a shade less friendly than "Dear Tommy," and friendship was the last thing in the world that was present. "Dear Sir"? That was quite wrong. The letter went to "Dear Smith."

I learn with regret that you are in trouble again. I have discussed with my solicitor your suggestion that a lawyer might be found to defend you at your trial. He informs me that in his view it would be useless. I am sorry I can do nothing in the matter.

Yours truly,
Marian Framley.

It was July when that letter was written. A letter in reply came some weeks later, in August. It arrived on the morning of the day she had arranged to go up to town to examine a book-shop in Theobald's Road which had just come into the market. The letter was overwhelming in its protestations of gratitude. It might have been imagined that Marian had not merely acceded to Tommy Smith's request for legal aid, but that she had employed the most highly paid luminaries of the profession. The letter announced the sentence that had been passed on him—six months. It gave the visiting-times in case Marian should find it possible to get down to Lewes. In any case, he hoped Marian would be so very very kind as to send him down some worth-while reading matter. He did not think Walpole so good, but he thought a great deal of Sabatini and Priestley, though he was well aware *tot sententiæ quot maris fluctus*. It was a ruled notepaper. Every line of all four pages was closely crammed. Yours gratefully, Till hell freezes (it ended), Tommy Smith.

It was impossible not to be embarrassed, but it was no good being irritated. That was the way Tommy Smith's mind worked, and it would go on working that way. She had asked for this. If it had been possible for her to ignore that first letter, there would perhaps not have been a second letter. She thought it likely there would now be a third letter, and a fourth, and a fifth, according to the number of times per month a prisoner is allowed to write letters.

She was going to Theobald's Road, and that was no distance from Ernest Latimer's flat in Mecklenburgh Square. It occurred to her that she ought to take the opportunity to talk over with Ernest this latest development. After all he was on the ground-floor, so to speak. But was he? She had been involved in this heart-breaking business before she had heard a thing about it from Ernest's lips, that night at dinner with Bill Hylan and the others. She had been involved not only because she had already had that seemingly trivial encounter with Tommy at the bus-stop, but because, ever since she was born, she had had an uncle named Matthew Browne.

What good was it going to do to anybody if she went round once more to see Ernest? He had not been particularly helpful last time, and, assuming that Tommy Smith had not got into touch with him again, perhaps Ernest was by now well on the road to forgetting all about the episode. What good would it do to remind him? Or his wife, for that matter? It would do no good to Tommy Smith. It would do no good to herself. She would probably have to go over the whole story, and that would be like lifting large stones and putting them back where they were. Then she would once again ask his advice, for that would be the whole point of the meeting. That would be awkward for him, for his own handling of the matter had not been very bright or brave. But supposing he could forget that, what would he say? He would say exactly what he had said last time, exactly what old Dunstable, the lawyer, had said more recently, though he would not use the same idiom.

She went to Theobald's Road, and approved the prospects there; then she came straight back and packed up a parcel of books for Tommy Smith. She enclosed a small note with it saying she regretted she would not be able to visit him in Lewes Gaol, and if it was in order for him to receive a further parcel of books, she would dispatch them.

A single theme dominated the third of the letters from Lewes Gaol. It could be stated simply in a familiar formula: Crime Doesn't Pay, or in the language he actually used, it is a mug's game. Sometimes blokes do jobs (wrote Tommy) and if they get nicked, well, they get nicked. They stuck their necks out, so who could complane if they got it where the chicken got the chopper? (It seemed to Marian that he was making a careful non-incriminating reference to a crime, or crimes, he might have committed since his release from Parkhurst, crimes of some seriousness which he had got away with.) But it just shows you (Tommy went on) that when the police have got it in for you, they've got it in for you. You can just be standing round looking at the dashboard of a car, when there's a hand on your shoulder, they've got you. There's nothing for it. You've got to go straight, and there's no going straight unless you get a job. So if Mrs. Framley could only do him the greatest faver that any human being could ever do for any other human being and get him a job to go to when he came out, he would be her slave for life and there wasn't anything he wouldn't do for her, going through fire and water wasn't anything to what he would be ready to do for her. The letter concluded with a quotation which could as easily have a bearing, as not have a bearing, on the situation:

Stone walls do not a prison make
Nor iron bars a cage

The embarrassment and annoyance which Tommy's earlier letters provoked did not fail now. She nearly shouted with temper. What does he think he could possibly do for me? she asked herself. What could he possibly do for anybody except get out of their lives, as far away as any transport could carry him? But she relapsed again into the numb depression which invariably followed the embarrassment and annoyance.

Dear Smith (she wrote),

I have received your letter, and I am pleased to learn that it is your intention to turn over a new leaf when you have served your sentence. I will give careful consideration to your idea that I might be of some use in getting you a job. I will have to give some idea of your past history to any employer I may be able to contact. It is possible that will disappoint you, but you will see I cannot do anything else. I hope you have found both profit and pleasure in the books I sent you.

Yours truly,
Marian Framley.

She re-read the letter. It was a priggish letter, there was no doubt. It didn't seem like her own voice at all. But what other sort of letter could you write? You couldn't talk down your nose, like a schoolmistress. You couldn't be jolly and full of bounce, like a boy scout. Anyway, she had written four versions already. She signed it and sent it off.

The letter that came in reply was surprisingly level-headed. One had the impression that Tommy Smith at last had realized that a situation could be seen from other points of view than Tommy Smith's. He was very grateful to her indeed, and, of course, an employer would have to know, and surely he would not kick a man when he was down. He forgot to say he could drive a lorry or car or anything, but, of course, he would be greatful for any kind of job to have a fresh start and get on his feet. P.S. He hopped he would be out in a few weeks, and he knew she knew he would not come to Oxford. She knew why. But please if it was all right he would write to her.

So Marian set to work to try and fulfil her promise. It was not easy going. It might have been a little easier if the Oxford area, where she naturally had the greater part of her contacts, were not totally out of bounds. Also, whatever contacts the daughter of an Oxford don might be expected to have, they are unlikely to include employers of labour on the lowest levels. St. Stephen's had certain connections with one or two public schools in the Midlands, and she might have landed something in those regions, but she did not think it wise or fair to commit Tommy's situation to black and white. She was therefore practically forced to confine herself to the Home Counties area, which was in itself not unpropitious, because she was now definitely making arrangements to transfer herself and the Easy Chair to London, where she had long wanted to be. (It was not going to be called the Easy Chair this time—that was altogether too languorous a name.)

For Cecilia Burton's young man had now returned to Cecilia and he was even going to marry her. She had been delighted to dispose of her share in the business and Marian was now in the last throes of winding it up and starting again in London. She had practically acquired a one-time stationers and tobacconists in Theobald's Road, which she proposed to stock with more serious wares. A small room behind the shop and another above it went with the lease. When she had first heard about these additional premises, it seemed to her quite wonderful. If she bought the shop, she would be buying herself a home at the same time. But on closer inspection the two rooms proved impossible. There was a sharing of bathroom and toilet with strangers, which, even if they were a lot more palatable than they were, was not to be thought of. Also the rooms looked out, beyond a narrow entry, on to a steep façade of dirty wall that extended away up and out of sight.

So she was faced with the problem of finding herself a flat, as well as finding a job for her protégé, Tommy Smith. Neither was easy going. She learned very soon that a request of the sort she was making in Smith's behalf causes considerable embarrassment, even when it is not complicated by special considerations.

It is easier to ask a business-man to enlist an employee of a high grade than of no grade at all. And, of course, there were the special considerations. The first two or three people she contacted turned her down out of hand. It was a galling experience. Two or three others said they would see what they could do, and it was obvious they would do nothing. No-one put it into so many words, but a few, at least, clearly felt that it was inadvisable for Matthew Browne's niece to be occupying herself with such a matter. At last she was directed to a total stranger, a certain Mr. Williams, a manufacturer of plastic toys in Putney. Nobody could have been more sympathetic than Mr. Williams. He undertook to find a job for Tommy Smith driving one of his lorries, without even insisting on a personal interview with the released prisoner. He was merely to present a note from Marian.

It was almost as much as Marian could do to say "Thank you." All she hoped was she would not start blubbering before she had left Mr. Williams's office. In fact, she managed to get to the main gates of the works before the tears started flowing. Then there was no stopping them.

"Poor girl!" sighed the man at the gate. . . . "So old Williams is up to 'is tricks again, the old basket!"

Tommy Smith was already out of prison by the time this contact was established between Marian and the estimable Mr. Williams. Within a few days of his discharge Marian had received a letter from him, addressed, as ever, *via* St. Stephen's College. He stated that it would give him more happiness than he could say if she could spair a few moments to see him when she was next up in London, or anywhere at all, except Oxford, she would know why. He knew that it was too much to ask for, and he would understand if she would rather not see him. He would be waiting news of any job she might find for him. A letter would always reach him c/o Mr. Bickers, at an address in Hammersmith.

She read the letter and placed it with the others. She did not know which distressed her more, the jauntiness of some of the other letters, or the abasement of this one. She acknowledged the letter and told him she was doing what she could. Shortly she was in a position to inform him of the kindness of Mr. Williams, the plastic toymaker. She enclosed a second note inside the envelope, for presentation to Mr. Williams. Within ten days, a note came from Tommy Smith, informing her that he had been recognized by one of the workmen as the T. Smith with a record. There had been unpleasantness at the works, and Mr. Williams had been forced to dismiss him. He was grateful to Mrs. Framley for what she had done, and he was not going to ask her to try again. But perhaps she would now understand a bit better than before. He did not specify what she would understand.

She did, in fact, try more than once, each time scrupulously informing Tommy's employer that the young man in question had a prison record. Each time she failed, the failure taking place either before employment, or within a short time after employment. It was driven home upon her that her determination to tell the truth was making it impossible, or almost impossible, for Tommy Smith to be placed in any sort of a job above that of casual dish-washer, and she doubted that that sort of job could restrain him long from reverting to his former interests. It might be possible to land him somewhere if one concealed his past, but that would be totally anti-social, and was unthinkable. In the meantime, the weeks were piling up. She herself was due shortly to take over the book-shop in Theobald's Road, and was exceedingly busy with her own affairs, seeing wholesale booksellers and publishers, and interviewing a series of young men and women who had answered her advertisement for a book-shop assistant. (It was her intention to let off the two rooms behind and above the shop by way of part payment on the assistant's weekly wage.) It was a pity this almost hopeless business of trying to find a job for Tommy Smith should be going on while she was so tied up with her own affairs, all the more as Robert and Anna, who could be generally relied upon to give her a hand in an emergency, had been abroad during practically the whole of the Long Vacation.

What is more, they had been away with Clifford Eckersley, of all people. There was no doubt about it, it was a piquant situation. She wondered what Robert and Anna would think if they found out that while they were holiday-making in Brittany with Clifford, Clifford's brother was serving a sentence in Lewes Gaol, and their elder sister was moving heaven and earth to find him a job. They would be surprised, but they wouldn't make too much fuss about it, of course. Their own uncle might be serving his latest sentence in the next cell to Tommy Smith.

CHAPTER VIII

I

IT WAS in the first term of Clifford Eckersley's second year that Robert and Anna, the Warden's twin children, first met the young man from Baxendale. That was, in fact, how a good many people called him—the young man from Baxendale. The meeting might well have taken place at Sunday lunch, for Eckersley was certainly Important, and Sunday lunch was the rendezvous of the Important, the best old Etonian and Wykehamist undergraduates, the smarter dons from the good Colleges, and the crested Relatives up on a visit.

But obviously Clifford Eckersley did not have the right sort of Importance, despite the book of poems which had won the highest commendation of Great Turnstile Street, and his rapid successes at the Union, and his formidable weekly "Scrutiny" in the *Isis*. So he was the guest, not at a Sunday luncheon, but at a Warden's tea-party, and the twins were there, too.

But at the last moment something had gone wrong with the tea-party. Perhaps the Secretary had gone mad. Instead of the pimply women lecturers and the gawking Scholars from Grammar Schools it was Debrett at its most rarefied. There was even Royalty there, though admittedly it was the wrong side of Suez.

"The Secretary's mucked things up a bit," said Robert irreverently later.

"And wasn't Daddy *naughty*," said Anna, blushing. Tomboy girl though she was, she blushed easily.

"Naughty!" snorted Robert. He was very angry. They were both very angry. The fact is that the Warden was a good deal more thrilled by his company than the Warden of an Oxford College had any right to be. He addressed ten words, perhaps less than that, to Clifford, and made only a perfunctory effort to introduce him to any of the other guests. Then he forgot about him. Mrs. Browne, the Warden's wife, had done what she could to retrieve the situation, but she was never any good at names, and she soon withdrew, disheartened. The twins were too young and too cross to put things right. Robert was in his first term, over at Magdalen, and Anna was just down from Roedean, and feeling very much out of it. Besides, Eckersley looked as if he didn't want any situation to be retrieved. He had his nose high up in the air, and his eyes sparkled truculently.

"How handsome he is!" Anna thought. There were not many people who thought that, but at that moment there was a certain grandeur about him.

"I hope you don't mind, Eckersley," said Robert diffidently. (His mother had introduced them.) "But I'd be awfully bucked if I could ask you some day about one or two of your poems."

Eckersley did not seem to have heard him. Suddenly he turned on his heels and was moving towards the door. It had not been an easy time for him.

The next time Clifford met either of them, it was Robert, coming up over the bridge towards Magdalen a few days later. Clifford was on his bicycle, and he came off so quickly on seeing Robert, it was obvious he had something on his mind.

"Excuse me, Browne," he said. "I *did* hear you."

"I beg your pardon?" said Robert, opening his eyes wide. Then he remembered. "Oh, please!" he begged. He might have been his sister the way he was blushing.

"If you really *want* to ask me anything about my stuff," said Clifford, "then, of course. When you like."

"Won't you have luncheon with me at the George tomorrow?" said Robert impulsively. "That's my sister and me," he explained.

Clifford stood and stared into Robert's eye for several seconds, as if to satisfy himself that the Warden's son wasn't paying out some conscience-money.

"Thanks," he said at length. "I'll be with you." Then he jumped on his bicycle and thrust off.

That was how the friendship started. It did not at first progress very fast. Clifford could not convince himself that the twins were not merely cultivating his acquaintance to make up for their father's unceremonious treatment. After a punctilious return luncheon, on which he presumably spent a good deal more than he could afford, he quite clearly avoided them. For their part, the twins were embarrassed by the fact that Robert was only a freshman, while Clifford was a second-year celebrity. None the less, they were not to be put off, particularly Anna, who always knew exactly what she wanted.

She accosted Clifford one day in the High.

"Hello, Eckersley," she said. "Don't try and pretend you haven't seen me."

There was nothing much to be said about that.

"Sorry," he murmured.

"Have you seen Robert the last day or two?" she asked.

"I don't think I have."

"He's got a black eye," she said.

"Oh, I'm sorry."

"It doesn't go very well with that fair curly hair."

"No. I don't suppose so."

"Do you know how he got it?"

"No," he replied, a little uneasily.

"He had a fight with someone who called you a bag of poison."

He bit his lip.

"I do wish people wouldn't——" he began.

"Don't behave like one!" she said, and swept on.

Next day he got a charmingly worded note from her. She and Robert had managed to get three seats for the Berlioz opera at the New Theatre next week. They'd be so distressed if he were engaged that night. He was free, and was with them.

From now on things went a lot easier. Robert down below, and Anna in the gallery, never missed a speech by Clifford at the Union; Clifford, who would have died rather than attend any athletic function at his own College, was an unabashed enthusiast whenever Robert played rugger, or went rowing. They both went out to see Anna do Portia's speech at the little Drama and Dance School in North Oxford, where a number of Dons' daughters were vaguely fitting themselves out for the Royal Academy of Dramatic Art, and, it was hoped, a stage career after that. The "Woodcote Group," they called themselves. Anna was not particularly keen about having them there, and Robert was not excessively interested, but Clifford was firm.

It was a pleasant triangular friendship, and it is quite likely that the Warden was aware of it, though he made no comment on it for some time. It was a difficult thing for him to comment on. He could either say he liked it or did not like it. Undoubtedly he did not like it. He preferred his children to have for friends the young people of impeccable social antecedents. He could not say he did not like it either. Academically the young man undoubtedly was an asset to the College. It seemed unlikely he would fail to get a First in both his Moderations and his Finals. He was an asset in extra-academic fields, too, though that was less important. There was no question of the reputation he had achieved at the Union, despite the Lancashire accent he seemed wilfully to hang on to, or, as some said, he had wilfully acquired; despite the falsetto, too, which he slid into when he was excited. Further, he had written verses which were well spoken of, and it was reported that a first novel was to be published in the purlieus of the waste land by the most austere of the London publishers.

So it wasn't at all easy to inform his children he would have preferred it if they had a lot less to do with Clifford Eckersley. However, in the last week of May, at a purely family tea, the twins made an announcement at the Warden's table on which it was impossible to withhold a comment.

"Oh, by the way, Warden," said Robert, as it were, casually.

"Yes?" his father asked a little suspiciously. He knew that Robert knew he liked his children to address him as "Warden," though it didn't happen very often. On the other hand, when they *did* thus address him, as often or not some sort of bounty was going to be asked for.

"About our walking-tour in the long Vac.——"

"We've decided it's going to be Brittany after all," continued Anna.

"Excellent, excellent," approved their father. "You'll remember to stuff Michelet into your rucksacks."

"I've heard the Bretons are not very careful about their drinking-water," observed their mother.

"We'll carry tablets," swore Anna. "And there's lots of cider."

"And shrimps," added Robert.

"Prawns," corrected Anna.

"*Shrimps,*" insisted Robert. He glared at her. She glared at him.

"Get on with your tea, children," the Warden said. "You can settle that when you get there."

"We've asked Clifford Eckersley to come with us," said Robert, as casually as he had initiated the conversation. The Warden had some tea inside his mouth and a cup up against it. It was evident it was as much as he could do to retain the one and set the other down without mishap. The tea went the right way down. The cup found the saucer. Then the Warden paused. Here was a time for considered speech if there ever was one. The remark he finally made did not do anyone any credit.

"But he can't afford it," said the Warden. Then he blushed. One knew now where the twins got their proneness to blushing.

"Oh, that all *right,* Warden," declared Robert enthusiastically. "He's going to spend the advance on his novel—it's come through!"

"And didn't old Fothergill screw them up, too!" boasted Anna.

"*Fothergill,* darling?" asked her mother, very bewildered.

"The agents!" said Anna reproachfully, though she had only heard the name herself that morning.

"Oh, I see, the agents!"

"I don't think it's quite suitable," said the Warden. The hot scone was like a flannel in his mouth.

"But why, Daddy, why?" asked his daughter. "Because Robert's a freshman? People aren't so sticky nowadays."

"No, it's not that at all!" said the Warden. "We're expecting big things from him at school. He ought to keep at it!"

"Oh, *Warden*!" Robert exclaimed. "You know he's been burning the midnight oil the whole year through. He *needs* a holiday! Besides, it's not going to be holiday all the time. As soon as we get to Floumantel, we're going to settle down to a real grind. Except Anna, of course. She can go out on to the moonlit sands and shake that lissome pointless clerical toe of hers."

"It's not!" said Anna. She had been thinking.

"Not what?" asked Robert.

"Not Floumantel. It's Floumanach."

"It's Floumanach. All right," he admitted with quite unusual generosity, though it was a little irritating that she was right, and he wasn't. "Floumanach!" He knew he was driving his father into a corner from which he could not emerge without surrender.

"What I meant was," explained the Warden, "it mightn't be quite fair to Eckersley. After all, it's one thing to be friends at Oxford, when you just meet for a meal now and again, but when you're brought together so closely, twenty-four hours a day——" He stopped. That, as far as his daughter was concerned, was clearly not a fortunate expression. "You see what I mean, don't you?" he went on lamely.

"*Daddy!*" cried Anna. "You don't mean because his people are poor and because he comes from a Grammar School? Oh, Daddy, you can't meant *that*!"

"You know perfectly well I don't!" snapped the Warden. "You know I recognize no social differences here at St. Stephen's!" Yes, of course. The Warden was the complete democrat from top to toe.

"Yes," recalled Anna. "The very first time we met him was in this very room, and there was royalty here."

"You see!" said the Warden. "To me it's of not the slightest importance that his father's a boiler-welder, or something of that sort. But it's different when it comes to going abroad. If it was only Robert who was going, I shouldn't mind at all. But a girl——" He closed his eyes. For the first time a new aspect of the situation had presented itself to him. "No!" he decided firmly. "No!"

"Daddy!" said Robert, changing the mode of address.

"Yes? What do you want?"

"I want to speak very seriously. Listen. I don't think in our family we ought to object to anyone just because he's the son of a boiler-maker. Please let us go."

"Yes, Daddy, please!" added Anna. "You don't need to

worry about *me*. Or about *him*, either. He's our best friend. We like him a lot and he likes us. It's going to be *such* fun!"

"Ask me next week!" said the Warden grumpily. "I'm busy! Go away, both of you!"

When next week came, one or the other of them asked their father for formal approval of the walking-tour. After all, he would have to pay for it.

"I don't see much point in saying 'No,'" said the Warden.

It was only a day or two later that the encounter took place, if it can be called an encounter, between Clifford and the strange young man, who may have been an undergraduate of Balliol, or an undergraduate of Pembroke, or an undergraduate of nowhere at all. The episode had upset both twins a good deal. They had gone striding up and down, up and down, between the Front Quad. and the Middle Quad. Then they had had a quarrel, because Anna said Clifford had behaved like an ape. The quarrel had been all the sharper because Anna felt very sick about calling Clifford an ape. Then they had turned their backs on each other, and had kept away from each other for some hours. Then Robert had sought Anna out, exactly at the moment when Anna was setting off to seek Robert out, because that is the sort of twins they were. They were seeking each other out because it had occurred to both of them at the same moment, that seeing the strange young man had been with Marian, Marian might know something about him. So finally they had called on Marian and asked her did she, in fact, know anything about the stranger. And Marian had said 'no,' she didn't know a thing. They both had had a vague sort of feeling that Marian *did* know something, whatever it was. And if she did, and was lying about it, what in heaven's name was it all about?

Obviously the only way to find out was by asking Clifford. But judging from the show Clifford had put up on the occasion of the famous meeting in the quad., it was just as obvious he wasn't going to like being questioned.

"Go on, *you* ask him!" urged Anna. "He's *your* friend."

"He's your friend, too," returned Robert. "Besides you're a woman. Women are expected to ask questions."

"I'm not going to stand up there and be snubbed."

"Any reason why I should?"

It was quite obvious that neither Robert nor Anna was going to face up to it. Several more days passed, when suddenly Robert saw a stocky young man in flannels with a Balliol scarf round his neck. Robert, Anna and Clifford were on the tow-path, the young man with the Balliol scarf was standing on one of the barges.

"There he is!" cried Robert.

"Who?" asked Clifford.

"Who?" asked Anna.

"Don't you remember? The man we saw——" Then he stopped. It occurred to him that whether the young man in the barge was the same as the young man in the Front Quad. at St. Stephen's, the less said about it the better.

"No, it isn't!" said Anna firmly. "You're bats. That's a Balliol scarf, not Pembroke."

"It isn't who?" asked Clifford, pale as death. "Who are you looking at?"

"Nobody, Clifford. Let's get a move on. I was seeing things."

Clifford by this time had identified the young man they were talking about. It was not Tommy, his brother. He turned and walked on. He looked as if he would fall into the river at any moment.

"Steady, Clifford!" bade Robert. "Aren't you well?"

"I'm all right," Clifford gasped. His lips were like the fingers of chamois-leather gloves.

The situation suddenly was too much for Robert.

"Listen, old chap!" he begged. "Get it off your chest. Who *was* that chap at St. Stephen's?"

Clifford turned away and was quiet for a long time. The way his shoulders were heaving, one got the impression he was going to be sick. At last he turned. His face was still twitching with fury.

"Listen, Robert!" he said through his teeth. "And this goes for both of you. If you ever bring up that business again, I'll never talk to either of you! Never! Never!"

"Sorry, Clifford!" muttered Robert. "I promise!"

"Me, too!" said Anna. Her eyes were sad and dewy with unshed tears.

II

From the Warden's point of view the Warden was, of course, right in objecting to the proposed walking-tour. If a young man and a young woman who are obviously fond of each other's company, are going to see a good deal more of each other than they normally do, and in the most agreeable circumstances, it is possible they are going to like each other's company even more than they did before. There is considerable danger in that. They might even fall in love, or delude themselves into thinking so, which is still dangerous. Both the Warden and his wife were descended from an impeccable line of clergymen, army and navy men, and those country solicitors who are still gentlemen of the county though they spend far more time among ledgers than among foxes. Out of the vast deep God had thought fit to fish up a squid and plant it in the bed of the Warden's mother and call it Matthew. The Warden was already sensitive enough on that score. It was impossible to retrieve the situation; but the next generation of his family could go some direction towards building a buffer zone between themselves and the family shame by marrying just as exaltedly as the children of an Oxford Warden might be expected to marry, with the exercise of some care and skill. It was regrettable that Marian, the eldest daughter, had not done very well for herself or the family. But it was war-time, and young Framley was a hero, and he had died a hero's death, as heroes should. She could still renew the tarnished lustre of the family name by marrying one or other of the admirable young men, one or two with old titles, who would obviously race to the altar with her if she flicked a handkerchief at them. But she did nothing of the sort, the baggage. She insisted on earning her own living. She managed book-shops. Well, the book-shop in the Broad, by all accounts, wasn't going well. She should soon be ready to consider a more permanent career.

As for the twins . . . yes, the twins, that was where his hopes lay. One did not need to think of Robert's marriage for years and years. Young men are no problem, though he would vastly have preferred it if Robert had consorted more with the best people in Magdalen (who liked him, as he well knew) instead of frequenting the company of this gawky, brilliant, embarrassing youth from Baxendale. But girls are different, particularly hot-headed youngsters like Anna. They should not be brought into close contact with eminently undesirable young men.

Of course, there was an alternative possibility to consider, and the Warden perhaps paid it too much consideration. The very proximity which was something to be afraid of might also turn out to be something to be grateful for. The fact is, and one must face facts, Anna was a lady, and Eckersley was working-class, and Lancashire at that (though the Warden seemed to remember the Registrar had said he had actually been born in Camden Town—quite as bad). His manners were sometimes regrettable. He was plain, there were times when he looked positively ugly. Surely it was the sort of face that must get on a nice girl's nerves quite soon, when you were looking at it many hours a day. And that *voice*! Surely one could trust that voice to work the trick, even if you heard it infrequently. Yet sometimes (the younger dons reported) Eckersley talked for hours and hours in that terrible voice of his. There was no stopping him. It was like an endless fusillade of hard peas fired at one's forehead.

Anna was too fond of the sound of her own voice for that. She would get heartily sick of Eckersley in a few days and the party would split up, north and south, or east and west. The walking-tour might well turn out to be a blessing in disguise. Perhaps the twins on the one hand and Eckersley on the other would hardly be nodding-acquaintances when next term started.

So the Warden did not withhold the finance which the twins had been promised for the walking-tour. Nobody could ever say of Henry Browne that he acted the heavy father. He got what he wanted in subtler ways.

But it did not turn out like that. The Warden's worst forebodings were realized. Anna and Clifford fell wildly in love with each other.

It is possible that they were in love with each other before they left for Brittany—but even if they were, it is quite likely that Anna would have hooted with laughter if the suggestion had been made to her, and Clifford would have been embarrassed and angry and refused to see her again.

"In love with *Clifford Eckersley*!" Anna might have said. "Don't be an idiot! Not if he was the last man in the world! He's a dish! He's enormous fun! I could listen to him for hours, and I've often got to! But in *love* with him? Dear me, you've a mind like a sink!"

And Clifford: "You make me sick! Can't a chap be seen with a girl without people starting to yap like puppies? It's Robert who's my friend, really. Anna's always *there*. They're twins. They can't bear to be apart. The man or woman who takes on the one will have to take the other on, too. Whoever Anna marries it won't be the adopted son of a metal-worker from Lancashire. Pappa has other ideas."

"Nobody said anything about marriage, Clifford."

A cold glare from Clifford. "When people are in love, marriage may well be considered part of the programme."

But no such conversation took place before the party went off to Brittany. Love came bounding out upon the young people like a tawny lion from the wild thyme in the shadow of the dolmens at Carnac . . . or came out like a sea-monster from the black Arthurian reefs that lie along the yellow sands of Brignogan, like the burned-out hulks of old galleys. Or sang to them faintly one night like a turtle-dove from the depths of a fir-tree that overhangs an old farm-house on the edge of the cliffs above Tréboul.

Each loved the other. Each knew the other loved in return. But their lips did not meet. Not even their hands went out to each other. Perhaps, at most, Clifford allowed his finger-tips to caress the tendrils of Anna's hair above the white neck that the sun had faintly dappled like the skin of a peach. They did not breathe a word. They had to tell Robert first.

They both knew this. They, and Robert, were lying full-stretched on a circular turf platform beside the small hotel west of Tréboul. There, eastward, the hill declines towards the beach and the bathing-boxes of the small plage, and, westward, the promontory marches, cliff upon cliff, breaking down in gorse and heather and thyme into the Atlantic, till the Points du Van and the Points du Raz, the last cliffs of all, stand ankle-deep in the wild Atlantic spray. Their coffee cups were beside them. The prawns were within them. (They had been prawns, not shrimps, though neither twin now knew whether he had been on the prawn side or the shrimp side.) It was warm as noonday. A bright silver plaque of a moon was high in the sky. The air swarmed with the odours the aromatic flowers gave off from all the hanging wildwoods.

Anna got up.

"I'd like to go for a short walk to the farm," she said. "Are you going, chaps?"

"I think I'll go in and read," said Clifford, "if you don't mind."

"I'll go," said Robert, and the twins went off.

The moths fluttered and flickered about their faces. The glow-worms lit up their tiny lamps and shut them off again. Below the sea slapped like hands against the rocks. They reached the level ground where the farm was on their left hand. A horse snorted in his stable. In the dairy, somebody clattered the milk-churns. Owls hooted from the barns and orchards.

"Robert," said Anna. "I've got something to tell you."

"What on earth?" asked Robert uneasily. "Are you bored?"

"Bored!" she exclaimed.

He misunderstood the emphasis. "Oh, Anna dear! I thought we were all getting on so well!"

"No, I'm not bored," she said gravely, and was silent. She turned her head, where some night bird talked out of the branches, as if he had a message specially for her.

"Well, then?" he asked, recalling her.

"Can't you guess?" she asked.

"What on earth are you driving at?" It would seem as if the famous sympathy between twins is not infallible.

"I'm in love with Clifford," she said.

He paused for a moment or two.

"In love with Clifford?" he repeated. "Well, why not?" That seemed to her something of an anti-climax. There was another pause. "Is he in love with you?" he asked.

"I don't know," she said. "We haven't said anything. What do you think?"

He considered the question.

"I shouldn't be surprised," he decided. "I suppose I'd still see as much of you as before?" he observed, with a momentary twinge. "If you were both serious about it, I mean?"

"Don't be *silly,* Robert," she reproved him. "Besides, you're taking things for granted."

"I'll ask Clifford," he told her.

"Oh, no! Oh, no!" she cried out. "He'll think I'm chasing him!"

"I suppose he'll tell me himself," Robert said doubtfully. "He usually does." He usually didn't.

"Oh dear, oh dear! What will the Warden say?" wailed Anna. "He won't like it at all."

"Considering the family we come from, we're jolly lucky!" Robert said brutally. "All right, I won't ask him. I'll wait till he asks me."

He didn't have to wait long, only till next morning, in fact. A voice came out of the other little iron bedstead at the other side of their bare wooden-floored bedroom.

"Robert!" This was Clifford.

From Robert sleepily:

"Morning, Clifford, are you awake?"

"I've been awake for hours."

"It's not time to get up, is it?"

"Robert! I've got something to tell you!"

(Here it comes, said Robert to himself.)

"You, Clifford?"

"I'm in love with Anna."

"Oh, are you? What do you know?"

"*Please* don't talk like that. I'm serious, Robert. I'm in love with Anna."

There seemed to Robert no more appropriate comment than the one he had made to Anna the night before.

"Well, why not?"

"Why not? There's lots of reasons why not. You and Anna know more about me than most people. You know my background, don't you?" (Robert knew some of the background. The Tommy element of the background had not been presented.)

"What's that got to do with it?" asked Robert. "*We've*

got a family background, too." (That was as near as they had ever got between them to any reference to the existence of Matthew Browne.)

"Suppose she likes me, too?" said Clifford. There was only one person in his mind.

"Well, supposing?"

"Well, I'd hope to marry her some day."

"O.K. So long as you can maintain her in the state to which she's been accustomed."

"Robert, be *serious*!"

"I *am* serious. We'd expect you to feed and house the girl properly."

"Do you think I have a chance, Robert?"

"Ask her, Clifford."

"I feel frightful. As if I'd taken advantage of this walking-tour——"

"I've kept my eyes skinned," Robert said virtuously.

"She's so *beautiful*, Robert. She's like a . . . rock-bird . . . you know, with lilac in the underwings. She's like . . ."

"Leave that to the poems," Robert ordered roughly.

"One doesn't do that sort of thing in poems," Clifford pointed out sternly. But this was not the moment to discuss the sort of thing one *does* do in poems. He came back to the greater theme.

"I've no right to think of her like that. I mean, I can't help *thinking* of her, but when it comes to going straight up to her and saying, in so many words: 'Anna——' "

"Now, now!" warned Robert. He was not very tolerant of the famous inferiority-complex which had often infuriated people close to Clifford Eckersley.

"And Lord God! The Warden! What will the Warden say?"

"Did I hear you say you had fallen in love with the Warden, or with my twin sister?" asked Robert coldly.

A loud howl filled the air. A pillow went with it. These were from Clifford, breaking down suddenly into irrepressible joy. His eyes were shining like a hilarious small boy, such a small boy as Clifford had never been. From the reverse direction another howl came, accompanied by another pillow. In a moment both young men had sprung out of bed, and were belabouring each other with pillows in the best tradition of the Fifth Form at St. Dominic's. The air was a snowstorm of feathers.

The door opened. Anna entered in her nightgown, looking like Aurora, or the young Ellen Terry.

"Go and stand in a corner, both of you!" she cried. "And do me five hundred lines before tomorrow morning."

But before tomorrow morning Clifford, at least, had another task to do.

It was after dinner again. The moon was coming up from beyond the cairns and the stony fields. The coffee-cups lay beside them, as last night, the prawns were numerous within them, washing in a pool of cider. There had been chicken, too, roast chicken with rice.

"How's everybody feeling?" asked Clifford.

Everybody felt fine.

"How about a little walk, both of you?"

"Bit tired," said Robert. "Swam out rather far this afternoon."

"How about you, Anna?" asked Clifford.

She hesitated.

"Go on, Anna!" urged her brother. "Don't let him go alone. He'll fall into a ravine or something."

"Oh, very well," she grumbled.

She rose, and went after him, along the narrow path, with the heather and the gorse on each side of them, and the sea pulling away below, pulling away, only to come thudding more vehemently against the iron cliffs. They got to the farm, and went beyond it, and reached the road that descended a kilometre or two away from the plage.

"Which way, Clifford? Through the fields or along the road a bit?"

"Let's stay here, Anna. Shall we? Here on this rock. It's odd. There's no dew." He took her coat none the less and spread it beneath them.

"Anna!" he said.

"Yes, Clifford?" She tried to make her voice as matter-of-fact as it usually was.

"I have a feeling that you know."

"I know *what*? There's an awful lot I don't know."

"You know, for instance, I love you."

"I thought you did."

"Do you love *me*, Anna?"

"What do you think?"

"I don't think I ought to let you," Clifford said.

"What can you do about it?"

"I'd rather not do anything."

"Well, then, what do we do now? I suppose you kiss me, do you?"

He still held back. She seized his head and brought it down to her mouth and they kissed until their lungs were empty of air.

She sighed profoundly.

"I suppose it's all right to call you darling, now," she speculated. "And really mean it, I mean. Not like Hermione Gingold and Henry Kendall."

"Yes, darling," he said humbly. "Did you think it could be so lovely?" Their fingers were intertwining like the tendrils of honeysuckle.

"I've never thought much about it."

He took her into his arms this time, and kissed her again, hard and long and deep, but not so long as before. He withdrew his lips suddenly.

"The Warden!" he exclaimed.

"To hell with the Warden!" said the Warden's daughter.

"What about your sister Marian?" exclaimed Clifford, some days later. "She's been awfully decent. Oughtn't we to write and tell her?"

"What do you think, Robert?" asked Anna.

"Oh, don't be so pompous, both of you!" declared Robert. "Besides you might hate each other's guts by the time the long Vac's over! Wait till you see her next term sometime, and tell her yourself!"

"Fine!" they both said, Anna and Clifford. But what with one thing and another, and Marian having gone up to London now, it wasn't till the last week in November that Anna, up in town for the day, telephoned Marian in the Doughty Street flat where she had installed herself, and said she would like to come round, she had something interesting to tell her.

So Anna came round.

"Hello, Marian."

"Hello, Anna."

The sisters duly kissed. That over, Anna scrutinized the flat.

"Quite a nice little place you've got here. What terrible curtains!"

"They're not mine. Mine are having new linings sewn on. And is that the interesting thing you've come to tell me?"

"Oh, no," she said easily. "I'm in love. I'm, in fact, engaged."

"Really? Well. It had to happen some time, though I confess you're rather young for these complications." She spoke with studied calm. The two Browne girls always discussed intimate matters with reserve. "Who is it? Do I know him, Anna?"

"Yes, you do. As a matter of fact he's in our College."

Then Marian knew at once. She would have been very obtuse not to. The friendship had been close for a year. That had been followed by the walking-tour in Brittany. One way and another, it was all asking for it.

"Oh, Clifford Eckersley?" she said. "Congratulations! He'll need a little looking after. He goes off the handle awfully easy."

"Don't be *heavy,* Marian darling!"

"I suppose I've got to kiss you again?"

"I suppose you have," agreed Anna.

The elder sister duly kissed the younger sister. "Oh, by the way," said Marian. "Have you told the Warden?"

"What do you take me for? He'd have a fit!"

"You're quite right," agreed Marian. "He'd have a fit! He was hoping for a Viscount, at least."

"Well, there you are," Anna said.

"Have you told Mummy?"

"No. There's no point in telling Mummy. She'd just go around with her neck lowered, as if she's waiting for the sword of Damocles to fall on it. We'll tell them both when the time's ripe . . . after Clifford's done his finals, and we have some idea what we're going to do. Clifford Eckersley! Funny, isn't it?"

"I don't see why it's *funny*," observed Marian. "I think you'll be very good for each other."

But, in one sense, it was a lot funnier than Anna knew.

"Now tell me about this shop of yours," said Anna. "When do you open up?"

"Next week."

"What are you going to call it?"

"Framley. Just that."

"Like Bumpus?"

"That's it."

"How are things shaping?"

"I think it's going to be all right now."

"Why now?"

"It's been such an awful job finding an assistant. No partners this time. Cecilia taught me a lesson or two."

"Have you found an assistant?"

"After a lot of trouble. Working-class, but she's got a degree. Sheffield, I think."

"Marian *dear*! You sound just like the Warden!"

"You're right, darling. I'm sorry. What I mean is that there's a sort of flat attached to the shop, which I want to throw in as part wages. Miss Jamieson thinks it's heaven, presumably because the little house in Sheffield where she lived all her life is so ghastly. She's worked in a Public Library up there, but she's always dreamed of working in London. She smells of soap and looks red and innocent and just a bit tasteless, like those big red New York State apples. She's keen on books, the ballet, and saving up enough money to go to the Stratford Festival. She's just right."

"Am I to have a cup of tea, Marian?"

"*Tea?* And you bring me news of your engagement? Oh, dear, my drinks haven't arrived yet."

"Next time, Marian dear. And Marian——"

"Yes?"

"If Miss Jamieson's a flop, remember us, won't you?"

"Us?"

Anna grinned.

"Clifford and me. We'll be wanting a *pied-à-terre* in London. I'll wrap up parcels."

"We'll both do better than that," smiled Marian.

CHAPTER IX

I

MARIAN did not do at all well with her assistants in Theobald's Road. Miss Jamieson was everything that Marian had said of her but one thing. She was red-cheeked and keen on books, and smelled of soap, but she wasn't innocent. When Marian discovered that Miss Jamieson was working downstairs by day as a shop-assistant, and upstairs by night as a tart, Miss Jamieson had to go. She was followed by a scholarly young man in horn-rimmed spectacles, whose references were as impeccable as Miss Jamieson's. But while Miss Jamieson's references had not interested themselves in her sexual character, this young man's never said a word about his inability to get up before two o'clock in the afternoon. The young man had to go. It was another woman next time, but she was dirty, and lasted only two days. It was now January, the time of year when Marian got in touch with one of her husband's most devoted hero-worshippers, a certain ex-Petty Officer, by name Wally Humphreys, a large and genial character. He had been a first-rate Able Seaman, and owed both his promotion, and on one occasion his life, to Bertie Framley. A good deal of the dog-like devotion that he had paid to the Lieutenant-Commander he had since his death transferred to his widow. He was one of those sailors who, while still in the Navy, talk night and day of what they are going to do when they get to Civvy Street, and when they get to Civvy Street talk of nothing night and day but of how great a life they had when they were in the "Andrew," as they call it. It had become Marian's custom in January of each year, since Wally Humphreys had come out of the Navy, to have a sort of memorial dinner to the Lieutenant-Commander. She rang up Wally, who had a small tobacconist's shop in Lambeth and Wally brought along from the pubs frequented by sailors any sailors on leave he could find who had had any association with M.T.B.s in general, and Framley in particular.

Marian, therefore, duly gave her party in January this year, and during the course of the proceedings threw herself on Wally's mercy. Was there any recently demobilized sailor, honest, sober, intelligent, who could help her out in Theobald's Road? Wally looked a bit embarrassed. He knew quite a number of honest ex-sailors, some who were intelligent, but he wasn't at all certain about the sober. Anyhow, he promised to cast around.

He cast his net as far as Peckham, where he drew up a character called "Tubby." "Tubby" was a sober ex-sailor now, though he had been very prone to "wallop," as he called it, till the doctor told him the beer was producing a heart-condition. He was brought to the shop; he was found to be intelligent, and there was no reason to doubt his honesty. But the moment he saw all those books ranged side by side on shelves, he had a relapse. They made his throat tickle, he said. He started drinking when the shop closed and it was running out of his eyes next morning when it opened. He left that day. Another aspirant left the week after. The future of the shop in Theobald's Road was not promising.

Marian's future there was made all the more distressing by her repeated failure with another ex-sailor, Tommy Smith. People did not want to give a job to a confirmed criminal, and who could blame them? As for Tommy Smith himself, he was silent. The letters had ceased. He had presumably given up heart that an honest job might be found for him—always assuming an honest job was really what he wanted, and there was no sinister ultimate intention in his reiterated appeals. Perhaps even once again the wheel had jerked one more stage on its deathly circuit. He was waiting trial somewhere, or had already been sentenced. Or perhaps he had teamed up again with her precious uncle.

Then one morning as she lay in bed, the idea came to her. It was two o'clock, as she ascertained by the illuminated fingers of her alarm-clock; though she could not determine whether she had first opened her eyes and registered the time, or whether, by some curious quirk of the divided mind, she had registered the time after the idea had come to her, piercing like a long thin cold needle through the serrated jointure of the skull.

She would herself have to give Tommy Smith a job, the job as living-in assistant in the book-shop in Theobald's Road. What right had she to expect anyone *else* to take on her guinea-pig criminal? The thing stood up straight and sharp as an obelisk. She had no alternative. As she looked back on the whole business now, she realized that deep down inside her she had taken him on, so to speak, the night that Ernest Latimer had declared that Tommy Smith had got him down. Of her own free will, assuming there is such a thing as free will, she had set in motion the train of circumstances which made the appointment of Tommy Smith as inevitable as the day. She had made herself again and again responsible for him before God and Society. In some obscure intuitive way, Tommy Smith himself had divined this. With Ernest Latimer he had tried and failed. He had been convinced that with Marian Framley he must try and, it may be, succeed. If he was in trouble still again, it was not he this time who had failed, but she.

Suddenly she recalled a conversation that night in Hatchetts, her uncle's small house in the woods. She was talking to another graduate from Parkhurst.

"Oh, talking about books," Matthew had said. "I seem to remember. You took over a book-shop in Oxford, didn't you?" She admitted it. "I've learned a lot about books," he told her; then after a pause: "While I've been in Siberia." (That exquisite joke they had.) "You may want to take me on, one of these days."

But it was the junior partner in crime she proposed to take on.

Then a further thought presented itself. It was so horrifying in the image it built up of herself as a creature in the grip of the forces she had herself first evoked, that she lay there sweating with fear.

Why had she determined to come to London to set up her new book-shop? Why not another shop in Oxford? Why not in one or two other towns she knew and liked? Was it only because of her handful of London friends? Or was it because she knew that as far as Oxford was concerned Tommy had given his promise to keep away from it, while, as far as London was concerned, it was his background, the scene of his operations?

And why had she failed so miserably with the assistants she had sought to employ? Would they still have failed, somehow, even if this one had not been a tart, and another had not been a lie-a-bed, and another had not been a soak? Did she feel herself compelled to ask Wall Humphreys to seek out some suitable ex-sailor for her because already deep down she knew she was committed to another ex-sailor, Tommy Smith, though the idea had not yet come up to a conscious level? Did that mean that if all the tried-out assistants had been as able and loyal as any employer has any right to expect any assistant to be—would they still have failed, because this was Tommy Smith's job and not theirs, because they did not need her, and Tommy Smith did?

She was very frightened that night and, remembering it was a long time since she had said her prayers, she got out of bed and knelt on the rug there, and asked for guidance.

II

The following letter was written and dispatched by note that day, in care of Mrs. Bickers, at the Hammersmith address:

Dear Smith,

I am sorry I have had so little success in finding a job for you, and I hope you have managed to keep things going. (She meant she hoped he had managed to keep straight.) *It might interest you to know that I have started a small book-shop in Theobald's Road, and I have had some trouble in finding the right kind of assistant. I have been thinking of you in that connection, and am aware of your interest in books. Please think the matter over carefully, and if you want to discuss it with me, please ring me up soon, some morning between twelve and one, when my present assistant, who is under notice, is out to lunch.*

She used the shop notepaper, which had the telephone number.

It was only when she had dropped the letter into the letter-box, and had taken an inevitable step, fraught with possibilities so far-reaching and, indeed, so dangerous, that the thought struck her that, after all, she and Tommy Smith did not live in a vacuum. She had relatives and friends, and so had Tommy Smith. Her own relatives and friends she could wipe out straight away. To a man they would think her imbecile, except, perhaps, the twins. Sooner or later she would have to try and give the twins, at least, some idea of what had been going on; they would probably still think her an imbecile, but they would be amiable about it. She might get somewhere with them.

Of Tommy Smith's relatives and friends, she knew one each, his friend and her own uncle, Matthew Browne, his brother, Clifford Eckersley. Matthew Browne could not be wiped off so easily. If he got to know about the situation, he might think it a tremendous joke, or he might take it into his head to be furious. He was, after all, losing a colleague to a member of that same outrageous family that had stolen his table-napkins. In either case, he could make a nuisance of himself. Well, if the worst came to the worst, she could have the police in. The police would take a dim view of a criminal who was trying to frustrate an attempt to reclaim another criminal.

That left Clifford Eckersley, the brother. It was to be remembered that Clifford was not only Tommy Smith's brother, he had fallen in love with Anna, her own sister, and she with him. They were both terribly young, but there was no doubt how much in earnest they were. How was Clifford going to take the new development?

Obviously he could not disapprove of her project in itself. No decent member of society possibly could. Considered in the abstract, he could only welcome it. But this situation was very concrete. The core of it was his brother, whom he feared and abominated. It was quite hopeless to try and keep the situation secret from him. If he was going north to Baxendale for Christmas, as he probably was, for he was deeply attached to the old folk up there, he might just as easily go home *via* London as *via* Birmingham, and if he came to London, he would certainly come to see the new book-shop, and buy something or other, as friends do and should. In fact, all three of them, Anna and Robert and Clifford, had threatened to descend on her *en masse,* as they had warned her in a recent letter. She could not possibly allow Clifford to come up to the shop and find himself face to face with Tommy. It would be an unforgivable outrage.

Well, she must tell Clifford about it. Whatever his reaction might be, she was not going to deviate from her plan. But he must know. How soon, then, should she tell him? Even before Tommy had replied to her letter? No, that would be foolish. For Tommy might turn down her offer out of hand, or might even never reply to it, and she would have inflicted a great deal of misery on Clifford without doing anybody any good. She must wait a week or two, then, by which time Tommy could be expected to answer, if he was going to answer at all. That would be the time to deal with Clifford.

Day after day went by and there was no telephone message from Tommy Smith. The assistant under notice went, and it seemed likely she would have to get in touch with one or other of the people who had answered her last advertisement. There was really more than an element of the grotesque in holding up the appointment of a new assistant till Tommy Smith, confirmed criminal, could get round to answering her note.

On the eighth day he rang up.

"Is that you, Mrs. Framley?"

"It is."

"I'm Tommy Smith. I've only just got back to London. I've just seen your letter. Do you really mean it, Mrs. Framley?"

"I'd not have written to you if I hadn't meant it."

"Do you think I'd be any good at it?"

"That's what I'd like to talk over."

"When can I come to see you? Shall I come straight away?"

"One moment, Smith. I'm afraid I'll have to ask you something."

There was a brief silence at the other end of the phone. Then: "Yes, Mrs. Framley?"

"It's not my business to ask you what you've been doing these last few days. If you've been up to no good, it doesn't make any difference where you've been."

Again there was a silence. She had the impression that he was fighting with a temptation to put the telephone down and slope off. Well, if he did, let him.

"It's been all right," he said. "I'll tell you when I see you, if you want me to."

"If it's all right, it's all right. I'd rather take your word for it."

"Do you mean that?"

A little sharply. "Of course I mean that. But I *will* have to ask you something."

"All right. Ask me."

"Since you came away from Lewes, has there been anything you've done. . . . I'd rather not say more on the telephone. But you know what I mean. If I determined to try you out, it would be a horrible business if someone came and . . . and wanted you to go off with them."

"Mrs. Framley."

"Yes?"

"Nothing can stop them doing that if they want to, whatever I've done or haven't done."

She thought that over.

"Yes, I suppose so. It's pretty horrible, isn't it?"

"That's how it is."

"You haven't answered my question. Have you, or haven't you, done anything of that sort since you came out of Lewes?"

"I've wanted to once or twice, but I haven't."

"Honest?"

"It's up to you. You either believe me or don't believe me. I don't see why you should."

"Can you come round here at five-thirty? I shut the shop then."

"Thank you, Mrs. Framley."

"You've got the address, I think?"

"Yes, Mrs. Framley." He hung up. She had a feeling a certain insecurity had come into his voice. Or he might have put it on, of course. She hung up, too.

III

She hung up, and at once a feeling of panic seized her such as she had never experienced in her life before. To what unspeakable adventure did she propose to commit herself? She would be entrusting her business, her rooms and the things in them, and not least, herself, to the care of a confirmed criminal. There would be prolonged periods of time, in this newly-established business, when she would be entirely alone with him, in this murky section of London. Had he already boasted to his friends that he had now got that dame, who had twice already let him wriggle out of a nasty corner, exactly where he wanted her? In this venture did he have all his friends lurking behind him in the shadows, waiting for a gesture from him?

And she? What friends had she? She had taken this unparalleled step without consultation with anybody. Her father was not to be considered, but should she not have made some attempt to get her mother, or the twins, to understand what she was about? Or any of her friends, above all, Ernest Latimer, who, at that moment was possibly only a few hundred yards away. The dilemma had been his before it had been hers. Had she not some claim on him to take a mite of the frightful burden off her shoulders? But she had spoken to him before, and he had been anything but helpful. There was one person, of course, Clifford Eckersley, who by the tie of blood was deeply involved, and, if only that were taken into consideration, should have been at her side ready to help her. But more than the tie of blood was involved. She expected anything but comfort from Clifford Eckersley. No, she was quite, quite alone. The room seemed dark of a sudden. Shadowy shapes twisted and writhed behind the couch, beyond the curtains. One shape was lying inert on the carpet, the head at an odd angle with the neck. The shape was herself.

She dug her nails deep into her palms, and washed her eyeballs with her own eyelids, as with a cleansing lotion, to try and induce some light into her darkness. She was like somebody groping on hands and knees along a barely marked track over a wilderness, and she had only her instinct to guide her. Her instinct told her that whatever violence there was in the young man, it was not the sexual violence; it was a violence of another sort, from which, as in the testing episode in St. Stephen's, she would be immune.

She looked up, as if somewhere, straight before her, there was some reassurance waiting to be bestowed on her. The reassurance was on the mantelshelf. It had the lineaments of Bertie, her husband. It was, in fact, Bertie's photograph in its silver frame. Her loved one was smiling. He was even talking, was he not?

"Have a go, girl!"

Then another voice spoke. This one, also, was inside her head. It was her own voice.

"You asked for it, you know, Marian. Don't you remember how anxious you were that day when Matthew rang up, pretending to be a duke or something? You asked yourself a question: 'How did he get that way?' Do you remember now? And that night, at dinner in his little house in the wood, it was like a swarm of bees buzzing. 'How did he get that way, the brother of the Warden of St. Stephen's, the son of Sir Arnold Browne, the eminent surgeon?' You felt, if you could only stick him on the slide of a microscope and if you studied him long enough, you might begin to get the hang of it.

"Well, Matthew is too slippery to remain stuck down on the slide of any microscope. Besides, he's your own blood. He's too close to you. Possibly you couldn't ever *see* it, if the clue showed up . . . the way you don't recognize your own voice after it's been recorded, because till that time you've been listening to your voice from inside your eardrum, not from outside. But Tommy Smith is outside you. Here's your chance, take it."

Then the voice changed again. It was a man's voice . . . the same words as she had heard once already.

"Have a go, girl!"

IV

Although her thoughts had so long been full of Tommy Smith, and it felt as if she had been with him a number of times, she recalled that it was over half a year ago since she had actually seen him, the time he had thrust away from her side towards a bus on the opposite side of the High in Oxford, across a clangour of outraged bicycles. What would he be like? Would he be down-at-heel? Would he wear the dapper protective mask of the fly boy? Would he have the uneasy furtiveness one would associate with a gaolbird?

It was a minute to five-thirty. A minute later he pushed the door open, and entered. He paused a moment as if to allow her to take stock of him. There was nothing of the spry manner she had seen in him on the Witney Road, or later in the Ritz, when he was being an air-crew sergeant. He was grave, looking a lot older than he had done half a year ago. He wore a dark suit, quite respectable, in fairly good shape. Only the bright sunflower shoes were awry.

"Good evening, Mrs. Framley," he said.

She came from behind the counter, and extended her hand towards him.

"Good evening. We'd better start off properly," she said. His hand was limp and slightly damp. "No," she reproved him. "Shake hands decently." He improved on his handshake, then let his hand fall.

"I was here half an hour ago," he said. "I didn't want to come. I turned back."

"I'm glad you're here," she assured him. She felt like death. She felt that if she didn't have a stiff double whiskey-and-soda, she would never get through this. But there was no sign of it in her steady eyes and easy manner. "But if you're afraid of a job," she asked him, "why have you kept on asking me to find you one? Why have you let me go on trying?"

"You won't believe it, Mrs. Framley. But I'm going to try to be straight, see?"

"I'm going to believe all you say. So if you want to lie, just lie. It won't be a very brave performance."

"What did I write those letters for, you want to know?"

"Yes?"

"Same reason as I wrote to Mr. Latimer."

"Well?"

"It was for something to do. It was like some people do the Lord's Prayer on a threepenny bit."

Her heart dropped.

"You didn't mean what you said?"

"I've written to you since I came out, haven't I?"

"What do you mean, then? Is it just something to talk about, to your friends? See what nice people I know." (She must never do anything with him but hit straight from the shoulder.)

"No. I've not said a word about you."

"You did about Ernest Latimer?"

"I got fed up. He was scared of his own shadder."

"Well, what do you mean it was something to do?"

"You do it, but you don't believe it's going to get you anywhere. Like the bloke with the threepenny bit. . . ." He could not quite formulate the thought.

"You mean, it had better be the Lord's Prayer than 'You are my sunshine?' You might get *somewhere* with the Lord's Prayer?"

"That's it!" he approved. "That's it!"

"You, too," she said. "It's got *you* somewhere, too." She looked round the stocked shelves of the shop. His eyes followed hers.

"Now, listen, Mrs. Framley. This might be the chance I've been waiting for. I told Mr. Latimer . . . if only *one* person could believe in a bloke, only *one,* it might do something to him. He might be different."

"Do you *want* to be different? That's the whole point, isn't it? Do you *want* to be different?"

"Sometimes you do. Sometimes you don't. It gets hold of you."

"Doesn't it get hold of you because you're there, defenceless? You're moving among people who think it right to smash jewellers' windows, and break open banks? Why are we standing up, Smith? Here. Take this chair."

They both sat down.

"What's the catch, Mrs. Framley?"

"You see, Smith, you can't get it out of your head that there's a catch in everything. It's not true, you know."

He looked at her for some moments hard and straight.

"Isn't it?"

"I can prove it. You do the proving for me yourself."

"I don't see what you mean."

"This is not going to be of any use to anybody unless we both try to be absolutely honest with each other."

"All right. Well?"

"There's your brother, Clifford. You're always sending him wads of notes. I'll want to talk about that some time, if you let me. What's the catch."

"There isn't any."

"There you are." She smiled wanly.

"I want to do it, that's all," he went on.

"I want to do this, too, for different reasons." He looked at her and waited. "I want to do it because somehow I feel I've *got* to do it. It's the way it's worked out. I didn't ask to meet you, but I did. You kept on cropping up in my life. First that night when you went to see my uncle——" He looked up. "Yes, my uncle. My father's brother. I'm in something of the same position as your brother, Clifford. . . ." She stopped. She let him get to grips with this new element in the situation, then she went on. "Then, that night when you telephoned Ernest Latimer. Then again, and again. You remember?" He nodded. "So it seems I've *got* to do this. You might let me down, of course. But I'm hoping you won't."

"I want to ask you something, Mrs. Framley."

"Go ahead."

"You're not going to preach at me?"

"Not more than I've done already."

"Or make me go down on my knees, go to church and all that? They're tried before, you know."

"That's entirely your own affair. There's only one thing I'm going to ask of you. It's a purely personal thing, entirely outside your job. If you want to say no, you can say no." He was looking at her thoughtfully. "It's this. I want to *understand*. Do you see what I mean?"

"I don't see."

"I want to try and understand how it all started."

"You mean . . . like those psychiastric blokes. I've had some some of them too."

"They're professionals. I'm not even an amateur. But the point is, I'm absolutely certain . . . I won't say that, how do *I* know? . . . my feeling is people start off all right, way back in the beginning. Somewhere, somehow, things go wrong.

I'd like to find out about the past, your parents, and your family and the people round you. Does all this sound hateful to you? Or maybe just silly?"

He shrugged his shoulders.

"I've had some," he said again. "It didn't seem to do no good."

"Will it be all right?"

"O.K. by me."

"There's not much else to say just now. Before you say yes or no to the job, I'd better tell you about it, I'll show you the place." She showed him the two rooms, behind and above, which she had had quite simply and pleasantly furnished. "Maybe it's a bit feminine just now," she admitted. "The first assistant was a woman. We can see to that. There's a bit of a kitchenette here, you see."

"It looks fine," he said. "Could I buy a few things, too?"

"Of course. It's your place. You'd have to look after it properly. But the important thing is the shop." She told him what would be expected of him: he would wrap up parcels, post them, deliver them personally when necessary. He would answer the telephone. Later on, as he learned the ropes, he would help her behind the counter. She explained about the wages. She said that outside business hours his time would be entirely his own, of course. She would never ask him any questions about that. She knew it would take him some time before he made new friends, and the old friends were quite likely to smell him out and come hanging round. She'd expect him to shake them off. It would be goodbye to all that. That was first and foremost and everything. She waited. Two or three minutes passed. Then she put it to him

"Would you like the job, Smith?"

He could not bear to look her in the eyes. It seemed as if he feared she might dissipate into thin air.

"If you think it's all right," he said, "I'd like the job."

A thought flashed across her mind.

"You don't think it'll be too slow for you?"

A ghost of a smile hovered on his lips.

"It's not Southend beach inside *there,*" he said. "Where I've been."

"Would you like a day or two to think it over?"

"It's up to you, Mrs. Framley."

"All right, then. You've probably got some things in your room, have you?" He nodded. "Bring them along. Nine o'clock, sharp."

V

Next morning at nine o'clock sharp, he was there, with a suit-case. He put his things away in a wardrobe and chest of drawers, and came down. She pointed out the things she wanted doing then and there, and others which should be done as convenient. He went to work quietly and efficiently. If anyone had told the customers who dropped in during the course of the morning that the young man around the place was a criminal with a very dark history, and that the young woman, his employer, knew all about it, they would have walked out angry and insulted. These things do not happen, they would have said. If they do, not with a young man like that. Nor with a young woman like that, either. The young woman looked quite sane . . . unless she was crazy with love. And that was not evident on the surface.

While there had been an assistant, she had gone out for luncheon, leaving the assistant in charge. Since she had been alone, she had locked up for the luncheon-hour. The first test of the trust she proposed to put on him was to be administered at once.

"It's up to you, Smith," she said. "You don't know much about the books, and may not want to take on the responsibility. On the other hand, all prices are either marked on the covers—you see?—or just inside the cover, in the case of those foreign-language books. Like this. I ought to say this is a good time for book-selling, when people take a stroll in their luncheon-time. Would you like to close down? You're inexperienced, and perhaps you ought to. I'll leave it to you."

"Please, Mrs. Framley. You ought to decide."

She had decided already. The risk this involved was minute compared with other risks she was running.

"I'd be pleased if you'd take over. Oh, the cash-register. Let me show you how to work it." She showed him, but she had a feeling he knew quite well already.

She went out, returned, and *he* went out. At exactly two he returned, and went on with his jobs. He moved about easily and handled books in a manner that suggested that his frequently-proclaimed feeling for books was genuine, so far as it went. It was difficult for her to suppress a certain feeling of satisfaction, even of pride, in the spectacle, though she knew that the first hour or two of the experiment was hardly a time to start crowing and flapping one's wings.

And a shadow hung over the place, and not one likely to be lifted. The shadow was Clifford Eckersley.

That evening at five-thirty, while she made up the day's accounts, Tommy tidied up the place. What cash there was in the cash-register, she left there, without drawing any special attention to the act of faith. Then, finally, she handed over the keys.

"Good night, Smith," she said. "I think it's been a good first day."

"Good night, Mrs. Framley. Thank you."

It was odd how verbose he could be in his letters and how tongue-tied in the flesh. A not unusual phenomenon, she was well aware. She went off to Doughty Street, and knew she could not settle down even to a cigarette before she wrote to Clifford Eckersley. She had to be up in Oxford this week-end, she told him, and would be staying in the room she had at the Warden's House, in College. But she wanted to talk to him on a private matter. Could they meet at eleven o'clock for coffee at Constan's, which was open on Sunday? She would assume it was all right, if she did not hear to the contrary.

He wrote, none the less. He would be there. He hoped she was going great guns at the new book-shop.

VI

Clifford was so obviously in a state of nerves she determined to have at it straight away.

"What on earth do you think I'm going to talk to you about?" she asked. "Please don't look so worried!"

"One of *two* things," he replied at once.

"*Two?*" It had not occurred to her there might be a second "Oh, no! What two things?"

"It can only be two. One's Anna and me. The other's . . . my brother."

"Good heavens! Anna and you? It hadn't occurred to me. Haven't I written to you exactly how I thought about it? You're young. You both know that as well as I do. There's going to be some awkwardness with the Warden. Apart from that—God bless you! I wrote that, didn't I?"

"So it's my brother?"

"Yes."

"And you had to come up to Oxford to tell me about it? Is he inside again? And if he is, what's it to do with me?"

"Not so fast, Clifford, old chap. I didn't come up to Oxford to tell you about it. I had to come up to Oxford in any case. And he's not inside again. Far from it. He's got a respectable job."

"What's it got to do with *me,* Marian?" he cried passionately. "I told you. I don't want to hear about him! I don't want to know he exists!"

"I understand exactly how you feel. I think his persecution of you with those gifts of his has had something quite ghoulish about it."

"That's the word. Ghoulish. Well, *please,* Marian. Why do you want to talk to me about him? Let's talk about something else. How's the book-shop going?"

"I'll come to that quite soon. I beg you to listen to me, Clifford. One way and another we're getting quite close to each other."

"All the more reason to forget *him.*"

"Oh, no. Don't delude yourself. It's not so easy as all that. He can't forget you, and you can't forget him. You're brothers, you know."

"Brothers!" he exploded.

"Yes. You hate him. You have every reason to. But he loves you, God knows why. You've done everything to discourage him, yet he loves you, morbidly and frighteningly. It's all wrong, all that hatred and all that love."

"Wrong? How can you say that it's wrong of me to hate him? And how can I help it if he 'loves' me, as you say. *Love?* If he had the faintest feeling for me, he'd get out of my life and push off to the end of the world."

"Some day he might, if he stays out of prison long enough. Give him a chance—I mean just that. Give him a chance."

"*Give him a chance?* Me? What are you talking about?"

"*I'm* giving him a chance. You could help. There's no-one else in the whole world who could help the way you could."

He leaned his back against the wall and eyed her with hostility. "What are you up to, Marian?"

"That's exactly what I'm here to tell you. I'm going to bring the story up to date. I mean the story so far as it concerns Tommy and me. You know a great deal of it already. I'll go back so far as is necessary." Once more, as she talked, he closed his eyes. An onlooker might have thought that the young man had rudely dropped off to sleep. But Marian knew this was not so, if only from the deathly pallor which always invested his cheeks when his brother filled his mind. She brought the account of recent events to an end. "There are two reasons why I feel I've got to tell you all this. One is quite obvious. I couldn't have you barge into the shop and come face to face with Tommy, without knowing he was there."

"And the other?"

"I know it's something almost impossible to hope for. I want your help."

"You'd like me to go along and tell him how naughty it is to rob safes and hold up banks?" He had opened his eyes. They were as bitter as the Dead Sea plain. His mouth was twisted quite odiously.

"Steady! Steady!" she demanded, and touched him on the arm. "I'm not going to do any preaching at him, myself. He's had a good deal of that already. What I'm after doesn't lie that way."

"What do you want then?"

"I want to *understand*. I want to go as far back as possible. I've told him all that. He thinks it's stupid, but he's going to humour me. I want to find out where it started off. I've been successful once already, as you know. I may be successful again."

"He's to be a guinea-pig for your psycho-analytical researches?"

She blushed furiously.

"I think, Clifford, you *must* have been asleep when I talked to you, both this time and last time. I told you quite clearly what my feeling is. I feel that my taking a chance with him, my trusting him, may have an effect on him. It may start something off. It may be a thin ray of light by which he may ultimately lead himself out of the jungle. I'm willing to take the chance, as Ernest Latimer wasn't, and as you aren't, though he's got more claim on you than on me. Don't interrupt me, Clifford. I say again, you've either been asleep, or you're being impertinent. I'm sorry, Clifford."

He was silent for some time, but did not seem in the least taken back by her reproof.

"You should know perfectly well that I didn't intend to be impertinent. I've far too high a respect for you, and I'm far too full of gratitude. The fact is, you haven't an idea of the amount of suffering my brother's caused me; and not only me, of course. You can't blame me if I talk savagely about him, or if I refuse point-blank to have anything to do with him, ever, in any circumstances. You've employed him in your shop. Well, that's up to you, Marian. If you want to let me come and see you in your flat, well and good. I won't go to your shop, not while he's there."

"Very well, then," she said, coldly. "You will obviously do as you please. If you happen to come up to town with Robert and Anna, it will take some explaining. I'll endorse any explanation you give them."

"Marian!" he cried. "Don't talk like that!" It looked as if tears would jump into his eyes at any moment. "I'll help you all I can, if you really want me to. I'll answer any questions you like. But I don't want to have any contact with *him*, that's all. You *do* understand?"

She was now on the verge of tears herself.

"We'll work it out, Clifford, old chap. Let's talk about something else. Are you still doing those wicked 'Scrutinies' of yours? Is it true the mob from Trinity is starting a rival paper? Oh, dear! there's one thing we must get straight. The twins said they're coming to give the shop the once-over—that's how Robert put it—just after the end of the term. They said they'd bring you. What shall we do about it? Shall I send him off for the day?"

"It's not fair to you. If he's in the shop, he's in the shop, and anyhow, I told them up in Lancashire I'll be going straight home at the end of term. It'll work out, Marian."

"Very well, Clifford, dear. It'll work out. More coffee? This is stone-cold."

But he was off again. His mind was not on the coffee.

"I want you to do something for me," he said. "You can do it."

"Anything I can do," she assured him.

"Please, *please*, beg him to cut out those horrible presents of his. You know what a nightmare they've been to me."

"I know," she said, quietly. "That's what I'm hoping. The source will dry up. He'll be earning a modest wage, no margin for extravagances." She smiled. "At most an odd ten-shilling postal order, at Christmas. It seems to mean so much to him."

He pounded his fist on the table.

"Nothing! Nothing! Nothing!" he shouted.

Again she touched him lightly on the arm with her finger-tips. At once he subsided.

"Your request will have first priority," she said, with a slight edge to her voice. She did not like people to fly off the handle in this way.

It was not hard next morning to find a quiet five minutes at the shop. The minutes were likely to be quiet for longer stretches for some time to come.

"I was in Oxford yesterday," she said. "I saw Clifford."

"I thought you might. You told him I was working for you."

"I had to, hadn't I? It wouldn't have been quite fair to let him come strolling in."

"So he said he'd never come here. O.K. by me. I can take it." He could not keep the humiliation out of his voice.

"He asked me to give you a message."

"He did, did he?" He looked at her suspiciously.

"He begged you to send him no more of those presents you've been sending him all these years. I was going to bring up the same subject myself, with your permission."

"He's gone all hoity-toity all of a sudden, has he? All right then, I won't, if that's the way he feels."

"You're forgetting, Smith," she reminded him. "There aren't going to be any more presents like that to send him. Isn't that the whole idea?"

He paused a moment, as if the thought hadn't been clear to him before.

"Yes, of course," he admitted. "But there's still a little bit in the kitty."

"Oh, there is, is there?" He did not get the tone in her voice.

"Yes. That's why I didn't get your letter no sooner. I've been away trying to find it. I still can't remember was it High Wycombe, or was it Great Missenden. When you turned west, there was a little white building on a hill, with pillars, like one of those posh wedding-cakes—I'm almost sure."

"You've been trying to find what?" she insisted. At last he smelled some sort of danger in the tone of her voice.

"Something I hid, a long time ago. It's all right. It looks like I'm never going to find it."

"You mean some stolen goods, I take it? Was it jewels, or maybe it was money?"

"A bit of both," he admitted sullenly. "I can't remember."

(Her heart was racing violently. How dreadful it was going to be if, during the next few minutes, some lout was going to come in and ask her to sell him some idiot book!)

"Tell me!" she asked. "Do you really mean to think Clifford would have kept it, if you'd sent him some stolen money?"

"I'd rather not talk about it, Mrs. Framley. I've got those parcels to do, haven't I?"

"But we *must* talk about it, Smith! This is absolutely crucial. Answer my question, will you? Do you think he'd have kept stolen money?"

"Why not? *He* didn't steal it. Besides, it's a long time ago! I can't remember myself what job it was!"

"That's not the point, is it? You've sent him packets of stolen money before, haven't you?"

"What if I have?" He kept his eyes down on the ground.

"Of course you have. Do you really think that he kept them?"

He raised his head sharply.

"Didn't he? I never got them back."

"Now just think a moment. You made it quite impossible to send the stuff back, didn't you?"

"I suppose I did. I wanted him to keep it. You mean to say he gave all that dough away? But it wasn't *his* to give away. It was *mine*. I nicked it. I stuck my neck out, not him nor anyone else. It's a liberty, I call it!"

"Please, Smith, don't run away with yourself. Clifford happens to be an honest young man. He knew the stuff was stolen. You should have known him well enough to realize he wouldn't keep it. All it did was to make him so miserable he nearly put his head in a gas-oven."

"What did he *do* with the dough?"

"He handed it over to the police, of course."

"He didn't! Well, I'll be——" He stopped in time. His cheeks were red with anger. "The cops? I consider it a damn liberty, that's what I call it!" It might have been a shade less outrageous, apparently, if it had not been the cops.

"You know, Smith," she mused, examining him with level eyes, "it's going to take some time, I think, before you understand how ordinary men and women feel about things like these. In the meantime, I gave Clifford a promise!"

"The young sod!" he muttered under his breath, some word of that sort.

"I promised I'd get you to give up sending him presents. He doesn't want them! He can get on along without them!"

"But I've *got* to!" he cried out suddenly, quite shrilly.

Her eyes had been averted from him. They switched back like a cat pouncing at a faint noise in a mouse-hole.

"You've *got* to!" she repeated. "What do you mean, you've *got* to?"

"Oh, I don't know!" he said, his voice quite rough and nasty. He turned away to the piles of books on the counter. She went back to the invoice-book. She had harried him enough for one day.

VII

Two days later, when she came back from lunch, he had another event to report, outside certain sales he had effected.

"A friend of yours called, Mrs. Framley," he announced. His face was without expression.

"Oh? Did he leave his name?"

"Yes. I know him, too."

Then she knew who it was.

"Mr. Latimer?"

"That's right."

There was a pause.

Then: "Did he look surprised?" she asked.

"He nearly passed out," he said. There was a grin on his face.

"Did he come in just to say how d'you do to me, or did he want something, too?"

"He wanted Geoffrey Scott's *Architecture of Humanism*," he announced proudly. "We have the cheap edition. I gave it him." He was thrilled that he could repeat the title so pat and that he had known where to locate it on the shelves. "He said he'd telephone you at the flat."

"That's fine." They went on with their jobs.

Ernest Latimer duly telephoned her that night.

"Marian!" he said. "I'm not making any mistake, am I?"

"No," she told him. "That was Tommy Smith. I've tried three or four other people out. They weren't any good."

"Marian! I ask you again. Are you stark, staring mad?"

"I may be, Ernest. I don't know. Seeing that we're being personal——" she hesitated.

"Go ahead, Marian."

"I think I've got a little more guts than you, that's all."

"A *little* more guts! Lord God Almighty! A *little* more guts. I'm going to ring off, Marian! I can't take it any more!"

"Goodbye, Ernest. I'm glad we had the Geoffrey Scott in stock."

"Yes, Marian. Thank you. Goodbye."

VIII

One week went by, two weeks. Marian came in in the morning, went out for lunch, came back for the afternoon spell. Usually Tommy would make a cup of tea for them both at four-thirty, unless they were busy, when he might make a cup of tea at five-thirty instead, after the shop closed. She welcomed that, it was easier to talk then.

A picture of his day-to-day life emerged, though she was careful to make him feel she was not submitting him to any sort of examination. That was his own affair, so long as it respected one cardinal limitation. She was interested in an earlier epoch, and he had agreed to let her discuss it with him, as mood and opportunity presented themselves.

He was reading a good deal, and books on a fairly high level, though without seeming to realize he was lowering the standard, he would sometimes read a crime or sex novel of the sort that is displayed at the entrance to underground stations. He would dance sometimes, and more often go to the movies. He established himself in a "local," for he was a good hand at darts, and would sometimes go "pubbing," as he called it, further afield. Once or twice it was clear he had a hang-over, after a thick night. There was no reference to women, but probably he was having his affairs. She did not, however, have the feeling that he was bringing any women back with him to Theobald's Road.

It was impossible for her to refrain from asking him whether he had come up against any of his old associates, the question being covered in the general terms of their understanding. Theobald's Road was not very far from his old haunts, and the "pubbing" might take him nearer.

"Oh, yes," he admitted. "You see them up and down. You can't help it."

"Do they know you've got a regular job?"

"They know. It gets around."

"They know where you are?"

"They may do. Nobody talks too much."

"Supposing they come round?"

"They'll have to sling their hooks quick."

She had the feeling it was all he cared to say on the subject, and she felt it was good enough. She would have liked to ask him whether her dear uncle had lately given any sign of life. But it was clearly far better to let any mention of Matthew Browne come first from his lips. Perhaps Matthew had already passed out into a limbo of those bad sad men he had rubbed shoulders with from stage to stage of his career, and already they were less than shadows. Or perhaps Matthew was in prison again. The family did not try to keep itself informed of his movements.

A picture of the remoter past emerged more slowly. Sometimes Tommy spoke with a reluctance which now and again verged on sullenness, but for the most part he readily honoured his undertaking. He seemed to retain a bitter memory of certain former questioners, but when this was submerged, he sometimes rattled on with an ease bordering on garrulity. He behaved not unlike those star patients in hospitals who are requested to recount the history and symptoms of their case to students and visiting specialists. And just as these expound details of intimate functions which they would ordinarily be chary of expounding, so with gusto and a naive vanity, Tommy would expound details of his earlier minor thievings and the major crimes into which they evolved.

But Tommy Smith was not a "star" patient, Marian realized, as her knowledge of these matters increased. He was a run-of-the-mill patient. Further, the accumulation of details merely described Tommy Smith, they did not explain him. Nor did they explain the fact that the parents of Tommy Smith were also the parents of Clifford, his brother. That remained as mysterious as the fact that the parents of Henry Browne, were also the parents of his brother, Matthew.

Tommy Smith was born early in 1921, being about a year younger than herself, though often he seemed half a dozen years younger, younger even than Clifford. (She wondered if the suspension of the moral qualities sometimes slows down the rate at which the physical qualities develop, so that for long the criminal retains a real aspect of irresponsibility together with an aspect of illusory youth.) The Smith parents were not married till several years after Tommy's birth, and that situation alone produced a good deal of that sense of insecurity in which (Marian was informed by her authorities) juvenile delinquency sometimes finds its early roots. Harry Smith, the father, did odd jobs in the catering line. Sometimes he was a kitchen-porter in one of the dubious hotels that spore like fungi in the damp darkness round railway termini; now and again he took a job in an all-night "caff"; and once or twice he even attempted to start one off on his own. But that did not prosper long. They were incurable drunkards, both the woman, Sarah, and himself, and they lost no time in boozing away their takings as they came in. He was weak in physique as well as character, and when the two fought, as they often did, it was he who retired with the mark of a poker over his eye, or the blood streaming down his face. He was immensely devoted to Tommy, both drunk and sober. When sober, the mother regarded Tommy with a cold and hostile eye, when drunk, she would smother him in an orgy of penitent kisses. But drunk or sober she made no bones about it that he was an accident; and after starting as an accident, he had become a blight. He blighted the career she was about to embark on as the girl-friend of an important band-leader. For the band-leader had discovered she was pregnant, and had thrown her over for a less encumbered doxy.

A grandmother from Stepney figured prominently in the picture. The boy was having so shocking a childhood, he was so rarely at school, it was agreed that the grandmother should take on the small boy. She was a more reliable person, it was to be gathered, than her son and her daughter-in-law, but she, too, was a drunkard, with an unholy addiction to gin. In her gin-sodden moods, she would threaten Tommy, if he "created" just once more, that she would bundle him off, bag and baggage, to his parents' home in Camden Town. Once more, despite the better food and the cleaner bed, there was to be no security in the domestic outlook of young Tommy. Yet, despite the dreadful mother, the sometimes-threatened return to Camden Town was not a wholly black prospect, not only because there was a good deal more excitement in the Mercer Street home, but because the father was the only human being who really loved Tommy. He loved him almost more like a lover than a father. He would hang about the playground of Tommy's school in Stepney, and heap presents on him, crayon-boxes, fruit, bags of sweets.

(*Heap presents?* Marian's mind paused. Is that how the

habit of present-heaping started which was to become the bane of young Clifford's life?)

Ultimately, the grandmother became seriously ill, and was taken off to hospital. The parents had by this time got themselves married. They were having one of their more respectable periods. Tommy was duly restored to the bosom of his parents.

Perhaps Sarah Smith was one of those women who are ready enough to go to bed with their husbands, but resent bearing children and the pains and risks of bringing them into the world. Tommy Smith had an incident to recall here that he put into words only with extreme difficulty. In fact, it was only by thinking about them later, and setting them into their content, that she finally got their meaning. The mother had sent the son out to get the equipment necessary for the abortion of the threatened child. It was some week or two later that the old woman from whom Tommy had acquired the stuff made clear what it was all about with many a wink and nudge. The lad had never known anything like such shame and humiliation before. He hated his mother, and this episode clearly had a great deal to do with his hatred. He hated the child whose appearance his mother intended to frustrate.

(*Hated the child?* That's strange, isn't it, Marian asked herself. The brother whom he now loves with a love so excessive? No brother should have for a brother a love so morbid, with so much terror in it, it must be considered pathological. He *hated* the child that was to come. Strange, isn't it?)

Big boy that Tommy was now, at the time of the attempted abortion, he threw himself in a storm of weeping into his father's arms. But the father, as ever, was rather more drunk than sober. He totally misunderstood the nature of Tommy's grief and resentment.

"Don' worry, Tommy boy," he mumbled. "When it comes to using it, she won' use it. She's too frightened. She says she will but she won'. So Tommy's going to have a dear li'l sister, after all, a swee' li'l sister? Who's going to have a dear li'l sister? Tommy is. She'll smell like butter. She'll have a dear li'l pink ribbon in her gold hair."

So Tommy tore himself away and celebrated his resentment in a manner more virile than tears. He went and stole a pocket battery from Woolworth's counter.

"Did you get away with it?" asked Marian.

"Yes."

"You wanted to pay them out for being unkind to you?"

"I suppose so."

"Was that the first time you stole anything?"

"I don't know. I may have pinched apples from barrows before, and all that. I think I pinched some raisins once in a shop. But it wasn't the last time. I went on pinching."

"I see. I see." She thought hard. "Was it exciting?"

"I suppose it *was*. It always *is*."

"I've no doubt. Then in course of time Clifford appeared on the scene. Did you feel different when he actually came? Was it fun to have a baby brother?"

He looked at her as if the reply he was about to make surprised himself as much as it might her.

"I hated him."

"Oh?" She sat thinking for some time. There was nothing really surprising in that. "You'd been very attached to your father, and now you had a rival."

"I suppose so," he muttered. "The only thing was——" he hesitated.

"Yes? The only thing?"

"I was glad he wasn't a girl. Smell like butter. Pretty pink ribbons in her hair. It made me sick."

"You were quite grateful to Clifford, in a way, for not being a little girl."

"Looks like that."

"And then gradually you began to like him?"

"I suppose I did. I must have done."

"But it didn't prevent you from going out and doing the things you'd already started doing?"

"Pinching and all that? No. I went in for it a lot more. I was getting older, see. Sometimes I'd go out with the boys, too."

"Not all the time?"

"No—not all the time. Usually I'd want to be on my own. They were yeller. Sometimes I'd do it for fun, too."

"What do you mean by fun?"

"Just for the fun of not being found out. It was more fun when it was really a hard place to break into. Somebody might be sleeping in the next room, or there might even be a dog. You mightn't even want to nick anything. But if it was something for Cliff, then I'd risk it."

"You mean as he got older?"

"Yes. When he got older. A few times I got into paper-shops where they have toys. But even then he could smell it if it was something I'd nicked. Maybe I was thinking things."

"You mean even as a child Clifford wouldn't have anything to do with stolen things?"

"Yes. Seems so."

"Your parents didn't mind?"

"Sometimes she lambasted me till I was that stiff I was like a poker. But she had men in the house much more often now. She didn't care any more."

"And your father?"

"He was always canned. Sometimes he talked to me, but it didn't mean anything."

"But what about Clifford? With all this going on around him, didn't he try his hand at a little thieving sometimes, when he'd go shopping, and so on? And, as far as you know, didn't he ever help himself if some loose money was left lying around?"

"It was as if he was somewhere else, miles away. He'd listen to music on the wireless, or he'd be sitting on the sofa, with a book in his hand, even before he could read."

(*It was as if he was somewhere else.* Do you hear that? Can it have been like that in the austere household of the eminent surgeon, Uncle Matthew's father? Had Uncle Matthew been somewhere else, too, in a very different sort of world?)

Tommy was continuing:

"Sometimes, when I'd brought him back something, and he didn't touch it . . . he didn't want things like trains, or tin soldiers, or puzzles, it didn't look like he knew he was there . . . I'd bash him till I nearly killed him. He didn't howl much, he just cried." (The memory seemed to cause him great pain.) "But later on, when he was seven or eight, it was just the same. I giv him books and compasses and all that. It was all the same. He didn't want my books or anything that I giv him, but he'd sit there, whatever anyone else was doing . . . the old man booming, or the old woman having one of her pals in and going off into the bedroom. Every once in a while, Dad would create. But it didn't get nowhere. And there he was, that little bastard, his ear at the radio turned down quiet-like. Or maybe he was scribbling in exercise-books. He used to do poetry and that, I think. I'd sometimes nick one of them, and they'd be all lines different sizes."

It wasn't all easy sailing for Tommy Smith in the years that followed. There were episodes at Juvenile Courts. The Probation Officer began to be a regular feature of the landscape. None of this did the young scoundrel any good. At sixteen, he was sent to an Approved School. (Clifford was nine at the time.) He broke away, was at large for a time, and did a number of robberies. These included a nice new bicycle, which a minion delivered for Clifford at Mercer Street, with love from Tommy. Soon after, he was caught and consigned to Borstal for two years. These were the two years just previous to the War. He escaped from Borstal—he paid no regard to the futility of escaping—and went wild. He had by this time become a really desperate character, if he had not been one for some years. When he was caught next time, though he was only nineteen, it was considered necessary to send him to prison. He served a sentence in Maidstone.

"Maidstone?" repeated Marian. "I think . . . our learned friend was there? At the beginning of the War, I think?"

He nodded.

"The old 'Prof.' Yes. In Maidstone. Not half a lad he wasn't." The *curriculum vitae* continued.

Tommy Smith came out of prison in February, 1941, and went to see his grandmother. By this time Clifford had left Mercer Street. He had, in fact, been taken away during the first year in Borstal. Tommy had made a great many efforts—as you can even in Borstal, or in prison, too, for that matter—to find out where they'd taken the kid. But he'd had no luck at all. However, when he came out of Maidstone, he marched straight to his grannie's bed-sitting room in Stepney, for she was still extant. He asked her where Clifford was. She refused to say a word. She had sworn to keep Clifford's whereabouts a secret. But Tommy had a bottle of gin with him, and that did the trick. At least, he found out the kid was up in Baxendale, in Lancashire, and that the people he'd gone to had changed his name to Eckersley. She refused to give the address. Perhaps that way she salved her conscience, or perhaps she genuinely did not know. Anyhow, he knew the kid was clever. If there was a Grammar School up there where you could win scholarships, Clifford would be at the local Grammar School with a scholarship. So up he went to Baxendale, just to say how are you to his own born brother, but the little squirt treated him like dirt. Tommy shoved off, determined never to have anything more to do with the ungrateful little swine.

"You didn't quite do that?" asked Marian.

"I sent him something. I needn't have taken the trouble."

"No," Marian assured him. "And then? You became a sailor, didn't you, about this time?"

"Yes," he agreed.

"Did they have your record?"

He looked at her with an expression of indulgent contempt.

"Not *my* record. Someone else's. That was easy. Some other bloke's identity card, and all that."

"I see," she assented. "And then?"

"So I was in the Andrew for a time, see. It was all right. I've never been so happy as I was then. The grub wasn't too bad, and there was those duty-free cigarettes, and the girls always touching your collar. Dead-easy. Then it got a bit monotonous, like things always do—all that dhobeying, and running across the parade-ground in full kit at the double." (She felt a curious nostalgic thrill twanging at her heart-strings. Yes. That was the way they talked, the youngsters of the lower deck from which her husband had risen. Those very words. Other things being equal Tommy might have been "Sparks" or "Stokes" on one of Bertie's small ships. Other things being equal.) "So one time when I was in London on long week-end I ran up against Frankie the Toff. He's not half a bloke. You might like to meet him some time. Address, Marble Arch. He can tell you a lot more about all this lark than I can. So this Frankie the Toff tells me about a job. 'It's as tough as they make 'em,' says Frankie, knowing I've always liked jobs with a bit of spice to them—and if Frankie don't know, who does? I felt I wanted a bit of a break after going straight so long, so I takes a chance. But Frankie was right, it wasn't half a tough spiel. So I came unstuck."

Off he went to prison again, as if that was his natural element, as water is to a fish. He said to himself that prison must be the right place and the only place for a bloke like him. He was all dead inside, like when a dentist had jammed something into your gum. And yet, sometimes, somehow, it was a bit different from the other times. Sometimes a nerve would start jumping inside the deadened gum. He began to tell himself more firmly than ever before that prison's a mug's game. He had always liked a decent book, but this time he began to take a real interest in them. This was the time he read three books of that Mr. Latimer, all in a row. He had a few talks with the Chaplain, and all that; not mocking him inside himself, like most of the blokes do, but talking serious man to man. The authorities thought when he got out of stir this time he might try and make a job of it.

So the year went by and, as usual, he got discharged before his time. He always behaved all right inside, he never gave trouble. Then, of course, they had to take him back to Chatham, to get his naval punishment. They don't really consider it genuine leave, he said, if you have to be away for a year, doing a stretch. And there he was in the guard-room one fine morning, and they were giving him half an hour's exercise walking round the yard there. When suddenly he sees through a window a Petty Officer's uniform hanging on a hook. Nobody's not taking any particular notice of him, so he just quietly steps inside, slips out of his duck suit, and slips into the P.O.'s uniform; then, natural as a cucumber, he makes his way over to the main barrack gate, and walks out into the street. What's more, the P.O. has kindly left a ten bob note in his trouser-pocket, so he gets into a taxi and says drive me to the station, please. A few minutes later there's a train to London, and Bob's your uncle. It's as easy as falling off a brick wall.

"I didn't need to have done it . . ." Tommy pointed out. "I'd have got my discharge in any case, I suppose, though I'd have been quite happy to have stayed on in the Navy. But what can you do? He leaves his uniform on a hook. You can't help it, can you?"

"Let me see now," Marian observed, without considering the question. "Isn't this about the time you met my friend, Mr. Latimer?"

"Yes, that's it," he said eagerly. Nobody could say he wasn't doing all he could to help his boss. "A couple of weeks later. I'm hanging round old Wolff's gym in Charlotte Street, keeping myself fit, when I come up against Andy Patten, training. *You* know, Andy Patten. One-time middleweight champion, he was."

"I know," murmured Marian. "I've heard about him."

"So Andy asks me round to his wedding at the Cross Keys, in Hornsey. And that's how I met Mr. Latimer, see. But you already know that, Mrs. Framley, don't you? Mr. Latimer told you, didn't he?"

"And so have you, for that matter."

"Yes, so I have." He was silent for some time. "So you see, Mrs. Framley, don't you?"

She smiled sadly.

"No. I wouldn't go so far as to say that. You've been awfully patient and helpful. We'll talk again, won't we, Smith?"

He shrugged his shoulders.

"Whenever you like," he said.

"Isn't the problem beginning to reverse itself?" Marian asked herself. "What else but Tommy Smith could the Smith family produce? The mystery is, surely, that against such a background a boy could grow like the boy I've known as Clifford Eckersley?

"But isn't it the truth that environment invariably produces, or is likely to produce, the sort of creature you would expect from it? How then would you explain Matthew Browne?

"We are no nearer than before. Is the evil thing already

present in the womb? Is there a moment when suddenly evil is, and it was not there before?"

She did not find that the early history of Clifford, of which Tommy had already given her some account, threw much light on these matters. Clifford spoke of them with grief, but with precision, for words were his medium. From early on there had been genuine concern among school-teachers and well-disposed neighbours regarding the upbringing of young Clifford, a concern which had been much less vocal with regard to Tommy, the older brother, who had at no time been a favourite in Mercer Street. Protests were made to the N.S.P.C.C., who sent representatives to visit the Smith home over a period of time. These issued increasingly grave warnings to the feckless parents; there were promises of improvement without improvement following. Finally the case was brought to court, where the Smith family were no strangers. Clifford was nine years old at this time. Tommy had lately been sent to an Approved School, Clifford was now sent to an L.C.C. Home for Children with unhappy backgrounds like Clifford Smith's. The School was in Surrey.

It happened that the Warden of the home was a Lancashire man, and a sturdy Methodist. Further, he was an old friend of another goodly Methodist of those parts, a certain Dan Eckersley, a sheet-metal worker, whose home was in Baxendale. Finally, he knew that Dan Eckersley had lately lost a son with double pneumonia, and that there was no likelihood of his wife presenting him with another child. It was the ardent wish of both parents to adopt a male child, if possible, of the same age as the boy they had lost.

This information was duly handed on to the visiting County Welfare Officer, a lady who passed it on further to her opposite number at a Children's Home in Lancashire. The second lady paid several visits to the Eckersley household in Lancashire, and had no difficulty in recommending the proposed adoption before the Children's Committee of the Home in Surrey.

The Eckersley parents were given the opportunity to see the young Clifford for themselves. They were touched and delighted, and thanked God from the depths of their hearts. The technicalities were got through with no waste of time.

In a month or so the boy was taken north by his father-to-be, and with a minimum of delay his name legally changed from Smith to Eckersley. For his part, Clifford was as happy with his new parents as they were with him. He would have been happy with parents less kind and thoughtful than the Eckersleys, if only they had let him get on with his reading of poetry and listening to music, as the Eckersleys did from the first day. They hoped he would in course of time become a good Christian, and a worthy Methodist. But they pressed nothing on him. They remembered the earlier boy, of their own blood, and held their hand. He won a scholarship in Baxendale at an early age, and in due course was elected Scholar at St. Stephen's College, in Oxford.

From that point Marian knew his story, or, at least that part of it which was bound up with Tommy, his brother.

IX

So much, then, for Tommy Smith. So much for his brother, Clifford Eckersley. But what about their parents? What about the people who had been round them in their childhood? What about the grandmother in Stepney with whom Tommy had lodged for a while, until a serious illness had compelled her to restore him to his parents' home? If it was possible to get into touch with some of these, what thing might be revealed, what quarry started?

Alas, she had much less luck here than might have been hoped for. Her serious illness had made an end of Grannie. The Smith father was dead, too. As for the Smith mother, a month or two after Clifford was removed to the L.C.C. Home in Surrey, she went off with a good-looking Irish labourer, no-one knew where. It might have been Ireland, America, Australia—or half a mile away in Marylebone.

What about relatives, neighbours? The two young men were unaware of any relatives. At all events, they could not remember any relatives who were anxious to claim relationship with either parent. The neighbour situation was complicated by the fact that a good deal of Mercer Street had been flattened in the air-raids; the neighbours that had not been evacuated were largely exterminated. Mercer Street had known not one land mine, but two; also one of the most mortiferous of the V2 bombs.

There was a schoolmistress still at the local Council School who remembered the two Smith brothers. She had nothing more to say than Marian knew already, namely that Tommy had been a scoundrel from an early age, and Clifford had always had his nose buried in a book. The line of inquiry led nowhere. She was more fortunate with a family named Hopley in the north end of Mercer Sreet, which had had less bombing than the rest of it. The Hopleys remembered the Smiths quite well. They remembered that Mr. Smith had been a drunkard, and that Mrs. Smith was no better than she should be. The elder boy was a crook, the younger boy was a bookworm. All that Marian knew already. But she gleaned one fact from the Hopleys which might definitely lead somewhere. First of all it led just round the corner to a room in Townley Street, where a certain Mrs. Purvis lived in the ground-floor front. This Mrs. Purvis, though herself quite old, was the younger sister of a Mrs. Lewis, who had lived in the first-floor back in Mercer Street during the early thirties, in the very home where the Smiths lived, when both the boys were growing up. Mrs. Lewis had long since left Mercer Street. She had, in fact, been evacuated to a place called Shenley, in Shropshire, early in the War. By the time the War was over, she was a sick old woman and had become an inmate of the County Institute.

"Is your sister alive still?" Marian wanted to know.

"I wouldn't be surprised," Mrs. Purvis admitted. "On the other 'and I wouldn't be surprised if she was dead, neether."

"When did you last hear from her?"

"I got a Christmas card last Christmas."

"Then she's probably alive?"

"Maybe. Maybe not. If you call it alive. In *them* places!" There was nothing to do, after cheering up Mrs. Purvis with the price of a bottle or two of Guinness, but get into touch with the authorities at Shenley. Yes, they informed her, Mrs. Lewis was still alive. She was a bed-ridden patient in the Institute Infirmary. Visiting-hours were between two and three on Wednesdays and Sundays.

It was all a little grim and discouraging. She found it hard to imagine what sort of clue she might expect to pick up in a conversation with a bed-ridden old lady in a workhouse infirmary who happened to have lived under the same roof as Tommy Smith fifteen and more years ago. It was even more grim and discouraging when she got to the Institute, which was a morose lavatory-red-brick travesty of an Oxford College. The style was Utility Ruskino-Gothic. There was a Porter's lodge, there were belfries and turrets, there were quadrangles. Keble! Keble! a wag from almost any other Oxford College than Keble might have called out. There were knots of elderly residents strolling, just as undergraduates do, along the cloisters and down the quadrangles. The males wore scarves round their necks and grimy flannels, just like undergraduates, and they had ill-smelling pipes in their mouths. Like women undergraduates, the females were dark and dowdy and wore spectacles.

There seemed to be no-one about who had any idea where the Infirmary was, not even the porter in the lodge, who was deaf, like everyone else she addressed. Or perhaps, she wondered wretchedly, it was the way she spoke the language. There seemed to be nothing to do but plunge into a network of passages, and trust to the smell of carbolic and bed-pans, characteristic of all hospital institutions, of every social grade, to guide her to the Infirmary.

After some time she found her way not only to the Infirmary, but even to Ward B, where, according to the card that had been issued to her, she would find the inmate, Ada Lewis, widow. It was technically Visitors' Day, but the place looked so deserted it was to be concluded that nobody in the world had the least interest in visiting the patients in the Shenley Institute Infirmary, at least in Ward B.

She knocked at the door, but there was no reply except a cackle of laughter. She knocked again. There was still no reply. She opened the door and entered. It was a very sanitary room. The furniture was sparse and austere, the walls smooth and pale as junket. At the opposite corner a nurse leaned over a patient. In the other eleven beds a series of old ladies were mumbling, twitching, or just lying. One was knitting a wool mat, another was nursing a rag doll. If it would have been possible to steal out of the Ward again straight away, Marian would have done so, it was all so evidently hopeless and useless. But it was too late.

"Yes?" a sharp voice asked. This was the nurse. "What do you want? Got your card?"

Marian held out the card before her.

"Mrs. Lewis, please. Which is Mrs. Lewis?"

The nurse indicated with her chin a bed in the corner. "That one!" she said.

"Oh, thank you!" She went up to the bed which had been pointed out to her. None of the other patients seemed to take any interest in her arrival, any interest at all. Mrs. Lewis was certainly an old lady, but she looked years younger than her sister in Camden Town. She had one of those diseases of old age which fill out the skin and make it smooth and plump and pink. The eyes were blue and childish. The hair was as fine as spun silver.

"You're Mrs. Lewis, aren't you?" asked Marian.

The old lady wasn't going to give anything away. She considered the question carefully.

"Eh, what's that? Who do you say I am?"

"You're Mrs. Lewis, aren't you?"

"What's that in the bag?" the old lady insisted on knowing. The eyes were not really as childish as they seemed.

"I'm a friend of your sister, Mrs. Purvis," Marian said, as she proceeded to take out the things she had brought—some fruit, some chocolate, a box of eggs.

"Don't let them see," demanded Mrs. Lewis. "Put them in my cupboard. I want a banana."

"Your sister, Mrs. Purvis, sends her love."

"You mean Beat?"

"Yes, that's right, Beat." (Probably the name *was* Beat.) "Do you remember the Smiths? The two boys send you their regards, too." The old lady was having some difficulty with the banana. Marian peeled it for her. The nurse was evidently struggling with herself as to whether she ought, or ought not, to make some comment on this dislocation of a patient's diet.

Mrs. Lewis popped an end of the banana in her mouth.

"Do you remember the Smiths?" Marian asked again.

"What Smiths?"

"You lived in the same house. You remember? In Mercer Street."

The old lady shook her head.

"No," she said. "No." Then suddenly a memory came back to her. She took the banana out of her mouth.

"Oh, *Lucy* Smith?" The eyelid closed over the blue eye. "She was a *fine* one, she was! The young cow!" She tittered soundlessly. The breasts swung and heaved under the flannel nightgown.

"But the boys," insisted Marian. "You remember them? There was Tommy. And there was Clifford. Do you remember?"

"Oh, that Lucy Smith!" Mrs. Lewis went on. "Yes. Yes. Oh, dear! She was nearly the death of me." The memories were crowding in on her. "She once sent a man into my room. 'E 'ad a violin. 'E was an Eyetalian, in the polishing trade. She wasn't 'arf a one, she wasn't."

"But Tommy. He was the elder boy. Do you remember? He got into trouble. Have one of these chocolates, Mrs. Lewis. They're nice and soft. You remember? Tommy?

The old woman's jaw set sullenly.

"I don't remember no Tommy."

"And there was Clifford, too."

That made no impact, either. The smile was coming back into her face.

"The young cow," she said again. "But it wasn't my business, was it? She gave me a lovely little bottle of whiskey once. *So* big." She measured with her hands how big it was. "Do you know Ernie?" asked the old woman suddenly.

"No," Marian said, wretchedly. "I don't know Ernie." A flutter of hope darted through her. "He wasn't a friend of Tommy, was he? You know? Young Tommy Smith?"

"I want another chocolate," the old woman whimpered. "A pink one."

It was no use, heartbreakingly no use. She tried again, and still once again. Then she gave it up.

"Goodbye, Mrs. Lewis," she said. "I've got to go now. I'll give your love to your sister."

But the old lady took no notice of her. She was at grips with a second banana.

X

At the same time as Marian pursued with extremely little success these personal lines of inquiry, there was other help she sought, and other sources she studied, in the elucidation of the problem which had so devouring an interest for her. She read the literature of juvenile delinquency and of crime in general; she haunted juvenile courts, frequented the company of probation officers, and made friends with several magistrates, in charge of courts both juvenile and adult. Through their influence, and sometimes in their company, she visited remand homes, approved homes, Borstal institutions, and prisons.

But it was not enough, and it was too much. It was not scholarship she sought, it was intuition, which you cannot find by seeking it. It was revelation, which does not reveal itself in the company of amiable Chaplains falling over themselves to be of service, or of courteous Prison Governors who knew your father at Rugby. It was necessary to make as many journeys as possible to the other side of the moon, to meet as many criminals face to face, alone, off their guard, as lay within the limits of the possible, if not the sensible.

It was not easy. She could not ask Tommy Smith to introduce her to his criminal associates who were for the time being at liberty, for those were the people whose company she hoped he would by all means avoid. There was another criminal quite close to her in the tie of blood, but she did not think he would be co-operative. She made the acquaintance of several of the local policemen in the Theobald's Road area, and from them she learned the whereabouts of a group of milk-bars and public-houses around the town which were stated to be the rendezvous of criminals. In the company of one particularly obliging young policeman, she paid a number of visits to these dens of wickedness, but she found it necessary quite soon to forswear his company; in the first place, because the young policeman was good-looking, and he developed the view that it was his good looks that she was interested in; in the second place, because the world of policemen and crooks is a rather close enclave, like Quakers, or the Faubourg St. Germain, where everybody knows everybody else. She became aware, whenever she entered one of these sinister places, that the customers were almost imperceptibly winking at each other or nudging each other in the ribs. It was obviously being deduced that she was either the young policeman's girl-friend, or a "copper's nark." She gave up the policeman, but it did not sensibly help the situation. She did not talk or behave as the other customers behaved; she did not look like them, and did not know how to dress like them. They still took her for a "copper's nark." At the best, it was concluded, she was a probation officer, or perhaps, most unhelpful of all, a writer. She gave up the milk-bars and public-houses. They took her nowhere.

There was, however, one of his associates, and only one, whom Tommy Smith, in a mood of unusual expansiveness, allowed her to meet. This was Frankie the Toff, of whom he had spoken more than once already. Tommy explained that Frankie was a reformed character these days, but that there was probably nobody in the country, inside or outside of prison, on the right or wrong side of the law, who knew more about crime than Frankie. His public name these days was Dawkins—Uncle Dawkins. He saved souls at Marble Arch.

"We'll have a little talk with him after the service any evening you like," Tommy suggested. "I can tell him you're another of these newspaper writers. He's got quite a few pals on the newspapers."

"Why not tell him the truth?" she asked.

He hesitated a moment. The habit of untruth was inveterate.

"Why not?" he agreed. "Then I can slope off. You could have a cup of tea together up Edgware Road, eh?"

"What do you have to slope off for?" she demanded. Tommy looked uncomfortable. "Is it the police?" she asked. "You don't like the thought of my being seen around with two bright characters like yourself and your friend? Is that it?"

"I suppose it is."

"But you're through with all that, both of you. So where can the harm be?"

"It'll look as if . . . as if we're talking something over."

"But we *won't* be! It won't *do,* Smith! You mustn't be so unsure of yourself! Of course we'll have a cup of tea together. Or a glass of beer, if you prefer it."

"He can't stand the stuff," said Tommy. "He'd run for miles."

So one evening they both went along to Marble Arch, and were members of Uncle Dawkins's congregation for some ten or fifteen minutes. Never had she found any man so instantaneously detestable. She was bewildered and frightened by the intensity of her reaction, and realized at once that there was little likelihood of any useful outcome of a meeting which must of necessity be odious to her.

She gave no indication of her feelings to Tommy Smith. He was, after all, doing what he could to be of use to her. The last hymn was sung, the last elderly maenad flapped away on loose soles to her next bout of redemptive ecstasy. Uncle Dawkins was about to stride off.

"Uncle Dawkins!" called Tommy, using the public name. Frankie the Toff did not turn.

"Tomorrow night, son, same time," he said over his shoulder.

Tommy made after him.

"Listen!" he whispered. Frankie whipped round.

"Oh, it's you!" he said. He lowered his voice. "What's this they're saying——"

"Mrs. Framley!" Tommy called out. She came up. "Here's a lady who'd like to meet you. This is an old pal of mine."

It was clear that Frankie the Toff was unaware whether it was Frankie the Toff who was being introduced, or Uncle Dawkins. But this *was* Marble Arch. He had just finished a service. Almost certainly he was Uncle Dawkins.

"Are you saved, madame?" he wanted to know.

"It's all *right,* Frankie," Tommy assured him. "How are you for a nice plate of cod and chips?"

They moved off out of the park and over into an Edgware Road eating-place, where a chalked announcement on a blackboard propped up against the door stated that at that very instant not only cod but halibut was frying. They entered and sat down in a cubicle.

"What can I do for you, madame?" asked Frankie the Toff, rubbing his hands like a shop-assistant about to discuss a handsome line in sweaters. He gave the impression he had been in the retail business before, with his stock-in-trade of criminal reminiscences.

"The lady'd like to ask you a thing or two," explained Tommy. He was not very much at his ease.

"By all means," said Frankie the Toff. "By all means. What would you like to ask me, madame?"

It was very ridiculous, and she was quite certain it would once again get her nowhere.

"Oh, please talk," she said miserably, "and I'll listen." The smell of the frying oil, and the sound of the oil in Frankie's voice, were beginning to make her feel squeamish.

"What about, madame?" he asked. "Prison experiences? Famous crimes I have committed? How I saw the light in Parkhurst Gaol?"

"Perhaps . . . I don't know . . . how it all started off?" she asked, thinking desperately to retrieve out of the wreckage one stick that might have value.

He cleared his throat, and started.

"Born in 1871," he declared, "I must have been the Black Sheep of my doctor's family of eight, because ever since I was sent alone to America at the age of eight I have had a yearning and a kink for crime. Steerage, in those days, was simply hell. With my father I called in at a shop in Malden Street, Cardiff, where he bought me a tin cup, a knife, a straw mattress and a blanket. Tearful goodbyes were said on the quayside, and I set out, alone, for the New World. A rough crossing. . . ."

"Excuse me," Marian interrupted. "It's not really your life-story I was interested in. It's how it all *started,* your actual urge to be a criminal. You know, you've passed it over. You said you were sent to America at the age of eight because you already had a yearning for crime." She stopped. She realized he had not been listening to her. He was merely waiting for her to end her interruption. She blushed. The words died on her lips.

He resumed.

"A rough crossing in the *Oceania* followed and fifteen days later we anchored off the Statue of Liberty and were soon taken to Castle Gardens. Ellis Island had not then been thought of. I can remember Jenny Lind singing 'Home Sweet Home. . . .'"

On and on he went, exactly like a book. Then she kicked her shin, her own shin, under the table. Of course, there was a book. With or without assistance from his writer-friends, he had written his life-story. Any minute now, he would ask would she like to publish it for him, and she could come in on the profits. The waitress, who had been a long time about it, set down the fish and chips for Frankie, a cup of tea and a slice of cake for Tommy, a cup of tea for herself.

She looked at her watch.

"Oh, this is dreadful!" she exclaimed. "I should have been in Knightsbridge ten minutes ago! Please excuse me!" She took a ten-shilling note out of her bag and thrust it under Frankie's plate. "I do hope you'll let me talk to you again! Goodbye! Goodbye!"

She talked to Frankie the Toff two or three times again. She told herself she had no right to allow her detestation for the man to prevent her trying to extract from him the morsel or two she might find of value. But the man was preposterous, and, what was worse, he was not a man, he was a set of gramophone-records. His vanity was inordinate. He was as proud of his impersonations, forgeries, hold-ups, as a big-game hunter is of the number of his trophies. His hullabaloo of soul-saving had as much conscience in it as a cat's stalking of young birds. The accounts of his exploits and penitences were inconsistent and, in a degree that varied from time to time, fabricated. It was impossible to get him to answer any questions. He could only put on another gramophone-record.

He was, all in all, a failure, like Mrs. Lewis before him, like all the people she consorted with, and all the books she read. She grew more and more despondent. And the greatest failure of all was Tommy Smith himself. What good had it done her, that she had succeeded in housing him, as it were, in a laboratory? The white moment had not come, the moment of wild rebellion, of shattering compulsion, the apocalyptic moment at the heart of which the clue dealt like a salamander, unconsumed, all-revealing.

She held him again, as it were in close-up, before her eyes. The early background history of Tommy Smith was a cliché, such as every text-book on these matters covered. In the columns of the Sunday crime newspapers scenes from the lives of such people as the Smith family were re-enacted every week-end. It was to be admitted that there was one unusual element in the case, and that was Tommy's desperate devotion to his younger brother. He stole and, from the proceeds of his thefts, showered presents on him. When he was asked why—by Marian herself, in fact, at this late stage—all he could answer was: "I've got to! I've got to!" But love is always like that, whether for man or woman, or brother, or creed. It has got to. It has got to. *Why* has it got to? If there is any finding out the answer to such a question, are we nearer to the solution of our original problem? Or are we merely side-tracking ourselves, getting ourselves lost in another thicket?

So at last she spoke to Tommy, one day of intense depression.

"You're making good here, you know that, Smith, don't you?"

He eyed her curiously.

"Are you upset about something, Mrs. Framley? Why do you bring that up? So I'm doing my job all right. So what?"

"I didn't expect you'd do it half as well. I thought you might get restless and give it up."

"I *have* been restless sometimes. I've told you. But I've settled down again."

"I feel, in some ways, I've got you here under false pretences."

"Why? Do you want to give me notice?"

"No, Smith. Please be patient. You're doing a good job, and so am I, I think. I'm proud of you. I don't like saying a thing like that, I know how embarrassing it is, but there you are. It's true."

"What have you got to say it for then? We're doing all right."

"I took on another job, too, when you came to give a hand here. Don't you remember?"

The shadow of a smile, and it was not a pleasant one, passed across his face.

"You wanted to find out how I became——" he spared her—"how I became one of the boys? Well, I've answered all your questions, haven't I?"

"Listen, Smith. I don't think I'm being fair to you. I've lost confidence in myself."

"What do you want to do, then?"

"Could you put up with going to a psycho-analyst? I've asked you once before. You weren't kind about it, so I've not asked you again. I know what a misery it is. Would you?"

"Mrs. Framley, I'm ready to let *you* poke about inside here all you want." He placed his finger-tips on his forehead. "You've been very good to me, and you said you wanted to dig around, so I said O.K. Dig in. But I'm not going to let any damn quack go mucking about. That's final."

"Very well, Smith. I won't ever ask you again. Let's wind up for the day, shall we?"

She went home and helped herself to a lot more gin and vermouth than was good for her. She was thoroughly out of conceit with herself. "I'm at the end of my tether," she told herself. "There's only one creature living who could be of any help to me. Clifford. But he's as likely to jump into the Isis.

"But I'm not giving up," she vowed. "Don't you believe it. I'm not that sort. Bertie wasn't that sort, either."

She helped herself to another gin and vermouth.

CHAPTER X

I

"Are you doing anything tonight, my dear?" the Warden asked Anna. "After dinner, I mean. I shall be dining in the Common Room."

"No," said Anna, "not actually." A little tack-hammer got up inside her head and started tap-tapping. "But one never knows," she said, helpfully.

"One had better know tonight," said her father. "I'd like to have a little talk with you."

"Certainly, Daddy," she said. "Unless one can do it now, maybe?" Perhaps it would be possible to get it over now, she hoped, whatever it was.

He got into his gown, gathered up his books, and moved to the door.

"Till tonight, Anna."

"Yes, Daddy. And you *are* going to come to our show, aren't you?" Perhaps if she was good, it might help to assuage his wrath.

He smiled.

"You're doing 'Comus,' aren't you?"

"I'm Sabrina."

"I remember. We'll all be there," he assured her. He meant not only his wife and son, but all the don parents and don brothers whose daughters and sisters would be putting the show on, and appearing in it . . . the Woodcote Players, in fact. The door closed behind him.

"That's torn it," she muttered. She followed after her father a minute later.

"Let me see now," she said to herself. "Where will Robert be now?"

She had an exact schedule of her brother's lectures in her mind, though she had never actually sat down to memorize it. He would be on his way to Wadham, she worked out, this very minute, to hear old Jolliffe on the Troubadours. If she flew, she could intercept him at the corner of Queen's Lane. He was, in fact, just turning the corner from the High.

"Robert," she gasped. "What do you think?"

"I think I'll be late again for old Jolliffe, if you don't make it snappy."

"He knows," she said, lugubriously.

"Oh, dear." His face fell. He knew exactly who she meant and what. "Who told him?"

"I don't know."

"How do *you* know he knows?"

"He wants a few words with me after dinner," she said heavily.

"Perhaps he wants to jerk up your allowance a bit," Robert suggested helpfully. "*You* know. The cost of living and all that."

"Don't talk rot!" she told him, and let him speed off to his appointment with the Troubadours.

Mrs. Browne was in her easy-chair, knitting. Anna was trying to get Russia on the short wave. That was not because she was a fervent disciple of the Russian teachers, but, when things were a bit sticky, she always felt it was a good way to get her own back on Fate in general, if she managed to establish even so tenuous and one-sided a connection as this between Moscow and Oxford. Mrs. Browne did not even say "Stop it!" as she would have liked to. She had long given up the habit, which had never been a deeply-ingrained one, of saying "Stop it!" There had been too much to say "Stop it!" to across the years. Her brother-in-law, Matthew Browne, had been more than enough, to begin with. Then there had been Henry, her husband, very devoted, but very self-willed. She had never quite forgotten the way he had got up very early on the morning after their honeymoon night. Very early. It was about five o'clock. They were staying in a hotel near the Tuileries. Out of the corner of her eye, she looked to see what he was doing. He was rummaging in his trunk. He was slipping on his running things. (He had been a Varsity half-blue for running.) In fact, he was going for an early morning run in the Tuileries' Gardens. "Stop it!" she had whispered, so faintly that he had not heard her, and probably it would have made little difference if he had. She had never really had much heart in saying "Stop it!" to her husband ever since. The same went with Marian. She would have liked to stop Marian opening up a book-shop in Oxford, let alone a *second* book-shop in one of the more sinister parts of London. She would have liked to stop Robert and Anna taking that poor clever Mr. Eckersley with them to Brittany. She would have liked to stop Anna trying to get Moscow on the radio. But she just sighed, and went on knitting instead.

The door opened.

"Stop it!" the Warden said. Despite all the squealing and the morse coding, he had identified the language which was coming across the sound-waves. It was not the content of the broadcast he was objecting to, though he thought that contemptible, and was sure it could not convince anybody. It was the accent he deprecated, an uncouth Ukrainian accent.

Anna stopped it.

"Have you had a nice dinner, Henry?" his wife asked solicitously. "What was the white wine like?"

"Corked!" her husband said. "And that garrulous whippersnapper was there, from All Souls'! Partington!" he pronounced the name as if anybody with a name like Partington was damned already, without being garrulous, and a whippersnapper, to boot.

("Oh, dear," Anna said to herself fearfully. "That's a nice beginning!")

"You won't mind, will you, dear?" the Warden said to his wife. "I just want to say a word or two to your daughter."

("*Your* daughter!" Anna's heart repeated. "Blimey! But it's not so bad. He's not hauled me off to the study. It's a bit inconvenient for Mum. But who cares about Mum?")

"Certainly not, dear," said Mrs. Browne. "*I* don't mind." She rose from her chair, trailing her knitting all around her, like a disheartened octopus, which has long since ejected all its ink, trailing her tentacles. She went into her own room.

"May I sit down?" asked the Warden.

("That's not too good!" said Anna to herself. "It's heavy sarcasm now." But, in fact, it wasn't. He was often punctilious in that old-fashioned way.)

She took a plunge.

"Yes, Daddy! We'll sit together on the sofa, and talk!" For two pins she'd rest her head in his lap.

"No. Stay where you are, Anna. I think I'll be more comfortable here." He sat down in his usual arm-chair, the bust of Socrates on a marble wall-pedestal behind his head. He went to it at once. "Do you know what I want to talk to you about?"

She opened her eyes wide.

"No, Daddy. What is it?"

He looked at her severely.

"You know very well, Anna, don't you?"
"Yes, Daddy."
"Well? What is it?"
"It's about Clifford Eckersley."
"*What* about Mr. Eckersley?"
(Oh, dear, he was doing his Socratic line. The Socrates bust always seemed to wake up and grin during moments like these.)
"We're in love with each other."
He pursed his lips and was silent for some moments.
"Thank you for telling me," he said. "It would be gracious if you had told me somewhat earlier."
She felt like warmed-up death.
"I'm sorry, Daddy. It wasn't easy, you know. We both know you don't like him." That meant both Robert and herself, of course.
"I admit I don't like him, but I'm well aware that that's an entirely personal affair. I certainly admire him a good deal. I can say I admire his pertinacity and his considerable intelligence."
"I *love* him a great deal, Daddy. He loves me, too."
"You hope to marry him some day?"
"When he can manage it."
"I'm sorry. I don't think him a suitable husband for you. I know how high-spirited you are, and he has his own brand of nervous temperament, too. I think it's an infatuation." He had made up his mind that that was all he was going to say, just that. More would be futile. And it might be dangerous.
"Yes, Daddy," she breathed. He was being rather sweet about it, on the whole, infinitely less unpleasant than she had imagined, than they had all imagined he was going to be. She wasn't going to argue with him.
"Tell me," he demanded sternly. "Did either of you know anything of this before you went to Brittany last summer?"
"No, Daddy, we didn't." Then she thought again. She was determined to be as truthful as she knew how to be. "Not consciously we didn't."
He seemed appeased by that. He knew she was not lying.

"And by the time you'd got back you knew . . . that that was the way you felt about each other?"

"That's right, Daddy."

"And Robert knew, too, of course?"

"Yes, of course."

"You didn't tell your mother?"

"We wouldn't tell Mummy without telling you, too."

"You thought I might make difficulties?"

"Yes, Daddy."

"Quite right. I intend to make as many difficulties as I can. You are not of age, of course."

"Yes, Daddy. I mean, no. Naturally, we intend to wait. We're both very young. And I know how you feel about it. And I'd rather you felt as little unhappy as possible. But I love him."

"All I can say is I hope you'll stop loving him and start loving somebody a good deal more suitable."

"Maybe, Daddy. I don't think I will."

There was a silence for some moments. Then he went on.

"I can only say I'd have been pleased if you'd talked to me about it yourself. I may be a crusty old don, but I've got eyes in my head, you know."

"Oh, Daddy, you *knew*? You *knew* all the time?"

"It would be more correct to say I had an unhappy feeling. Then one caught a word or two at High Table, and once or twice in other Colleges. But I only made up my mind to talk to you about it yesterday."

"Yes, Daddy?"

"It was after the Hebdomadal Council. Professor Pirtle came up to see me. Professor *Pirtle*!" (He seemed to dislike the names of the people he disliked more than the people who bore them. She wondered dimly if it would have been different if Eckersley had been Robinson or Smith.)

"The one whose teeth rattle?" she asked ingenuously.

"Yes. He wanted to know how soon you and Mr. Eckersley were going to be married. I realized it was necessary to talk to you."

"What do you want us to do, Daddy?" (She meant—"You're not expecting us to give each other up, are you?")

"I do not expect you to give each other up, perhaps not

for some time. I merely request you not to behave in such a way in public as might lead Professor Pirtle, and other people like him, to ask impertinent questions."

"Oh, *Daddy*!" The blushes raced furiously across her cheeks. "I can't believe you'd be so wonderful, so absolutely shatteringly wonderful! Yes, yes." She had thrown her arms round his neck, and was trying to kiss him. He was trying hard not to allow himself to be demoralized in this dishonourable way, and he wanted her to know she was very much under-estimating his objections to the situation. "I will! I will!" she cried, and kissed him furiously. "What a pet you are! You may be just a wee bit of a snob, but what a ravishing pet!" She removed her arms, looked at him again, then kissed him, tenderly this time. Then she flung off to the door.

"I'm going off to tell Clifford!" she cried. "He'll die!"

"But I don't approve of it at all!" he called weakly after her.

But she knew that already. She took no notice of it.

As she flew to the Porter's Lodge she remembered her bicycle had a puncture. Perhaps there would be a bus, a taxi, in the High. There was neither bus nor taxi. Bullingdon Road was just not far enough away from St. Stephen's to thumb a hitch-hike. She ran out of the High, over Magdalen Bridge and into the Iffley Road, with almost the speed of her own father, in the days when he was a running half-blue. When she was almost there, she suddenly remembered she was not at all sure Clifford was in his Bullingdon Road digs. He might be in somebody else's rooms, or at the Union. Well, anyhow, it was not a Debate night. He might be at one of his Clubs, or in the Isis offices. She stopped in a panic and turned round. Then she turned and continued to Bullingdon Road. He was likelier to be there than anywhere. He was working like fury for his Finals. The sort of Degree he got would have a lot to do with the time he could get married.

The landlady opened the door. She was Mrs. Thexted, very much a Warden Browne name, the sort of name he pronounced as if he was chewing a rotten hazel-nut.

"Is Mr. Eckersley in?"

Mrs. Thexted stood and thought for a moment. Strictly

speaking, young ladies should not be calling for undergraduates at this hour. She herself, Mrs. Thexted, was a respectable woman, but, also, she was an advanced one. Moreover, Miss Browne was the daughter of the Warden of St. Stephen's.

"Certainly, Miss Browne. By all means wait for him. He's not in very late these nights, he's working that hard." She turned and went along the narrow lobby, and threw open the door of Clifford's sitting-room. Then she snapped the light on.

"Very cosy, I think," she said, "*and* up-to-date." She felt it impossible not to announce that she thought her front room very cosy. She had been announcing it to successive generations of undergraduates and their friends for thirty years or more. "*Do* sit down!" insisted Mrs. Thexted, and went off.

Anna looked round with a renewal of that fascinated horror which the room never failed to evoke in her. Cosy? Perhaps. Up-to-date? No. The poor woman tried hard. But she was always a round ten years too late. She had long since given up "Love Locked Out!" and "The Fighting Teméraire." She had reach Van Gogh's "Sunflowers" now, and ceramic masks with crinkled hair. Great sprays of plastic and twisted-wire flowers, very self-consciously non-natural, bloomed from Heal vases. Any day it would be Paul Nash's "Sea-Wall." Impermanent as these decorations were, compared with them how brief a tenure on this lamp, this chair, this table, each undergraduate had, before his swift successor came loping in on winged feet!

"It'll be your turn to go soon, Clifford darling!" she breathed. "And I'll go with you."

She closed her eyes. The room—and most of it was not Clifford—was easier to bear that way. She laid her head for a moment up against his typewriter, as a dog lets its muzzle lie against his master's boot. It was not comfortable, so she removed it quite soon. But she loved that typewriter, and was very proud of it—all the poems that had gone round and round in its inside, like milk in a churning-machine.

Clifford came in half an hour later.

"Anna, darling, *hullo*! Anything wrong?" Such a visitation had not happened before, certainly not at so late an hour.

"Clifford, darling, hullo! I've got something to tell you!" She could not bear to string this out. "He *knows*!" she proclaimed.

"Your father?"

Her face was radiant.

"Yes."

"Isn't he furious?"

"He's not ecstatic, but he's certainly not furious. He was an absolute darling. It never occurred to me he could be such a brick."

"Does he approve?"

"Oh, no, he doesn't *approve*! The great thing is he's not stinking mad. He hopes we'll get tired of each other, and all that. But he doesn't propose to turn me out into the snowstorm with my baby."

"Well, that's immense, Anna! Robert said only last week——"

"Robert was right. Aren't you going to kiss me, you idiot?"

He looked round anxiously, as if Mrs. Thexted could see straight through the wooden door-panels, if she chose to look. Then he kissed her. It was a slightly furtive kiss, as a good many of their kisses had had to be. He didn't like the room they were kissing in, though Anna disliked it a good deal more than he did. But he did not know that he had ever been so happy kissing her before, anything like so sweetly, deliciously, heart-poundingly happy before . . . not that time when they pounced together on the first fritillaries in Port Meadow, and instead of fastening their hands on the flowers, their mouths fastened, each on the other's mouth; nor that time when they had both suddenly realized together that the Uccello in the Ashmolean was too beautiful to be true; nor that time when they came free-wheeling down from Farringdon, and they said they were riding on air, where *were* their bicycles?

Then the kiss ended. He remembered what the kiss was all about. The formidable Warden, the Marquis-hunting Warden, was not going to be such a pain in the neck, after all.

Mrs. Warden was going to be able to lift *her* neck, too. The sword of Damocles had come down, and it was as gentle as a sheet of typing-paper.

"Didn't he say *anything*?" he demanded incredulously. "No advice, no warning, nothing?"

"He said we weren't to be seen necking in public, so that no gentleman named Professor Pirtle could go up to him and ask him when we're going to get married."

"We'll see what we can do," said Clifford, "to spare Professor Pirtle's feelings."

"And Mrs. Thexted's," agreed Anna reluctantly. "You'd better see me home."

"One more," he demanded.

"One more," she admitted.

Then he saw her to the gate of St. Stephen's. Very light and lovely it looked that night, as if it were floating on a stream, like an unanchored water-lily.

She waited a moment at the small door inside the large door, as the night-porter swung it open for her. Clifford blew her a kiss, as she had hoped he would, in the teeth of all the Professor Pirtles. She threw a kiss back to him, and disappeared.

He turned to make the return journey to Bullingdon Road. He was happy. How happy he was! Anna was happy. Robert was happy. The Warden was comparatively happy. With a bit of charm and sweetness, now that the bars were down, and he could go all out to show how good a charmer he could be, Mrs. Warden would be happy, too. Everybody would be happy. Everybody. It was quite late at night, but it felt like bright morning. Skylarks were singing in the middle vault of the sky between the spire of St. Mary's and the tower of Magdalen. Univ. was behind him on his right, Queen's on his left. He was almost at the Examination Schools, when something happened. It was like stumbling on a stone, but no stone was there. The skylark song, which, as a matter of fact, was not there, switched off suddenly like a water-tap. The sky was silent. Not everybody was happy. No, Marian was not.

He had seen Marian only a few days ago, the previous Sunday. He was on one side of the High, she on the other.

She was walking straight on, obviously to St. Stephen's. It was clear to him she was pretending she had not seen him. Oh, no. He was not going to allow anything of that sort. When you once allow entry to the thin edge of an estrangement, you never know how broad the wedge is going to be. It wasn't good enough, not with Marian. Not only was she Anna's sister, but she was one of the loveliest people in the world. He hurtled over to her.

"No, Marian," he said. "Don't try that on. You saw me."

She was beautifully honest, as always.

"Yes, Clifford, I did. I didn't feel up to it."

"Have you got ten minutes? Have you come up to do anything special?"

"I thought I'd like to have lunch with Mother, that's all."

That was like her, too. Nobody else went out of their way —moreover, London was a good distance off—to have lunch with Mother.

They crossed the High back to the Queen's side.

"Addison's Walk?" he suggested.

"Very well." They turned into Magdalen.

He came out at her suddenly.

"How's it turning out?" he wanted to know.

"It's a great success," she assured him.

"Well, what are you looking so unhappy about?"

"Don't be so ridiculous! I'm not unhappy."

"I'm not going to beat about the bush. Are you quite sure he's playing the game?"

"What do you mean? Is he being honest?"

"That's exactly what I do mean."

"No. He's not robbing the till. He's not hiding books under the counter to sell them to review-copy dealers. He's being absolutely scrupulously honest."

"How do you know, Marian?"

"In a small business like mine, one *knows*. I think I'd know in a bigger business, too. I mean, when once your nostrils are on the alert, you'd smell it."

"You've never——" he stopped.

"I've never left money lying around, to see if I could trap him? That's what you mean, isn't it?"

Oh, dear, this woman was always a jump ahead of one.

"Yes, that's what I meant, Marian."

"I haven't. Forgive me, Clifford, you *are* being an idiot. If he was still a thief, he wouldn't go stealing shillings from me. He works for bigger stakes."

"I see. I suppose you're right."

"I *know* I'm right. Besides . . . if there was anything wrong I'd know about it. I have a pretty cast-iron system of book-keeping and stock-taking. I thought it would be useful, after my experience with Cecilia, poor dear. I got the system into gear before Tommy was taken on."

He stopped a moment and looked at her, almost goggle-eyed with admiration.

"You're terrific, Marian. You're terrific. Do you think there's anything in it?"

She raised her eyebrows.

"In what?"

"I mean . . . you remember you told me. First it was Ernest Latimer, then it was you. If only somebody'd give him a chance, he'd go straight. That's what he told you both. Is there anything in it?"

She looked at him fair and square.

"As far as I know, Clifford, it's working out. I'm quite certain he's completely honest at his job. I don't ask him to give an account of what he does in his spare time, but I just don't see how he can be doing anything he shouldn't do, after we shut the shop. Why should he? He's got the chance he asked for. Nobody put the idea up to him, neither Ernest Latimer nor I. It was his *own* idea. He may break down sometime, but I don't see any sign of it."

"And still you're not happy about something. What is it, Marian?"

She kicked her heel into the grass verge.

"I don't get any further," she said. "What I really want to do is to find out what it's all about. You know what I mean. What put him wrong, if he didn't set out hopelessly wrong from the beginning. I don't feel anybody's really safe, not him, nor me, nor you, nor anybody, till someone's got down to the root, the final deep root. As for myself, I'm not getting there."

"Has he been keeping to his side of the bargain you made with him?"

"Do you mean has he talked up whenever I asked him questions? He's been first-rate. I know sometimes he felt like smashing my head open with a volume of the large Britannica. But he kept control of himself. He even allowed me to meet one of his old friends."

"What? *Marian!*" he cried out in alarm.

She smiled.

"I shouldn't worry," she said. "He's an old man now. He was no end of a tea-leaf in his day. Thief, I mean," she said, apologetically. "You'd be surprised at some of the words I know."

"You shouldn't, Marian! Really, you shouldn't," he grumbled.

"Such a miserable spent volcano. All that's left of the old fire now, is a single red carnation in his button-hole. He's got religion now. I'll take you to listen to him some day at Marble Arch. His name's Frankie the Toff."

"Well? Did he help?"

"I'm a very ambitious woman," she said sorrowfully. "And I must be a very stupid woman. He didn't help. I found him conceited and wicked and immensely loquacious. He'd talk the clock round for two rashers and a couple of fried eggs. But he didn't help. Nobody helps. I don't get any further." She looked at her watch. "I ought to be getting to College, Clifford. They'll think I'm not coming."

"Marian, I'm a swine!"

"No, Clifford, no! Don't be violent!"

"I owe you such an awful lot, and when you asked me to give you a hand, I turned you down flat!"

"I've forgiven you, Clifford. I know how you feel about the whole thing. I don't suppose anybody knows as well as I."

"Nobody, Marian."

"And you're both so happy, you and Anna. I don't want you to let any shadow fall across your happiness. Who knows if you'll ever be so happy again!"

"We will, Marian!" he said, fiercely. "We will! Nothing can get in our way! Not even my brother! Somehow he doesn't matter so much now—now that I have Anna!"

She wondered if he had unburdened himself of his miserable secret to Anna. But that was his own affair. She dismissed the thought.

"Marian!" he exclaimed.

She turned to him.

"Yes?"

"Scrub it out!"

"Scrub what out?"

"You asked me to meet Tommy sometime. I said I never would. I will, Marian!"

Her eyes shone with pleasure.

"Do you really mean that, Clifford? I think if anything could do the trick, that could. He'd feel less like a pariah. He'd feel he belongs somewhere. He'd feel he had roots. When, Clifford? What's your idea? Would you like to come to the shop? Or should we have a meal in a nice noisy place? You know, near the band? Nobody'd have time to be embarrassed, the band would be making such noises in our ears. Or the Zoo, maybe? One of you told me you'd once been to the Zoo together. Was it you?"

She was so excited, she was running away with herself. She was again about to embark on the circuit of Addison's Walk.

"Marian dear, we'd better go," he said quietly. "May I think it out? *You* know. It's a bit revolutionary!" He put his hand to his heart as if the project had already speeded it up twenty to the dozen. "I'll write to you in a day or two. O.K., Marian? You go on to College. I'll go walking round a bit more."

"So long, Clifford. I'm beginning to think Anna's a very lucky girl."

He made a face at her, and went off.

He wrote to her two days later:

Marian dear,

Not a meal, please—even at the Corner House. It would be the wrong sort of distraction. We'd all come thrusting back upon ourselves like tapirs. I fear I express myself obscurely, even incorrectly. No, and not the Zoo either. (Did that put the concept, tapir, into my head?) Animals are all right up to a point, and decidedly inadequate beyond it. Besides, I am afraid of the nostalgic note you struck when we talked the matter over in Addison's Walk. The associations evoked might be intolerable, and I'd be bounding off, like a gazelle. Or goat, if you prefer it.

It ought to be something with some value per se, *with which we might all merge ourselves, as, and whenever, it became necessary. I gather you feel he is something of a highbrow. I myself have not kept pace with his intellectual evolution. What about the Old Vic? (No newspaper at hand. I'm trying not to read newspapers till after my finals.) Is the Old Vic on? Or the Ballet? There's the dancing if the music's too tinny, and the music if the dancing's not up to scratch. And the backcloth, and the costumes, and the funny people in the audience with beards. God's plenty for all of us at the Ballet. Shakespeare would fill the bill, too, if anybody's doing any Shakespeare.*

Oh, by the way. We're all desolated you can't be up to see "Comus." Excepting Anna, who pretends she's delighted, and begs us all to go and see Errol Flynn instead. You and your First Nights! Isn't this a First Night, too, Anna's First Night? Though, of course, Sabrina isn't a very long *part.*

Love,
Clifford.

The reply came by wire:

It will be Ballet, darling. Exact time and programme later after seduction of Keith Prowse, Chappell, etc. Love,
Marian.

II

It was Saturday afternoon, some four days after the performance of "Comus" by the young ladies of the "Woodcote Group," in North Oxford. Anna had been Sabrina. Even Clifford, love-dazzled though he was, could not but feel that there might have been Sabrinas as good before, and Sabrinas as good might be again. But none had ever been, or ever would be, so lovely. None ever had, or ever would have, a head like Anna's head, that poised itself so fair and firm and free, so exactly like a flower's head. And who could ever again recite so bewitchingly:

> *Brightest Lady, look on me!*
> *Thus I sprinkle on thy breast*
> *Drops that from my fountain pure*
> *I have kept of precious cure;*
> *Thrice upon thy finger's tip.*
> *Thrice upon thy rubied lip. . . .*

They were walking that afternoon in the meadowy country by Yarnton. For Anna had insisted that Clifford must take a rest from his books, and had threatened to burn them if he didn't. They had taken the omnibus, for it was Clifford's bicycle that had the puncture this time. They were walking slowly, hand in hand. If anyone had come up upon them, even from behind where he could not see their faces, he would have been very obtuse not to see that they were lovers.

Someone did, in fact, come up behind them, someone on a bicycle. They drew over towards the left of the road to let the machine pass. So deeply engrossed were they in their own conversation they would probably not have been aware whether it was a man or a woman who rode it, if the rider had not dismounted. It was a man, with a silky-brown Vandyke beard. He was wearing a corduroy coat and jodhpurs. He looked like a painter, or an author, who was getting on in his country cottage with some job he had in hand.

"Excuse me," he said courteously. This was addressed to Clifford, in the way a well-bred man addresses another man who is with a woman he would like to speak to. Clifford nodded. The man turned to Anna.

"You must forgive me," he said. "You *are* Miss Browne, aren't you?"

"I am," she said. She saw no reason why she should deny it.

"You see," the man explained. "I saw your performance the other night with the 'Woodcote Players.' I thought you were excellent. I *do* hope you don't mind my saying so."

"Not at all," she said. She was puzzled. She was just a little frightened. "It's very kind of you." She didn't like the man. He was just a little too suave. She wondered how soon he would get on his bicycle again. But he seemed in no hurry to move off.

"I was also delighted with the little *corps de ballet*. They were charming. Who arranges the dancing?"

"Miss Slocombe," Anna replied.

"You see——" the man with the Vandyke beard said apologetically—"I hope to be taking up ballet in a big way. I know the Colonel well. Colonel de Basil," he supplemented.

"Oh, yes," said Anna.

The conversation was for a moment at a standstill. Clifford was never at his best with strangers. Anna was not very good, either. The man made a move as if to get on to his bicycle again, then he stopped. He had caught sight of the tie Clifford was wearing. It was the St. Stephen's tie.

"Oh, St. Stephen's," he said. "I'm an old St. Stephen's man myself," he pointed out. "Oh, a long time ago. Before you were in rompers. My name's Fordyce. What's yours, may I ask?"

"Eckersley," said Clifford.

"How do you do?" He held out his hand. Clifford held out his hand. Mr. Fordyce's hand was not a pleasant hand to hold. Clifford dropped it. The man then made a move as if to proffer his hand to Anna, too. Anna seemed to see no reason why she should go round shaking hands with smarmy strangers, even if they came from St. Stephen's. And, anyhow, this fellow didn't seem a St. Stephen's man at all, not even a Pembroke man. One reads about these people, saying they came from Eton, or King's, and they're bank clerks, or the funny sort of clergymen, just out of prison.

She turned to Clifford.

"We'll be going, Clifford," she said.

The man with the Vandyke beard was determined to retrieve the situation.

"Excuse me, Miss Browne," he said. "It *is* Browne, with an 'e.' Aren't you the daughter of the Warden?"

"Yes," she replied, her lips tightening. But the realization had not come to her yet.

"Oh, you *are*, are you? Then this isn't the first time we've met," he proclaimed delightedly. "Once—you were not a day over three years old——"

Then suddenly there was an explosion in her head. A dazzling light went with it.

That time when Matthew Browne had phoned up from beyond Witney somewhere. He wanted his table-napkins, he said. He wanted them at once. And Marian volunteered to take them to him.

Then Marian came back.

"What's he like?" Anna had asked her.

"He's got a Vandyke beard," she said. "Brown and silky." She had changed the subject at once. It had never been brought up again.

Anna was yelling at the top of her voice, there in the road between the meadow and the wood.

"You hateful creature! You horrible crook! Get out, will you! Get out, or I'll scratch your eyes out!" She meant it, too. To Clifford, at least, it was a shattering revelation that a girl, so frail, so exquisite, could look so like a Billingsgate fish-wife! But, oh, what a glorious fish-wife, with those burning eyes, and those scarlet cheeks, and the nostrils twitching like a rabbit. The man hesitated. It was too quick a transformation of the situation, even for him.

"I beg your pardon, young lady," he said, with an attempt at stiff dignity. "You're making some dreadful mistake. I don't believe you're the daughter of my old friend at all. You're an impostor!" He was quite off his stroke.

Clifford took a hand now. Clifford hadn't the least doubt who the man was. It could be one man only in the whole world. He put two hands on the crossbar of the man's bicycle.

"If you don't want me to smash this over your skull, you'd better beat it!" he affirmed.

Without a word, with, at most, a sniff, Matthew Browne climbed into his saddle.

"Lancashire, I observe!" he called over his shoulder, when he was three or four yards off. A little further on he had something more to say. This was to Anna. "Tell your disgusting father I still want those table-napkins! And I'm going to get them!"

Then, smiling, restored so quickly to the best of good

humour, he waved his hand, pedalled off, and disappeared.

By this time Anna was sitting on the grass verge and howling away like some frightened child whom some idiot had given a whiff of ammonia. Clifford threw himself down beside her.

"Anna, dear. You mustn't cry, you mustn't! The horrid creature! You mustn't let him upset you, you mustn't!"

Her words came with difficulty between her sobs.

"You know who he is, Clifford dear? You *do* know? I don't have to explain."

"Yes, Anna darling. I know. Dry your eyes. Here's your handkerchief. No. Take mine. It's bigger. There now. Forget about him."

"You've known all along, haven't you?"

"Yes, darling. Don't think any more about him. What harm can he do to anybody. Shall we have some tea?" he asked.

"I'd like some tea, awfully. I think it's wonderful of you to know and never to show a thing. I do love you, Clifford. Kiss me."

He kissed her, made her place the tip of her tongue on a corner of his handkerchief, then wiped her eyes.

"You'll need a little something out of your bag, too," he said. He opened the bag for her, took out her vanity-bag, then held the tiny mirror up while she put her face right. At last they rose from among the grasses and the speedwells and tiny stars-of-Bethlehem, and walked back towards Yarnton, where there would be a tea-shop. They found one soon, not a very smart tea-shop, but the tea was excellent. The rock-buns were less good. They drank three cups each.

"Are you feeling better, darling?" he asked.

"I could show a bull where he got off," she said, meaning she wasn't frightened any more of Matthew Browne.

"Very well," he said quietly. "Then you can walk a bit along the road instead of taking the bus?"

"All the way, if you like."

"We'll see. Sweet one," he wanted to know, "have you ever heard of Tommy Smith?"

"Who?"

"Tommy Smith. My brother."

"I never knew you had a brother."

"You're going to know now," he said. For he had made up his mind, over the drinking of the tea and the eating of the rock-buns. There was now only one secret between them, and soon there would be none at all. It was ridiculous to try and hide Tommy Smith from her, as it had been ridiculous to pretend he knew nothing about Matthew Browne. The one could make exactly as much difference in her love for him, as the other had made in his love for her. He was made of tougher fibre than a year ago, and it was love that had toughened it. As for Anna's fibre, she had shown that more than once, this girl, gentle as gossamer, tough as steel.

"It's a long tale, Anna dear," he said, "painful, and with many complications. I'll try and keep it as simple as I know how. It'll shock you and might even frighten you. I might have been frightened, too, if I didn't believe in you as I believe in the earth and the sky."

"What of, Clifford? What would you be frightened of?"

"With any other girl but you, Anna, I'd have been frightened she couldn't take it; it would be such a jolt to her——"

"I'll kick you on the shins, Clifford. You mustn't talk like that. Please go on."

He told her of the Smiths of Camden Town and the Eckersleys of Baxendale. He told her of Tommy, his brother, whose love was an incubus. He told her of the prison sentences, and how Tommy Smith had met Matthew Browne, and how then it was decreed that if he, Clifford, should come to Oxford, he should come to St. Stephen's. He told her that at first he had cursed the odd quirk of the brain that had brought him there. But it was Anna's home, and he loved every stone in the walls, and every blade of grass in the lawns.

That was not the whole story. Marian, the valiant, the redoubtable, was tied up in it. At this very moment the young man who was Marian's assistant in her new book-shop was Tommy, no other than Tommy himself. Anna had rubbed shoulders with him each time she had gone down to Theobald's Road.

"No," marvelled Anna. "Is that true?"

"You *had* seen him once before, darling, let me remind you."

"Oh, Marian!" whispered Anna. "Splendid Marian!"

He went on to discuss the situation as those two were concerned, Marian, her sister, Tommy, his brother. He told her that Marian had stated that the mainspring of her action was her consuming curiosity regarding the origin of the criminal impulse. How do they get that way, she terribly wanted to know. The case of her uncle had long mystified her, as it undoubtedly mystified everybody who knew about him. Marian's curiosity had attained its climax that night at Hatchetts, the small house in the wood, as she gazed with fascinated horror on the silky-brown Vandyke beard. Then she had met Tommy for a first time, then she had met him again, and still again, as if Fate had expressly brought him to her. So this preoccupation of hers had transferred itself to Tommy, he had become the central point of her meditations and her practical experiment.

He, Clifford, believed that Marian was not deluding herself. Undoubtedly she was as possessed as she stated herself to be by this intellectual passion. But he believed the deeper truth was simpler than that. She believed that buried away somewhere in all human beings, even the wickedest, was a seed of goodness, deep under ruin and rubble. With the sweat pouring down the cheeks and the eyes starting from the head, the seed could be reached if you dug hard enough. It could be vivified. That was the heroic labour to which Marian had devoted herself, with what success he would not dare to say. He paused, and looked away from his sweetheart as if he were a little shy of the sentiment he was about to utter.

"You see, Anna," he said quietly, "I think Marian is a saint, in the full theological sense of the word. I shouldn't be at all surprised if miracles were performed with her relics."

Anna did not smile. She looked very serious indeed.

"I'm thinking," she said. "Let me think." He did nothing to hasten her. "It all fits in." He waited. Then suddenly she turned to him. "There's a lot in what you say," she said. "But it's not the whole truth. Of course she's a decent sort, she's tops."

"I said she's more than that."

"All right, darling. She's a saint. But she's something else, too. You've forgotten."

He was curious. "Yes?"

"It's going to sound too easy to make much sense to you. She's a woman."

"Of course."

"There's no of course. You never knew Bertie, her husband, you see."

"Of course, I didn't."

"You didn't see the way she loved him. I think, perhaps, she loved him more than he loved her, because that's the way she is. And when he was killed. . . . Oh, Clifford, it was dreadful!" She caught hold of his arm, as if she might stumble at the mere memory of her sister's grief. "You've seen those bombed buildings in the East End, just shells? That's what she was like. In a way it's what she's been like ever since." He looked sideways at his love's face. At this moment how wise she seemed, wise and old, like an old woman. "I think she's building up something inside the shell, to make up for what was burned out."

He meditated long on what she had said.

"I still think she's a saint," he said. "Are you tired?"

She was on the defensive at once.

"I could walk *you* off your feet."

"Of course you can." He was no Robert to argue with her. "Talking about Robert——"

"Yes?"

They had not been talking about Robert, still less *to* him. But in a sense he was always there.

"We'll tell Robert, of course," he said.

"Of course. It's only like me knowing."

"I feel I could die for you, Anna. For both of you, if it comes to that."

"You'll do no such thing!" she ordered him. "You'll get the best Double First since Asquith. Or Gladstone. Or who was it? Then you'll become Editor of *The Times,* and we'll live in Egerton Crescent." She had had an eye on Egerton Crescent since she went to a party there last Christmas.

III

A letter came from Marian the following Tuesday:

Clifford dear,

Having suffered a Fate worse than Death at the hands of all three, Keith and Prowse and Chappell, I am to announce that I have acquired three seats for the Ballet, for a week next Saturday night. It won't be terribly long before Schools, but it will take you out of yourself. We have front seats in the Stalls Circle—not too grand. I always think them the best seats for Ballet. Meet us in the foyer ten minutes before the curtain goes up. If we feel like it, we could have a snack. If you get back to Oxford a bit late, tell Mrs. Thexted you went to the Ballet with the Warden's daughter.

Love,

Marian.

So it was to be the Ballet, after all. Well, let it be the Ballet. He would have preferred it to be the Old Vic, not because he didn't prefer the Ballet to anything, but because the most recent association with Ballet in his mind was the execrable Matthew Browne, the intimate of de Basil, the founder-to-be of a new Ballet company.

But there it was. They were going to the Ballet. Matthew Browne probably has as much use for Ballet as he, Clifford, had for dirt-track riding. He would probably be trying the french windows of some country house out Oxford way the night they were going to the Ballet.

And suppose the one in the million chance came off and Matthew Browne decided to go to Covent Garden that same night?

Well, what then? Suppose Matthew Browne saw the three of them together? Marian wasn't going to talk to him. Tommy wasn't. He wasn't. Besides, Tommy's name was Smith. His own was Eckersley.

Then a memory plunged into his heart like a needle.

Matthew Browne knew that Tommy Smith had a brother. Tommy Smith had told him long ago, when the two had first met up, in Maidstone. Faintly, like the sound of bicycle-bells tinkling across evening meadows, his brother's words came back to him across the years:

A Professor he was, from St. Stephen's College. He could talk ten languages. I told him I had a kid brother. He could say all "At Flores in the Azores Sir Richard Grenville lay" at seven years old.

Well, supposing Tommy really *had* said what he pretended he had said, supposing the "Professor" remembered a thing so trivial after so great a lapse of time, supposing Matthew Browne put two and two together and concluded they were two brothers, Tommy and himself? Supposing. Well, what then?

Anna knew.

Robert knew.

Marian knew.

Yes, but the Warden didn't know. Well, if the Warden got to know, the Warden would have to put up with it. For his own part he knew that Anna was beside him and he was beside Anna to their dying day. And who was the Warden, anyhow, to make a fuss about having a crook in the family?

Just the same, he would have preferred it, if it had been the Old Vic, and not the Ballet.

IV

It happened the very day Clifford received from Marian the letter just quoted, that Marian herself arrived in Oxford. She might have saved herself the stamp. She had quite forgotten, she had so many things on her mind, that she had been summoned to Oxford by old Venables, the lawyer, to go through certain legal documents which required their joint attention. The business duly discharged, she felt she could hardly return to town without calling in upon her devoted parents, and getting lunch out of them. It would be a better lunch than she would get anywhere in Oxford, and in most places in London. The table of the Warden of St. Stephen's was a matter which received the special attention of the Warden.

Her parents were delighted to see her. They were aware

she was putting a lot of time and energy into her shop, but they admitted she looked well on it.

"Oh, by the way," her father said. "I'm going to take the chair for young Soames in Gower Street, in a week or so. You remember Soames, of course? Hittites."

She did not actually remember Soames, but there was no point in admitting it.

"Yes, of course, Hittites," she agreed.

"It's an afternoon lecture, and I'm terribly busy. But it'll give young Soames a leg-up. They were particularly keen I should come."

"Certainly. A leg-up for the Hittites, too."

He smiled indulgently.

"I won't be very far from where you are, will I? You *did* say Bloomsbury?"

"Well, practically. Theobald's Road."

"I thought I might come in and have a look round, Marian. How would you like that?" He sounded as if he was preparing a visit from Santa Claus or a film star.

She thought quickly. Tommy Smith would certainly be there, unless she sent him out, and she certainly wouldn't send him out, as if he was tainted. Of course tainted was exactly what he was, but to treat him as incurably sick was not the way to heal him.

She could say nothing about it, that was one way of handling it. Just: "Daddy, this is Smith, my assistant." But that wasn't quite good enough. She had just arranged that Clifford, after all these years, should acknowledge that he had a brother. She saw no reason why the whole family shouldn't know that Clifford had a brother, and that the brother was working for her. After all, he was doing the job well.

"What are you so silent about?" the Warden demanded. He was hypersensitive. He was always imagining people were thinking things they didn't want him to know about.

"I wasn't silent, Daddy. I was just thinking."

"Thinking what?"

"How nice it'll be to have you there. Are you coming, too, Mother?"

"No, dear. It's a bit of a rush for your old mother."

She turned to her father again.

"I've not told you about my assistant, have I, Daddy?"

"I don't think you have. I seem to remember you were having a lot of difficulty finding one."

"Oh, that's all over now. I've got a first-rate young man. He lives in, you know, in that flat that goes with the shop. You remember I told you about it?"

"Did you?"

"It was me you told, Marian dear," said her mother.

"Maybe Daddy's forgotten about it. And isn't it odd?"

Her father looked up.

"Yes?"

"This young man's a brother of one of our own undergraduates. Clifford Eckersley."

"*Who?*" He hoped his ears had betrayed him.

"Clifford Eckersley."

"Clifford Eckersley," he growled. "Wherever I go, Clifford Eckersley. I'm not at all sure it's right."

"Why, Daddy?"

"That the brother of one of our most prominent undergraduates is a shop-assistant. It'll get around."

"Supposing it does, Daddy. It's no disgrace. Some very distinguished members of Society are shop-assistants, and have been for two or three generations. In New York there are one or two ex-Kings who are shop-assistants. Oh, no, nobody worries nowadays. Besides, this is different. It's a *book* shop."

"Humph! Ha! Hum!" her father went. "You know best, as usual. It's just a bit embarrassing for me, that's all."

"You don't have to meet him often, Daddy. I don't expect you to ask him to the Senior Common Room to take port. Can I have that Camembert, Mum? It looks just right."

Mrs. Browne passed the Camembert.

V

They were to meet in the foyer ten minutes before the curtain went up. How exactly right Marian always was, Clifford said to himself. Fifteen minutes would be too long a time to hang around in; ample time for everybody to get hot around the collar. Five minutes would not be long enough; there would be a fuss about getting to the seats before the curtain went up. He arrived, in fact, ten minutes too soon, and went off in a sudden access of nerves round the corner beyond the stage door. He came back at exactly the right time, and found they were already there, on the left of the foyer, near the book-stall. He told himself he would have to put his chest out. It couldn't be any easier for Tommy than it was for himself, and it wouldn't be ice-cream for Marian, either. It was up to both the men to give Marian as easy a time as possible.

Before they sighted him, he gave a quick look among the people gathering in the foyer, the grand ones in tails or diamonds, the discreet ones in black ties or plain frocks, the artistic ones in long hair and cropped hair. There were, of course, men with beards. These were mostly in their early twenties, and very artistic. There was no Matthew Browne, with beard or without.

"Ah, there you are!" It was Marian calling out. They were approaching him. It would be only a few seconds before he and his brother were toe-to-toe. Speculation whirled wildly in his mind. How *would* she arrange it, the brave, the clever, woman? Then another thought came down on that like a hammer and flattened it. It was himself must do the arranging.

They, in fact, addressed each other simultaneously, Tommy and Clifford.

"Hello, Tommy!"

"Hello, Cliff!"

Their hands did not move with the same simultaneity. Clifford's hand went first, Tommy's hesitated the fraction of a second, and followed. He was acutely conscious, as ever, of the feel of hands. Tommy's hand was dryer, firmer, than the hand a week or two ago proffered by Matthew Browne. It was possible to hold it for several seconds.

"I just managed to make it," lied Clifford. *"Patineurs.* Dear Meyerbeer! Dear Constant Lambert! I'm dying to see it." As between Tommy and himself, it was he who must make the going. "Have you ever been to the Ballet before, Tommy?"

"I haven't," Tommy said quietly. "Mrs. Framley's been telling me all about it. It sounds fine."

"I've been making him read Haskell and Beaumont till they came out of his ears," Marian proclaimed. Her eyes were sparkling. If this was not a moment of triumph, what was?

Through the corner of his eye Clifford saw a man; and the man was Matthew Browne's height, and this man had a beard. He wanted to turn and make sure whether it was or wasn't Matthew Browne, but he restrained himself. The man would be passing in a moment or two. Above all, Clifford said to himself, she mustn't know I've got this silly ant in my hair.

"And *Checkmate,* too," added Marian. "So there's something for both of us. And we start off with *Lac des Cygnes* for Tommy." (The book-shop was off duty. She must call one Tommy if she called the other Clifford.) "Not only for Tommy," she insisted. "For all of us, I hope! Where would Ballet be without *Lac des Cygnes*?"

(The man with the beard had gone. Of course he was not Matthew Browne.)

"I'm sorry, Marian. I was trying to think who wrote the music for *Checkmate*. Bliss? Yes, of course. What did you say about *Lac des Cygnes*?"

"I said I hoped it's something for all of us."

He smiled. "Of course it is. Anyhow, it might have been *Sylphides,*" he said.

"Highbrow!" she reproved him. "Shall we go on? Or do you want to see more funny people?" But the attendants were calling out: "Take your places, please!" They gave up their tickets and went in.

"Ah!" This was from Tommy, bathed for the first time in the immediate enchantment of that rose-pink twilight, treading for the first time upon the footfall-muting carpets, beholding the secret alcoves, the populous theatre-curtain, the shimmering wraps, the austere white waistcoats, the ardent eyes of the *illuminati.* They got programmes and found their seats, Marian placing herself between the brothers.

There was no doubt that so far as the outing as such was concerned, it was already a success with Tommy. He leaned forward to try and glimpse the orchestra as it filed in, he looked up from tier to tier of the crowded theatre with pleasure, and anticipation of more pleasure to come. If the meeting with Clifford was causing him any further embarrassment than he had shown in the first moments in the foyer, he was concealing it with the skill of a master. The three of them buried their noses in the programme, for there would not be much time to come to grips with the contents. From the sunken orchestra-pit little phrases, like birds in tree-tops, cooed and chattered. A few moments later a flurry of applause flickered among the upper tiers.

"Who's that?" whispered Tommy.

"That's the leader," Marian told him, "the first violin." The oboe proffered its bitter-sweet A. The strings matched themselves up to it. A reed moaned and fluttered. There was a faint shudder of drums. Marian looked at Clifford through the corner of her eyes. He was not immersed in the programme. He was looking round as if he expected someone might be there, peering out over the orchestra stalls, up into the boxes of the Royal Circle.

"Are you looking for someone you know?" asked Marian.

The reply, if any, was drowned by the louder burst of applause that greeted the appearance of the conductor. He took his place, bowed to the audience, the lights in the house went out. There was an array of brightness showing along the base of the curtain, where the footlights caught it. The conductor raised his baton. The sweet tide of music slid out upon the air.

"So far, so good," Clifford said to himself.

The words were not in Clifford's mind alone. They were in the minds also of his two companions. But whatever they had been expecting, how else could it possibly have been but the way it was—"Hello, Tommy" and "Hello, Cliff"? Of course it had been an inconceivably different encounter, the last time the brothers had been within some yards of each other. But neither, then, had been expecting the other. Each was then as startling to each other as a skeleton walking. And things had happened since then to civilize both the brothers. And both felt a tremendous sense of responsibility to Marian. Marian must not be let down.

It was only Tommy who saw much of the Ballet, and heard much of the music. He sat enraptured, or so he seemed.

"I think it's going to be all right," Marian was saying to herself jubilantly. "I can relax. Oh, what a strain it's been! If there's anything there, anything worth retrieving, tonight will seek it out. He can't resist all this, these months of complete trust in him, these violins, the floating wisps of sweetness, this superb gesture of the brother to whom he's been anathema for so long. Did I read somewhere of a mediaeval exorcism, and the spells were put on a peasant boy who'd gone filthy rotten, and with great retchings and heavings he at last brought up a toad from the depths of his bowels? This is a kinder treatment, but sooner or later, I think, the toad will come hopping out."

"He seems to like it," Clifford was saying to himself. "He's not putting on an act, is he? I suppose nobody can be entirely putrid who can be touched by music like this, even if it's the showier sort. And Marian thinks there's something decent deep there, inside him. Who would dare to argue with Marian? And he's been under her influence for some months now. Perhaps the whole thing's not so pitiful and ludicrous as I've thought.

"I wish I weren't so jumpy about the odious Mr. Browne. She's already spotted that I'm restless. I'll have to tell her one of the dons said something about coming up to the Ballet tonight. That's not him in that row along there? Don't be an idiot! That's the wrong sort of beard. It's a *Chambre des Deputés* beard. If I go on carrying on like this, I'll *evoke* him. I'll make him come to the Ballet tonight, even if he's in Newmarket at the moment, wondering what there is in doping horses."

Lac des Cygnes was over. There was applause, a curtain going up and down, ballerinas receiving bouquets, a male dancer standing aside for the ladies to go before him away from the rosy public lamplight and the joy cascading down from the high gallery. The curtain stayed down now. The orchestra-pit was empty.

"Well, Tommy?" Marian asked.

He blinked. "Good-o!" he said.

She smiled indulgently, as she always smiled when he brought out his navy phrases.

"It gets you!" Clifford conceded grudgingly.

"You dreadful highbrows!" Marian reproved him. "Let's have a drink upstairs in the Crush Bar." They all rose.

"I wish she hadn't thought of it," Clifford said to himself. "If he's anywhere, that's where we'll bump into him. But I can't say don't go. This is an Occasion, after all. How respectable and correct my brother looks! That woman sizzling with diamonds, they're shoulder to shoulder now. Would she have a fit, or wouldn't she, if she knew she's rubbing up against one of the toughest thieves of our time. Marian, Marian! You know what you're doing, don't you, Marian?"

They went down into the foyer and up the red carpeted staircase to the Crush Bar. The great mirror on the landing caught them and held them for a moment or two. "Was there ever a trio like this ever reflected in this mirror before?" Clifford asked himself. "Who knows? Perhaps this johnny with the white tie murdered his wife last week."

As far as one could see there was no Matthew Browne in that press of people. With some trouble they got to the bar itself. No Matthew Browne.

"What'll you have, Marian?" asked Clifford.

"This is my party," Marian insisted.

"I'd like to pay for drinks," declared Tommy.

"Fine!" the others said. It was better not to dispute it. For the young men a lager, for Marian a gin and vermouth.

"He might be anywhere among those people," Clifford was saying to himself. "It wouldn't do any harm to find out. I *know* it's all sheer idiocy, but the thing is to go after it, and scotch it. If he's here at all, this is where he'll be, here in the Crush Bar."

"Marian, let's see if we can spot people. It might be fun," Clifford said, lightly. "Come on, Tommy!" They came away from the bar and into the salon beyond. "That's Olivier, Tommy, do you see?" he whispered.

"Where?" asked Tommy. "Oh, I see. Smashing!"

The pushing and scrambling yielded three other celebrities and an author. It was all such fun. It yielded no

Matthew Browne, of course. They went down again and back into their seats. *Checkmate* was fun, too, though Tommy looked a little puzzled and deflated when the Ballet was over, Bliss or no bliss to him. Marian assured him that some ballets get you at once, others are a bit slow about it. This was one of them. They all three rose again. "A smoke?" Marian suggested. "We might go out for a breath of air."

"A drink!" said Clifford firmly. "His turn before, my turn now!" He turned to his brother. "Isn't that so, Tommy?" There was no getting away from it, the affectionate diminutive stuck in the throat a bit.

"I'm easy," said Tommy. Once again the naval phrase. Once again Marian almost purred.

But it wasn't merely because it was his own turn to pay for a drink that he insisted on this second visit to the bar. He had time to think during *Checkmate*, as one has, from stage to stage of that ballet. And he had made up his mind he had been a perfect idiot. This time he wouldn't be looking round for anybody. He wasn't interested any more. He just wanted a drink, and the other two could do with one, too. Certainly Tommy could. And Marian liked her little drop of gin. They'd drink, then they'd come down again.

It was on the way to the bar, rather less crowded this time than it had been during the first interval, that a voice called out "Marian!" and a moment later you saw the mouth that had uttered the salutation. Or rather you saw the brown silky Vandyke beard first, and then you saw the mouth above it. Matthew Browne was leaning with one elbow on the bar, a glass of champagne in his hand. He was in full evening dress. Beside him a lady in a ravishing concoction, twinkling with sequins and shimmering with feathers, stood and adored. In her hand, too, was a glass of champagne. The shoulders were very bare, the corsage low-cut. It was a young dress, but the lady, who was at least sixty, should not have worn it. It made her look older than she was.

"Excuse me, dear," said Matthew Browne to his friend. He was perhaps discussing with her the idea of founding the new ballet-company of which he was to be the English de Basil; for he, too, among his various avocations had been a colonel. He advanced two steps, the distance which separated him from Marian Framley's group. "My dear Marian!" he cried, though he made no attempt to hold out his hand. "Fancy meeting *you* here!" One might have thought it was Marian who was prevented by frequent residences in prison from doing homage to the Ballet. "And the young Eckersley!" he said. "Anna's fiancé! How charming!"

Marian was conscious of a convulsive lunge at her side. It was Tommy. She put out a hand and seized his arm. Above all, dear God, no scenes! Perhaps, even, if Tommy could manage to remain silent as a stone and turn his head away, Matthew would fail to see who he was, because, surely, this was the last place in the world where he might be thought to be, and these people the least likely in the world to be his company. But even in the moment that she realized, with a sort of electric shock that seemed to singe her cheeks, that no place was an unlikely place to find either Matthew Browne or Tommy Smith, because the last time, and the only time she had seen them together, it had been the Ritz—in that same moment, the damage was done.

"Well, on my soul!" Matthew cried joyfully. "But there is my old friend, Tommy!"

They were still silent, all three. Even the bedizened lady at Matthew's side seemed to be conscious of the deadly tension in the air.

Then a sparkle of delighted recognition danced in Matthew's eyes. It was said by the members of his profession that no-one was more expert than the "Professor" in putting two and two together. And no-one had a more flawless memory, all the long road between Maidstone Gaol and Newport in the Isle of Wight.

"It's the kid brother, Tommy? Or am I mistaken?"

The brief word that Tommy hurled at his old friend had rarely been uttered in the Crush Bar of the Royal Opera House before. A great many more ears heard it than the two they were intended for. Blushing like butcher's meat, Marian turned away. Clifford seized Tommy's arm and with all the force he had dragged him towards the door.

"Sorry, Mrs. Framley!" Tommy brought out from the depths of fury and penitence. "I'll smash him up! You'll see!"

"I don't know," said Marian helplessly. "Perhaps you'd

better not. Shall we go down again? The last ballet's *Patineurs,*" she said, feebly. She looked as if her knees would give under her any moment.

"We'll take a taxi to Paddington," said Clifford. There was nothing for it. Though he felt like a soggy wisp of straw, it was up to him to be the strong man of the company. "There's a good pub at the corner there. It's the Bag o' Nails."

"Yes," muttered Tommy. "I know it."

"We'll have a few drinks, and you'll see me off to my train. Is that all right?" He very much wanted it to be all right. He had no idea whether or not Marian had intended Tommy and him to be alone for a time, but tonight, at least, he could not take it.

"Yes," whispered Marian, more abashed and miserable than she had ever known herself to be. "Let's do that." It was good that somebody else, for a change, was making decisions.

"Cheer up, both of you!" commanded Clifford. "It was a bit of a frost, but whose fault was it?"

"I'll smash up his bloody place," said Tommy through his teeth. "There won't be two sticks left standing. And his face, too!"

"Please don't," she begged. "It's my aunt's place! My poor Aunt Edith!"

"That sort of thing isn't going to do anybody any good," Clifford pointed out severely. It was queer how one evening had made an elder brother of him. "Here's a taxi!"

They did exactly as Clifford bade. They had a few drinks at the Bag o' Nails, then they went over into the station, and saw Clifford to his train.

"I'll come up to see you both after my Finals," said Clifford. "If that's all right by you, Marian?"

"It's all right by me."

"The Ballet as Ballet was fun," he went on. "Thank you, Marian."

The conversation on the platform was desultory. Was Tchaikowsky as saccharine as all that? Perhaps he was. Perhaps he wasn't. Marian sighed. Tommy was silent. The train drew in.

"Goodbye, both of you!" Clifford said at the carriage-door. He bent and kissed Marian, never having kissed her before, and shook hands with Tommy. It was easier than it had been earlier on, in the foyer of Covent Garden.

"Good-bye!" they called after him as the train set off.

"What the hell does it *matter* if the greasy swine knows we're brothers?" Clifford asked himself, as he settled in his seat. "It would be different if the Warden knew. That *would* be a kettle of fish! But how on earth could the Warden ever get to know? Oh, to hell with the Warden! One thinks altogether too much of the Warden getting to know! The Warden has troubles enough of his own."

As the train moved off, he settled down in a corner of the carriage, and took a small tome out of his pocket. But the light was not good, and he was too unsettled to read. He raised his eyes, because he knew a man had just come in from the corridor and sat down in the corner opposite.

But the man was not Matthew Browne. It wasn't anything like him. And the man who came light-footed after him up the Bullingdon Road in Oxford was not Matthew Browne, either. After all, Matthew Browne was way back in London, discussing like Diaghilev, and Colonel de Basil before him, the formation of a new ballet company.

CHAPTER XI

I

THOUGH he had enjoyed his evening of Ballet, Tommy Smith had found the air of the Royal Opera House a little rarefied, and he looked forward with more than usual pleasure to his visit on the following Wednesday to the Kismet Palais de Danse. In the same way, though he doggedly read his latest highbrow novelist to the end, he was relieved to give himself a holiday with Zane Grey.

He was also looking forward to seeing his "party" again, as he termed her, a little waitress named Doris whom he had got to know last month in a Holborn tea-shop. Doris was fast attaining the dimension of a "steady." If things kept going the way they were he hoped to introduce her one of these days to Mrs. Framley.

He got to the Palais in good time, and Doris got there a minute or two after. They had an orangeade and some cut cake, and then went out on the floor, where the "Scarecrows" were beating it out real hot that night, with their battered silk-hats and their dented saxophones. It was after the third dance that he saw Johnnie the Quiff waving to him from the edge of the floor. There was nothing to do but to wave back, though he would have preferred that Johnnie hadn't chosen this particular evening to come to the Kismet. However, Johnnie spent most of his nights at the Kismet, when he was out of prison, so there was nothing to do about it. And if you're going to go round trying to find dance halls where the "boys" *don't* go, you'll wind up in the Y.M.C.A.

The dance ended. Johnnie the Quiff was coming round the edge of the floor.

"Excuse me, Doris," said Tommy. "Just wait here. An old pal of mine wants to say something." The obedient little girl stayed put, exactly where he left her.

"Well, what is it, Johnnie?" Tommy asked; his voice was not too friendly.

"Who's the dame?"

"Hands off!" requested Tommy. "What do you want?"

"I saw the Prof. last Sunday in Maidenhead. You know, that posh joint on the river? I did it in seventeen minutes from Chiswick High Road." (He was addicted to severe understatements in matters of this sort.) "Have you seen my new M.G.? Oh, boy!"

"You said you saw the Prof. last Sunday. Fine. So you saw the Prof. So long. The girl's waiting."

"He gave me a message for you."

"He did, did he?"

"He knows you've gone on the level," Johnnie the Quiff winked, meaning that he knew it was a good thing to take on an honest job now and again, if you could get it. It looks good in the record. What you may be up to on the side is entirely your own business.

"What do you mean, he knew? You mean you told him. Who told *you*?"

Johnnie fluttered his eyelashes.

"Nobody told me. All the boys told me."

"So what did the Prof. want?"

"He knew you'd gone into the book-shop business. But he didn't know it was the business owned by a relation of his. So he told me to tell you she's a nice girl, you mustn't do her dirt."

Tommy's eyes darkened.

"Tell him to mind his own mucking business."

Johnnie grinned. "O.K."

"Well, so long," said Tommy.

"There's one thing more. Tell Tommy, he said, I've not forgotten those table-napkins. Tell him I expect them one of these days."

Tommy turned away without a word, his face black as a storm-cloud. He came over to his girl.

"Doris!" he said. "I've had enough! Let's get out of here! Let's go to the pictures!"

II

When Marian came into the shop next morning, she saw at once that something heavy, and something new, lay on Tommy Smith's mind. The encounter with Matthew Browne had obviously upset him a great deal, but by the time Monday morning had come round, he was wearing his usual poker-face again. It was Thursday now, and the poker-face had slipped. He was very moody all morning.

It got worse rather than better, and after lunch she determined to talk to him.

"Smith," she said. (In the shop it was natural to slip back into "Smith.") "You're worried about something. If there's anything I can do, you know I'll do it. Is there?"

"There isn't."

"Don't look so glum. You'll frighten the customers away without buying anything."

"Sorry, Mrs. Framley."

It did not need much divination to conceive a link between Matthew Browne and Tommy's present mood.

"This has something to do with Matthew Browne?" she suggested.

He looked up sharply.

"How do you know?"

"I don't know. It just makes sense. Has he been after you?"

"He sent a message through a bloke."

"One of the 'boys,' I suppose?"

He nodded.

There was a sudden flicker of alarm at her heart-strings. "He doesn't know where you work, does he?"

He caught the alarm in her voice.

"There's no need to be frit, Mrs. Framley. If he puts his neck inside this door, I'll twist it, quick."

She smiled faintly.

"There'd be other ways of dealing with him," she murmured. "So he *does* know where you work?"

"It seems he knows you kept that other shop in Oxford. And seeing me with you, he thought I must be working for you. He knew already I was working in a book-shop. The boys had told him."

"He doesn't miss a stroke, does he? Well, what was the message?"

"He's loopy."

"But there *was* a message," she insisted.

"You remember those table-napkins?" he hesitated. "I was supposed to get them. You know." He looked away, quite uncomfortable.

"Yes, I remember those table-napkins." Her heart began to droop and sag like a tallow candle in a very warm church. "Well?"

"Oh, to hell with him! Please, I want to forget about him! He won't show up here, I can tell you that!" He went on with his work.

It was quite clear what the message was. Tommy had failed to get his odious table-napkins on another memorable occasion. He had been asked to get them some time or other. The napkins were, of course, purely symbolical. They were the symbols of the association that Matthew Browne and Tommy Smith had entered into in Parkhurst. It was evident that Matthew was not going to allow the association to dissolve into thin air without making some sort of a nuisance of himself. And suddenly a more frightening thought presented itself to Marian. Perhaps the napkins were not the only symbol. Tommy Smith was a symbol, too. He must be aware that Tommy Smith had held down this job of his for several months already. He must be aware that Tommy was trying to go straight, and she, Marian, was giving him his chance. There was no doubt that the man was an adept at fitting pieces together.

In other words, Tommy Smith must henceforth be considered a *casus belli,* with the forces of decency tugging in one direction, and the forces of the underworld in another. She threw back her head. If he wanted a fight, he could have one. She had been fighting a pretty tough fight for some time now. Her dead husband, too, had given her a wrinkle or two about fighting.

But how could there be any fight worth speaking of? So long as Tommy remained straight and loyal, in a way he gave every appearance of doing, how could a known crook like Matthew Browne, who must be under the perpetual surveillance of the police—how could he possibly get anywhere? Everything was *for* Tommy, and *against* Matthew Browne. Matthew had cracked his whip. You could expect that of him. But this time the bear wouldn't take any notice.

She turned to Tommy.

"You're not worrying, Smith, are you?"

"No, Mrs. Framley. Not now I've told you."

"I just want to say this. If there's any monkey-business from the... *Professor*"—her voice underlined the description—"we'll put the police on him. Get that straight, please."

Tommy shrugged his shoulders. Perhaps he was not convinced that recourse to the police was an infallible answer to all problems.

III

A year had passed since the telephone-call with which this narrative opened, the telephone-call from Matthew Browne in his dream-villa, to his brother, Henry Browne, Warden of St. Stephen's. Matthew Browne had said he wanted his table-napkins. He still wanted his table-napkins, though he had had most of them, and been paid at least once for the rest. But, of course, one cannot live on table-napkins. One must have a lot of other things, too, and one must spend a certain amount of time and trouble getting them. Not too much time, nor too much trouble, for that would be almost tantamount to earning an honest living, and that was unthinkable. But one does this and that. One has one's contacts up and down. One has one's hand in so many things, one might call oneself a centipede, if the creature went in for hands instead of legs.

The most that can be said for one is that a whole year has gone by and one hasn't been "nicked" again, as one's commoner friends put it. Well, quite likely, sooner or later, one *would* be nicked again. One has already been pretty lucky once or twice to get away with it the way one has done. Well, if one gets nabbed, one gets nabbed. Off comes the nicely-pasted, faintly-curling, sweetly-smelling hair. Off goes the topping little beard. Farewell to Dow '05 and Niersteiner Riesling, 1923. Farewell to Whitstable oysters and roast partridge with bread sauce. Hail to skilly, hail to cocoa. One raises the portcullis, or somebody raises it for one, and one sits behind it safe and pretty. No nerve-strain, my dears. It's really a good deal more tolerable than you imagine it to be. Try it sometime, won't you? Some of the best people *have* tried it, you know.

And Edith? Well, well. Poor dear Edith! I suppose she'll still take me to her skinny chest and forgive me when I cry down the cleft which practically isn't there, and tell her that *this* time I've learned my lesson, *this* time a ray of light kissed me on the forehead one evening in the prison chapel. So she'll forgive me again, and still again, as she did last time and the time before.

Really, the donkeys that women are! The people one brings to the house, and one says one's going to start up a garage with this one, or a travel-agency with that one. A man would have smelled prison soap a mile off. *How* it lingers! Fancy being taken in by Skippy, because he has red cheeks, a check waistcoat, and breeches. Such a nice country type, Matthew dear! And you're going to breed Angora rabbits together! How nice that will be for both of you!

Or Tommy Smith. Remember that time Tommy Smith came down to Hatchetts? A bit common, of course, he was, but what a nice kind open face! And you're going to collect fruit from our dear little orchard, and he's going to sell it in London on barrows? No middle-man! *Such* a clever idea!

Or does she really know deep inside her that Skippy and Tommy Smith and Willie Yamton are dyed-in-the-wool crooks, as tough and nasty as you make them? And does she know that all this being so frightfully busy with car-selling one month, antique-peddling the month after, estate-agenting the month after that, is all my eye and Betty Martin, whoever *that* lady was? Does she know, and she just sticks her head two feet deep in the sand waving her legs in the air and showing her scraggy bottom?

Well, maybe she knows. So one day she'll stick her head in the gas-oven instead of the sand, as she threatened to do only last week, the night she had too much whiskey taken and her broth of a boy out wandering on the great hills. But we're on electricity. We don't have gas laid on out here. Love will find a way, Edith darling.

The gas not having been yet installed, one eked out the situation with a little gift from time to time. As, for instance, flowers. What can be more thoughtful than flowers? And what more economical when the garden is full of them? One was economical of labour, too, for the butler made up the bouquet.

"Oh, Matthew," said Edith Browne, hatred burning at her heart. "Really, *you shouldn't*." Perhaps, in a way in which the last prison sentence wasn't, and the next prison sentence might not have been, the home-grown posy *was* the last straw.

"Just a little thing," Matthew said, with accuracy. "You'll be glad to know the Ballet project I told you about is going very nicely. Mrs. van Dommelen is being very co-operative. I wish her face was less like a pig's snout."

"Yes, dear." She wondered how he described *her* face to Mrs. van Dommelen.

"We've practically fixed up an exchange system between our leading ballerinas, Madame and I."

She raised her eyebrows.

"Madame?"

"Madame, dear. Ninette. Ninette de Valois. Where were you brought up?"

She would have liked to have said she had not spent the greater part of her time being brought up in His Majesty's prisons. But she was a long way from such insolence yet.

"Oh, by the way, dear. I've some interesting family news for you."

"Yes, Matthew?"

"I don't think I mentioned I saw your Anna some time ago, did I? You know, Henry's twin?"

"No, Matthew."

"She was with a boy friend. They looked so much . . . *that* way about each other, as people say."

"I hope he looked a nice boy," said Edith.

"He looked nice enough," Matthew admitted. "What fun it would be if there were a family wedding! It's about time, isn't it?"

"Yes, it is, I think."

Perhaps Henry could be persuaded to let bygones be bygones, and it would be a real family affair, a gathering of the clans. After all, no-one could do more than I'm doing to wipe out the past. One can't do more than keep to the straight and narrow, and turn an honest penny here and there."

On that she felt she could make no comment. She returned to the matter of Anna and the young man.

"You don't know whether there's anything official about it?" she asked.

"It wouldn't be in order to drop Dorothea a short note of congratulation? She's always been so terribly sweet to us. They all have."

His eyes darkened. He always thought it damned impertinent on the part of his brother's family to go slopping and wheezing around his wife during the periods in which he was enjoying his enforced leisure.

"No," he said shortly. "It might be a bit premature." Then his face lightened again. "I found out something more last Saturday night. At the Ballet, of all places. Marian was there, and this young fellow who's sweet on Anna. His name's

Eckersley. Yes, Eckersley. He's a St. Stephen's man. That's how they met, of course, Anna and he."

"Oh, Marian was there," she murmured. He was allowing her to be quite vocal this evening. "She's a dear."

"Yes. She's a widow, too. It's taken her quite a long time looking round. You know, of course, she gave up her bookshop in Oxford?"

"Yes."

"And she moved off to London somewhere. Theobald's Road, as a matter of fact. She told me. We had quite a long talk."

Perhaps that, at least, was true. Marian had been friendly enough to come all the way out to Hatchetts to deliver those silly table-napkins that Matthew was always making such a fuss about. Perhaps she *had* opened out to Matthew. At the Ballet who would suspect who Matthew was? He always looked so distinguished. There had never been any doubt of *that*.

"Is she doing well?" asked Edith.

"Tolerably. Tolerably. And if she *is* doing well, she owes it all to her partner."

"Really? One of her Oxford friends?"

"No!" he chortled. "One of *my* friends!" Her heart sank.

"How did that happen?"

"I thought it would be doing them both a good turn," he said. "But that's not what I wanted to tell you about. *Such* a coincidence. I found out that my old friend is the brother of this same Eckersley as he calls himself. You know my friend, as a matter of fact. You remember a young fellow named Tommy Smith? I suppose one or the other of them changed his name. Tommy got here late one night just about a year ago. Do you remember?"

Yes. She remembered.

"A nice fellow, with a good war record, a first-rate air-crew sergeant. Rather older than he looks. Not out of the top drawer, you know." He flicked a speck of dust from his coat-sleeve. "None the worse for that. We can't all be top drawer." He paused to ruminate on top drawers.

"Well, I'm glad dear Marian's nicely fixed up," Mrs. Browne ventured.

Matthew smiled darkly. *Fixed up.* She had hit the nail exactly on the head, as she sometimes did, the haggard old runt. The smile did not leave his face.

"Such a coincidence, as I was saying, that my young friend's brother should become an undergraduate at my brother's college. And yet, perhaps, not such a coincidence. After all, I kept on dinning the superiority of St. Stephen's over all the other colleges so loudly into Tommy's ears, he would have felt there was only one place to send the boy to, when he was the right age. Don't you think that's likely?" He didn't wait for an answer. "And now, my dear," he said, with one of the quick changes of subject that were characteristic of him, "perhaps you'll ring the bell and ask Johnson to mix me a whiskey and soda."

"*I'll* do it," she said, and half-rose. Sometimes he was angry if she didn't volunteer, sometimes he was angry if she did.

"No!" he snapped. "I said Johnson. He'd better do *something* to earn his bread and butter."

He was very silent as he sipped his whiskey and soda, He sat so long, and remained so silent that at last she got up from her chair.

"I've got one or two things to do, dear, if you don't mind," she breathed.

He made a gesture with his left hand. She was dismissed.

"Clever young bastard, old Tommy," he was saying to himself. "How *did* he fix it? He met her with me that time at the Ritz, of course. And I suppose he got round her, the crafty one. I must hand it to him. Well, anyhow, there he is, with his claws right into her, good and hard. Maybe she's fallen for him. She doesn't look the sort that runs around easily, and it would be a long time since she's had a man. I didn't know Marian had money. But perhaps she has now. Perhaps she's inherited it from somewhere. They don't keep me as well-informed as I should like on family developments."

Then another thought, and in its way an intriguing one, presented itself.

"Maybe they're in love with each other. Maybe she's trying to make him go straight, and he's fallen for it. I've not heard he's brought off any of those jobs lately that he was always so good at. Wait a moment. That actress's flat in Pont Street? No. If it was Tommy, it hasn't got around yet. There wasn't anything in it, either, nothing like smart enough for Tommy.

"Tommy go straight?" he said to himself again. "Tommy go straight? I'm seeing things. I think I'd better have another whiskey and soda. Oh, dear, that means getting up and ringing. Oh, to hell with it! I'll shout."

"Johnson!" he shouted. Johnson came in. Matthew held out his glass. Johnson filled it.

He drank half of it at a swig, and felt better. He was pretty certain now that the distasteful idea of Tommy Smith trying to go straight had nothing to it.

"But whatever it is, I want to be in on it," he said to himself firmly. "After all, she's my niece, isn't she? And it was I who introduced them, wasn't it, that time at the Ritz?"

IV

It was a few days later, and Marian was returning from lunch along Theobald's Road. As she got within four or five yards of the door of the book-shop, she heard the door slam hard and saw a young man leave in something of a hurry. He was a blond young man, with a sort of Veronica Lake droop of the blond silky hair over the right eyebrow. He was wearing a long "drape-cut" jacket, as it is called, and pale tan gabardine trousers. There was a kingfisher flash of American tie and Scottish sock. But the face held the attention. It was an angry face, and rather a frightened one. It did not seem at all as if the owner had gone into the shop to buy a book.

Marian entered. Behind the counter Tommy Smith's eyes smouldered and his chin was thrust forward most unpleasantly.

"What is it, Smith?" she asked. "Who was that fellow?"

"Johnnie the Quiff, if you want to know." He was always ill-mannered when put out like this.

"You must not be unpleasant to me," she expostulated reasonably, "if one of your old friends comes in and upsets you."

"He's a tick," said Tommy.

"I think I know what you mean," she observed. "And I agree with you if the gentleman's anything like his clothes." She looked round. Everything was shipshape.

"No, I didn't hit him," said Tommy.

"I'm glad. Is there anything more you'd like to say about your visitor, or should we get on with things?"

He half-turned as if to get on with them; then suddenly it spilled out. The nerve-strain he was being subjected to lately was making him lose his old self-control.

"The 'Professor' sent him," he exclaimed. "If he doesn't keep his snitch out, I'll do him!"

"May I ask what the Professor wanted?"

He hesitated. It's probably an automatic reflex, she thought. They've been conditioned not to answer questions about colleagues.

"Very well," she murmured, and turned off towards the book-shelves.

"No!" said Tommy. "It isn't anything like what you think it is!"

"What is it then?"

"He said I should go and have a drink with him, in one of his pubs. He says he wants to talk things over."

"I see," she paused. "If it isn't now anything like what I think it is," she went on, "it might easily be, later on!"

"Yes," he agreed. "I don't see what else he'd want me for."

"What are you going to do? Has he got anything on you?"

He hesitated.

"I think everything's been taken into consideration." That was the police-court phrase, of course. "He can't hang anything on me."

"What are you going to do, then?"

"Nothing."

"Very well," she said quietly. "You know you've got me behind you, and Clifford . . . and us all." By "us all" she meant all the forces of law-abiding society.

"Yes," he agreed.

"We'll pull through, Smith."

She looked as calm as if she were talking to an old woman in an alms-house. But her heart was full of foreboding.

"Where is all this leading to?" she asked herself. "Is there no God who's ready to give a hand to a soul that's trying to lift itself from the pit of damnation? I won't believe it!" she told herself. "He knows what's going on. He'll be there, when we most need Him."

It was a full month later that Johnnie the Quiff again approached Tommy Smith with a message. This time Johnnie was at the Kismet Palais, which was his home ground. Also, he had taken the precaution of suggesting to two of his most stalwart friends, who were among those dancing there that night, that they might come along with him while he had a word with Tommy Smith, and hang about in the background, just in case. . . .

He approached Tommy diffidently.

"Look here, Tommy, you've got no call to be wild with me just because I bring you along a message from an old pal."

"Who asked you to be a bloody Mrs. Go-Between? Hasn't he got a tongue in his head? Can't he write?"

"Tommy!" There was real sadness in his voice. "You know the Prof. never writes, excepting on cheques! And then it's never in his own handwriting!"

"Well, I'm through with him," proclaimed Tommy. "I'm through with the lot of you."

"Oh?" murmured Johnnie mildly, raising his almost invisible golden eyebrows. "O.K. by me. The boys will miss you."

"You know what they can do with themselves." He turned away.

"Listen, Tommy. I *must* tell you what he said. He gave me a message for you. Don't let me down."

"Well, what?"

"He said you was to be in the Red Bull next Wednesday night, at eight, or. . . ."

"Or what?"

"That's all he said."

"What else did he say?" Tommy insisted.

"'Or else.'" That's all he said."

Tommy expelled a foul oath, and turned on his heel.

Tommy Smith did not turn up at the Red Bull the following Wednesday night.

It was not the first time that Matthew Browne had been stood up by Tommy Smith in a public-house, but this time Matthew Browne was determined that it should be the last. Tommy Smith had had his chance to be taken back into the bosom of the Old Firm. He had thrown it away and spat on it. Tommy Smith was going to be made to see that you do not lightly spurn the "Professor" in either business or social relationships.

Matthew Browne was toweringly angry, so angry indeed that even the toughest West End louts kept away from him. Those who knew him realized that someone had let him down, and someone was going to pay for it. There was a general awareness who that someone was. They spat on their hands, and hoped they would be present when the next meeting took place. It was going to be interesting. Those who did not know who the "Professor" was, at first imagined, judging from that fine appearance and the too-well-trimmed beard, that he had come into the public-house for a different purpose. A closer view of those furious eyes and tight-drawn lips quickly undeceived them.

The "Professor" was angry for various reasons. He was used to being snubbed by magistrates, and prison governors, and wardens, but that was part of the game. He was behind his portcullis. He could take it. He had his armour on. But he was not going to be snubbed by his associates, least of all by whipper-snappers like Tommy Smith, and whipper-snapper as well as guttersnipe he certainly was, though their association went back so long a time. Smith had let him down not only in his own sight, but in the sight of the boys. That helped to swell the account. But perhaps the aspect of the case which he found most exacerbating was the thought that Tommy had beaten him to it. He had got in on a racket, whatever it was, without bringing his old friend in on it; and a racket, moreover, tied up with his own niece, to whom he had himself introduced him at the Ritz. He could kick himself black and blue with annoyance that he had ever brought the two of them together.

He was going to get his own back on Tommy. There were

various ways of doing it, but a man is a fool who lets out all his rope at one time. It's good to keep a nice bit of slack in reserve.

The "Professor's" lips were working in a way which would have made strangers think he was a nerve case, instead of being a party quite celebrated for his total absence of nerves.

"What gets me most," he was saying to himself, "is the shameless way he's trying to gate-crash into our family. First of all he arranges to send that weaselly brother of his to Henry's College, just because he expects he might do himself a bit of good through my connection with it. Then a lot of finaigling goes on, and he gets my little niece, Anna, tied up with that same brother. As if I'd stand for anybody in my family getting hooked up with a Lancashire lout whose family are a lot of spivs from Islington, or wherever it is. Then he gets well in with Marian and they start off a book-shop together in London. What do they sell under the counter, anyway? Nylons? Dope? It isn't books, I'll bet my bottom dollar, unless it's dirty ones. The next thing is he'll be leading her off to the altar. Not so fast, Tommy boy, not so fast!"

He started thinking, and as he thought, another figure took possession of the foreground. It was a natural transition from the Junior to the Senior College. The figure was, in fact, that of the Warden, Henry, his brother.

At once the tension slackened. The lips stopped writhing, like a mess of worms in a saucer. A sort of sweetness took possession of his face.

"Well, Henry, my dear," he said to himself. "You've landed yourself in a fine pickle, haven't you? I've always been such dirt you wouldn't touch me with a barge-pole. You thought it was pretty horrible to be the brother of a crook, didn't you? Well, how about marrying off your daughter to the brother of another crook? Probably he's a crook himself. Probably the two of them are in cahoots together." (One eyelid drooped. It was the way it often went when a crafty idea came to him.) "I wonder whether dear Henry knows anything about all this? Maybe he doesn't even know his gold-haired little innocent is pulling a fast one on him with a crook's brother? Poor Henry! What a shame to be led up the garden path like this! You know what? I'll drop him a little note. That'll keep dear Henry busy. And sweet little Anna, too. What about butter-won't-melt-in-my-mouth Marian? Well, Marian will keep for the time being. We may get round to Marian, later. There's no point in spoiling a good racket you may come in on. Hold your horses, Marian can wait."

Two mornings later, the Warden of St. Stephen's received a letter. The envelope was type-written and non-committal, and bore a London postmark. It was marked Personal in the top left-hand corner, but the Warden had long ago given permission to his secretaries to open all letters addressed to him marked Personal. More particularly those marked Personal. The Secretary duly opened this one, but, in virtue of the nature of its contents, she felt herself compelled to hand it over to the Warden and not, as she had done on earlier occasions, use her discretion as to whether or not it should be destroyed.

Dear Henry (the letter read),

I know you will be surprised to hear from me again after so long a silence. (In fact it had not been so long a silence as all that.) *But when you read what I have to say to you, you will realize I was absolutely compelled to get into touch with you.*

You may say to yourself I am the last person in the world to have any right to talk about the honour of the family. As far as I myself am concerned, you are right, and I would not argue with you, even if my belief is, with some authorities, that tout savoir c'est tout pardonner.

But when it comes to the honour of the women of the family, that is another matter, and I refuse to keep silence. It is my painful duty to bring certain facts to your notice in connection with young Anna. You may or may not be aware that she is keeping company with an undergraduate of your college. The name is Eckersley, or that, at least, is the name he goes by. I do not even know if the affair is serious, or if it is merely one of those boy-and-girl affairs which soon blow over. Whatever the facts may be, I must tell you that he is the brother of a confirmed gaolbird, by name Thomas, or Tommy, Smith. It may be that the name, Smith, is an alias, and Eckersley is the real name. That is unimportant. The fact is that I have known Smith for a good many years, though he is still under thirty, I think. The circumstances in which I have known him you may work out for yourself. He has been associated with me in a number of undertakings.

I feel constrained to write this, partly for Anna's sake, and partly for your own. Anna perhaps may be trusted to look after herself. She is, by all accounts, a capable young woman.

But the case is different with you. I know how you have suffered all these years through having a brother who has been a criminal. You may think it unwise to bring still another so close to the bosom of your family.

Your affectionate brother,

Matthew Browne.

V

The Warden let his brother's letter slip from his fingers on to the table. Then he went over to the armchair to the right of the fire; hardly went over so much as shuffled over. It seemed to take a long time to get there. Then he sat back, and closed his eyes. His face was bloodless.

He was a Christian and believed in God; he believed that men do not wholly have the ordering of their own affairs, but that God, in His inscrutable wisdom, has a great share in it. God has seen fit that a notorious criminal should be born into the bosom of a decent, God-fearing family of piety and substance. But He had not been content with that. He had ordained not only that he, Henry Browne, should have a criminal brother, but that his ewe lamb, his sweet young daughter, Anna, should consort with the brother of another criminal, an associate of Matthew Browne's. He had only Matthew's word for it, but on this occasion he knew in the depths of his heart Matthew did not lie.

One could not enter into abstract metaphysical debate within one's heart as to what sin, sinned by whom, was being paid for, at this day, in this coinage. In humility, he did not see how he himself had deserved it, or his poor wife, or their fathers or their mothers before them, or any of their kinsmen back into the depths of time. It was God's plan, one could say no more. Yet even if it was God's plan, it did not mean that God appointed that he, Henry Browne, should bend forward and offer his shoulders to the deadly burden, supinely, without prayer or protest.

To whom he should pray was manifest, and then and there he prayed. But to whom should he protest? In what words, by what deeds? To the young man, Clifford Eckersley? Was he to say: You are brother to a criminal. I will not ever have you speak a single word to my daughter again? He could not do that, not on those grounds. He certainly thought the friendship between his daughter and Eckersley undesirable, but that was for different and very adequate reasons. But with respect to the shame of Eckersley's family, he, Henry Browne, had suffered enough, through a fault which was not his own, to wish to inflict similar suffering on another creature as unfortunate as himself.

Should he speak to Marian, and bid her dismiss her assistant because he, her father, had discovered Smith to be a criminal? But, surely, the very reason why Marian had given him the job must be because she had some idea in her head of reforming him. Perhaps she would succeed, perhaps she would not. No-one had ever succeeded with Matthew. It seemed impossible to imagine how anyone ever could have done. But perhaps this brother of Eckersley, this Smith, was more malleable. If he was right in his thinking, Marian would not give up her experiment with Smith, because no-one had ever succeeded, even if it had ever been possible to try, with Matthew.

No, it would not be easy to talk to Marian on any such lines. She was a grown-up person, and the matter of the people she employed was entirely her own affair. She had always been a very independent young woman, and had not grown less independent with the years.

But, Anna—that was a different thing. He would *have* to talk to Anna, sooner rather than later. Fundamentally what he wanted was that Anna and Eckersley should give up whatever serious intentions they might have about each other. He had a strong feeling that if he forbade the friendship on the ground of Eckersley's misfortune, he would arouse in Anna all she had of chivalry and quixotry and it was a great deal. It might well be a disastrous card to play. But there were other cards to play. Yes, soon, as soon as possible, he must talk to Anna.

VI

Since his second meeting with Matthew Browne, the meeting which had identified him as Tommy's brother, Clifford Eckersley had not had the slightest doubt what the logical consequence would be. He did not need to trace out the line of Matthew Browne's mental processes. Perhaps not even Matthew Browne himself could do that. But he knew with complete certainty what would happen. Matthew Browne would make it his business, either through an intermediary or a letter, to let the Warden know that the young man who loved his daughter was the brother of a criminal. Matthew Browne was evil, evil incarnate, and evil must follow its own law.

Clifford did not see how the Warden could behave in any other way than peremptorily forbid the association between himself and Anna. Legally she was still a minor, and would be for a couple of years. Legally, too, she could do what she chose in the matter when she reached her majority. But that was no matter of Law. This was a matter of a rose to which a canker had been brought. It was a fiddle with the strings wrenched and the case broken. The light had gone out of the sun.

He slapped his hand hard against his forehead. Nothing had happened yet. Matthew Browne had not yet conveyed any information to the Warden. The Warden had not *yet* said: "Go! Get out of my sight!" Besides, Anna, though she was nineteen, was no sloe-eyed gazelle. She had a mind and a tongue of her own. He must talk to her. He had tried to find excuses for not talking to her. But he must not shirk it any longer. He must seek her out

He gave Anna in exact detail an account of the meeting with Matthew Browne at the Royal Opera House. He conveyed to her his conviction that Matthew Browne would write all about it to her father. He told her that he did not see how her father could hold his hand any longer. They would be forbidden to see each other. "Supposing he does?" he asked. "Supposing he does? What shall we do?" His face was drawn with pain.

"Exactly what we're doing now," she said, and brought his mouth over to hers.

"How can I take the responsibility of asking you to disobey your father?"

"I can," she told him. "Besides, you don't make me. I make myself."

"You're a child," he pointed out.

"I'm twice your age," she returned. "Who's behaving like a school child, you or me?"

"Do you think it's fun for me to talk like this? Do you think I'm playing games?"

"You like to torture yourself a bit, don't you, darling?" she chaffed him, twisting his hair round and round her finger. "He hasn't written yet, has he? Matthew, I mean."

"Not so far as I know."

"When he does, Daddy will deal with it."

"I suppose he will," he said miserably.

"And if he tells me to give you up, I'll say: 'Don't be a lunatic, Daddy!' And he will say 'Humph!' and look very cross, and bury his nose in some mouldy old book. And that'll be that."

Clifford was not convinced. Nor was Anna, for that matter.

The weeks went by. It was June. It was July. It was early August now. Clifford had long since got the First in History that everyone, excepting himself, had so confidently anticipated. Various Colleges were interested in him. If a Fellowship were not offered him at his own College, it might be offered to him at another. Perhaps it was likelier at another, for it was known that the Warden of St. Stephen's used his weight in favour of aspirants who had come up from more exalted schools than Eckersley's Baxendale.

For various reasons Clifford had not yet gone down to Baxendale this Long Vac. He was sketching out a play in verse, he was engaged in some independent research in the Foundation and History of the Hussite Movement (for the Eckersley parents had not been wholly without influence on the line of his academic interests). And there was Anna, of course. He wanted to be near Anna. That was the chief reason.

He was still at Bullingdon Road, though his first novel had been quite successful, as first novels go. It was therefore to Bullingdon Road that the St. Stephen's College Messenger delivered a note from the Warden one day in early August. The Messenger was to wait for a reply.

The Warden's House,
St. Stephen's College.

Dear Mr. Eckersley,

I understand that you have not gone down yet. A matter has come to my knowledge which I urgently wish to discuss with you. Perhaps you can come along here at eleven tomorrow morning. If that is not convenient, please inform the Messenger whether or not you can be here later in the day.

Sincerely yours,
Henry Browne,
Warden.

"Please tell the Warden," said Clifford, "I will be there at eleven tomorrow morning." There was no doubt at all in his mind what the matter was that had come to the Warden's knowledge. He and Anna had intended to go out for a bus-ride somewhere that evening, and dinner on the river. He knew he would be bad company, and sent her a letter begging her to excuse him. He had a headache, he wrote, and that was quite true.

Next morning at eleven o'clock he was shown into the Warden's study. The Warden rose from his chair at the desk.

"Good morning, Mr. Eckersley," the Warden said, indicating an armchair. "Will you sit down?" Clifford had never seen the Warden look so drawn and haggard. He had never seen him look drawn and haggard at all. The devoted attentions of his wife and the College servants, combined with those ample reservoirs of College port which even two wars had not seriously depleted, had served to keep him pink and hale.

"Good morning, Warden. Thank you," murmured Clifford. The Warden transferred himself to the other armchair on the other side of the fireplace.

"Perhaps you would like to smoke, Mr. Eckersley?" He pushed forward a large box.

"Thank you." Clifford helped himself.

"I have already told you how pleased we all were with your First. It's only what the College expected, of course. That puts us level with Balliol this year."

("When is he going to get on with it?" Clifford was asking himself.)

"And there is a new literary work in hand? Another novel?"

"No, Warden. It's a play in verse."

"Excellent. You are in the trend, I see, in the fashion. H'm."

("I suppose it isn't an easy subject for him to embark upon," mused Clifford. "Look at those drops of sweat glistening on the dome of his forehead.")

All of a sudden the Warden was away.

"Mr. Eckersley. I want to establish one thing first. You are aware of the existence of Matthew Browne, who he is, and the sort of person he is?"

"Yes, Warden."

"Yes," the Warden repeated heavily. "I did not expect otherwise. The fact is I have received certain information from that quarter, and it is only fair to you to make quite sure you know the sort of person it came from."

"If it's going to make it any easier, Warden, may I say I can guess what the information is?"

"It's very kind of you, Mr. Eckersley. You do, indeed, make it a good deal easier for me. You can guess what a dreadful shock it's been. Clearly it would have been painful enough if the circumstances had not been . . . so complicated. The complication makes everything a lot harder to bear, though I would hardly have thought that possible." He kept his eyes averted, as if he were telling his doctor some details of his own physical or moral weaknesses of which he was intensely ashamed.

"We've both suffered a good deal, Warden, and in exactly the same way," said Clifford. "You're older than me, of course, and have had longer to suffer. And you occupy a much more important place in the eyes of the world." They were talking very much as man to man. "What do you wish me to do? Have you called me to tell me I must give up all hope of marrying Anna, and to ask me never to see her again?"

"Mr. Eckersley. I'm a tired man. I've been living under a great strain for a good many years. Sometimes the strain has been less than at other times. I was almost unaware of it. Then something would remind me suddenly, and with great force. Now, with respect to the present situation, I know that I've neither the right nor the power to ask you to give up any hopes you may have of marrying Anna. You're aware that for various reasons I consider that you wouldn't make the right husband for my daughter. Anna disagrees with me, and so do you. Very well. But all other considerations go over into a new perspective for me now that I've received this latest information. I'm trying hard to look at it from Anna's point of view, though naturally it's exceedingly difficult to disentangle it from my own. I put it to you, Mr. Eckersley. However young and headstrong and carefree Anna may seem, you can imagine the family shame has not left her unscathed. Supposing, in addition to that, this further shame were added on to her. Do you think that's a fair thing to ask the child? Don't you feel it's likely to cut into the very foundations of your married life? Please don't think it necessary to answer at once. I beg you to give the matter your most earnest consideration."

"Warden, I've already considered these matters very carefully. You're treating me with great courtesy, and I deeply appreciate it. But I know you won't expect your courtesy to affect my answer, one way or the other. The issues involved are too important to both Anna and myself."

"Of course not. That's the last thing I should wish. Then tell me now, if you prefer to, exactly what you think."

"First of all, with your permission, I would like to tell you what Anna would reply if faced with these questions."

The Warden looked up sharply.

"I wonder if it wouldn't be more satisfactory if she were allowed to talk for herself?" he suggested.

"By all means, Warden. I think it's only fair to say we've already thrashed the situation out between us."

"She *knows* all this?" the Warden asked. He seemed hardly able to believe his ears.

"She knows all this. I tried to keep it dark from her . . . that I had a brother with a prison record, I mean. But an event recently occurred . . . I felt I had to tell her with the least possible delay. It was, in fact, the occasion when Matthew Browne first realized the relationship between my brother and myself." He was about to say that it was at a performance of Ballet at Covent Garden, to which Marian had invited them both. But he stopped in time. He did not know how much the Warden knew, and there was no point in getting Marian mixed up in all this. "It was at a theatre," he said simply.

"So you told her," the Warden said mournfully.

"I told her. After that evening I had a feeling that something like this would happen, and it *has* happened. I told her that Matthew Browne would write you a letter."

"And he's written it," the Warden sighed, and shook his head. "What did she say, Mr. Eckersley? You said you'd tell me, you remember."

"I can't give you her exact words, but this is the sense of them. She doesn't see that two wrongs make a right, Warden. She doesn't see that because your life has been bedevilled by a miserable relationship—she doesn't see why hers should, or why mine should either. And as you can imagine, Warden, that is exactly how I feel myself. You can't conceive that I could feel otherwise."

The Warden was silent for a long time; five minutes, perhaps, but it seemed far longer than that. At last he spoke.

"Who knows why his sorrows are visited upon him, Mr. Eckersley? That is in the disposition of a Plan of which we cannot begin to see the details or the intention. I only know my own sorrows have been hard to bear. You must try not to believe that I'm appealing to you for pity. I've never done that to man nor woman in my life before. But these events have worn me down. I'm terribly aware of the responsibility that lies upon me. I'm aware that Anna is a child, still legally under age. But I don't feel strong enough to exert my authority. I'm afraid of the effects that it would have—not on you, for you are a man, and I could cope with you, and you could cope with yourself. I am afraid of what Anna might do, what fatal indiscretion she might lead you both into. I am afraid, Mr. Eckersley. That is all I have to say to you. I must leave you and my daughter to work this out for yourselves." Clifford seemed about to make an effort to say something, but the Warden raised a hand to stay him. "I would rather you said nothing more now, Mr. Eckersley. I would rather we both said nothing more. You'll talk this matter over very soon with my daughter, I do not doubt. Be as forbearing as you can with an old man who has suffered much. If it's possible, be magnanimous. Whatever happens, my blessings will go with you. Good morning, Mr. Eckersley."

"Good morning, Warden," Clifford said, and went out. On leaving the Porter's Lodge, he left a note to be delivered to Anna, requesting her to come down to Bullingdon Road as soon as she could make it. He would wait for her until she turned up.

"Well?" said Anna, almost before she was in the room. "What happened? Did he threaten to horsewhip you if you ever darkened his doorstep again?"

"Anna, darling, I want you to be serious. *He* was. *I* am. Don't make it too hard for me."

"What?" she cried. "Has he been appealing to your better nature, darling? Has he got you to promise to be a Boy Scout and give me up?"

"Will you let me tell you what happened?"

"Will you let me tell *you*?"

"Anna, if you're going to behave like this, I won't say another word. It's not fair to your father, and it's not fair to me."

"Sorry, darling." She looked very penitent. "You mustn't take any notice of me. That's the way I always am, when I'm feeling things a good deal."

"Do you really want me to tell you what happened? I've got to, whether you want me to or not," he said, rather pitifully. "Do you promise not to interrupt me?"

"I promise."

"All right. Listen, Anna." He gave an exact account of what had happened in the Warden's study. Despite his *farouche* exterior Clifford was a tender-hearted young man, and he was almost in tears by the time he had finished. She kept her word, and did not interrupt him once.

He came to an end.

"Well, Anna, that's what he said. He leaves it to us, he said."

"So that's what he said, is it?"

"Yes."

"What would *you* like to do about it, Clifford?" She raised her eyes innocently.

"*Do* about it? Exactly what we're doing about it now. Do *nothing* about it. But that may not go for you, Anna. That's why I've been at such pains to try and remember your father's exact words." He paused. There was quite a long silence. Then he spoke again. "Well?" he said. "Aren't you going to say anything?"

"What do you expect me to say?" she wanted to know.

"I know what I hope you'll say."

"And isn't that the same as you expect me to say?"

"Well, I suppose it is."

"Well, it is."

"I'm very relieved, Anna."

"You don't want me to hit you on the jaw?"

"No, why should I?"

"How dare you say you're relieved?"

"Well, I am, that's all. But I feel pretty bloody about it, too."

"Why? Don't you love me any more?"

"Don't be an idiot! I mean about your father."

"Oh, the Old Boy? I shouldn't feel so bloody if I were you."

"Why not?"

"I know the Warden better than you, you know."

"Of course you do. What are you trying to make out?"

"You'll probably throw me through the window."

"Go on. Speak."

"It's one of his lines. He's got several. This is, on the whole, the most successful—till you get used to it. He can be an awful old fox, you know."

"Honestly, Anna?"

She shrugged her shoulders. She had said as much as it was necessary for her to say. He thought a moment. He recalled a disreputable story they told in Junior College to the effect that the Old Man had only been appointed Warden because he cried at the final Fellows' meeting. In that way he had got the Fellows to bypass several of his colleagues with better qualifications. It was nonsense, of course. The Head of a College is appointed in strict seniority, except in those cases where gross senility makes it necessary to waive the rule.

"You know him better than I do," Clifford said. "But I still can't admit it."

"Tell me. Just one thing. Did he say a word about Marian? Do you think he knows who her assistant is?"

"Marian told him Tommy was my brother that time he went to take the chair in London for some Hittite or other Don't you remember?"

"That's right. She did," Anna remembered. "Didn't she say he pointed out how alike you two were." She paused a moment. It was as if something cold and alive and strange had alighted upon her neck. She shivered. He looked at her with fear in his heart. But she was going on. The moment was over and done with. "So now the Warden knows there's a second Bad Boy in the family—or pretty near it. And you say he said nothing about it to you?"

"He had something more important on his mind than Marian's shop-assistant. He was concerned about a possible son-in-law."

"I suppose he'll talk to Marian herself some time. Don't you think?"

"Perhaps. I don't know. Perhaps he won't. It doesn't seem to get him very far." He gazed at his sweetheart with a proud smile.

"No, I don't think he will. Parents are beginning to learn

they mustn't interfere in their children's lives the way they used to. What are we going to do, darling?"

"This." He kissed her.

"I don't mean *that*. What are we going to *do*?"

"What about yesterday's bus-ride?"

"Beautiful."

"And we still love each other?"

She threw her arms round his neck.

"To the death?" he wanted to know.

She tweeked his nose, and pulled him out into the bright sunshine.

CHAPTER XII

I

THE first meeting of Tommy and Clifford had taken place, the first meeting, that is to say, after many years (and it was hardly correct to call the encounter in Baxendale a meeting). Marian had not hoped that it was to be the first of a series of meetings that would from now on be repeated at short intervals. At the very least, Clifford was up to his eyes in work for his Finals. Moreover, for a considerable time to come the embarrassment on both sides would be acute. No, the intention was with this meeting to break the ice, and, even more important, it was to serve as an attestation that Tommy need not henceforth think of himself as a pariah, an outcast from society. He had a brilliant younger brother, rapidly making a name for himself, and this brother acknowledged his existence and approved the efforts that were being made, both by Tommy himself and by Marian, to make a decent citizen of him.

From one point of view the evening at the Ballet had turned out a ghastly experience. There was no doubt of that, and there was no point in trying to pretend it was anything less than that. But from the point of view with which the evening had been organized, namely the getting together of Tommy and Clifford, the evening had been a real success. It would have been still more successful if the Matthew

Browne adventure had not taken place. She had intended to take the two brothers on to supper at the Toasting-Fork, where a good deal of further progress might have been chalked up.

Well, it had not turned out like that. But the ground gained had not been lost. Meanwhile, at the book-shop, they went on with the daily round. She was pleased to be able to report to Tommy that in a brief letter Clifford had sent her he had also sent his regards to his brother. Considering Clifford's nightmare hatred of Tommy, which seemed to go back to the very earliest of his emotions, that was a good deal. It would have been too much to hope for that Clifford might actually himself address a note to Tommy, though it would have been of immense moral value. But there was no doubt that Clifford's gesture had deeply impressed Tommy. He did not say much, but there was almost at once a difference in his bearing.

It was obvious that all was not to be plain sailing in the rehabilitation of Tommy Smith, and she knew she would have been an imbecile to expect it. The two encounters with Johnnie the Quiff, which were merely to be considered as long-range encounters with Matthew Browne, had upset him considerably. None the less, within a matter of hours, he was on an even keel again. She made a point of suggesting to him some films and plays he might go to, which he might otherwise have missed; and she would herself have liked to take him to one or the other sometimes. But she knew how important it was to retain very strictly the employer-employee relationship. The excursion to Covent Garden had been a different matter, of course. That had been a family affair, with one of her guests a leading junior member of her father's College.

It was a morning in late August when she came in to find he was having difficulty with his preliminary jobs, which included, apart from a certain amount of cleaning up, the packaging of books which had been asked for late on the previous day, and the unwrapping of books which had arrived that morning. He had his arm in a rough sling, and he was evidently in a certain amount of pain. When asked what was wrong, he said it was nothing; he had been roller-skating the night before, and happened to fall just on the edge of the rink, where somebody had only a moment before dropped a lemonade-bottle and broken it. He admitted it had hurt the wrist-bone quite a bit, and when she insisted on seeing what sort of a cut it was, there was no doubt about it, it was quite nasty. She insisted on doing up the wrist there and then with whatever materials there were on hand, and sending him round to the morning surgery of his panel doctor. She also telephoned the doctor herself, for Tommy was not likely to report it to her if the doctor was perturbed about it. The doctor didn't like the look of it, either, she learned. He insisted that Tommy should come in and have it seen to every other day during the next week or so.

It was during one of these absences at the doctor that Marian had an alarming, and totally unpleasing, visitor. This was none other than that distinguished reformed criminal, Frankie the Toff, whom she had met several times, with whom she had, in fact, broken bread, if the bread was nothing more palatable than an Edgware Road rock-bun, but who could not by any stretch of the imagination be considered a friend of hers, and one from whom she would welcome a social call.

But, in fact, it was not on her that Frankie the Toff had called. It was on his young friend, Tommy Smith. The black morning-coat shone as green and greasy as ever before, the black clerical hat was more disreputable, the red carnation bloomed as boldly.

"God bless you, madam," he said, as he entered the shop, for he had got religion. "God bless you, and good morning."

There happened to be a certain Mrs. Pickard in the shop, who had already made one or two purchases on earlier occasions. "What on earth will Mrs. Pickard think?" Marian asked herself. "What sort of a shop will she think this is?" She went on discussing the matter on hand. When would Mr. Deeping's books all be back in print again, Mrs. Pickard wanted to know. She couldn't bear the thought of missing a single one. As far as Marian knew, there were a number of titles in print. She would be glad to find out the exact situation from the publishers. ("Take yourself in hand!" Marian told herself. "How is the woman to know that the queer old creature beside her has been one of the most masterful criminals of the century? She obviously doesn't like to be in the same place as he is. He certainly smells like cats. But she probably thinks he's some sort of religious crank, which, in a way, he is. He's come in, maybe, she thinks, to buy some book on the British-Israel movement. She's getting restive. She'll be leaving any moment now. What am I going to do? I don't want to be left alone with him. The Devil take Tommy Smith for telling him where the shop is.")

"Yes, Mrs. Pickard, I can find out. Certainly. A standard edition? Of course, I'll find that out, too."

("Perhaps it isn't Tommy Smith who's told him. He wouldn't be so foolish, so impertinent. It must have been one of his friends. These people know everything. Ought I to scribble a note to this woman and ask her just to breathe a word to the nearest policeman? Lunatic! She'd scream and run for miles. Besides, he's probably just come in to borrow a shilling or two. Don't behave like a panic-stricken schoolgirl!")

"We have your address, haven't we, Mrs. Pickard? Good morning. Good morning."

She turned to Frankie the Toff. Her voice was flat and uninviting.

"Yes? Can I do anything for you?"

"He does work here still, doesn't he, ma'am?"

"You mean Smith, my assistant? Yes." The sooner this man was off the better. "Can I give Smith a message for you?"

"It's a bit on the urgent side. How soon do you expect him, please?" The man was smooth and well-spoken.

(What sort of a message could Frankie the Toff have for Tommy Smith? From whom? What connection could there possibly be between the two men?)

"He's gone to the doctor. One can't tell how long he'll have to wait."

"I do hope there's nothing much wrong with him. I'm afraid I don't remember your name, ma'am."

One gained nothing by being positively uncivil.

"I'm Mrs. Framley," she said.

"Thank you, Mrs. Framley. What did you say was wrong with him, ma'am?"

"He fell and hurt his wrist. The flesh has gone septic, too."

"Oh?" Frankie the Toff opened his eyes wide. He considered the matter. "Then that would put it out of court at once, I think."

(In Heaven's name *what* would it put out of court, the fact that he had hurt his wrist? What other sort of activity was Tommy Smith engaged upon that required two wrists in proper shape? She felt the floor slightly unsteady beneath her feet, as if she were on the deck of a ship at sea.)

"Don't let this fellow see he's taken you out of your depth," she told herself. "Keep control of yourself, Marian. A darkness has come into the air. But don't let him see anything. Don't let him think you know less than he does."

"Oh, no," she said easily. "I don't think he's as badly hurt as all that. I should imagine he'd be all right in a day or two."

"But he wants him tonight," said Frankie the Toff.

"Who?"

Frankie the Toff paused and looked for several seconds deeply into her eyes.

"You're on the up and up?" he said at length.

"Well what do you think?" she asked.

"Naturally, I thought you were. People don't go in for this sort of thing——" he looked round over the rows of books—"to make a living."

She laughed.

"Of course not." She remembered a phrase which seemed helpful. "You've said it." Then she remembered a snatch from another conversation. It wasn't a conversation in the flesh, so to speak. It was a conversation over the telephone. The context then was books, too, Tommy Smith is talking to Ernest Latimer, the novelist, whom he had recently met. "I thought you was running some racket, you and them two others." "But you know perfectly well," replies Ernest Latimer, "that I'm an author." "Oh, I know you're an *author*. But what do you do for a *living*?" At the same time as these phrases, this snatch of conversation, passed through her mind, she was aware also that her heart was transfixed with a pain so poignant, that it was beyond the register of immediate perception. Slowly, hideously, her whole being would be flooded with it, as the jaws are when all the teeth have been removed, and the whole gamut of nerves has been deadened with cocaine. But soon the nerves will quicken, one and the next, and the next, till they are all twanging and twittering in a shrill imbecile chorus.

"He's a deep one," Frankie the Toff said. "The boys were saying the dame he was working for—that's you, ma'am," he bowed, "was trying to make a job of him. You know, straighten him up." He winked. Marian winked back.

The thing that was most immediately and disgustingly shocking was this man's easy assumption that because she, Marian, was in an association with a crook, she, therefore, was a crook, too. Once again the analogy with Ernest Latimer's experience was exact. Because Ernest was a guest at a wedding where at least a few guests were villains, Tommy Smith had assumed Ernest was also a villain. This creature here in the shop had had at least one moment of misgiving; but only a brief one. They were all criminals together. She had asked for this degradation and, by Heaven, it had been meted out to her.

But not yet had the grief, the frustration, the humiliation, made themselves felt as anything more than shadows of their own dreadful substances, lurking like wild beasts in a covert from which soon enough they would pounce in all their fury. She was still preoccupied with Frankie the Toff, playing him, holding her own with him. But that was not difficult, because he believed her to be playing on his side.

"Would you like to wait for him, or shall I give him the message? By the way, who's the message from?"

"The Moocher. *You* know."

"*I* know."

"But honestly, I don't think it'll be any good if his wrist's bad. You know, it's a climbing job. You know how he likes them."

"Can't resist them."

"I wonder where he messed himself up. I've not heard. He's losing his touch, you know. Maybe he's in love," he said, coyly.

She smiled. She had a terrible fear that the smile might

remain on her face for ever and ever, all the teeth showing, as in a death's head.

"He got it roller-skating. He slipped on a lemonade-bottle."

"Ha, ha, ha!" Frankie the Toff whinnied. His face was very frightening when he smiled. She wished the Lord joy of His recruit. "You wouldn't know the time, please?" he asked. "The least I can do is to nip along and let the Moocher know."

But the opening door interrupted him. It was Tommy Smith returned from the doctor, with his wrist done afresh. With one glance he brought into focus Marian Framley and Frankie the Toff and the fatuous mistake he himself had made. But what man who ever lived does not make a mistake sometime? He had taken Mrs. Framley to meet Frankie the Toff, because he wanted to help her out in those cock-eyed studies she was making, and somehow he had failed to tell Frankie the Toff that that did not mean *he* was at liberty to repay the compliment and call and see *her*, if ever he got the address. He should have told Frankie he would get a knife between his ribs if he ever came and pestered her, whether he himself was or was not in. He should have told him and he hadn't told him. That's all there was to it. Well, then, what had Frankie come for? What bleeding mucking brick had he dropped?

The faces of Frankie and Marian came slowly through the red mist of anger, Frankie's grinning a welcome, Marian's grey and hard and cold.

"Who the hell asked you to come here?" he wanted to know.

Marian gave the reply. The voice was as thin as a blade.

"The Moocher. He wants you to do a job with him."

Tommy opened his mouth as if to say something, but the few sounds he uttered were like a deaf-and-dumb man trying to get a meaning across. Then slowly his head drooped. They both heard him shape two words from above his breast-bone.

"Get out!"

"Listen, Tommy," urged Frankie, and put out his hand, as a pastor might put out his staff to a restive sheep in his flock.

There was such a glare in his eyes as Tommy lifted his face, that Frankie the Toff, a much older man, felt himself constrained to get out without delay. He said not a word. He knew he had got things badly wrong, somehow.

Marian and Tommy Smith were silent for a long time. Tommy's head was down on his chest again. She stood and stared at him and wondered how a human being could be so base as this. Then suddenly she moved over to the door and locked it. She did not want any customers to come in and interrupt the business ahead—not that it interested her if she ever sold a single book again. As she passed near him, he shrank as if he expected the lash of a horse-whip over his shoulders. Only a moment later a customer came to the door and tried to open it. He could not do so, and rapped at the glass panel with his knuckles, for he could quite well see two people inside, presumably the people who ran the place. He rapped again, and rattled the handle. But the two people took not the slightest notice of him. The customer shrugged his shoulders and went off. It was clear the people were stark raving mad. Or maybe he had interrupted them at a moment when their true love was not running smooth.

No. She would not talk first. Let him talk. She had done enough talking. She felt she would rather she had talked herself into her grave than into this moment.

At last he spoke.

"I wouldn't have gone," he said. She did not get the meaning of the words at first, then they came to her.

"You mean you wouldn't have gone on that job of thieving with your friend, the Moocher?"

"Yes."

"You expect me to believe that?"

His eyes were still on the ground.

"I've never told you a lie."

"No?"

"Not since I've been with you."

"Did you hurt your wrist at a roller-skating rink?"

"No."

"Where *did* you hurt it?"

"Doing a job. The drainpipe came away."

"So you *did* tell me a lie?"

"That's different."

She could not begin to work out at that moment when, in a mind like Tommy Smith's, a lie is not a lie.

"You've been out thieving, then, since you've been here?"

"Twice. I went alone. That's different. I wouldn't go with nobody else."

"Why is it different?"

"I had to do it." '

"Are you mad?" The glibness of his answers infuriated her.

He shrugged his shoulders. That seemed to suggest the idea did not startle him.

"What have you stolen from me since you came here?"

He turned round and faced her.

"Nothing. You know that. You've no right to ask me."

"I know nothing. I thought you'd play the game by me. What have you done with the proceeds of your robberies?"

"They didn't come off. The first time the people were up. The other time the drainpipe came away and I fell."

Again there was silence. She wanted desperately to cry, but that would be coming later. She must keep back the tears now. She must stop her lips from quivering.

She was not really very curious now, because it was all over. But she might as well ask him any questions that came into her head, there would never be any opportunity again.

"What would you have done with the proceeds of your thefts? Would you have sent them to Clifford?"

She saw him wince, as a puppy does in the shadow of a raised boot.

"I won't ask you if you're sorry about what you've done to yourself. Aren't you sorry about what you've done to Clifford?"

His face was screwed up in its grief like a screw of paper.

"Don't tell him, please! Don't tell him!"

"How can I help it? He was to be here in a few days. Why should I go on sparing you? Have you spared me?"

"Don't tell him! Don't tell him!"

"But when you go away, and start up again with your old pals, he'll be reading about it for himself, won't he, sooner or later?"

"Shall I pack my things now? Would you like to see I don't take anything that doesn't belong to me?"

"I'd like you to get out as soon as you can."

He went upstairs and started moving about. One could hear feet up there quite plainly. After a time the feet stopped moving. Ten minutes, fifteen went by. What was going on up there? Was he stretched out on his bed crying? Was he capable of remorse? Or had something else happened, something grim and horrible? A numbness began to creep along her heart. She tried to move her feet towards the back-room, where the staircase led up to the front-floor room. But her feet were like stone mill-wheels.

"Smith!" she called out. Her cry was not above a whisper.

Then at last she heard his feet moving again. Some minutes later he came downstairs with his suitcase. He had not many possessions, at least in that flat, apart from a number of books; and it did not seem that these had been packed in the suitcase.

"You haven't got your books," she pointed out. "Have you?"

"I've left them," he said. "I won't be reading books again."

"Here are your papers." He held out his hands and took them. "I'm sorry," he said, then. That was all. Then he went out.

II

He went out, and it was like a second death in her life. First, there had been her husband, Bertie Framley, and the war had killed him. Now there was Tommy Smith, and he had killed himself.

This Tommy Smith had in no sense taken the place of the fine lad who had died, excepting in the sense that she had devoted to him a great deal of thought and energy, as one does to a lover or a husband. Much more, he had taken the place of the child she had never had, a child who was born with, or who, at some stage, acquired a deadly illness which she had sought so bravely to cure in him. But she had not succeeded. The illness would kill him in the end. For her he was dead already.

She did nothing more in the shop that morning. She left things exactly as they were, went out, and locked up. She started walking, and went on walking, for three hours or more, from Theobald's Road into Southampton Row and Woburn Place, round into Euston Road and far off into Paddington. She was not aware of any moment at which she had consciously set her mind on going back to her own flat in Doughty Street. But at a certain moment there she was; she had taken the front-door key out of her handbag and was letting herself in. She went up to her flat, which was on the first floor, and automatically went along to her kitchenette, for that was her habit whenever she came in. But inside there, her hand on the frigidaire, she realized she was not hungry. She seemed to remember that at some point somewhere she had bought herself a roll and butter and a glass of milk. No, she wanted nothing to eat. Instead, she went into her sitting-room, and took the gin and vermouth bottles out of the cupboard, and, with trembling hands, mixed herself a large drink. When she had had a second, and a third, she felt a little better. Also it occurred to her that she was quite alone now, she could let go. So she started crying. The tears went flowing for a long time, as if the reservoir of tears were inexhaustible. Now and again she helped herself to another gin and vermouth. Suddenly she felt she was sleepy. She lay down on the sofa then and there, and passed out of herself. It did not last for a long time, only about three-quarters of an hour to an hour. She felt rested when she got up, and much stronger than she had expected, for she had had next to no food all day. But she still did not want any. She was light-headed, rather drunk, in fact. But she knew exactly what she wanted. She wanted to talk about Bertie, her love, and there was only one person in the world who was anything like such an expert on Bertie as she was herself, and that was the genial Wally Humphreys, the ex-Petty-Officer who had been with him in small boats all the way up from Able Seaman. Wally Humphreys and his wife, Edna, kept a small newsagent's and tobacconist's shop in Lambeth. His wife looked after the novelties and magazines, he looked after the cigarettes and tobacco. They were not doing so badly, either. They were, for instance, on the telephone. She looked at her watch. It was a quarter-past-eight. Business for the day was long since over. Either Wally and Edna had gone to the cinema, or Wally was round at his local. If she phoned up, Edna would tell him, and, if necessary, go and bring him round to the telephone. It was not the first time that Marian had felt an overwhelming necessity to have a word or two with Wally. Both he and Edna understood perfectly. They were first-rate people.

As a matter of fact it was Wally himself who answered. You could hear Ted Ray two feet or so away on the Light Programme.

"Hello, Wally, is that you? It's me, Marian Framley." She was herself conscious that her speech was not so clear as it should be. She heard the switch-off of the radio.

"Who? Did you say Mrs. Framley?"

"Yes, Wally, it's me."

"Is anything the matter? You don't sound too well." What he meant was "You sound a bit tight. Am I right?"

"I'm feeling frightful. I want to see you, Wally, please. Do you think Edna can spare you for an hour?"

"Oh, Edna's all right," he said, with profound conviction. She heard the sound of a female voice, but it was too far from the telephone to hear what it said. "Is that Edna?" she asked, knowing it must be.

"It is. She said if you want to talk to me, of course I should go over. I'll put my boots on and come straight away." It was obvious he realized there was some urgency in the matter. Mrs. Framley was not the one to upset a quiet domestic evening without good cause. "There's just one thing——" he started. Then he stopped.

"I'd promised to see Jock later this evening."

"You mean *our* Jock?" she asked with delight. "Jock Dunbar? Is he on leave?" This was another of Bertie's boys, and one of the gayest. He was a few years older now, of course, than in Bertie's day, but he was still a card.

"Yes, he's on leave. I could see you, then I could nip along and see Jock, and come straight back. I've *got* to see him, you know. He's dead broke, and I'm holding his last pound for him. You remember, he often gives me a pound for next leave, so he can have something to fall back on."

"Of course you've got to see him. I'll go along with you."

"As a matter of fact he's fixed himself up with a party at the Nelson Arms. He told me to go along there and hand over. If I could get in touch with him, I'd ask him to come along to the Old Horseshoe. But I can't. I don't know where he is. He's with an oppo., and they're doing a bit of a pub crawl."

"Well, we'll meet at the Nelson Arms, and we'll all have a drink together. Why not?" She stopped. He was quite sure he heard the gurgle of liquor poured into a glass. "It would be fun," she went on. "We could talk and talk." That was O.K. by Wally. He liked to talk about the Lieutenant-Commander just as much as she did. But not in the Nelson Arms, the one in Denman Street. It wasn't a fit place for the likes of her. She would need a bit of handling, evidently. She was as chokker as they make them, as blue as cigarette-smoke.

"Look," he said. "We'll meet at the Old Horseshoe first. Then we'll talk about it. Are you ready? I could make it in half an hour. Can you make it? You can? Fine! I'm coming chop-chop." He rang off.

He arrived at the Old Horseshoe dead on time. Marian had not arrived yet. He gave her five minutes, ten minutes. There wasn't too much time. It was nine o'clock already, and he had to break up the evening by going over to the Nelson Arms and giving Jock his pound. He would bring Jock back with him, too, if Jock was in a fit state to talk to a lady, but he didn't think that very likely. "I'd better ring up her flat," he told himself. He rang up, and there was no reply. He gave her another five minutes. Then suddenly he realized what she must have done. He was quite certain of it. She had gone straight over to the Nelson Arms. She was feeling absolutely down-and-out, and she must have made up her mind that the Nelson Arms sounded more like the place she wanted to be in tonight than the comparatively staid Old Horseshoe.

He clapped the money down for his drink, and rushed out. It was quicker to walk than to take a taxi the way the traffic was. He was in the Saloon Bar of the Nelson Arms in less than five minutes. He was absolutely right. There she was, the centre of an animated group of sailors, including the redoubtable Jock Dunbar, who could knock back more pints of beer, or vino, or pastis, or glycerine-and-water from the wheelhouse than any three other members of the crew put together. They were all drunk, and she was as drunk as any of them. Her eyes were not quite straight in their sockets, and her hair was falling all over the place. There was quite a handful of the regular women there, and she looked more like a Denman Street harlot than any of them. They were looking at her sourly, their thin bright mouths pressed tight together. They resented this stranger from another parish poaching on their preserves, and making such a huge success with the matelots, whom women of that sort consider the best of clients, because they are ready to get rid of all the money they have in one smash-up evening, and because they bring so much gusto into their love-making; so much gusto, in fact, that the women are sometime ready to forgo payment, or to postpone it till a time which might not come.

Wally Humphreys, ex-Petty-Officer, rolled in like an outraged walrus. He did not, in fact, have any moustaches, but at that moment you could have sworn they stood out bristling for twelve inches from each side of his face.

"Hello, Wally!" cried Jock delightedly. "Wha' dae ye knaw?"

"Look who's here!" shouted Nobby. "Old Bill Humphreys!"

"Old Bill himself!" shouted Stokes.

Several of the sailors there had met Wally up and down, here and there, across the seven seas, for long-service sailors sooner or later bump into each other *somewhere*, if it is not in Rosyth, it is in Trincomalee, and if it is not in Trincomalee, it is in Singapore or Freetown. The other may not have actually met *that* Wally Humphreys, but they had met some Wally Humphreys exactly like this one.

A shrill feminine voice detached itself from the deeper voices, the voice of Marian Framley

"Here's my love, my pet, my own Wally Humphreys!" She half-rose to her feet, but they slipped down from under her. She sat down again, and reached her hands out. "Come on, Wally dear! You're late!" she cried. "Have a drink!"

Jock was sitting on one side of her, Nobby, or somebody, on the other. Wally gave Nobby a shove that nearly sent him into the bar, and sat down by Marian's side. He was furious, and ashamed, and immensely miserable. What would the Lieutenant-Commander say, he was asking himself, at a sight like this? He felt profoundly guilty, though Heaven knew he was not much to blame. His mistake had been to mention the name of the God-damned pub. She must have been more than half-soused by the time she had got here. It had taken a lot of liquor to get the poor lady into a state like this. Poor dear Mrs. Framley! Something had got hold of her, something had bitten her good and hard to make her this way. Had she suddenly got hold of a mislaid photograph in the pages of a book? Was it some old bunch of letters she had been reading? Poor old Bertie, he hadn't had time to write many letters to anybody, before he was done in. She was talking. She was trying to tell him a story. She couldn't keep the thread of it. She was waving her glass around. Someone filled it from a private rum-bottle produced mysteriously out of the depths of the pair of bell-bottoms. "You're not drinking!" she was saying. "Give him a drink, you!" Then she swung round bleary-eyed to Jock. "You tell him! I can't! Such a funny story! You never heard such a funny story! Bertie would have laughed his head off! Dear Bertie! Sweet Bertie!"

"There now! There!" said Wally, putting his arm round her shoulder to comfort her. "Shall we come out and just have a little breath of air?"

"You tell story. Damn funny story!" she insisted. "If you don't, I'll crown you!" she threatened him with her glass.

Jock started off. It was not a coherent story, but it was funny enough. It was all about a man ashore at a place called Leghorn, and the boys went on to two places called Pisa and Rome. And Jock had seen that Leaning Tower, and they had all had a few wets of vino and some other wine; well in a state of uncon—uncon—in a state of frivolity, they had gone up to the Tower. There was a notice written in every language under old sol, saying "don't ring the bell," so Jock rang it and there was a deafening peal, and people shouted and looked tower-wards, but the copper gave a big grin, and they went to Rome as well, and the Catholics went to see the Pope, and the others went to the pictures, but Jock and his oppo. went to have a few more wets. . . .

By the time that Jock had got to the end of his story, if the story had an end, a long time before that, Marian was asleep on Wally's shoulder, her face flaming-red, her mouth wide-open. Jock was now telling the tale to himself, but the scene had changed to a brothel in Lemnos by now. Jock was too drunk to stop and everybody else was too drunk to stop him.

Everybody but poor Wally Humphreys. He felt very much like crying, but refrained from doing so, because it would have been thought he was drunk, too. But he was not drunk, and he was not going to be. He had a precious burden to look after. Soon, when things quietened down a bit, he could take her out and walk her round a bit, before taking her home in a taxi. It would soon be closing-time, anyway.

Besides Wally Humphreys there was another young man present that night in the Saloon Bar of the Nelson Arms who witnessed this episode with embarrassment and concern. It was a Rhodes Scholar from South Africa, by name Jan Kleewe, an undergraduate from Brazenose now in his second year. He was older than that sounds, for he was already a graduate of Cape Town University. He was a serious young man, and had more than once bought a book at the Easy Chair in Oxford, till the easy manners of Cecilia Burton, one of the partners, had frightened him away. He knew the other partner, Marian Framley, well, for he had met her once or twice at parties, the parties where movements are founded and have no further history.

What Jan Kleewe was doing in the Saloon Bar of the Nelson Arms that evening need not detain us. He may merely have wanted to pick up a woman, which is made exceptionally easy for the diffident in the Nelson Arms. Or he was merely gathering material for some sober fictional study of the Underworld of London. If asked, he would probably have said the second was the reason. The fact is, he was there. There usually *is* someone there, someone who knows who we are, when we behave badly in public places, however obscure we are. And Marian Framley was not as obscure as some. She was the daughter of the head of an Oxford College, which means meeting people, and twice over the guiding spirit of a book-shop which means meeting plenty more.

It can be imagined with what feelings this serious young man from South Africa witnessed the spectacle of a Warden's daughter publicly strumpeting in a notorious pub not many yards from Piccadilly Circus, swigging down mixed potations of gin and rum, and being pawed by a sequence of lusty sailors. The climax was as distressing as anything—the appearance on the scene of the huge *maquereau,* Wally Humphreys, in fact, who immediately asserted possession over her, and was evidently living on her immoral earnings.

The South African did not arrive on the scene till the Warden's daughter was well ensconced in the bosom of the lower deck, with the pints and the shorts, the gins and the bubblies, following each other in rapid succession. He was a Rhodes Scholar, and hefty, but as against that he wore horn-rimmed glasses, without which he was useless. There was a long struggle inside himself as to whether he ought to try and extricate Mrs. Framley from this horde of young satyrs, take her somewhere till she sobered up, then attempt to get to grips with her on the matter of the disgraceful profession she had chosen. She was a lady, and she was Oxford. She was the daughter of the head of a College. Was it nothing to her that when her parents found out, as find out they must, she would bring down their grey hairs in sorrow to the grave?

On the other hand, she seemed a thoroughly lost soul already. And how would the sailors like it if he sought to snatch their prey from their slavering jaws? And what a bore it would be if he lost his horn-rimmed spectacles in a mêlée! None the less, he determined to risk it. He drained off a second glass of beer—he never took more than one, normally —and went straight over to Mrs. Framley.

"Excuse me, Mrs. Framley," he said. "Do you recognize me?"

His heart leapt when he found she did.

"Books!" she cried out. "B.N.C.! *What* a College! Public lavatory! Give him a drink, someone!"

Sailors are very friendly people. At once they sought to rope him into the circle of their festivities, but he managed to extricate himself from the scene, without precipitating their rancour, a difficult thing to do sometimes. "La-di-da!" they say with frigid disapproval, and have been known to bring a pint-pot down upon your head.

The South African then withdrew to the furthest corner of the Saloon Bar, and continued to be a spectator of the lugubrious proceedings. When, finally, the large ex-boxer barman called "Time, gentlemen, please!" for the thirtieth and positively the last, time, Jan Kleewe, always keeping a discreet distance, followed the party of sailors, and the helpless harlot, out into the street, to see what would happen next.

It was exactly as he feared. He saw the large *maquereau* hail a taxi, and drive off somewhere to their love-nest, in the depths of the depraved London night.

CHAPTER XIII

I

It was about eleven-thirty the following morning.

"An undergraduate from Brazenose College to see you, Warden," said the Secretary. "He says it's exceedingly important. He's a Rhodes Scholar. I imagine," she took the responsibility of adding. One ought to try and bear in mind the fraying bonds of Empire.

"Tell him to go away!" said the Warden. "I'm busy!" What was Oxford coming to, when undergraduates, *undergraduates,* from Brazenose College, of all places, thought they could disturb a Warden of St. Stephen's during his meditations.

"In a way of speaking, Warden, I told him to go away, and write for an appointment. Or he could telephone me, I said. He said he had come specially from London to see you. He *must* see you, he said."

"Up from London?" Fear gripped the Warden's heart. "Did he tell you what it was about?" Had Marian's assistant stolen all the cash and bolted? Had he perhaps murdered her? "Bring him in at once!" he ordered.

The young man from South Africa was brought in. The Secretary went out. The Warden kept his eyes glued on the papers before him, then he raised them. The interval was to give him time to make of his face the mask it usually was.

"Yes?" he said. "Sit down." He waved to a chair.

The young man did not sit down, he was evidently in a very nervous condition.

"Well, sir? What is it?" the Warden shouted. He was rarely so ill-mannered as this. "Who are you?"

"My name's Jan Kleewe, sir, from Brazenose. I'm a Rhodes Scholar. You must forgive me."

"Nothing to forgive," said the Warden, his heart thumping away. "Will you tell me what you've come for? I understand you've come up specially from London."

"Yes, sir. I was in the Saloon Bar of a place called the Nelson Arms last night——"

The Warden banged his fist down on the table.

"Will you spare me the history of your debased frequentations? What do you wish to tell me? Does it concern a member of my family?"

"As a matter of fact, it does, sir."

There was dead silence for some moments. Perhaps the fellow had come in with the story of Matthew's latest chicanery, in which he had somehow got himself involved, and had come to ask him, the elder brother, for some redress. Perhaps it was not Matthew. Perhaps it was Marian, after all.

"Which one?" the Warden asked. "Which member of my family?" His voice was very quiet now, almost inaudible.

"Your elder daughter, sir. Her name's Mrs. Framley, I think."

"Yes? What have you to tell me about her?" The Warden's knuckles on the table before him were as white as wax.

"Dr. Browne, I wish I hadn't got to tell you this, I wish there was some possibility of my being mistaken. But I've thought the matter over till late in the night, and I didn't see how I can possibly be. You'll make your inquiries, of course. But I'm proud to be a member of this ancient

University, and I'm a Christian, and I've felt myself compelled to take this step."

"Is my daughter well, or is she not well?" the Warden asked, in a rising tone. The young man opened his mouth, perhaps to explain that that was an ambiguous question. "Quiet!" said the Warden, though the young man had not said anything. "Will you kindly say exactly what is in your mind? You need not think of sparing me."

"Very well, sir. It was like this."

The young man from South Africa proceeded to tell the Warden exactly how it was, or how it had seemed to him that it was. His narrative petered out, like the last drops from a water-tap. Then there was silence for a minute or two. By this time the Warden sat half-turned away from the young man. His hand was over his eyes.

"Is there anything more you wish to say? Is there anything more you recall?" He did not remove his hand.

"No, sir. That's all I can remember. It was all very confused. I hope you'll forgive me, Dr. Browne. I think you'd have acted the way I did in similar circumstances. Isn't that so, sir?"

"Thank you, Mr. Kleewe. It must have been very painful for you, too. I am very grateful to you. Will you please go now?"

Without a further word, the young man tip-toed to the door, opened it, and walked out.

II

Almost an hour later the Warden rose from the chair where he had till now sat unmoving as a stone, and touched the bell which summoned the Secretary. She came in. He took care to keep his face averted from her as he addressed her.

"Is Miss Anna in to lunch today, Miss Burnley? Is she in already?"

"I'll find out at once. I believe she is."

"Will you ask her to come to me straight away? Please tell Mrs. Browne to hold over lunch till I say I'm ready."

"Certainly, Warden." The Secretary went out. Three minutes later, Anna came in.

"What's the matter, Daddy? You look like death. You wanted to see me?"

"Please sit down. I'm not feeling very well. I want you to bear with me."

There was a seriousness in his voice which was not of the pontifical sort she was thoroughly familiar with. He looked ghastly. Her own stomach began to turn over inside her.

"What is it, Daddy? Please sit down." He did not sit down.

"I hoped this moment wouldn't come, Anna. But it's come, and I've got to face up to it. So have you, my child."

"Please, Daddy, don't keep me in suspense." She had her handkerchief out of her handbag, and was twisting it till it looked like chewed string. "What is it all about? Is it about me and Clifford?"

"It is, of course, as you guess. But for the moment it's more about Marian . . . and Clifford's brother."

"What on earth are you trying to say, Daddy? Has he tried to rape her or something?"

He turned sharp round to contemplate for a moment this child, his own child, who talked with such fantastic and dreadful flippancy.

"No," the Warden said. "I should imagine not."

"I should think so, indeed. You don't know Marian. She'd clout anyone over the head with a flat-iron. Rape, indeed!"

"I never thought any such thing, or used any such word. Will you control yourself and listen to what I have to say?" His voice and manner were extremely grave. It would be as well to respect them. "I had a visitor today, an undergraduate from another college, but a mature man, not a boy. He is, in fact, a Rhodes Scholar."

"Yes?" She was not impressed.

"He came in to describe a scene he witnessed last night. Yes, only last night, in one of the most depraved public-houses, I was given to understand, in London's West End. He had considerable difficulty in telling me what happened. I will have a good deal more. But I have no alternative. It is my duty to repeat the young man's report, as far as I can bring myself to, before my daughter, and a daughter so young as you are."

"Only one thing, Daddy."

"Yes!"

"Did the young man *have* to come telling stories of a girl's night out?"

"Night out, you call it! *Night out!*" His voice rose angrily. "Well, you shall judge for yourself. I will ask you if *you* wouldn't have felt yourself forced to come and tell me about it, if by some terrible freak of fate *you* had happened to be in that place."

"Daddy, all I can say is, Marian's the straightest, cleanest, loveliest woman in the whole world. Anybody who says anything about her is a mealy-mouthed pussyfoot, a spy, and a liar!" Her cheeks were bright red. Her eyes sparkled angrily.

"Will you be quiet!" her father roared at her. "I told you, I will tolerate no interruptions! Listen! This is what happened!" He went on to give her, now at second-hand, an account of the party at the Nelson Arms. The rims of his ears were fiery-hot as he spoke. Sometimes his lips quivered so uncontrollably, he was almost unintelligible. Clearly the man was beside himself. At last the account came to an end. Suddenly all the fury which had been accumulated within him seemed to leave him, like the air from a great gash cut at one stroke in an inner tube.

"Well, Anna," he breathed. "Was the young man right to come and tell me? Tell me, Anna"—he looked beseechingly into his daughter's eyes—"wouldn't you have come to me yourself if you had witnessed all this?"

She hesitated a little time before answering.

Then: "Tell me, Daddy," she said. "Do you really want to know what I think? Or have you now so completely made up your mind on the matter that there's no point in my saying anything at all?"

"Of course I want to know what you think," he replied. "Well?"

"I think Marian was feeling blue yesterday, for one reason or another, probably connected with poor old Bertie. If anyone knows her in these blue moods, it's Robert and me. Nobody else. And she won't let even us be in on them if she can possibly help it. So my view is she took a nip or two in her own flat after work——"

"You mean, you *know* she drinks on her own, in her own flat?"

"People do, sometimes. They either drink at their own place, or someone else's. Last night she went to someone else's. A pub, in fact. The nip or two at home didn't do her any good. So she went to a pub, and there she fell in with a bunch of sailors. So they all got pickled. And that's all there is to it. That's *my* view of the thing, Daddy."

His eyes stared glassily out at her.

"You mean you *condone* such conduct as this?" he shouted.

"I'm not condoning, Daddy, I'm explaining," she said, wearily.

"And you can explain why she was lying there shamelessly drunk in the arms of a man? You can explain why she went off with him when the orgy was over, in a . . . *taxi*?" He used the word "taxi" as if it were a word one normally sees written on lavatory walls.

"I should imagine it was one of the sailors in civilian clothes," she said. "And he was just seeing her home to see nothing happened to her."

"And that's your explanation, is it? *Is* it, I ask you?"

"Yes," she said. She might as well say "yes." For, in fact, it was.

"Well, it isn't *mine*!" he shouted. "It isn't *mine*! I'll tell you what my explanation is!" From phrase to phrase his voice spiralled higher and higher. It was a good thing that it was vacation, and the rooms adjoining the Warden's house were empty. There was no doubt his wife could hear him, and his secretary, and anyone else in the house. "My explanation is: you can't touch pitch without being defiled. Your sister's seen fit to consort with a gutter-rat for I don't know how long, and a criminal gutter-rat, and now she's crawling in the gutter herself. I wanted to warn her, but I failed to do so. May God forgive me! I told myself she's a grown-up woman and she knows what she's doing. Now we all know what she's doing. She goes into the public-houses of the West End, and gets drunk, and picks up men. I'm not going to let you go that way. Do you hear me? No. I know what you want to say. Keep quiet! You're going to say that this Eckersley is a different sort of a person, just as I'm different from Matthew. That's true! But Matthew's got gentle blood in his veins, however warped and twisted his mind is. This Eckersley's from the same gutter as his brother. If you insist on consorting with Eckersley, you'll go the same way as your sister. Once and for all now! I forbid you to have anything more to do with Clifford Eckersley. You may go! Do you hear? Get out!"

By the time he had come to an end his face was bright red. The sweat was running continuously from his forehead, down his nose and cheeks. His breath came in short gasps, like a boxer who has had a gruelling time in the ring against a fierce opponent.

Anna had risen from her chair. She said nothing. She just stood there and stared incredulously, as if a man had masqueraded as her father, and imitated his voice, and used his tricks of speech. He went away from her, his right hand winnowing the air as if it sought something. His hand came to rest on the back of a chair.

Then he stopped and listened, perhaps for the sound of an opening door. He heard nothing. Then he turned.

"You heard me?" he asked. "Let me be!"

"No, Father," she said. "I'm afraid I can't do as you say." Her voice was low and quiet. He turned his head to her, as if he genuinely had not heard.

"What did you say?"

"We've discussed this before, Father. I won't give Clifford up. I love him."

The Warden sat down as if otherwise he would have fallen down. She heard him speaking, not to her but to himself, and he was almost inaudible.

"I can't. Years and years! My own daughters! I can't stand it any longer! All these years!"

She observed there was a bubble of spittle at the side of his mouth. The bright red of his face was purple now, streaked with fine white lines. She saw his head fall helplessly to one side. A moment later he had fallen sideways off the chair on to the carpet, his head narrowly missing the edge of a revolving bookcase. The chair went with him.

"Daddy!" she cried. "Daddy! Daddy!" She flew over to him and raised his head, and, finding a cushion within reach, propped the head up with it. She loosened the collar and chafed his hands, then looked wildly towards the closed door. "Mummy! Miss Burnley!" Then, at last, the door opened. It was her mother, and the Secretary close behind her.

"Darling! What is it?" cried Mrs. Browne. "*Henry!*" She was over beside him, feeling for his pulse, pulling back the eyelid. But he was alive. The breath came and went in short puffs. The Secretary ran out, came back with ammonia, a bowl of water, a decanter of brandy.

"Fetch a doctor! *Do* something, Anna!" cried Mrs. Browne. "Oh, how could you? Your own poor father!" she wailed. "What have you been saying to him?"

But it seemed as if the Warden would be all right, with a doctor or without. The face was resuming its natural colour again, the breath was steadying in his windpipe and lungs.

"I'll telephone," said Anna. "Dr. Carew will be here in a few minutes. If not Dr. Carew, somebody else."

"You stand there talking about doctors," Mrs. Browne moaned. "What happened? Is nobody going to tell me?"

"Father asked me to give up Clifford Eckersley. I said I wouldn't, and this is what happened." Her voice was cool and contemptuous. "Well, I will. I'll do what he says. I see I have to. You can tell him that when he comes to himself. I'll telephone . . . then, after that, is there anything else you want me to do, either of you?"

Her mother said nothing. The Warden's weight was heavy against her chest.

"We'll manage," said the Secretary. "I think perhaps you ought to go and lie down."

"Very well," said Anna. She telephoned from the extension in the sitting-room, and learned that Dr. Carew was at home and would be on his way immediately. Then she went into her own room and locked the door.

She hated her father, as she had never hated anyone before. She thought she had learned all his tricks, but found now she was mistaken. If he did not get what he wanted, he had now showed he could throw a fit, wholly convincing because it was entirely genuine.

If she did not give up the boy she loved, he would take one final trick out of the bag. He would die, quite deliberately and, of course, irreparably. She could not allow that to be on her conscience, nor could she allow it to be on Clifford's. He had had a bad time, the old man, and she was sorry for him, though she hated him. From now on she would always hate him.

Perhaps, when her father died, Clifford might still love her, as she was certain she would still love him. And, in that case, they might get married. But probably it would be a long time from now. The heads of Oxford Colleges are a long-lived species. It was a sad and an unjust thing for the young to sacrifice themselves to the old. But the young had their youth, if there was any consolation in that.

Precious little, to see the way the small face twisted, to hear the dry sobs that shook that frail and lovely body.

Some time later, half an hour or so, she took her writing-pad, and wrote a note to be delivered by the Porter at Bullingdon Road, as soon as his errands took him round that way.

III

Excitements were not over for the day at the Warden's House in St. Stephen's College, though this particular excitement was kept dark by the Secretary till the people whom it concerned more than it concerned her were more in a state to learn about it.

At about half-past three in the afternoon the telephone-bell rang, and the Secretary answered it. Mrs. Browne was with the Warden in their bedroom, Anna was in hers.

"Is that the Warden's House at St. Stephen's?" a man's voice asked.

"It is."

"Who is that, please?"

"This is the Warden's Secretary. Who are you, please?"

"My name is Dr. Senior, from Witney. May I speak to the Warden, please?"

"I'm afraid not, Doctor. He's quite unwell. He had some sort of heart-attack. Is there anything I can do?"

"And the Warden's wife?"

"If it's at all serious, it would be better if I handled it, Doctor."

"Very well. I'm speaking from Hatchetts. You know the house, don't you?"

"I know about it. Yes?"

"Mr. Matthew Browne lives here. He is—I understand, the brother of the Warden."

"That is so." She wondered why it was a doctor telephoning, not a policeman. One had expected a policeman would be ringing sooner or later.

"Mr. Matthew Browne has been attacked with a dangerous instrument, a chisel. He has been seriously injured."

"I'm very sorry, Doctor," the Secretary said primly. She was not very sorry at all. She knew enough about the Warden's brother to know that whatever injuries he had received he had richly deserved. "Is it known who attacked him?" She was not really very interested. Doubtless one of his prison associates had a grudge against him, and thought a chisel a good way to settle it.

"Oh, yes," the Doctor said. "It was his wife. The manservant overpowered her and called in both the police and myself."

"The police?"

"Yes. They knew Mr. Browne is the brother of Dr. Browne of St. Stephen's. So did I, for that matter. But I don't think the police will take the matter any further. Mr. Browne is not likely to press a charge."

"No."

"The matter's now in my hands. I wanted to get in touch with someone who can help Mrs. Browne. At first she refused to say a word. All her own people seem to have disowned her long ago. Then finally she brought out something about a certain Marian. That's the Warden's daughter, isn't it?"

"Yes. What happened, doctor?" Then she had her pad at the telephone as if she were taking out notes about some furniture that was to be delivered.

"He was obviously very drunk, and apparently he insulted her. Perhaps not for the first time. She went for his face and made a pretty bad mess of it. She seems to have made a dead set for the beard. She had been drinking, too. May I take it you will contact Miss Browne?"

"Mrs. Framley, the name is. I will."

"Thank you. This is my telephone number."

The Secretary wrote it down on her pad and replaced the receiver.

IV

It was about two hours later, and tea was coming to an end at Clifford Eckersley's rooms in Bullingdon Road. Miss Thexted's last "hotter" had been eaten, there was no more raspberry jam in the pot, and the tea was thin and cold, with the tea-leaves floating around like bacilli on a slide.

"Well, thanks for tea, Clifford," Robert Browne was saying. "Up to the best Thexted standard. Say that quick, Clifford. Best Thexted standard."

"Mrs. Clifford Eckersley will do better," Clifford assured him with a smile. "Can't I squeeze one more cup out of the pot? Just one more?"

"I hate to say no. *Such* tea. *So* much sugar. All the milk you want. But I've got things to do. And it's family dinner tonight. So long, Clifford. Thanks again. Don't forget tomorrow. After lunch, two o'clock. And I'll bring my gramophone."

"I'm not so sure of that. Ought people to play gramophones on the river? Is it kind? Is it decent?"

"You can bring *your* records and I'll bring mine. You'll have Palestrina, I'll have Bing Crosby. Fair's fair. And you ought to give yourself a break, Clifford."

"Very well, Robert. Where shall we meet? Magdalen? There was a knock on the front door. Mrs. Thexted came up from the room at the back of the house to open it. One heard a word or two, then the door was closed again. There was a knock on Clifford's door.

"Come in!"

Mrs. Thexted entered, holding out a letter.

"From College, Mr. Eckersley," she said. "The College Porter. He was not to wait for a reply."

"Thank you," Clifford said, and took the note. "Hello! It's Anna's writing What's this in aid of?" He opened the envelope. "I suppose she's suddenly got tickets for that show. She said she'd try for returns." Then he read the note, which went as follows:

Dearest Clifford,

I wish I was dead. It has happened. The Warden has beaten us. You will never forgive me, but there is nothing else I can do. Somebody came up from London and said they saw Marian drunk in a pub. I suppose she was. You know she has bad times. He said other things, and I am ashamed to tell you what. So Father called me, and said it was through having people like your brother round her. Then he said the same would happen to me, and said I must give you up. I told him what I thought of him, then he crumpled up and had a heart-attack. I am quite sure he wanted to have the heart-attack, but there it is. He has become quite a madman about the whole thing. I suppose the terrible strain of the Matthew business has a lot to do with it. I am slap sure that if I do not break it off with you, it will kill him. I mean just that. It will kill him, and I will be responsible. He will not live for ever, but you will have stopped thinking about me long ago. Try not to hate me too much. I love you. I will never love anyone else.

Good-bye, my darling,

from yours,

Anna.

Clifford read the letter but did not raise his eyes. Good-bye, my darling. From yours, Anna. From yours, Anna. From yours, Anna. It was like a gramophone record with the needle catching. With one immense effort he lifted the needle away from the obstruction, and thrust his eyes upwards towards the beginning of the letter. Dearest Clifford. I wish I was dead. It has happened. It has happened. It has happened. The needle was caught again. He let the record fall to the ground. It did not break. It was paper, not wax.

"Clifford, old boy," he heard his friend whisper from a long way off. "What's gone wrong? What does she say? Can I read it?"

Clifford's tongue was thick and dry and he could hardly move it.

"Yes," he brought out, and pointed to the letter where it had fallen on the floor. Robert stooped and lifted it. Then he looked at Clifford again.

"Sure you want me to read it?" he asked.

Clifford nodded.

"Read it."

Robert read the letter and put it down on the table. For a long time he said nothing. Then he spoke.

"We can't stand for this. It's absolute nonsense. I'll talk to her."

"*Please,*" begged Clifford. He found some saliva in the recesses of his mouth, and sent it round, so that it should be possible for him to speak. "Don't you see it's no good? Don't you see, if she could write like this, it's all over? Please leave her alone. It's bad enough for her already. Please leave me, too, now. Will you, Robert?"

"How can I leave you like this, Clifford? I'm your friend, aren't I?"

Clifford spoke, but he did not answer the question. His mind was not with his friend, but with someone closer to him, in the bond of blood, at least.

"I knew it would happen that day I saw him, in the Front Quad. there. We were so happy, Anna and you and I. He'd been chasing me all those years, and then he stopped chasing me." He turned to his friend. "What did I do, Robert, that he should do this to me?" Then once more he seemed to be talking to himself. "It's all over. There isn't any sun in the sky."

"Clifford!"

There was no reply.

"Clifford!"

He shook his head, as if shaking off a sleep he was falling into.

"Yes, Robert?"

"Come out! I'll get a car! I'll drive like mad! It'll take you out of yourself!"

"No, no, no!" Clifford pleaded. "I want only to be quiet."

"Yes, of course," Robert agreed. "You want the river, the quiet of the river. The willows trailing in the water." He nodded his head as if the suggestion of the river came from Clifford. "A good idea, Clifford old boy! Why don't we go out and get a punt or a canoe? We won't take the gramophone, if you'd rather not. No. You can just be quiet. We'll have a drink somewhere on the river. What about it, Clifford? Would you like to change? Oh, no. It'll be all right in grey flannels, and we'll take our coats off." He waited. "Yes, Clifford?" He looked with mournful anxiety into his eyes.

"Tomorrow!" said Clifford. "Please! Tomorrow! Let me be by myself today!"

"Very well, Clifford. When would you like me to come? In the afternoon? Or before lunch, and we could have lunch on the river?" He kept on repeating it. The river. The river. Like an incantation.

"The afternoon, Robert, I think!"

"Oh, listen, Clifford!"

"Yes?"

"Why don't we get hold of Marian and find out what really happened in London?"

Clifford smiled wanly.

"Do you really think that has much to do with it?"

Robert could not bring himself to answer the question, though he knew what the answer was.

"Well, I'll go now," he said. "Tomorrow, at two." He opened the door, and went, leaving behind him the heart-broken boy, and the smooth ceramic masks glaring eyeless from the walls.

V

It was not a gay household that Robert came back to. The doctor had ordered the Warden to bed, Mrs. Browne moved from room to room, moaning, and wringing her hands, and Anna was in her rooms with a bad headache.

"Anna! It's me! Can I come in?"

A very faint voice:

"Yes, Robert, if you wish to."

Robert came in. Anna was lying on her bed, her face blotched with weeping. She turned her head away as Robert came in.

"Robert, you've not come to tell me what a swine I am?"

"No, Anna, I don't see what else you can do."

She turned her head towards him for a brief moment and flashed at him a smile in which she conveyed all she felt of love and gratitude for his flawless understanding.

"There's one thing I've got to tell you," she said. She was more in control of her voice now."

"Not anything *more*?"

"They've rung up Miss Burnley."

"Who have?"

"The doctor!"

"What about? No! Nothing wrong with Marian?" His heart almost stopped beating.

"No! It's Uncle Matthew this time. Dear Uncle Matthew! Aunt Edith has had enough. She got up in the middle of the night and——" Suddenly laughter took possession of her. She was hooting like a drunken owl. He waited patiently. Young though he was, he knew how people suffering from profound grief suddenly break down this way with an almost lunatic laughter. The laughter died down. At last Anna could speak again. She felt round for her handkerchief and wiped away her tears. "Aunt Edith got up in the middle of the night," the girl repeated, "and hacked off his Vandyke beard with a chisel. He'll never be so pretty to look at again. Ha, ha, ha! Ha, ha, ha! Oh, dear! How awful!"

"Is Aunt Edith all right?"

"We've sent for Marian."

"Of course. When's she coming?"

"She arrives at two tomorrow afternoon."

"Oh, damn!"

"What is it?"

"I've got a date I must keep. Tell her I'll come along as soon as I can make it."

"I'll tell her. Robert!"

"Yes?"

"Thank you, Robert! I don't feel so bad now."

"Shall I stay?"

"Just stay. But don't talk. Read a book."

"Yes, Anna." He looked round and picked up a book and pretended to read it. She had done the same thing for him in her time, when he had needed the reassurance of her presence by his side.

VI

At two o'clock as arranged, Robert shining in flannels arrived at Bullingdon Road. He had sweets, because he and Clifford both liked sweets. He had cigarettes, because Clifford liked cigarettes, and it was quite likely Clifford would forget his cigarettes. He had no bathing-costume, because, though he himself adored bathing, Clifford apparently detested it. Anyhow, he never went bathing in public places. It was a perfect afternoon for a bathe, but it was not the sort of afternoon on which Robert wanted to do anything that meant leaving Clifford out of it.

"Hello! What's this?" cried Robert, as he entered Clifford's sitting-room. Clifford was sitting in a chair, no book before him, not even a cigarette in his mouth.

"Hello!" said Clifford, raising lack-lustre eyes. The lids were heavy and swollen. He had obviously not slept much.

"This won't do!" proclaimed Robert. "You've got a date!"

"Have I?" asked Clifford.

"You *know* you have! And I've scratched one with Greta Gynt specially to come out with you. Come on! This isn't going to get you anywhere. Get out of that chair! You've not *really* forgotten, have you?"

But Clifford had really forgotten.

"We're going canoeing, you fixed it yourself! Get cracking!"

Clifford rose. He looked down at his sports-coat and flannels.

"Shall I change?" he asked.

"Just as you like," said Robert.

Clifford changed. That already did something to him. They went down to the boat-house and stood for a moment meditating what sort of craft to take out.

"A punt?" asked Robert. "Then you can take it easy."

"No," Clifford said, as Robert thought he would. "Let's take a canoe each." Clifford had always liked canoeing better than punting, for, being no athlete, and pretending a mild contempt for athletics, canoeing none the less gave him an appearance of not being totally useless with his body. He was really quite dexterous with a canoe, and would like to forge quickly ahead in sudden minnowy flashes or by sharply back-watering bring the canoe to an almost dead stop, as near as might be to a braked bicycle.

They thrust off from the bank and paddled along side by side in silence for a minute or two.

"All right?" asked Robert at length.

"All right," Clifford said. Certainly no stranger would have perceived from his expression that the young man was racked with heart-break. Although he could handle a canoe tolerably well, it meant a fair degree of concentration. A butterfly dickered towards the bank across their bows.

"Look!" Clifford cried. "A Clouded Yellow!"

"No!" maintained Robert, though he rather thought it *was* a Clouded Yellow. It was with Anna he usually conducted his arguments, not with Clifford, who had a habit of being right on matters like this. But today he thought it wouldn't be at all a bad thing to argue with Clifford. "I saw it first!" he exclaimed. "It wasn't a Clouded Yellow! It was a Painted Lady!"

"It wasn't at all," insisted Clifford. "It had fewer spots than the Painted Lady has, and they were bigger and yellower, too."

"Very well," said Robert. Have it your own way! But it wasn't, you know!" They compromised by hurling a slap of water at each other, and paddled on.

The minutes went by, the butterflies flickered among the spiky blooms of willow-herb, the water-wagtails rose abruptly into the air, and dropped down again among the tree-roots, their black and white tails twinkling. A small dark water-bird came darting out of a covert of reeds, jerked zig-zag this way and that, and went back where he came from.

"Pretty creatures, coots!" said Robert.

"Yes, aren't they!" Clifford agreed. It was, in fact, a moorhen, but he was getting a little tired, too tired to argue. Robert at once spotted the fatigue in his voice. At the best of times, Clifford did not have the strength to maintain a physical effort for long, even a suave one, like canoeing.

"Let's tie up, shall we?" Robert suggested. He knew that

Clifford would not make the suggestion himself. He was of the sort that goes on till it drops.

"Yes, I'd like to," agreed Clifford. "I might even shut the old eyes for half an hour or so." After all, he had not had much sleep last night. A little drowse in the warm afternoon, among the reeds, in the green twilight of the weeping-willow branches, would be helpful.

"Me, too," said Robert, though he felt quite fresh. "It won't do me any harm, either." But the great thing was it was doing Clifford quite a lot of good. Robert looked at his watch. Yes, Marian would have arrived some time ago. She would have quite a lot to handle, and very capable she was of handling it, too. There was no hurry. He didn't quite see what use he could be helping to straighten out the worm that had at last turned, if that wasn't a harsh way to describe Aunt Edith: and an inadequate way, too, for worms don't go about hacking off beards with chisels. He could safely leave Marian to it, for another hour or two, anyhow. He felt he was doing a good job with Clifford.

"Shall we tie up here, Clifford" he called out. "It's nice and shady!" But Clifford was not visible. "Hello, Clifford! Where are you!" he called out.

"I'm inside here," came back the voice of Clifford. "The canoe just drifted in. Where are you, Robert?"

"I coasted downstream a bit. I'll be with you in a minute."

He back-watered towards the sound of Clifford's voice and found him ensconced there, deep among the reeds, his rope tied to the roots of an elder. He followed suit, and tied his own rope to a root not many yards away. So they settled down and talked for a while, on quite a number of subjects and people, excepting the one person they both had uppermost in their minds. Gradually their voices failed. To talk seemed merely convention, while the water did the talking for you, not to mention the faint sound there was among the reeds. If that wasn't enough—splash, that was a water-vole. There were birds here and there—a pigeon or two, crooning musically in the denser tree-tops, a little distance away the muted midsummer voice of a blackbird, suddenly, somewhere, quite alone, a robin twittering, the way a robin suddenly strikes up again, late in August.

"Let him shut his eyes a bit," Robert said to himself. "They'll be open again tonight, and maybe the night after, and many a night to come. But his misery will pass. He's young and, God help us, the old man's old. Clifford will be Clifford again."

He allowed his own eyes to close after all, it was so warm and comforting inside there, the water chuckling and the twigs and leaves coming from up river, and fallen petals of ragged robin and brooklime and forget-me-not winding round among the reeds till they touched the side of the canoe, and for a moment or two they stayed with you, then they went on again, winding through the reeds, into open water again. And at last, sooner or later, they were out in the broader river. And then it was meadows on each side, with cows standing in them, and the edge of the river gay with marsh marigolds. Then there were houseboats beside the river; and bridges over it. The towns were bigger. But still these small leaves and twigs, these fallen petals of ragged robin and brooklime and forget-me-not, retained their minute identities even in the surge of a river now grown noble, one of earth's great rivers: and it had all started here in a backwater of the Cherwell, and they came, the twigs and the leaves, and the petals winding round among the reeds, till they touched the side of your canoe, and stayed with you, and went on again. . . . And my own thoughts, he said to himself, are like the twigs and the leaves and the petals. And they are like the water which has carried them, and has become the great river; and yet they are the same small stream, with the willow-branches hanging down, and the reeds all about you. . .

Then Robert heard a splash as something of some weight slipped down into the water. It was not a branch falling. It was not a water-vole slipping out of his den in the bank. Because he knew exactly what it was, and because the knowledge was terrible beyond words, for a period of time which cannot have been more than a second or two, he allowed himself to say to himself it was a branch, it was a water-vole; or perhaps some dog had come down into the water from the meadow; or someone was bathing somewhere beyond the thicket.

But he knew it was none of these things. He dared at last to turn his head. Clifford's canoe was there, of course, for it was tethered to the tree-roots. But Clifford was not there.

"Clifford!" he cried out in terror. "Clifford! Clifford!"

There was no reply. How could there be from the depths of the thick water? And why should Clifford reply, when he had made up his mind, there in the dark night of his soul under the bitter willow-branches, to call out to no-one ever again, and never to answer if anyone called.

In an instant Robert had heeled over from his own canoe, and was thrusting through muddy water and the soggy pulp of leaves towards where Clifford, on the stream's bottom, clung to a root down there with all the pertinacity which friends had admired and enemies deplored, all his young years. But this time, with the heart thumping and thundering, and with the eyeballs exploding in the sockets, it needed a far more desperate resolution to hold firm, than ever was needed before.

No, Robert could not pull him free. He rose to the surface for air, and cried "Help! Help!" for he knew that here was a task he could not achieve unaided, and he would very surely need help himself.

Once more, he struggled in the depths down there, but Clifford's hands round the under-water roots were as hard and gnarled as the roots themselves. It had been enough, and too much for him. I have lost my dear, I have lost my dear. That was the bitterness in the hollow of the tongue, and the grit between the teeth. I have lost my dear. I will not live without her. It was like thunder rolling among the mountain-tops, the heart behind the ribs, thumping, thudding. Then there was a sweet thought; a sweet sound, oozing through the ear-drums like a dribble of warm honey. It is a long way from her, but it is a long way from him, too. Down here he will not be able to find me, my loving brother. Down here he cannot find me, cannot find me, ever again . . . can . . . not . . . find . . . me.

Now Robert had come up for the third time, and had gone down again, and even if he thought to give up the attempt to disentangle Clifford's hands from the roots, he could not any more have disentangled himself from the snaky, slimy weeds. His strength was gone. He, too, remained under the water now, and did not rise.

But the cry for "Help!" had been heard, for the Cherwell in these reaches is not an unfrequented stream. Some holiday-makers in a punt, and in a second punt, came up, and saw the two empty canoes. There were hefty young men among them, who went to work at once. Robert was landed quickly; Clifford was a harder job, the hands were so tightly knotted to the roots they held.

It was possible with hard work to bring Robert to life again. But not Clifford.

CHAPTER XIV

I

By the time that day was ended, Marian Framley found she had a great deal more to do than handle the matter of her unfortunate Aunt Edith, not to mention her unfortunate Uncle Matthew (for it is no small thing to have your face hacked open with a chisel when your good looks are a great part of your stock in trade). It is not the novelist's purpose to expound grief for its own sake, unless the grief is dynamic, and impels his story into fresh courses. But Anna's grief for Clifford, and Robert's grief for Clifford, led nowhere, except to a more deadly dislike for their father than they, or he, had known before.

In the face of calamity on such a scale as this, the Warden's wife showed herself surprisingly courageous. One realized with surprise that it might well be from the mother that Marian inherited some of her most valuable qualities, rather than the father, though he had gone so far in the gratification of his academic ambitions.

But Marian was admirable, as might have been anticipated. If anyone could see Anna through the thorny wood of grief, in which she was tangled and lost, it was Marian. If anyone could edge Aunt Edith into a nursing-home, rather than into any gloomier institution, it was Marian. For Robert, and for all of them (including the poor Eckersleys, who had come up from Lancashire), she made the ordeal of Clifford's inquest, and the weeks that followed, less intolerable than they might have been. With two people, however, her exertions were less heroic. She hoped her father might at last learn, at this most grievous cost, that one does not meddle in the love-lives of one's offspring, for, if one intends to, one might as well not have produced them. Also she did nothing at all to mitigate Uncle Matthew's sense of outrage that his wife, to whom for so many years he had been so loyal and devoted, could turn upon him in this highly unpleasant way; nor did she seek to console him for the irreparable damage that had been done to that beard which had so bemused her, on the fatal night when she had gone down to Hatchetts to hand over to him the table-napkins he had asked for, the night when she had first met Tommy Smith, the night from which all these consequences flowed.

For, of course, Tommy Smith was tied up in these events, in all of them. She did not intend to let the matter go by, so far as she and he were concerned. He was going to be told exactly how she viewed the situation, and in her view it was Tommy Smith, no one else, who was ultimately responsible for the death of Clifford Eckersley.

She did not expect it to do any good to Tommy Smith. The shock of the death of Clifford put everything in a clearer light for her, and she determined that Smith was going to see everything as clear. She remembered with disgust that she had been weakening in her attitude towards the ex-convict. She had suffered a disappointment and a humiliation far beyond anything she had known. It had made her behave, on the evening of the day when she had thrust Tommy Smith from her door, like a sailor's doxy, in a low pub. Yes, she was, apparently, an incurable sentimentalist. Smith's words during their last conversation kept on coming back to her again and again: *I had to do it. I had to do it.* She had heard those accents of compulsion before. "Why did you send presents of stolen money to your brother?" she had asked him. "I had to do it," the reply had been. "I had to do it. I had to do it."

Was there, in fact, some secret compulsion which, with a little more patience, and faith in her own theories and ideals, she might have stumbled against? Had she made the whole course only to shy ingloriously at the last fence? Oh, what arrant nonsense all that had been shown to be! The fact was that, in the day of hang-over that followed the sailors' party, and the days of gloom that had followed that, she had begun to slip into a slough of rank sentiment, and shocking frivolity—for those excuses and palliatives could not be conceived as anything but sentimental and frivolous now.

When she could decently get away from Oxford, she must find a way to dig out Tommy Smith from whatever rat-hole he might be hiding in—unless he was out in the country now, promoted to Flight-Lieutenant after his grounding in the humanities in Theobald's Road. She would dig him out and give him his family news. It was quite likely that he would get it from no other source. She knew that he did not read newspapers, and therefore had probably missed the newspaper accounts. No one else would give the news to him, for, as far as she was aware, no one else knew that the drowned Oxford student, Clifford Eckersley, was his brother—except Matthew Browne, who, when he recovered, was not likely to be very communicative, and, even if he spoke, was not likely to be very intelligible.

No. It was her duty, and in a certain monstrous way, it would be her pleasure, to give to Tommy Smith the news of what had happened to the brother he had loved so much.

After a couple of weeks, she felt she could safely leave the family for a few days, at least. Her mother had shown herself astonishingly brave and Miss Burnley, the Secretary, was a tower of strength. She could attend to her own affairs for a short time with a good conscience. She had lately been lucky over at Theobald's Road. (She felt it was high time that in that region a bit of luck came to her.) A couple of days after the debacle, a young lady came in, one Alice Moore, an ex-Roedean girl, who had not the least idea that this was the shop of an old friend, the Marian Browne that had been. Alice Moore's husband had gone off to Kenya. He was, apparently, not the sort of husband you go to Putney with, let alone to Kenya. Alice Moore was at a loose end. Marian invited her then and there, to come and join her in the bookshop. She was thrilled to come in and learn the ropes at once.

She took over gallantly when Marian was summoned to Oxford. Somehow she was carrying on now. She might even come in on some sort of partnership basis later on, for Marian now realized that it was not the idea of partnership that had been wrong in Oxford, so much as Cecilia the partner.

So Marian went back to London. She found Alice Moore had been carrying on admirably. Nothing could be more pleasing. But it was after other game than Alice Moore that Marian had come to London, gun in hand.

She knew exactly how she was going to find Tommy Smith, if he was to be found in London at all. One person would know, for he knew everything. That evening she went down to Speakers' Corner at Marble Arch. It was a bright gay evening, and the Speakers were all in good form, including Uncle Dawkins, the black-coated, carnation-wearing, religious leader, or Frankie the Toff, as others knew him. She hung about on the outskirts of his congregation and joined in the singing as lustily as the next. When the meeting was over, and he was about to stride off on his long shanks into the mysterious world he dwelt in, she went up to him, and pulled his coat-tails. He turned round, the automatic snarl on his face. The snarl was replaced by an almost as disturbing smile, when he perceived it was an attractive young woman who had sought him out. Then the smile was succeeded by a look of apprehension as he recognized who the young woman actually was, the young woman who had been Tommy Smith's employer.

"Good evening, ma'am," he said, a little diffidently. "Very pleased to see you, to be sure. Have you been listening to our hymns, maybe?"

"I've been singing with you," Marian assured him. "A very stirring experience."

"Thank you, ma'am, thank you. Though you must understand that it is chiefly for those who haven't yet seen the Light——"

"Do excuse me," said Marian earnestly. "It isn't the Light I want to talk to you about. I want you to find Tommy Smith for me, if he's anywhere around."

"Hush," motioned Frankie the Toff, and placed his finger on his lips. Tommy Smith evidently lived in another world of reference than the world of the Cross and the Blood of the Lamb. And there were police around. The police were still Tommy's world, till *he,* too, had seen the Light.

"It's all right," said Marian, wondering whether Frankie the Toff imagined she was trying to find Tommy so that he might pull off some job for her. "I've got some urgent family news to give him."

Frankie the Toff looked doubtful. He did not remember Tommy Smith as being one consumed with curiosity about his family's welfare.

"Now look here," Marian assured him. "Tell him it's some terribly important news about his brother. You can take it from me he'll come when he hears that."

"Very well, ma'am. And thank you, thank you." This was in response to a ten-shilling note she had slipped into his hands.

"How soon do you think you can find him?"

"I have reason to believe he's in London," said Frankie the Toff, mysteriously, and a little pompously. "I ought to be able to contact him tonight, if he's not otherwise engaged. If not, tomorrow sometime. When would you like to see him, ma'am?"

"I'll make a point of being in at my flat—my *flat,* tell him, not the shop you came to——"

"Yes, ma'am?"

"I'll make a point of being there at six in the evening for the next three nights. If he doesn't come, I'll contact you again."

"He'll be there," said Frankie the Toff.

Two evenings later, at six in the evening, Tommy Smith was there.

II

It had been very harrowing waiting for him to come, first the one day, then the next. She had the instinct that he was the sort of person who could come on time, if he was going to come at all. But would he come the first day, the second day, the third? If he did not, was she to spend the next few months wondering whether, suddenly, one evening at exactly six o'clock, he would turn up from Heaven knows what morose or garish world, to demand what the message was she had for him?

She smoked a good deal in the hour preceding six o'clock in the evening of that first day, but she gave him up half an hour or so after six o'clock had gone by. She had quite a horrid little heap of stubbed-out cigarette-ends to turn out into the waste-paper basket. On the next day she again started chain-smoking about five, and went on, till there was a ring at the front-door bell, one floor down, at exactly six o'clock. The street-door, as she knew, was open. A moment or two later she heard feet climbing up the flight of stairs, moving along the passage. They stopped. There was a knock. She was waiting, just behind the door. She opened it. It was Tommy Smith.

"This way," she said, and took him along the passage to the sitting-room. She was now so nervous, she knew she had to exercise the utmost control over herself, to prevent herself collapsing. She was not frightened of him, she had no fear of physical violence. But she had vowed herself to accuse this desperate young man—always she thought of him as a "young man," though he was practically her own age—she had vowed herself to accuse him of atrocious conduct; not murder, but conduct which inevitably leads someone, somewhere, to self-murder. He was not going to get away with it. He had got away with his putrid ingratitude to her. He could get away with a burglary, either by escaping with his loot from the scene of his crime, or by being caught and liquidating his crime with a prison-sentence. But this, the cutting off of the brilliant and pathetic Clifford Eckersley in his prime, this he would not be allowed to get away with. Though she was at the moment as weak as a kitten, she would stand and face him, and pay out to him the wage he had earned.

"Sit down!" she ordered, and motioned him to a chair. He sat down. She sat herself down in a straight chair with its back against her writing-table. She would feel more capable of her task if she was not lounging in an arm-chair. Behind her head, on the upper elevation of the desk, half a dozen sulphur-tipped copper dahlias raised their heads out of a large vase. The sun striking through the window caught their petals and made each of them flare like the flame of a match.

"What does my brother want?" he asked at once. It was clear he had not got the slightest notion of what had happened.

"Your brother doesn't want anything," she said, evenly, fixing her eyes on him. Her cigarette was burned down to its stub. She placed the end in an ash-tray behind her on the desk, already half-full of stubs, and lit another cigarette. "No, he doesn't want anything," she repeated. The words had an ominous ring to him. He turned his eyes away. His feet were shuffling uncomfortably on the carpet.

"Well, what have you brought me here for?" he asked. "Isn't he well, or something?"

"He's dead," she said.

It was as if the words did not mean anything, as if he could not allow them to mean anything.

"If he isn't well," he complained, going on in the same direction of thought, "what can I do for him? He won't let me do a damn thing. You know that."

"I tell you, Smith, Clifford is dead."

It was impossible for the barbed words not to bite home this time. He turned to her, his eyes full of fear.

"No!" he cried. The sound was not like his voice at all. "No! It's not true! You're trying to pay me out! He can't be dead! He wasn't ill!"

"You're right," Marian said. "He wasn't ill. But he's dead right enough. The story was in the papers. You've apparently missed it. He drowned himself in the Cherwell, in Oxford, just over two weeks ago."

"He *drowned* himself?" His face was puckered like a child's. "You're lying to me!"

She reached for her handbag.

"I have the newspaper account here, if you like to see it." She was opening the clasp of the bag.

"No! Don't!" he cried, putting his hand to his eyes, as if he were actually shutting out from them the sight of a drowned body. "Why did he drown himself? What did he have to do that for?"

"Don't be a coward, Smith! Drop your hands! Turn round! I'll tell you!"

He turned.

"I know what you're going to say!" he cried. "It's my fault! I did it! Well, it's not true, that's all! He's known I've been a crook all these years, and he never had to drown himself before. He didn't do it because of me, I tell you!" His fists were pounding away at the arms of his chair. "He didn't! He didn't! He didn't!"

"When you stop whining," said Marian, "I'll tell you what happened. It won't do you any good. The one influence which might have meant something to you, the influence of your brother, is lost, gone for ever. Nothing can do you any good! You're rotten through and through!" She took in a great puff of cigarette-smoke in her rage, and nearly choked. It took a minute or so before the spasm went. But she started up another cigarette, as soon as she had wiped the tears from her eyes, and she could speak again. Tobacco was now a drug, apparently, without which she could not function at all.

His mood had changed. The voice was petulant and piteous.

"Why did he have to drown himself?" he asked. "You didn't tell him I'd let you down, did you?"

"No, I did not. He drowned himself only two days after I sent you away from my shop. I hadn't spoken a word to him, or got in touch with him in any way."

"Did somebody else tell him about me? Tell me. Did they?"

She paused, and stared at him. What right had *he* to be asking questions? Did he imagine he could frighten her into telling him a single word more than she had a mind to? Had she finished her job, she asked herself? He now knew exactly what had happened. She had left him with not an atom of doubt that it was he, he and no-one else, who was responsible for his brother's death. If she went into further details, wouldn't he take the chance of arguing, whining, explaining away? Hadn't she already provided him with a bitter enough cud to chew for all the rest of his years, wherever he spent them, and there was no doubt at all that there was only one place where he would spend them, and that was prison, one prison, and the next, and the next, and the next?

A vision flashed across her mind of the lad under the dark green water, his knuckles grasped around the submerged roots, and the teeth deep in the lower lip.

"Oh, no," she told herself. "It isn't good enough. The cud isn't bitter enough. He shall know all there is to know."

"Listen!" she commanded. "Do you hear me?" She clenched her fists tight because it was extremely distasteful and difficult for her to be talking to him in a mode other than disgust and contempt. "You know my sister and your brother were very much in love with each other?" She waited for a word from him. There was none. She repeated the question.

"Yes," he brought out. His jaws were hanging loose like a village idiot's.

"When my father got to know about their engagement he had no idea who Clifford's brother was. Then he found out." She waited a moment. "Someone told him."

Tommy Smith's lower jaw swung loose. Then it jerked into place again.

"Who told him?"

"You can guess," she said. "After that meeting in the theatre."

"I see," he breathed. His skin was like dirty dough.

"He ordered my sister to break off the engagement. She refused."

"Well?" he asked again. The inference was, if the girl refused to break off the engagement, and still Clifford threw himself in the river, how was he, Tommy, to be blamed for what happened?

Suddenly the indignity of the situation was more than she could bear, the indignity of disentangling the complex threads before this lost and malign creature so that he could see them clearly, one by one. It was like a gob of fatness in her throat.

"It was *you*, I tell you!" she shouted at the top of her voice. "And you have the impertinence to ask me questions! It all goes back to you! It was because of *you* my father made Anna give Clifford up! Because of *you*! And because of *me*! You let me down, everything I did for you, all my belief in you, all my schemes for you, and I was so smashed up I went and got drunk like a common tart! So they went and told him about it. This time, when he spoke to my sister. . . ." She stopped. She could not longer continue her exegesis, the shame of the old man, the tragedy of the boy and girl. "It's *you*! It always goes back to *you*! You're the evil genius of us all!" She was puffing wildly at the cigarette between her lips, but there was no life in it. She fumbled round the desk for a box of matches, took one out, and with trembling fingers lit up her cigarette again. She blew at the lit match and put it down in a receptacle behind her.

"It was *you* who drowned him!" she went on. "It was *you* who held his head under water! Why, for God's sake, were you ever born?"

He spoke, but it was not in answer to her words. He had his right arm thrust before him, pointing beyond her shoulder.

His eyes were protruding from their sockets. "He's burning! He's burning!" he cried, in a voice thin and shrill with horror. She swivelled her head round swiftly where the finger pointed and saw a gush of flame in the pen tray. It was the fountain-pen blazing. The match-flame she had blown at she had not extinguished, and it had set the pen alight. Even as she swivelled her head round again, for she did not wish to lose him from her sight for more than the fraction of a second, she raised the pen by its further end where it had not yet caught fire, and carried it to the flower-vase, where she dropped it into the water between the stalks of the dahlias. The quenched flame hissed like a snake.

The thoughts were careering through her head like broken twigs in a mill-race: *I've seen him once before like this. It was that time in Oxford, over a year ago. That time when I found out about the brother, that there was a brother he loved so consumedly. His lips were quivering and twitching. He was trying to close them so that he could speak, but he wasn't able to. The green glitter in his eyes was like lead. A clot of spittle was bubbling at the corner of his mouth.*

I think the moment of discovery has come again, as it came once before. This is why I called him back again. It wasn't to kick him to death. That was my excuse to myself. I had to give myself, I had to give both of us, one more chance. I must swoop like a hawk, as I did then. Something has startled the secret out of its undergrowth . . . the secret I was never clever enough to ferret out. . . . I told myself there was no secret there at all. It's there, rustling down in the dark grass. I must stoop and seize it before it bolts into the bolt-hole for ever.

She laid her hands on both his shoulders.

"Listen, Tommy!" she demanded softly, urgently. "Who's burning? Is Clifford burning?" (Who else, what else, could possibly be burning?)

Tommy nodded, like a patient in a trance at a hypnotist's bidding.

"Clifford's burning!" he moaned. "Clifford's burning!"

"A long time ago, wasn't it?" she asked.

"Clifford's a baby. Poor Clifford. He's in his cradle, burning." The words were coming in spasms, their consonants muted, as they had been before, that time in St. Stephen's College, in June, over a year ago. His skin was grey and blotched with goose-flesh, as it had been then.

"What happened, Tommy? Why was Clifford burning?" And even as she asked the question, she knew that she knew the answer. Her heart was riven with horror and pity.

He was seeking to give vocal substance to the shadow of words in his mouth. But the words stayed there. They would not come.

"Yes, Tommy," she urged, digging her finger-tips into the flesh of his shoulder-blades. "Get it said, Tommy. Once and for all. Then it will never pain you any more. Yes? Yes?"

"I wanted . . . to kill him. Father and Mother were both out. We were alone, me and Clifford. There was a coal-fire. I took a stick to the fire and lit it. Then I put it . . . among the bed-clothes. The clothes started burning. Oh! Oh! Oh!" he moaned. His grief was dreadful to look on. He placed his hands before his eyes as if at this very moment the cradle were in the room, blazing, as the fountain-pen had been, a few moments ago.

She shook him fiercely.

"It's all right, Tommy! I tell you it's all right! Nothing happened to him! He was all right! Take your hands away from your eyes! Take them away, I tell you!" He did not. He could not. They seemed nailed there. She seized them by the wrists and tore them away. "There now! Look at me! Straight in the eyes! Tell me exactly what happened! Why did you want to kill him?"

"I was jealous. I hated him. Before he came, Father loved only me. Then he forgot about me. He loved only Clifford. I went out stealing. I wanted him to hit me, take notice of me. No. Only Clifford.

"Yes, yes, I see. Who put the flames out, Tommy? Was it you? Perhaps you put the flames out, and you've forgotten? You see, perhaps you saved Clifford's life? Did you?"

The sweat was pouring down his cheeks in steady streams. He had the face at this moment of a wretched old man decades older than himself, scored with deep lines of guilt and remorse.

"No. I ran out of the house. There was a fog and no one saw me. I ran and ran and ran."

"You were frightened to come back? Isn't that so, Tommy? You didn't come back till a long time later?"

The head jerked sharply in affirmation, like a puppet's.

"And somebody came in just in time? Was it your father? Or your mother, maybe?"

"Mrs. Lewis," he said. "She lived upstairs."

Her heart stopped. Mrs. Lewis. The woman she had gone to Shropshire to see, all the way to Shropshire, the old woman who had been so coy and lewd and silly. Oh, the tragedy of it! Was it not probable that, if the woman had not become so cretinous, she would have brought up this tale of the burning cradle, and the child in it? Was it not at least possible, given that clue, that she herself might have tracked down Tommy's secret months ago to the lair it skulked in? And, if she had tracked it down, would not Clifford have been living at this moment? Perhaps at this very moment Clifford and Anna might have been walking hand in hand along the meadows of the upper river!

But the key to the secret had remained undreamed of, inaccessible, behind the babbling lips of Mrs. Lewis. And Tommy himself had forgotten the old woman's name all these long years ago; that is to say, he had thrust it into the furthest recess of his unconscious mind, along with every other memory of the episode.

"Mrs. Lewis," Marian repeated. "Yes, of course. Mrs. Lewis." There was nothing to do but to go on from that point. "So you see no damage was done, Tommy?"

"He was burned," Tommy said. There was a moue on his face like a hurt child's. "Here." His hand made a feeble gesture in the area above his left hip-bone. Yes. She remembered. Something had come out at the inquest about a huge purple weal in that part of Clifford's body. She remembered thinking that that may well have been the reason why Clifford did not play College games, for, hypersensitive as he already was, he would suffer further agonies of shyness about revealing that hideous scar in dressing-rooms and on the field.

"And tell me this, Tommy," she demanded. At that moment she did not know what particular thing she required him to tell her, when there were so many things to tell. Her brain was cracking with the effort she was making to fit all the pieces into pattern. And it must be done, quickly, oh, in these few seconds, while her finger was at the white-hot heart of the flame of the mystery, and his defences were vulnerable, the defences he had built up across the years, the defences pierced by his monstrous grief for his drowned brother, battered by the sledge-hammer abuse with which she had assailed him, and undermined till they were all tottering around him by the burning fountain-pen which had equated itself in the deepest depth of his mind with the burning cradle. It must be done at once, before the threatened defences made themselves good again and from now on finally invulnerable.

But they must labour at it together, he and she. It seemed possible, that, as Smith, the criminal, might once have been *made* in a matter of moments, now, too, in a matter of moments he might be *unmade*. But he must be *with* her. His own eyes, as well as hers, must penetrate into all the dark corners, till not one was left that was not flooded with bright air like hill-tops in the morning.

"Tommy!" she cried suddenly. "Tommy!" He was leaning forward, and in a moment it seemed he must fall flat on his face. She seized his arm again, and thrust him into a chair. "Wait!" she demanded. She darted into the bedroom and came back with a hand-towel. "I'll wipe your forehead! Is that better?" She was thinking furiously the whole time. Suddenly the whole line of attack was palpable before her, like an inspired chess-player seeing the inevitable programme of the game through all its moves. She seemed to tower over him, and he himself to be curiously shrunken and wizened in the chair.

"It was like this, Tommy. I'm going to tell you. You felt so miserable and guilty and frightened after you ran out into the fog, you wanted to kill yourself. That's true, isn't it? I *know,* Tommy. I know how it all happened. It's true, isn't it?"

"Yes."

"But you didn't kill yourself. Of course, you didn't. You had to come back and find out what happened to Clifford. And with a terrible, terrible sense of relief you found that he was all right, except for that nasty burn he had."

"Yes, yes," he whispered, nodding his head again, and then again.

"But you had to come to terms with your own sense of guilt. Besides, you had to make it up to him for the danger you had put him into, and the pain he was in, which probably lasted a long time. Isn't that so?"

"Yes, yes."

"So you felt you had to shower presents upon him. But you were very poor, of course, weren't you? Where were you going to find presents for him, or money to buy them with? So you started stealing. I mean, you went on stealing. You remember, you'd started already. You'd been stealing in order to attract attention to yourself away from the new baby. There probably was a bit of childish stealing still earlier on. There often is, I once told you, but it doesn't mean anything much. So there you were. Nobody cared whether you stole or did not steal. There was nobody around to tell you that stealing is really rather silly as well as rather horrid. In the last resort, it's really only yourself you steal from. You steal your own life from yourself, months and months of it, years of it. You know what I mean, don't you, Tommy?"

"Yes, Mrs. Framley," he said. He was emerging now from the state of semi-trance. He was listening now with something of his conscious mind as well as with his unconscious mind. The shivering was beginning to calm down. He looked less like an old man now than a very subdued small schoolboy in the presence of a formidable yet benign schoolmaster.

"Perhaps it's *more* silly than horrid," she went on. "Many children go through a phase of it. I did myself. Yes, yes, I did. It's almost a children's complaint, like mumps or measles. It may even be as prevalent. I don't know. Some get over it earlier than others, if the conditions are favourable. If they're not favourable, some never get over it. But *you* will, Tommy. You're still young. There may be a danger of relapse from time to time, but I think the danger will get less and less as time goes on. You had a shock when you were a small boy, and it was largely responsible for what came after. You've had another shock now, and things are going to be different, Tommy. Do you hear? Altogether different."

He looked up. There was exactly the same expression of doubt on his face, as a doctor will sometimes see on the face of a depressed and disheartened patient, after he has promised him a certain cure.

"I'm sure of it," she said, with passionate conviction. There was, perhaps, a shade more conviction in her voice than her heart. Then she remembered the one sure dart she held in her hand. "It's only in that way you can put yourself right with Clifford. You owe it to him to go straight. Think of him if ever the temptation comes again. It will, of course. The 'boys' will be after you. They'll always be after you till you get right away, as far as you can go."

"Why did he hate me so much?" he cried out suddenly. "I never did him any harm!"

It was necessary to eradicate that nonsense straight away.

"You never did him any harm?" she asked coldly. "Don't be ridiculous! He carried the harm you did him on his body till his dying day!"

The tears rushed to his eyes like the gush of water from a choked rain-spout. A moment later he was on his knees beside her, his head against her knees. She might almost have been his mother, and he her small, excessively naughty, son.

"I killed him," he sobbed. "It was my fault! I tried before but I didn't kill him that time. So I went after him, and I tried again and again, and then I killed him!"

She had had a feeling this would happen. It was a good thing it should happen. But it must be over and done with, at once.

"Quiet!" she cried peremptorily. "Quiet!"

But still he went on sobbing, and crying out: "It was my fault! I went after him again and again, and then I killed him!"

"Quiet, I said!" she shouted, and slapped his face hard. "You're a man, aren't you? Let's be grown-up!" He quietened down at once. He got up from his knees, and stood unsteadily on his feet. His collar and shirt were soaked as if they had fallen into a bucket of water. "Sit down again!" she ordered. "I'll get you some brandy, then I'm going to tell you a few things." She went to the sideboard and poured out for him a good stiff dose. "There you are! Now listen! It's all crystal-clear, Tommy, it's clear as a glass of water. . . .

"You went out stealing. You were only a child of eight, and you went out stealing. You are not a *born* thief, Tommy. Some people *may* be born thieves. I don't know. Nobody knows very much about it. Perhaps my Uncle Matthew's a born thief . . . your old friend, the Professor. Or everybody may be born a thief, and they grow out of it, as the grown-ups round them start telling them the difference between right and wrong. All I know is—you weren't worse than anyone else. And then certain things happened, the things you've been telling me about.

"You went out stealing to give Clifford presents. Not for yourself, Tommy. Get that straight. It was for Clifford. But Clifford wouldn't have anything to do with the things you brought him. He just wouldn't. Why? Perhaps Clifford knew with his unconscious mind you had tried to damage him, just as you knew yourself, with *your* unconscious mind. Nobody knows much about these things. Probably very small children know a lot more about things than people imagine they do. Perhaps, also, Clifford was born honest, as some people may be born crooks. He was afraid of you, for what you'd done to him. He hated the things you brought in for him, the things you'd stolen. He ran away from you, and from your presents. In a way, he was doing that all his life.

"Don't forget. You were only a child. You couldn't possibly think these things out for yourself. It's only a great stroke of luck that I'm in a position to work them out for you. You went on stealing. The more he turned down your presents, the more you felt if the presents were only big enough, he'd take them. You remember? How often did you think of that slap-up car you were going to leave for him outside the steps of St. Stephen's? And you remember where *that* landed you? You never really wanted money and gold cigarette-boxes for yourself. You took your living-expenses, of course. But you've never spent money in a big way on yourself. You'd even forget the hidey-holes where you stored the stuff away. You stole it all for Clifford, and when he turned it down, you couldn't stop stealing all at once, as you're going to be able to do, from now on. You had to keep right on. It was an excitement, Tommy. It was a drug. It made you forget how unkind Clifford was, turning everything down you tried to give him. It made you forget something much deeper down than that. You know what I mean. No, don't shiver like that. You've got to face up to it. You've got to keep it before you in the light of day. Then it won't poison the roots of your life any more. Aren't I right, Tommy? Tell me. Aren't I right?"

"Yes, Mrs. Framley, you're right."

"Let me go on. I don't think you'll feel any urge to go on stealing any more after today. You stole for Clifford, and he's not there any more."

He brought up a sigh from the depths of his heart.

"What's there left to go straight for, Mrs. Framley?"

"Come, come!" she gibed. "You didn't go *straight* for Clifford! You went crooked!"

"Yes, that's right!" he smiled faintly.

"Apart from anything else," she pointed out, "it's more sensible to go straight. Where does going crooked get you? Think for a moment of your friend, Frankie the Toff. Where's it got *him*? And I've always taken your word for it that he's the cleverest crook of the century. And he's lucky. Think of the old men at this moment eating their hearts out in prison, if they've got any hearts left. It's no *fun*, Tommy!

And it's *mean*! Padding up like a rat at night out of the gutter. It's dirty!"

He thought for some moments, then he raised his head with a quick jerk.

"What do you think I ought to do now, Mrs. Framley?" he asked.

"Oh, no," she said. "Oh, no." She took his glass and went over to the sideboard. "Try to work that out for yourself. I'm going to give you another drop of brandy. I think I could do with a drop, too." She felt weak, and she feared, if she did not take one herself, she would pass out. "I'll help myself first," she said. "That's better." She was suddenly conscious of a wild impulse to get down on her knees and deliver a hymn of praise, like the yelling votaresses in the Park; but she controlled it, she did not wish to embarrass either herself or him. She poured out a second dose of brandy for Tommy. "The other one was medicine," she told him. "This one is just a drink." Another thought had taken possession of her in these few moments. After all the solemnities, the follies, the frustrations, the Mrs. Lewises, the Frankie the Toffs, she was aware she had triumphed. She had triumphed over Tommy Smith. She had triumphed over wickedness and over luck itself. She tried to keep the triumph out of her voice, because she was afraid, if she did not, she would scream and bring in all the other tenants of the house, and maybe the neighbouring houses, and this matter did not concern them.

He sipped the brandy, and thought, and was silent for some time. Inside her skull triumph went on exulting, like a carillon. She did not hurry him. The bells swayed and swung. Still he was silent. Then the bells quietened. A modesty and humility filled her heart. It was as if she had been constrained to put forth her hand and check the bell-ringer as he tugged the bell-ropes.

"I must get this straight" (she told herself). "What have I done, with God's help? I dared to hope I'd dig my way down to some universal truth that has eluded the philosophers and scientists of crime. What folly that was! How does it all start, I kept on asking myself? I don't know now any more than I did at the beginning. But I think I've found out how it started in *one* human being. And I'm grateful for